# BLUE FUTURES, BREAK OPEN

BLUE FUTURES: DEITY & DUTY

# BLUE FUTURES, BREAK OPEN

A NOVEL

## ZOË GADEGBEKU

WEST VIRGINIA UNIVERSITY PRESS · MORGANTOWN

Library of Congress Cataloging-in-Publication Data

Names: Gadegbeku, Zoë, author.

Title: Blue futures, break open : a novel / Zoë Gadegbeku.

Description: First edition. | Morgantown : West Virginia University Press, 2025.

Identifiers: LCCN 2024038411 | ISBN 9781959000396 (paperback) | ISBN
      9781959000402 (ebook).

Subjects: LCGFT: Novels.

Classification: LCC PS3607.A35335 B59 2025 | DDC 813/.6—dc23/eng/20241028

LC record available at https://lccn.loc.gov/2024038411

For EU safety/GPSR concerns, please direct inquiries to WVUPress@mail.wvu.edu or our physical mailing address at West Virginia University Press / PO Box 6295 / West Virginia University / Morgantown, WV, 26508, USA.

Book and cover design by Than Saffel / WVU Press

For my mother, and her mothers, and their mothers

*We, outside of time, thinking of you, singing you this story*

*The spirit who was, is, and will be love and vengeance,*
*who is also Lucille*
*The spirit who was, is, and will be saltwater and sound,*
*who is also Serena*
*The spirit who was, is, and will be sweetness and luxury,*
*who is also Viví*
*Mawu-Lisa, a vast and plenty God*
*Ayida Wedo and Damballah, the most powerful spirits*
*who were serpents*
*Ndɔkutsu, who we are still trying to understand*
*Amegawó, Blue Basin's elders*
*Antoinette and Sans-Souci, lovers of each other and parents to Raphael*
*Vendredi or Friday's Child, eyes low, saying little but making much out*
*of just his hands and pieces of wood*
*Elsie Loiseau, the beautiful goldsmith*
*Miss Yvonne, of blessed hands and sorrowful spirit*
*Ma-Reine, Lucille's friend like a sister*
*Mama Hadzila, Ma-Reine's storyteller grandmother*
*Mama Aida, Ma-Reine's mother*
*Glory, Ma-Reine's husband*
*Samedi/Saturday Amegbetɔ, wearing this hat, in this weather?*
*Miss Geneviéve—please be sure to pronounce it correctly—*
*and her grandchild, Beau-Soleil*
*Nouvelle, Samedi's friend*
*Miss Mathilde, the midwife*

*You, inside of time, dreaming of us, listening for us*

# GLOSSARY

.......

*Words and phrases are shown here as they appear in the text.*

*A note on pronunciation: the character "ƒ" can be best described as what it sounds like to blow out a candle. "Ɖ" and "ɖ" are used to indicate a hard "d" sound as in "dog," whereas the "D" and "d" are a softer "d," almost like a heavy "th" sound. "ŋ" is like the "ng" sound you make at the back of your throat in "sing," and "ɔ" is akin to the "aw" sound in "awesome" but a little less drawn out.*

Aƒeme – home

ago blanket – a type of velveteen blanket found in some Ewe households

agoo – a greeting; used, for example, to announce one's presence at another person's door

akpe – thank you

à lòt bò dlo – (Haitian Creole) on the other side or across the water

basa basa – messy; scattered

Blewu – slowly; slow down

Daavi – young miss; used to address a younger woman; sometimes used as a term of endearment

Ɖa foɖo gã – Madam or Mother Big Belly; intended to be pejorative, not that she cared

ɖekákpùì – young man, but used in this novel to mean young person in a gender-neutral sense ɖevi, ɖevíwo – child, children

Ðo ŋtsi nam – answer me

Ðo to – be quiet

e nya kpɔ vava – She's very beautiful, or something more
    emphatic than English can convey

E se a? – You hear [me]?

E se egɔme a? – Do you understand?

Efo – address for elder brother, but also used generically for any
    young adult male; sometimes used in this novel as a term
    of endearment

Egɔme ɖe – What does it mean?

Énya kpɔ – You look/it looks nice

eze mela – potter

gbetɔ – person

kete – Ewe kente cloth

Kpɔ ɖa! – Look! or Attention!

Kpɔ wo ɖa – Look at them

lekee? – How is it? or How are things?

lwil maskriti – (Haitian creole) Haitian castor oil

Ma kpɔ ɖa – let me see

Mawu! – an exclamation; [my] God!

Me be ɖe – literally, "I say that!" Used to emphasize something
    surprising or unbelievable in conversation

me ɖe kuku – Please, or I beg your pardon

Me ɖe kuku na wó – I beg you

Me gli toge na wò – I'll tell you the story, or I'll spin a yarn for
    you (figurative, meaning I'm going to narrate a long story)

Menyo kra kra kra o! – It's not good at all!

Mia tɔwò – our people

mia tɔwò Eveawo – our Ewe people

Miawoezɔ – You (plural) are welcome

Mia yi, mia va – we'll be back (literally, "We're going to come.")

Míe se egɔme – We understand

Ndɔkutsu – sunshine

Núkà dím ne le? – What are you looking for? or What do you want?

Núkà e ma? – What is that?

Núkà edzɔ? – What happened? or What's the matter?

Nyateƒee? – Is that true? or Is that so?

nye sí – a combination of Ewe and English meaning "my sister"

nyɔnu – woman

siká gbede – gold smith

Taflatse – no offense; used before saying something potentially cutting or rude about someone else

tomefafa and dzidzeme – peace and contentment

Tɔnye – mine

Tɔwo – yours

Tsúkúnɔ – an insult; describing someone as having gone mad

Tutu gbɔvi – opening words of a popular Ewe lullaby; no specific meaning when translated into English. "Tutu" is a short form of "atuuu atuuu," a term of endearment when welcoming a loved one in embrace; "gbɔvi" is a short form of "gɔnyevi" (little child under my care)

Va yi – go on (as in leave, not as in continue)

Víví – sweet, sweetness

# PROLOGUE

.......

We are the never-satiated, the enraged, the vast, the danger-ous, the ungovernable, the unbroken, the ones who set fire to the corporeal self so the soul could be free, the ones who took flight before it was too late, the ones who stole away with spirit and flesh still unified.

We are outside of time, and you are in places like "Louisiana"—those people the color of the soles of a feverish person's feet, those we call yevú or sly dog, thought so highly of their pitiful selves, they named land not their own after themselves and their kings—agoo, we greet: Natchitoches, Caddo, Natchez, Osage, rightful and careful custodians of that land. We see you there on the inside of time in "Jérémie, Grande'Anse"—we mean Ayiti—in Keta, "Gold Coast"; those other names taste bitter in our mouths. You are there inside of time, living in the afterwards, in what came next after the universe shattered and we all fell through. You are living in moments like 1804, two-thousand-and-something, 1992, fourteen hundred-and-something, times that may seem eternal to you in their disarray but are only a twinkling to we who are able to see the entire breadth and beyond of time's horizon from where we stand.

You call us ancestor, dadá, lwa, spirit, holy, black magic, runaway slave, formerly enslaved, maroon, oracle, elder, African-black-not-anybody's-negation. We are also called Sans-Souci, Friday's Child, Yvonne, Ma-Reine, and other names we gave ourselves that you will soon come to learn. We see you tending to cut flowers like they are sickly children: fresh water, spoonfuls of sugar, loving whispers to stay and not to wilt, because you know we like something sweet to smell when we visit. We see you: looking for us in every crevice of your current life, in the painfully brief moment between just waking up and forgetting last night's dream, in song lyrics that never drop from the tip of your tongue no matter how hard you try to remember, in the closed faces of strangers all walking the same direction towards soul-splintering days in lives too narrow for spirits like you and like us. We are watching you there, there, there; we are outside of time dreaming of the day the way will open so you will join us here.

We send moonbeams through your shuttered windows on a night when no earthly crescent could have spilled so much light. We wait for you to clean the altar you built in our honor—replacing the week-old water and washing the glass clouded with oily fingerprints and dust—so we can take a seat watching for the candle, the tingle of clear or dark or sweet liquor; our tastes are as varied as the manifestations of our spirits. We prepare you for free living, sometimes slamming doors so you can catch glimpses of the wings folded behind your back waiting to be discovered and put to use, sometimes holding your hands and pulling hard to remind you escape is possible even without the wings, sometimes opening every door possible between the inside and outside of time until you gather enough courage inside your chest to run through and burn the threshold in your wake so your captors cannot follow. We believe in scorched earth. We are waiting for you on this land patched together from seabed and shoreline, in a place outside of time protected—as much as is possible—from the violence of your time by blue paint on veranda ceilings, blue paint on the walls, indigo blue for our clothes, deep blue to mark our skin, all kinds of blue mixed up and running together so that any of the white evil pursuing us think it to be the sea, and too scared to drown, they do not follow us here, nor will they follow you.

In fact, the way is already open. You are just in need of the right key, the speed of the wind just so, the feathers oiled so black they shine silver, the light to leak through the wooden side of a house at the perfect angle with the perfect shine, and then you will be air-bound, your destination the latter side, the outside, the free side, where you can also be unbroken like we are. You may feel we have left you flailing in cruel winds, but we are with you and we feel and laugh and weep when you do.

Because the way is open, when you dream of us from the inside of time, our ears itch here on the outside; sometimes, we startle at the sensation and break the plate we were washing. You laugh, and the tune of your favorite song plays on our spirit for a week. You place fresh bowls of water on your altars before kneeling to call on us, and we feel seafoam tickling the soles of our feet as the waves retreat. When you cry, the black and blue stains on our fingertips run out of our skin and seep into the bedsheets, and the deliberate scars carved into our cheeks and around our hairlines grow tender and start to hurt. When your bodies ache from the pink-skinned specters' whips and bats, we feel it in our lower backs. The earth quakes and caves in on itself and on top of you our beloved in Ayiti, demons in uniform shoot children in their sleep in "Louisiana" and on the "Gold Coast," and where we are, the moon rises in place of the sun, and the walls of our houses begin to flake then chip then crumble in response. As much as we do not want to put these words into the air for fear they solidify into reality, we must admit we are also terrified that life inside of time will become so dire for you, our beloveds, that the damage to the place we are preparing for you outside of time will be irreversible.

In the meantime, we whisper tales to you about people who can fly; about blue flowers on the Saturday night dinner table; about blue candles like pillars; about waters so blue it hurts the eyes and mind to perceive them; about you yourselves, in places called "Jérémie" and "Provencal" and "Boston" and "Jacmel" and "New Orleans" and Keta and "Port-de-Paix" and somewhere on the road from "Cave Hill" to Aburi; about sister spirits who became flesh to prepare for us all a place to land: love and vengeance, who would name her self Lucille; saltwater and sound, who would name her self Serena; and sweetness and luxury, who would name her self Víví. We speak in the background of your daydreams like an echo, in a minor key, troubling the flow of your thoughts so they run in circles and not in straight lines, round and round like this story we are trying to tell you just now.

Can you hear us? Entendez-vous? E mía nkɔ sem a? We are outside of time dreaming of you and holding the way open for your arrival.

# 1

*outside of time, before the break*
*when Mawu-Lisa shared the sky as moon and sun and spirits*
*roamed far and free*

Before anyone could fly, before there was anything called time, there was the Big Wide Blue water, and then there was God. God was vast and plenty, both moon and sun in one being. Their name was Mawu-Lisa, and they lived in a dark, quiet house in a town surrounded by sea and lagoon and by yellow sand. The town was usually empty, because the spirits and souls who lived there were busy being born; entering rooms where they were being mourned; ruffling curtains; lifting up the sheets used to cover mirrors; tapping on hunched and heaving shoulders; planting grit in the grinding jaws of people who had wronged them in life; dancing in the flicker of candles lit in their honor; or crowning the heads of the devoted who struck matches to light their way.

Of all the spirits who were serpents, two of the most powerful were Ayida Wedo and Damballah. They were witnesses when Mawu-Lisa took eight days to speak life to fill the void that existed before the universe. They were there when Mawu-Lisa rolled out the sky and scattered the clouds across it, when they fashioned bodies for the spirits who would be sent to live on earth and painted the landscapes that had their own spirits contained in smooth pebbles at the bottom of clear pools of water, in all the trees waving and bending to the will of the wind, and in all the waters—sweet and salt.

When Mawu-Lisa was finished, they gave Ayida Wedo and Damballah their instructions in a voice that sounded like the center of a storm: "This part is most important. Almost more important than the creation itself. E se egɔme a?"

"We understand."

"Do you know you will be the only force making sure our work does not fall into pieces and back into the void?"

"Yes, we understand. Míe se egɔme." Ayida Wedo and Damballah began to unravel themselves. They stretched and unwound until they were both at their full length, and then they looped their coils, thousands of them, around the pieces of the universe Mawu-Lisa had made. They were wound so tightly it would have been impossible to tell where one ended and the other began, had it not been for the color of their scales. Damballah had a white diamond-shaped patch in the center of his head right above his eyes. It stood out starkly against his black scales, so shiny it was as if each one had been polished individually. Ayida Wedo had silver scales that showed rainbows in the right light.

They remained together for two eternities and two more, side by side, but not unified. Although venom dripped plentifully from her fangs, Ayida Wedo was often the one to resolve the conflicts that occurred between the two of them when their tempers rose in their throats and fell off the tips of their tongues in insults and curses. Damballah was a terror when he preferred to be, which was often. His emotions swung wildly between compassion and violent rage, and his ever-changing disposition caused searing sunshine on earth one day and devastating tempest the next. So extreme did these rages become that one day, Ayida Wedo asked, "Can't you see what you are doing? Should Mawu-Lisa's children suffer because you can't control your self?"

Damballah looked slit-eyed at Ayida Wedo and turned his head as far away as he could from her. "Who do you think you're talking to? You think you're more powerful than I am? Are we not here tied up together, tied up in the same task?"

"Is that what I said? All I am asking is for you to calm down before you destroy Mawu-Lisa's children. You know, maybe you aren't strong or trustworthy enough for this kind of responsibility."

Damballah ignored Ayida Wedo, still refusing to look her way.

As they continued to shout at each other, each became more interested in winning the fight than focusing on the worlds they were carrying between their coils. Their grip loosened, and they continued to shout. They didn't notice the universe slipping and splintering light-years beneath them.

*** 

*inside of time, at the moment of the break*
*Keta, "Volta Region, Ghana,"—agoo, we greet, mia tɔwó Eveawo, rightful and careful custodians of the land—1777*

*Before the break, there was once a narrow spit of land like a sliver of skin cut from one of Mawu-Lisa's fingers. The people who came to build their homes there, wove their fishing nets there, tended to their laughing children there, decided to name it Keta. They chose that place to bring forth more life because the wide, waving waters of the sea on one side and the lagoon's stable surface* on the other were perfect protection from any outside threats that loomed. Keta was also shielded by forces only fully witnessed by the priests, keepers of secrets and custodians of shrines to Mawu-Lisa and all the other celestial beings ruling the universe. A bundle had been buried at the entrance to the town on the first new moon and prayed over every new moon that was to follow, until the day they went to pray and saw a hole gaping like a guilty mouth on the verge of confession where the ground should have been whole and holy.

Ndɔkutsu was sunshine's namesake. After his people had waited the eight days following his birth to make sure he would stay in the world of the living, they swore they saw the sun itself shining out of his face. He grew loud and alive with all the other children among the pale yellow sandbanks in front of the raging Gulf of Guinea, all slip and shine with saltwater, sweat, and the morning yɔkumí, raw shea butter to protect from the sun and to close any open cuts or wounds. It wasn't until he had seen many moons swell and die, when he was an adult, a little more than 30 years old, that gold flecks began to appear in his otherwise brown eyes. His mother had been right about the sunshine, her ego expanded like rising bread.

"Kpɔ da! Look at those eyes and tell me you can't see the sun shining."

Her neighbors kissed their teeth behind their hands, but whenever they greeted Ndɔkutsu on the way to or from market or their nets, they made sure to keep his stare as long as they could, so dazzled they forgot that in their own words, the sun didn't simply shine, it burnt.

Just like the other people of his age in that clan who were fit for war, he went to battle again and again, at first against familiar enemies from further inland, where the loose seaside *sand gave way to rich black loam and endless forests like green fortresses with walls that never ended. Later, they went to fight a different kind of enemy, one with strange skin so pale it looked like it glowed, skin that held their secret weapon, making them near impossible to defeat, or so it was said. Ndɔkutsu was never seen again afterwards, and everyone in the town believed the war had ended him. He wasn't the only vanished one. What happened to that other young man, who left handsome and returned red-eyed and silent? The town grew still with so many missing or most likely dead. Even the mangroves they had planted to keep the greedy water at bay no longer swayed to the wind's whim. Some of the old people said it felt colder, the night longer and denser, the laughs fewer and further between, and hollow too, like the low roar inside sea shells.*

*Ndɔkutsu might as well have been gone permanently from the world of the living, because if those people who had called him this name and admired his light-giving gaze had seen him, they would not have recognized him. Where his eyes had been honey or golden sky or failing fire's embers depending on the day, they were now a flat, glossless brown, his skin dull and dry like he was expiring from the inside out. The sun must have set behind his head for good when he decided to become one of those who interpreted their language into something the yevú could understand. The people of the town would never know Ndɔkutsu, one of their own laughing children turned grown, had been the one to dig up their protection, that this act of betrayal smashed his pride and spirit beyond repair, that after he dug up the bundle and threw it into the lagoon, it refused to sink, and he jumped in, disappearing below the water's surface with his body curved around it to protect it from damage already done.*

*If they could see him, if they knew, they might have asked, "Ndɔkutsu, were you ever that hungry? Did you not eat the sweetest coconut and the saltiest fish? Ndɔkutsu, what in this world was irresistible enough for you to do us this way? Ndɔkutsu, what did they give you or threaten you with? Was it worth it?"*

*The townspeople understood that with or without the few among them like Ndɔkutsu, the pink-skinned specters had come to take and take and take, to play god without any of the benevolence and wisdom of the gods of that land, to throw the universe off its axis, to end their world as they had known it because the yevú bloodlust and desire for more gold and spice and flesh knew no end. The blame first had to land leaden and undeniable on those specters' heads. By the time those yevú murderers marched into Keta with metal strapped across their chests, Keta was already lost to its former life forever. The invaders marched up and down the coast farther east and farther west than Keta, barking at each other in a language nothing like the people had heard, nothing that could be human. They dragged still-sleeping people off their mats and out of their doors, flung babies far from their parents' sides, separated lovers mid-embrace, and lit deadly fires in the heads and chests of the warrior clan members scrambling for their weapons. And as the serpents fought each other above and let slip the world from their grasp, so too did the people below lose hold of their freedom because of the yevú's greed and un-humanness.*

\*\*\*

Mawu-Lisa called three sister spirits; one who was, is, and will be love and vengeance; one who was, is, and will be saltwater and sound; and one who was, is, and will be sweetness and luxury. God called them from far beyond the universe's horizon, beyond the sky, beyond life itself. The three sisters could not live in Mawu-Lisa's town because they were too boundless for its walls and its low-roofed houses huddling together between waters. When the sisters stood up tall, their feet landed on opposite sides of the universe.

The spirit who was, is, and will be love and vengeance was living somewhere outside of time in a house next to a sea that never rose into high tide nor threatened the land because she said and made it so. She left her windows uncovered so the light could find its way in without restraint and so she could hear the cries and invocations from those who devoted themselves to loving with a vengeance. She was sitting there in her house admiring her self and the impressive things she was able to stitch together with those hands of hers, each fabric much more than something with which to adorn one's self but, rather, an occasion unto itself. Kete: brown, gold, white, and green, like an abundance of fields rolling ahead and out of sight. Black velvet: the tight parts of newly braided hair and the fingertips that linger down and across. Pink lace: the warm and waiting inside of a lower lip. Blue brocade: the seas as seen from flight, the sun splitting the water's blues into greens and silvers before fusing them back to blue again. Next to her works were the tools that made them possible: a loom, a tin box filled to the brim with spools of thread and needles thin and thick, her scissors with their gold finger rests. These things were more or less where she always kept them, but at this moment in a more alarming disorder than what they would look like after she just got through using them. The scissors were scattered on her worktable, blades and finger rests spread far apart from each other as though they had never been whole. When she bent forward and brought her face closer to the fabrics spilled over themselves and over the table's edge, she saw a steady fraying she knew could not have been because of some imperfection on her part. Her works, and her fearsome divine self, were always without flaw. Then, she heard someone calling her like a child crying for a parent missing from home much later than they promised they would return. Someone was calling the spirit to come forth, and she knew it was not her sister spirits, but she went because she felt she was needed. She stood up with her legs astride the universe, one foot in beyond and the other in what-has-already-been. And then, she went forth.

The spirit who was, is, and will be saltwater and sound knew there was something off-kilter because all her instruments had fallen out of tune. When she pressed them, the keys on her keyboard made flat, thudding sounds rather than being airy and light. All her horns—clarinet, sax, flute—were not letting wind in and out the way they should. Instead, the notes squeezed themselves sideways and stumbled over each other into discord. The likelihood of saltwater and sound's music sounding flat or not sounding at all was nonexistent. Saltwater and sound could play any noise ever heard or imagined. She could open her mouth and sing the ring of bells to celebrate new life or life just come to an end. She could clap and conjure the sound of hearty slaps on the backs of long-time-no-see friends. She could whisper, and you would hear light rain falling onto iron roofing sheets. The spirit who was saltwater and sound was outside of time, somewhere on the opposite side of the horizon from where the spirit who was love and vengeance was in her house by a still sea, and now she took her favorite cane chair and sat it far enough from her backdoor steps that she could forget about her faltering music and close enough for the incoming waves to break around and wash her feet without threatening to carry her away, letting it take her dirt and her tired back out to sea. The water swelled and foamed before her, approaching and retreating as if in prostration for three seconds or three thousand years, until its waves pulled back and back and beyond, almost folding onto the horizon from where they came, leaving behind gasping fish, their silver bodies so quickly exposed to their last gleam of life, they were dead before they knew it. She stood up and chased the receding waves until the water reached her waist, but not high enough to get the ends of her locs wet. She listened hard for what the silence wasn't saying. She listened so hard she was bent over at the waist. Then she stood up tall, legs astride the universe, her feet planted in the break between silence and expression, in the painful quiet to be found in the deep breath right before a sob wrenched from the floor of the soul. And then, she went forth.

The spirit who was sweetness and luxury set down her scissors on the vanity in front of her and ran her hands through her freshly cut hair. She watched her self through narrowed eyes, trying to catch any uneven spots from all possible angles, in the small round mirrors to the right and left of her, and in the large rectangular one behind her, the one with the cracks spreading across its glass like wrinkles on an aging face. This spirit who was la luxe embodied, e nya kpɔ vava, had her image shining back to her self all over her house not just as a function of vanity: she was beautiful in all the ways there are in the universe to experience beauty but also needed her mirrors to see the divine way, to know what had already come to pass and what was still yet to unfold. Because she was concentrating on her haircut—snipped scalp-close and just long enough for her coils to stand out neatly from each other when wet—she didn't notice at first that her selves reflected around the room were moving just a beat slower than her self in life. Her reflections were lagging behind, like her mirrored selves were trying and failing to move through heavy thunderstorm air. Even more worrying was that beyond her own image, her view of her two sisters sitting outside of time just like she was also distorted, the fronts of the usually sparkling mirrors turned milky. So she stood up tall, legs astride the universe, her feet planted in the break between agony and ecstasy. And then, she went forth.

The sister spirits tore through the air for seven days, and Mawu-Lisa sat with their hands folded across their chest waiting for the sisters. Their arrival troubled the water, and the sand, and the shingles of the flat roof, and the flimsy cloth like a mass of cobwebs in the windows and the ancient dust stuck in the corners of the speckled tiles. And still Mawu-Lisa waited, sitting still except when they lifted their hands to adjust the brown scarf they wore, carefully, so their nails wouldn't catch on the gold threads that had come loose from the scarf's weave. On the eighth day, the wind stilled and Mawu-Lisa stood up and stretched their stiffened limbs. It was dawn, and the sun was bursting orange out of a grapefruit sky.

"Sisters. We have called you here, and you have finally come after eight days of flying wild. Welcome. Miawoezɔ." Their voice was usually in disharmony, so Lisa would often begin to speak a few moments before Mawu joined in.

The wind the sisters had brought with them had turned into a breeze whispering at first and then hanging quietly in the room, like the warm glow remaining at the end of a fire's life. The spirit who was love and vengeance answered first. "We came like this, wild in the wind, because it was clear you needed us desperately. Isn't that so?

"But it took you eight days, as long as it took for us to bring the universe into being, as long as it takes for a spirit newly ushered into the world to decide whether it will remain on the human plane or return to us."

The spirit who was sweetness and luxury had all the bite of a too-ripe lemon in her voice when she said, "Well, we are here now. What do you want?"

The spirit who was saltwater and sound sighed, her breath reverberating calm around the walls of the room. "Mawu-Lisa, you wouldn't have called, and we wouldn't have come if it wasn't something terrible. What is it?"

Mawu-Lisa stayed quiet. The last time they had seen the sister spirits, they were threatening to grind Mawu-Lisa's town into ash. The sisters felt themselves too infinite to remain in the same place as the double colossus that was God. Mawu-Lisa couldn't believe these spirits would dare to be so defiant, and that they refused to make themselves small in front of Mawu-Lisa's might. The sisters had left to their respective places outside of time, where their selves had no limits.

Finally Mawu-Lisa was able to push the taste of their resentment into the side of their cheek long enough to say, "The world has shifted. The spirits who are serpents were not as powerful as we thought them to be."

"What's the meaning of this? Egɔme ɖe?" The spirit who is love and vengeance sounded hoarse, like all the forest fires crackling; all the ferocity of retribution had settled under her tongue. The heat she created was a room inside of the room in which they all stood, so solid they would have suffocated were they mortal.

"We are saying that the spirits who are serpents have failed. They couldn't be at peace with each other, and so they dropped all they were holding in place." Mawu-Lisa continued, their double voice melding more into one the longer they continued to speak. "All they were holding in place, our beloveds: an old man wearing one gold earring sitting in the same place on some road somewhere, smiling at any somebody who would smile back; children dancing in a ring, each hand clasped to the next; the people swaying with hands in each other's pockets, under the watch of a million and one winking fireflies, conspirators, witnesses to love and desire. All of it. Nothing else but horror can lie at the other side of this."

The sister spirits understood the reason for Mawu-Lisa's summons but still wanted to hear them say it. Just because they were divine, grander than the entirety of the universe and unimaginable to the human mind, didn't mean they would not be just a little petty and a little more stubborn.

"Sisters. Spirits. This break means that the man with the gold earring; and the smiling, dancing children; and the swaying lovers have now gone through a kind of death, a death in spirit if not in body, and both for some. Cruel somebodies—the pink-skinned and some of our kin who became their accomplices, some at the threat of being stolen or dying themselves, some spurred on by shortsighted greed— have turned precious life into objects to be sold, flesh to be weighed and evaluated for how much it can endure, enslaved in perpetuity unless. . . ." Mawu-Lisa was just as proud as the sister spirits, but the sense of urgency and doom that had been building inside their dual self exceeded the need to show the sister spirits who amongst them was most powerful. "Sisters. Spirits. Love and vengeance. Sweetness and luxury. Saltwater and sound. This is no time for bloody-mindedness. We called you because there has been a break in the world. We know what is to come, and we need your assistance, standing outside of time as you are. We need you to stand inside the break to make some sort of elsewhere for them to escape to and to open the way for them to find it."

# 2

*outside of time, after the break, in the void where Blue Basin was formed, where love and vengeance would become Lucille, where saltwater and sound would become Serena, where sweetness and luxury would become Vivi*

The spirit who was love and vengeance wanted to start with the bones. She knew this was no way for these souls to spend an afterlife. She was standing on a narrow shelf of rock shifting from one bare foot to another to keep some feeling in them. It wouldn't be an easy task to recover the remains from the watery no-place and other nowheres to which they had been cast. The bones had been forced to dwell for what might as well have been several eternities and a few days more, bearing the enormous weight of the sea in molding boxes abandoned between castaway furniture and decaying paper or trapped in the wreckages of twisted vessels. These remains deserved reverence and ritual before the spirit could set about preparing a place for those beloveds who were enduring all kinds of evil inside of time, after the break, but still had a chance to fly towards a free place outside of it. She had to approach the only entity more powerful than her self and Mawu-Lisa, this giant Blue Sea God—with a belly so deep no being could ever fill it to satisfaction—for permission to recover and care for these bones.

The rock jutted out above the waves that were sometimes lazy, most times raging, and the spirit stared downwards, hoping her sight could pierce the ocean's swirling unknown. She spun her self around, looking over the waves frothing and breaking in the same exact motion each time, a dormant God retracing her steps obsessively, forward and back, forward and back, day after day, whether humanity was there to witness her movement or not. For eight days, the spirit who was love and vengeance had done every conceivable ritual to appease the Blue and to gain access to the burial grounds she was keeping submerged in her deepest reaches. The spirit had prayed without ceasing, from the time the sun rose to its peak until it descended behind the horizon.

"Our souls can't rest. Wandering souls need rest. Wandering bones live yet."

It absolutely had to be eight days, the number of days Mawu-Lisa spent turning divine impulse into creation; the same amount of time it takes to see if a child would remain on the living side of the portal between spirit and flesh; the time parents would wait to name their child once it was certain the child would choose to live—a sacred number, eight. She chanted and cried through her pleas, hoping for a sign that she could enter the sea and emerge alive and not sink to rest forever with the bones she was trying to recover. "Vous êtes grande. Most powerful water, permit me to do right by these souls, to do what we spirits couldn't do while they lived."

And again, "Mawuga! Deèsse, vous êtes grande! Our souls can't rest. Our souls need rest."

It was now the eighth day, and her conviction was less taut muscle and more a tremor, like the heat melting the air in the distance and making it dance. It seemed she had failed after all. The soles of her feet were raw from stamping on the rock, and hunger groaned deep inside her so strong and so loud she could barely hear her own thoughts. Sustained solely by her goal, she hadn't needed food or water. She was weary, and she was wearing the signs of defeat all over her body. She sat down and stretched out her legs before her, noticing for the first time the scratches and insect bites, the faint trails of dried saltwater interrupting their otherwise unscarred brown. Her head dropped towards her chest. She would take a short rest before resuming her prayers.

Then, there came a low fizzle like feet shuffling slowly across a floor. It grew louder, until the volume was unbearable, pressing against her eardrums and waking her with the same amount of force as the giant wall of water that crashed over her head. The water carried her away from her resting place on the rock and snatched her along with it. She was certain she would be ripped away from her own body. She shuttered her eyelids tightly against the salty sting of the sea running into her every crevice. The spirit was so tense she didn't realize the wave's fury had calmed to a gentle caress, setting her back on the rock. Was this a warning? Permission? She assumed the latter and dove head-first into the sea. The universe had broken open, and she was the only one able to stand in the break, because she was the spirit with the grandest stride and stance, the one who curled her self into the hot ears of the never-satiated, the enraged, the dangerous, the yet-to-be-unbroken, the ungovernable. She had no more time to spare.

Thrashing her arms and kicking her feet at panic speed, she tried to complete her mission before the great wide Blue could change her mind and turn her tides. She had no idea what she would find: burial mounds decorated with seaweed or crosses fashioned out of driftwood, maybe sea shells spelling out names to neither be forgotten nor fully known. She swam farther down still, ignoring her lungs screaming for air they could not have and the grit from the sea's own sand itching her eyes and the back of her throat. She swam until she was close enough to the bottom and crawled along with arms outstretched, her eyes narrowed to make her vision as precise as she could.

She came upon the first set of bones by accident, when her toes knocked against some solid and unrelenting thing, not wood, nor rock, nor even metal. From there, she found where the rest had settled, bones with grooves and nicks cut into them, bones with scraps of hair still hanging on. She gathered as many as she could fit into her embrace, wide like the whole world, and returned above ground, and back again, and again, until she was sure she had recovered as much as was possible, was necessary, was vital to memorialize, to lay to rest as their lives deserved.

Even as day dimmed into evening, she could clearly recognize the remains before her for the people they had once been. She ran the roughened tips of her fingers over the skull she held in her lap, lingering over every dent and chip where the bone had given way to time and decay. By following contours only previously touched by flesh, she was already treading too close to the boundaries of the sacred and unforgivable, threatening to rouse souls that had never attained the decent rest they deserved.

She lifted one skull in her hands up to touch her forehead, as if to stare into eyes that once squinted against the sun's last piercing of a fading sky; eyes that once grew wet with joy tempered only by the fear of death reclaiming a child as quickly as it had allowed her to land on earth; eyes shuttering closed to complex internal worlds, pathways and dead ends lined with death freshly planted like tree roots twisting inwards on themselves; eyes aching with the call of sleep and held open only by the kind of childlike curiosity that never rests.

The spirit who was love and vengeance untied the white linen from around her waist and laid it over the rock's uneven plane. One after another, she placed each skull in a neat row, using both hands for the ones with cracks running all over their surface, the ones that looked like they would turn into powder if she pressed too hard in the wrong place. In her palm, she cradled jaws set in tight clenches like it was possible to soothe away the anxieties they had suffered in life. These jaws once sat in faces that routinely burst open into laughter and were caressed by the slender hands of a loving somebody, with fingers for cutting and trapping little pains, fingers for traveling love's familiar path once more before daybreak. She let out a low whisper a lot more like a sigh, as if the dead could still listen, never able to unhear the horror of battle, as if they still had ears eager to grow full with more wonder than any mind could grasp.

She stood up out of the awkward squat she had maintained to inspect the bones and the echoes of lives they held still, stretching her body backwards and side to side to ease her muscles pleading for relief. She sent her arms outwards like she intended to take flight, her palms facing the heavens, the tendons in her muscles tightening and hardening in anticipation. Through her nostrils and her open mouth, she drank as much air as her lungs could hold and jumped off the small shelf of rock back into the water. She propelled her self deeper and deeper, closer to the seabed, her feet and arms never falling out of sync. She passed all kinds of wondrous life, fish darting like bright flashes of color in front of her face, fish with deadly spikes sticking out of their scales, fish with eyes almost as big as their heads. She trawled the ocean floor in her search, the motion of her swimming disturbing spiny creatures attempting to camouflage themselves from their predators between rotting wood and tangles of seaweed.

The spirit who was love and vengeance saw her sister spirit, saltwater and sound, sitting on the sea floor just ahead, her shoulders rounded and head folded towards her chest, like she too was prey hoping to evade discovery. Her bare back glowed reddish brown overlaid with fluorescent blue.

"Sister, it's time."

Saltwater and sound didn't hear love and vengeance, so love and vengeance stretched her self closer, her hands barely brushing the ends of saltwater and sound's long locs streaming behind her.

"Sister . . . sister, is this the place?"

Saltwater and sound swept her hair out of her face and from about her shoulders onto her head, nodding as she did. She had swum close to the seabed looking for the right place to pull and waited there for love and vengeance to arrive. She uncrossed her legs and stood. They only had a short amount of time before the pressure of the water weighing on top of them would become unbearable. Even they could only withstand so much. Together, they looked down at the mass of rock and coral jutting out of the ocean floor and glanced at each other before love and vengeance reached down and began to pull. Love and vengeance pulled and pulled and pulled, until the water seemed to vibrate in reaction to her power. She pulled as water washed over her, resisting what seemed to be the sea urging her to abandon the task.

Love and vengeance was not there to take back the land and her people who had lived and died there as things to be owned and not as human. That land was stolen many a time over—agoo we greet you: Taíno, Natchitoches, Natchez, Osage, Caddo, Eʋe, Fon, Yoruba, Ga-Adangbe, Kru, Malinké, Serer, rightful and careful custodians of the land. Love and vengeance could and would not take these lands, but she could pull up as much of the seabed as she needed to give the people somewhere to go without resorting to cowardly pursuits: theft or murder or war. She pulled until the piece of land saltwater and sound had chosen broke completely away from the ocean floor's expanse and broke the surface of the water into the open air. Love and vengeance swam with her body turned sideways and one arm still pulling the land, until it came to touch the rock where she had prayed and waited and tried not to despair, stoic and in readiness for this event. Love and vengeance finally fell onto her back on the land and began attempting to massage the strain out of her aching body.

The third sister, sweetness and luxury, stood above her, her arms lifted with her hands folded one over the other on top of her head, her stance rigid with waiting. "What took you so long?"

Saltwater and sound had followed love and vengeance back up to the surface, and they both squinted upwards into the parts of sweetness and luxury's face that weren't covered by the shadow of the sun behind her.

"Don't move for a moment," love and vengeance said slowly. "Your body is shade for me."

Sweetness and luxury released her arms and flung them in the general direction of what she perceived to be apathy in a moment where urgency should have been pounding a maddening rhythm into their eardrums, strong enough to rattle their teeth.

"We don't have much time! Get up!" she shouted.

Love and vengeance lifted her self into a sitting position and glared at sweetness and luxury through the wet tangle of her eyelashes, still clumped together from her dive. "So now that I've done the hard work, you want to give me orders?"

"All I'm saying is, eight days is about to turn into nine."

The spirits who were saltwater and sound and sweetness and luxury could not deny the immense weight love and vengeance had carried, but it was not like they had just been sitting on their hands watching time tick by while love and vengeance alone worked hard. The nature of their work was different, not necessarily more or less difficult, but also important for opening a way for the yet-to-be-unbroken to land. Besides swimming along the seabed looking for the perfect piece of land to pull, saltwater and sound was making sure the people did not arrive in an empty nightmarescape. She gathered all the small pleasures the yet-to-be-unbroken had felt and would ever feel from the first day Mawu-Lisa had called the universe into being until the break—praises for the unique turns of a lover's left ear; laughs that sounded like bells and horns and whistles; riddles and rhymes for teaching children lessons that would keep them safe; keys in a lock after a while away from home; a baby's first cry on the earthly side of life; seafoam fizzle—ready to release into the air when the land was ready. Sweetness and luxury made it so that this new place would be full of all the beauty and sweet things the people had enjoyed and would ever enjoy, despite-despite: the flow, fragrance, and feel of almond oil on the body; fresh pawpaw, green-skinned and deep orange on the inside; sandalwood perfume lingering on clothes long after they have been worn, washed, and worn again; anything deep-fried and doughy, so long as its outside is crunchy and brown and its inside pillowy; the weight of a thick braid on the back of one's neck; kisses good night, goodbye, and just because.

The sister spirits swam in three different directions, far enough that they could no longer hear but could still see each other. Love and vengeance towards the Gulf of Guinea, saltwater and sound towards the Caribbean Sea, and sweetness and luxury towards the Gulf of Mexico. They were looking for the edges of the sea, the part of the horizon they could touch so they could move the water itself, and each knew when they had found it because they stopped swimming and stood upright. At the oceans' seams, they pulled at the waters and drew them together until part of the Caribbean Sea poured its crystalline blue self south and eastward into the Gulf of Mexico's silvery mass, which in turn flowed east into the storm sky blue of the Gulf of Guinea. They pulled until the water totally surrounded the piece of seabed love and vengeance had surfaced, blinking fast against the sand and creatures scattering into their faces. They pulled until they had made the place that would become Blue Basin a possible destination out of many for the beloved souls to fly to and land, to lay to rest all those long-suffering bones, neither paradise nor purgatory but an elsewhere they could live free and easy.

# 3

*outside of time, after the break, on Blue Basin*
*first full moon, or the beginning of the year on Blue Basin, or a*
*place where the arrival of a full moon signals a new month and*
*eight full moons make a year, or what is time when you are*
*outside of it*

The people had been dancing all day, defying the cresting and waving exhaustion that tempted them to stop for a rest. They began dancing early in the morning, when the sun's heat emerged more searing than was normal for that time of day, as if it too knew the day was just a bit more special. The parade started at the bottom of the hills in the Katye de Lasyrenn, on the northwestern end of Blue Basin. The younger and less experienced revelers winced and raised their legs, marking time, trying to relieve the feeling of hot pebbles burning bare feet in the same spots for such a long period, like hot needles to flesh. "I can't take it! When will we start moving?"

The elders also felt the discomfort, but the soles of their feet had long hardened to the burning sensation from the ground. They rained mocking laughter into the scowling faces of the young. "Chin up! The number of times we have celebrated the fête is bigger than your age, yet we don't complain!"

Their teasing was drowned out by a strident trumpet sound, signaling the beginning of the next song,

*Volez, volez, volez!*
*Petit oiseau, volez!*
*La fête, c'est pour vous! Volez*

Blue Basin's people would spend the day marching their joy past the small, flat-roofed homes behind low walls in the Katye, some with outbursts of flowers, hibiscus, and bougainvillea spilling over, others with the washing draped over to dry. The people formed a never-ending body stretching across the land, trembling and bristling, a mass of human life rippling with the constant motion of waving arms and heaving chests, of impatient legs surrounded by what looked like a light haze but was actually the dust risen off the ground and hovering, as restless and impossible to pin down as the people's stomping feet. They would move on past the islanders who were not taking part, those standing in the shade of their verandas, holding enthusiastic babies back so they couldn't poke their hands or heads through the spokes in the fences and chastising those who they were too late to save. "Eh heh! What did I say? Didn't I tell you to keep your hands to your self?"

They marched along the Gran Promenade through the Paroisse, a heavily perfumed garden in the middle of the island, grateful for the momentary coolness in the shadows of the rows of neem trees that grew in an arch over the road that led into this part of the island, with its narrow two-story houses sitting behind metal gates that might as well have been taken off their hinges since they were always left thrown open for neighbors and friends to come in and out with ease.

*Volez, volez, volez!*

*Petit oiseau, volez!*
*La fête, c'est pour vous! Volez!*

They danced so they would remember their various arrivals. They danced in the same steps as had the people before them, their footfalls following traces left for them by their mothers and their mothers' mothers, mimicking the kick, kick, turn, and repeat that more work-worn feet had taken to make their selves and their lives possible. They had not all landed at once. They had come sometimes in twos, partners who had dug and picked and scattered and again side by side. Sometimes they had come as whole families, or rather, families reordered out of who remained. Sometimes they had taken solitary journeys, lonesome fugitives with only the creaks and whistles of nighttime woods and the steady swishing of the wind around them as company. They had not all landed at once, but many of them knew what it meant to wear the night like a shroud; to beg their own breath to still into an imperceptible nothing; to feel the damp of swamps and ponds weighing them down from the inside, too long standing in unmoving, muddy water; to blend sans trace into the dawn so the shrubs and trees looked more alive than they; to wait for the sound of a benign cracking branch to turn into a dog's vicious barks of discovery; to flee; to smell the stink of desperation even on their babies' breath, the same stench clinging to the insides of their mouths and their nostrils even when their wide and wondrous tomorrows were open before them, even when flight was now.

And so again they sang:

*Volez, volez, volez!*

*Petit oiseau, volez!*
*La fête, c'est pour vous! Volez!*

Lucille stepped out onto her balcony with its black metal curling onto the side of the house. Leaning over the edge of the railing, she showed just as much wonder in her face as that of Sans-Souci and her toddler, Raphael, who were next door waving at the procession and clapping in time to the music. Lucille found the child hilarious in the delightfully unintentional way that children could be, especially when they weren't screaming dissatisfaction or hunger, and especially when they were someone else's responsibility. The child's red and white hat, part of the costume Lucille had sewn for him, was far too big—perfect for him to grow into—and it slipped past his eyes with every earnest, offbeat nod of his little round head to the marching band's music. She enjoyed the naïve comedy of children and their antics in general, but Sans-Souci's child was especially dear to Lucille because he was born in her house in the wake of his mothers'—Sans-Souci's and her love Antoinette's—arrival on Blue Basin several moons earlier. Lucille had heard the baby's first wails and bore witness to Sans-Souci naming her self anew. Sans-Souci hated that she had been forced to answer to "Marie-Ange" inside of time, and even though she could remember the name she had been blessed with, Afi-gā, older Friday-born, that self was no more, and she could not imagine going back for that name. That self lived in a time before she and her mother lost her baby sister, the day a dog crossed their path and brought with it the end of their world, somewhere along that endless march, that passage through a low door like a closing coffin on the way to becoming the walking dead.

"Cou cou! Bonne fête! How's my baby doing this morning?"

Sans-Souci held the baby's tiny fist and waved it towards Lucille in response. It was the best they could do because the fanfare on the streets below swallowed most of their spoken greetings. Sans-Souci was trying to see if she could spot Antoinette, top-hatted and cane-twirling in the parade. The day of their landing, Sans-Souci and Antoinette had fallen just shy of the shore and swam up onto the beach in Keta Afeme, convinced the only reason they had survived was for the as-yet-unborn life of which they would be protectors. And so the child was born on the island, avec les ailes ouvertes, with a future as wide as the horizon they had crossed to reach Blue Basin.

Lucille looked away from her neighbors and over the swell of bodies and music moving together, mostly in contest for which one could be most exuberant but also in beautiful concert, drumbeats spurring on rolling hips, arms waving rowdy praise in thanks for the band's chaotic serenade. She wanted to be right inside the joyous whirlpool, to be able to inspect and admire the costumes, her handiwork, up close. She strained her neck to see if she could spot her younger sisters, though she already knew it would be a wasted effort. The whole world and her wife were on the streets, but Lucille, marveling at her own creations, would be incomplete without a good view of what was always her best work every year: her sisters' outfits. The youngest, Víví, always carried her self a step behind or a step ahead of everyone else's rhythm yet still proudly flaunting the awareness of her allure with every rock of her hips and chime of the tiny bells and jewels circling her ankles. Her headdress fanned out above her head like the plumage of some rare bird, arrogant and rightly so, because she was aware of her rarity, less commonplace and far more grandiose than some regular peacock. Serena followed behind, powerful grace personified, in the same style she requested every fête, a floor-length tiered skirt with windows of lace sewed into the join where each tier began and a matching off-the-shoulder blouse with short, ruffled sleeves, all white and all the better to set off her skin.

The routine of coaxing Serena to try something more extravagant for once was as infuriating as it seemed obligatory for the annual festival preparations. Víví usually led the way with her self-assuredness as her sword and shield, and Ma-Reine, a friend of Lucille's as close as she could be without being one of the sisters, was right behind her. "Serena, ma belle, this style would be perfect on you!" Víví made grand flourishes with her hands in the general direction of the headless mannequin Lucille had pulled into the room for the fitting session. Ma-Reine continued, "You know I can draw anything you like? I can sketch something for Lucille to sew, something even more grand, something that will make the flowers and the fancy birds jealous on their best day."

"First of all," Serena began in her low and steady voice, "Víví, that's your outfit. And Ma-Reine. Please don't waste your time or your gift. You all know I'm not going to wear whatever you're talking about." She brushed her heavy locs away from her face, her impatience amplified by a heat much harsher than was usual for the time of day, and by having to take part in this silly playacting they all knew would end with her sticking to what Víví called plain boring.

Serena plucked one of the feathers on the bust of the one-piece, and Lucille looked up at her from the skirt she was hemming, "Baby, I'm just trying to make sure everyone looks good, but don't let fire tempt you to rip that thing. You know how long I spent on it?"

And on and on, enclosed by the day's unforgiving blaze, the people sang:

> *Volez, volez, volez!*
> *Petit oiseau, volez!*
> *La fête, c'est pour vous! Volez!*

And again:

> *We did not fall. We will not break.*

The islanders flashed and preened the feathers they wore on their backs, on their shoulders and arms, spilling forward and to the sides from the tops of their heads, more full of flair than the wings that had carried them to this land. Their former selves had kept their wings hidden under packed mud, slipped between warped floorboards, folded like praying hands underneath bales of hay and discarded sackcloth. They had spirited them away from uninitiated, unseeing gazes, so they would not be clipped. The unfortunate ones had only the sore, always unhealed wounds on their backs between their shoulder blades where the wings had been. Some knew of the bite and sting of whip and rope only in memory, but the will and ability to fly were still pressed deep into their consciousness, waiting to take off on a day when safety and peace felt too unimaginable for them to continue to stay grounded inside of time. Still, they were all capable of flight, clipped wings or otherwise. Some hadn't brought wings with them from the home side of no return, from the loving side, but they had brought spirits coiled within the center of themselves, always fluttering and waiting for the day they would step out and ride the wind's currents towards a place outside of time where living free was possible, where free was the only way to live.

Blue Basin was always dancing for its life. Not to save it but to relish its fullness, full and brimming over like the moment in a symphony where the strings' sound rise and swell to heavens. Depending on who you asked, you were likely to get a different explanation of the fête, each bearing little specks of truth in their colorful details. What preceded their flight and arrival, how the land had come to be, they could argue forever, a flicker in their eyes matched only by the center of the flame they sat around to argue and to tell lies and stories, piecing their beginnings together so maybe the truth would seep out of the spaces where the tales did not quite fit.

Lucille's watching followed the wake of Blue Basin's elders, the Grandes Dames or Amegawó, Saint-Antoine and her wife Toussaint, and Saint Pierre and Saint Christophe, who brought up the rear of the entire winding line. She recognized every drape and fold of the heavy blue and white kete over each of these women's shoulders, with the silver thread woven into the fabric winking each time the sun hit it. The heft of the cloth produced in the elders a stately sort of walk, a careful pace that concealed the less impressive reality that some of them were already tired and struggling to keep up with the rest of the dancing crowd. The Amegawó were the most difficult to dress, even more so than the children who could not be begged or threatened to stand still even if it meant a bissap icy as a treat afterwards. Lucille tolerated the Grandes Dames turned-down mouths and tongues clucking disapproval because their early arrival on the island commanded respect, even if they did not always regard her with the same. She kissed her teeth low, like there was any chance they would hear, not out of fear but irritation. She was no one's junior. But no one dared to say so aloud, because inside of time, growing stoop-backed, soft-handed, and white-haired meant you were worthy of reverence—often true, though there were also those elders whose long living didn't necessarily guarantee noble behavior nor command respect. The Amegawó had simply chosen to grow old on Blue Basin, but like everyone else on the island could choose to do, they could have remained as young as the day they landed had they desired, their hair never growing flashes of gray near their temples, their spines remaining unbent.

Because the flying islanders had died once already when those monstrous pale ones had turned them from person to property, they began their second lives approaching old age and death without fear but rather with the clear-headedness that came with the knowledge that they could control it. They did not fear death because it was no longer total, no longer as all-consuming as the darkness of a moonless night. Death for them was something continuous, a series of beginnings, a becoming over and over, unending. They could decide to send their spirits back inside or outside of time as anything in the world they wanted, like the feeling of cool water running down one's scalp while someone else washed and massaged the stubborn dirt away, or as the welcome heat from lemon ginger tea spilling down a sore throat and spreading across the chest on the inside. They could also choose to return as thunder and vengeance in pursuit of revenge against those who had snatched their humanity and tried to break open their souls.

If they chose to age and not to send their spirits back, they could grow old, like the Amegawó, and die naturally, to be buried in the hills standing over the Katye with the other ancestors. They could rest easy knowing they had died this second time in full and glorious possession of their lives, beholden to nothing and no one except their own selves. Whatever they chose, the most vital fact was that no one ever died on Blue Basin unless they chose to, and they always had the freedom to choose how.

Some of the smallest revelers skipped back and forth in line before coming to a standstill to mimic the imposing dignity of the Amegawó or running ahead to try to blend in with the ɖekákpùì, the young adult crowd, with flimsy pieces of cloth around their waists and upper bodies left bare, apart from the half-moons drawn neatly in white chalk all over their shoulders, chests, and backs. The fabrics they used were a spread of all sorts of blue, navy with splashes of white from tie-dyeing, or spotted with geometric shapes in green, or stamped with drawings of blackbirds surrounded by white ovals. Lucille could spot every gold button and epaulet, every bright red jacket fit tight on the marching children. All had passed through her hands at some point in the weeks leading up to the fête, and she still bore the remnants of her work, flecks of blue dye embedded under her nails and roughened patches on her palms impervious to pinpricks and cuts.

Some of the people had painted one side of their bodies in a vertical white stripe and the other in blue, their faces masked by white chalk and retreating under the shade of fringed umbrellas. Others sported sequined costumes with huge wings fixed to the rear, so realistic they looked like they could sail into the air if they stood long enough on a high enough cliff. The jewels blinked with every movement they made, reflecting beams of light in every direction, each dancer their own firework. They skipped and stepped and footworked together, neither brother nor sister, but nɔvi, sibling, neither soft nor toughened but a blend of all kinds of ways of being that were wonderfully complex and made them whole. Even from the height at which she stood, suspended over the festivities on her balcony, Lucille could feel the tickle of the feathers on her face, the pinch of broken beads underfoot, the grit of chalk and dust between her teeth.

*Volez, volez, volez!*
*Petit oiseau, volez!*
*La fête, c'est pour vous! Volez!*

And as they sang and danced—we did not fall, we will not break—they got lighter with every step forward. When they landed, all those many yesterdays ago, they were loaded with all the prayers for good fortune and safety they had packed into their pockets and sewn into the hems of their clothes: copper coins with holes drilled through their middles, heavy brown beads that clicked together when bunched into a fist, dried bones of animals killed very young, sea glass. They landed with shoulders sagging like they had carried the Atlantic drop by drop from its seabed to another place. They landed heavy, feet thudding to graceless stops. They landed smelling like inside of time, salty Bight of Benin, with black Natchitoches soil stamped into the cracks of their heels, and "Jérémie" fried fish lingering greasy on their tongues. They landed heavy but at the same time free and easy, knowing that the waters over which they had flown were now barrier and fortress, impassable stretches of blue over which the pale demons tormenting their former lives could not cross.

*Can you hear us? Entendez-vous? E mía nkɔ sem a? We are talking about:*

*Blue as in endless, as in an impossible sky whose other side you can only imagine if you are flying to your free futures. Blue like the bruises left where you folded and crammed your wings into unthinkable shapes to hide them from the clippers' glint. Blue as in your skin swallowing star light and moon shine. Blue like open palms, like ink tattooed and spilling from the lower lip and all over the chin. Blue like veins in uncut wrists—don't end your self, child, the world cannot lose you. Celestine blue like water so clear you could count the cracks in your fingernails through it. Blue like cobalt so rich it hurts just to glance at it, like winter breath turning visible on meeting the air. Periwinkle blue, like grandma's birthday cake and the icing you swiped and licked off your left pinkie until you were caught and caught a scolding. Blue like look what you did, mashed up those berries across the front of your church dress and now we will miss service. Blue like clean sheets and a towel for a work-weary body. Blue like noon sky is sitting high above your head, full of promise and I love you. A blue that will protect you because the evil cannot pursue where it does not understand, cannot chart the trajectories of your wide futures where it cannot see. Blue like maroon mountains, blue like quilombo, blue like we're outside of time dreaming of you dreaming of us, blue like we'll be here waiting on you.*

Oui, they landed heavy, but as to how the land got there, they could no longer tell, if they ever knew or remembered. What they knew was that Blue Basin was there, waiting for their arrival. So now they draped themselves with the same blues they used to paint every flat surface, every non-living plane—the walls of their houses, their front and back steps, the ceilings of their verandas, the tiles in their kitchens—so the devils they had left in the after-current of their flight would mistake all the blue for part of the water and would forever be stuck back there à lòt bò dlo, back where rising to a new morning felt like dying. And so they cheered, with no more regard for the song's tune:

> *No day for the devil!*
> *Whistle*
> *Fire on his head!*
> *No day for the devil!*
> *Whistle*
> *The devil is dead!*

And again:

> *We did not fall. We will not break.*

When new people arrived mid-celebration, the joy would not dull nor diminish. Instead, whoever happened to be closest to the landing place would slide out of line, smooth like a perfect hem concealing the working that kept it together, easing themselves out of the fête's forward-moving current and towards the new neighbor, who, more often than not, would be still shivering and more than a little afraid. Dancing arms turned steady and reassuring. Sometimes, they even recognized as friend, neighbor, sibling, lover, the people they received with arms and spirits cast wide: *Woezɔ, you are welcome, we've been waiting.* The arrivals were mostly peaceful, mostly tomefafa and dzidzeme, and even when they weren't, there was still relief breathing deeply behind the panic of "What would we have done had there been nowhere to land?"

But when the people were still, in between steps or pausing for breath mid-dance, or on days and nights where the heat was so thick it muted sound and made movement near impossible, inside the stillness they could hear people yearning for them from inside of time, people imagining their faces, people wondering what they looked like now, people questioning if they would still be recognizable to those they were wondering about. They were a part of each other, those who had flown off and now danced outside of time, and those yet-to-be-unbroken still moving inside time's forced straight line. A cry ringing out inside of time echoed outside of it on Blue Basin and in the spirits of those who had landed there. Any break, any crack, any fall of one of their own inside of time meant chipped paint, crumbled brick, a warped window on Blue Basin. So they mended and built and re-built always in anticipation of the eventual arrival of their wondering and wandering yet-to-be-unbroken beloveds.

Every day on Blue Basin was as monumental as the one before, even if nothing happened except the same comings and goings. Every day was monumental simply because it came to pass on this island, a most impossible place. But fête day was more than sacred; it was life's wonder distilled into hours that felt like they would never subside. It was also Lucille's birthday. But her itch to strut and leap and spin was squashed underneath the more pressing duty to remain available and ready for last-minute outfit emergencies. Between trombone blasts and tambourine shakes, the young and those who only had the taste of youth left on their cracking lips would hurry up the metal stairs, in and out of Lucille's house for her to see to their damaged headdresses or to find quick fixes for ruined seams and drooping sleeves.

"Careful with this outfit! You hear me? Don't let my cuts and bruises be for nothing. E se a?"

She would send them off with a wave of her hands and slight irritation twinkling behind mischief in her eyes. There were definitely many other people who could sew on the island, but none in the way she did, at least so everyone insisted. And even as her spirit self was raging revenge and turning Love's Face all over the worlds of the yet-to-be-unbroken inside of time, caring for them until they found a way out, her flesh self was here, outside of time, anticipating anything in need of mending. So, for the moment at least, she would remain.

*break open*

*inside of time, after the break*
*"Jérémie, Grand'Anse," Ayiti—agoo, we greet, mia tɔwò Taíno,*
*rightful and careful custodians of the land—1801*

*Can you hear us? Entendez-vous? E mía nkɔ sem a? We are called so many names we gave ourselves for all the many lives we have led:*

*Before she called and felt her self "Sans-Souci," before her free-flying baby, before being greeted by a lungful of saltwater and sand, she was Marie-Ange digging the big toe on her right foot into hot sand. She was surrounded by the sort of night so thick it could be a lake choked by reeds and slow-growing moss. Marie-Ange was waiting, half her self already on the other side of gone, the remaining half aching with impatience, with the fear of standing still in that hot sand for good.*

*"Ma chère. Suis-là, I'm here. Ready?"*

*"Antoinette. I thought you were leaving me here to die. It's hard to stand up tonight, but I'm ready."*

*Antoinette was Marie-Ange's mirror image, her complement, except wild. Marie-Ange's hair was wound with black thread and tucked into a small basket crowning her head, just like her maman had taught her to do for her self and for her little sister before they were taken away to work and die on some different land. Marie-Ange had red cloth tied around her body, stretched across her ballooning middle. Meanwhile, Antoinette's appearance was an accumulation of all the places she had run and hidden and crawled, tatters ripped into her cloth so it gave way to glances of brown beneath, scratched and bleeding in places. "Mon ange. Did you think I had died? Or you thought I'd go without you, especially with the child coming?"*

*"Antoinette. We are already dead. And how was I to know? Maybe you changed your mind. Maybe you thought me and this belly couldn't make it. How was I to know? I could have dug my*

*way out and come out somewhere else in all this time I've been waiting."*

*Marie-Ange scratched an insect bite at the side of her neck impatiently, so hard she was close to catching her own flesh and blood under her nails. She tilted her head in the opposite direction from her scratching hand and then jerked straight like she had been zipped up along her spine by an unseen somebody, then folded back over like that movement had spent the last of her strength. "Antoinette. I can barely stand upright . . . I haven't been able to for a long time. The damp . . . it settles. . . . I thought you would not come."*

*Marie-Ange had spent each of her dying days up to her elbows in dirty soap suds and near-boiling water and the wet and the heat had soaked into her body, sitting just beneath her flesh but deep enough that she could not dig it out, like she was slowly becoming stuffed with the never quite dry linens of which there seemed to be an eternal supply. Her bones themselves felt like mush, incapable of holding her frame together, so one day she was sure she would collapse into her self, a pile of skin and membrane too fragile to remain unified.*

*Her heart was leaping out of sync with its usual beat. This could not be good for the child. At first, Marie-Ange had barely acknowledged the existence of this new life pending, standing at the border between spirit and something like human, because this would mean acknowledging her "husband" who had not been a partner at all but a stranger she had shared begrudging space and unending nights with. The white man with the twisted soul in the once-grand house felt that by virtue of paying for their lives and their bodies, he could alter and designate their fates, and he* had forced them together so he would have more people to render undead, more hands to labor and carry and plough the dry land he owned. Being with her "husband" was like clutching at air, like his soul was miles away from the termites eating away at their cabin's wooden walls too close together for comfort, away from the raffia mats, from the slow burn of their daily drudgery. And the smell . . . sickly and sweaty and dying all at once. Marie-Ange's "husband" often looked at her like there was a hole through the back of her head, like he wished she was not there, but Antoinette loved all of her and Marie-Ange knew Antoinette would love the child.

"Y a pas de souci. There was no way I was leaving without you. I just had to be careful I was not spotted. I'm sorry. I'm here."

Marie-Ange stepped as close as her belly allowed and settled her arms over and around Antoinette's shoulders. The wind had started rushing urgently around them, but they didn't notice it lifting cloth and leaves and dust alike until it raged so much they felt it inside their chests. The wind rocked and pulled and tossed. Their feet left earth. The only sign that remained of their having been there was a shred of red cloth stuck to a thorny bush and the shallow dip in the soil where Marie-Ange had tried to bury her toe.

The wind was so chilling they thought they would never feel what it meant to be warm again. There was the cold, and there was a total night running over and around their bodies like oil, and they could not see where it ended or if it would ever give way to light. Their fingers had grown numb, and if it had not been for the weight of the other person's bulk, they would have thought one of them had fallen.

Marie-Ange spoke over and around the wind's howl, "Maman

*told me we will know when we reach. There will be a man with a hat sitting high and pipe hanging onto his lower lip and a crossroads. She used to sing me his praise song but I have forgotten . . ."*

*"Ange of mine. I thought it was a woman with a knife in hand and big wings folded at her back, so shiny they look silver. Her name . . . I have forgotten."*

*They did not have time to fear that their destination would not exist. If they had allowed doubt to chew away at their faith, they would probably still be rooted on the ground, doomed.*

*"Maybe a whole host of spirits will be waiting under some trees in a clearing somewhere, or by a lake, or by a blue diamond sea. Maybe it's Guinen, and my maman and my sister—my small me, my Afi-vi—will be waiting for us."*

*Standing in that total night was almost as frightening as the day Marie-Ange's world broke beyond repair, when she and her mother and sister were wrenched away from that quiet town, that spit of land between waters, and marched to a boat and another ocean that, unlike their stately, silent sea, roared like it could swallow them into its unimaginable below. The only thing more powerful than the fear threatening to freeze her to the spot on the wrong side of free was the dream that Afi-vi—Who was left to die because her little legs could carry her no further? Who lost her way? Who was pulled roughly by the arm into another line of people?—was somewhere between that final day in Keta and wherever and whenever Afi-gā turned Marie-Ange found her self now.*

*Antoinette responded, "Maybe. I heard it's a place where every wall is blue and where the sea doesn't spit out the dead—"*

*If there was such thing as a time that could be divided and apportioned into minutes and seconds and understood by the earth's compulsive rotation around a rising and setting sun, Marie-Ange and Antoinette were outside of it. They didn't know what time it was when they left; they knew only that it was dark and they had little time before the hounds set after their vanishing shadows. They did not know how long it had been since they took flight, nor did they know how much longer they would be airborne. Most urgently, they did not know how they would tell when they had arrived.*

*The night turned fluid, now more like silk than oil, and swaddled them so they thought they could fall asleep mid-air. They had broken time in half and stepped beyond it towards freedom, and they were dead tired.*

*"Cherie, you heard that?" Marie-Ange could barely see past the tip of her own nose but stretched her neck as far as she could over Antoinette's shoulder hoping to follow the sound where her sight could not go.*

*"No, I didn't. Careful, Ange. We cannot fall."*

*The something Marie-Ange heard sounded like a child's hands clapping together in play; it sounded like a tomorrow with a placid sea hugging up to the land before retreating and shifting the sand slightly like smoothing down someone's hair; it sounded like bare feet trying to cross a freshly swept floor—softly softly— in the middle of the night. The something Marie-Ange heard sounded like an arrival, but she just didn't know it yet. The wind gathered itself around Marie-Ange and Antoinette and drew them downwards. They both began to panic when they felt the harsh drag of salty air in their nostrils. They had flown too far to end up back in the same hell wearing paradise's face and yet, was it possible? Was it some sort of cruelty?*

*"Antoinette, I can barely hold my self together."*

*Marie-Ange gasped and tried to tighten her hold around her love, but her muscles turned limp, expired. They were running out of faith in a safe landing place.*

*"Careful, mon Ange," Antoinette repeated, but their shared terror made her words come out disjointed, like the beats their hearts were missing. Their panic meant the wind would have to work harder to steer them to land. Their panic meant they did not notice the wonder of the place sprawling below them. If they had looked around and beyond fear, they would have seen where three different seas flowed into each other and the land sitting inside this meeting of waters. Then again, they might have seen and not believed.*

# 4

*outside of time, after the break, on Blue Basin
first full moon, or it makes sense that Lucille would choose to
celebrate her self whenever the island celebrates too, or what is
birth to a person who has called her self into being, spirit made
flesh made somebody beyond human understanding*

Sturdy and determined adult hands eventually pried the
children away from the fête frenzy, scrubbed them down with
black soap, and smothered them with lwil maskriti to keep dry
air from cracking their young skin too early. The children went
to bed with mugs of hot chocolate, some still clutching in their
fists shreds of the raffia and feathers they had worn during the
day. Right before the sun ended its decline through the sky, and
before they fell into bed from too much merriment and too
much food, Blue Basin's people would take bottles from their
places on dead trees planted in the ground outside their homes
and clean them with seawater from the island's three coasts
before returning them to their various branches, verandas, and
balconies to ward off any ill-intentioned spirits too stubborn to
be stomped away beneath the islanders' dancing feet or repelled
by all the blue. The freshly washed bottles gleamed beneath
moonlight, but their use was far from ornamental. They were a
form of divine protection, a shield against unseen evil, at once a
warning and a trap.

Sans-Souci reenacted the tug-of-war she and Antoinette

eventually won against their son, who refused to part ways with the red jacket Lucille had sewn him, so taken was he with its gold buttons and chains hanging from the shoulders. "You should have heard him!" Sans-Souci caught her breath between laughter and imitating her son's wobbling away from her as fast as his new bones could take him, which wasn't very fast at all.

The crowd rumbled with laughter and sighs. They laughed harder still because they knew Sans-Souci was only at the beginning of what was an annual campaign for other parents on Blue Basin attempting to compel their children to abandon their finery, a months-long spectacle that usually involved these beautiful terrors sprinting down the Katye hills as fast as their naughty, breathless giggles would allow, with one mother or one uncle stumbling over loose sand and pebbles behind: "Mawu, this child! Il va me tuer! At least let me wash it!"

Among the people assembled for Lucille's birthday celebration, there were still a few infants clinging to a parent's hip here or tied firmly to a back there, too young to be left in the care of their older siblings. The babies were so worn out, only being able to stand so much excitement in their little bodies, they didn't stir at the noise from their parents' continued merrymaking. The bubbling and breaking of laughter and tipsy shouts were muffled inside the house, where Lucille was turning her sharp eye on her own appearance. She had sewn her self a white dress and stood in front of a full-length mirror edged in brass inspecting every inch, the heart-shaped neckline, the seams pointing down towards her waist, the fabric following the round of her belly and her hips before billowing to the floor like a scarf into wind. Her resplendent self was projected off every wall in her sister Víví's sitting room, their yellow paint almost completely obscured by mirrors of different sizes, with metal frames twisted into floral patterns and others with plain bands following their shape. She could already feel the humidity wrapping itself around her hair, thwarting the smoothening efforts of the handfuls of aloe vera she had slathered on to pull it back into a bun. All she would have to show for her efforts were a few sore spots where the pins would scratch and a fine halo of frizz crowning her head. She was exhausted and aching from her wrists to the small of her back, through her body down to the arches in her feet. A wreck, but she absolutely would not allow her self to look like it, especially not today. Not now, when she was content with what she was seeing and finally had the chance to let her self loose to les bons temps.

Outside, Víví glided between the guests, the white film of fabric she wore for a dress held up with straps so thin it looked like a whisper of a thing, or so the prim ladies whispered from their shaded corner, Misses and Madames who insisted on wearing white satin gloves for fancy occasions, no matter how high the heat. The gown trailed behind her, occasionally getting caught on someone's bracelet or under the heel of a sandal, yet still remaining without any stain or tear. Lucille knew Víví relished the role of host, as it gave her a chance to not only feel the vibration of other people's collective pleasure but to enjoy the fact that she and her hospitality were the reason for their pleasure. In her form as the spirit that was, is, and will be luxury and sweetness, Víví—or Sweetness, and very rarely, Vivienne, depending on who was calling on her—was inside of time everywhere a grandmother was wearing perfume to bed or putting a gold ring on next to four others, or where there was a flower opening full and bright into the world from a bud, but she was also here, outside of time, making sure no enjoyment was spared in any of their lives.

Every year, with the regularity of the seasons lapsing from monsoon to dry heat and back again, Víví insisted the party was the only way to close Fête Day. Lucille always kissed her teeth, so sharp and so loud that she almost convinced the others she was truly annoyed, although she loved the sunlight Fête Day brought out of Víví and everyone else on Blue Basin Island. Serena, the middle sister, let her soft and knowing laughs roll over each other, "We baby her. Then complain. Then let her do it anyway. Go ahead nye sí. What are you feeling like for cake this year?"

From where she stood indoors, Lucille could see the party guests dodging and dancing around the lawn chairs scattered in clusters across Víví's back garden. She caught fragments of harmless talk and shards of nastiness thrown by those guests who could never be satisfied no matter how lavish the affair.

"When can we eat?"

"I didn't come for mosquitoes to come and chew on me."

"Taflatse, is this for her or for Lucille? Regardez comment elle s'habille . . ."

Víví squeezed her way between the complaints and into the center of these conversations, patting her slicked-down finger waves for non-existent flyaways and smiling slyly, "Tout va bien? Get you another drink?"

She rolled her eyes as she pranced away to refill glasses still half full. Some people never had enough.

A smooth voice spun her self around the record player and wound her way out of the white wooden shutters before wafting over the heads of the people, swaying them, flowing beneath the high and low tones of their conversations rather than overpowering:

> *Sweetness, sing for me*
> *Sing for me sweet birdie*
> *Sing a little sweet song for me, sweetness*

Víví continued her rounds through the guests, pretending she didn't see the petals of her precious morning glories being crushed deep into the mud that was being churned up from underneath the grass by never-still feet. She paused by the table of food, her eyes roaming over the platters overflowing with crawfish, crab, corn cobs, several kinds of rice speckled with reds and greens from the vegetables, and bowl after bowl of Lucille's favorite domedo, the pork roasted to its crispiest and spiced until it could knock out the back of your throat. They had already feasted the day away after the dancing was done, but there was always room for more, especially if Víví had done the cooking. The centerpiece was, as always, the cake, this year with icing carved and fashioned into ridged shapes like crystals as yet unrefined, sitting on top of a white rock. Víví eyed the cake up and down, looking for marks in its creamy surface or other imperfections that were not there.

Lucille heard thump-break-thump, Víví hurrying up the porch stairs two at a time, and she knew the warm haze of camaraderie and alcohol was no longer enough to cover her absence from the party.

While the spirit that was, is, and would be saltwater and sound was somewhere inside of time in both salted water boiling for rice and the noise of the water frothing into the fire, the version of her that was Serena was outside of time by her sister's porch door, rocking her self in a wicker chair, singing along to the music in her own key, a melody unlike anything a person has or will ever sing anywhere inside or outside of time. A small group of people had gathered around her, sitting on the floor with their knees drawn up to their chins, enthralled by her voice, but from the way her eyes were shut and the tiniest of smiles flickered on her face, it was obvious she was not bothered by the audience. An odd sort of storyteller Serena was, one who could take or leave public attention because she narrated tall tales and sang mainly for her own satisfaction and for those she loved most dearly, her sisters. If Lucille and Víví were the rumble and rush of the sea before a storm, Serena was the stillness of low tide, saying little unless she was singing or storytelling. To Blue Basin people, young, old, and old in body but not in soul, Serena's stories were more than magic: they were the entire world and all the sparkling unknowns that lay beyond it. She had the answers to everything—why it was not wise to whistle at night, how to arrest ill-meaning spirits with only a small bottle and a piece of string, and why mosquitoes loved the thin skin on human beings' ankles most of all. Serena could call each star by name and pluck it from its place in the constellation to give the children a better look, to explain how it came to be at all. She could hold the moon in her wide, steady palm and point, "Do you know where this comes from? Me gli toge na wò. Let me tell you."

When Víví reached the top step, she glanced up at the porch ceiling, painted the color of the early morning sky. She winced a little when she noticed tracks left by ants attempting to find a way in to nest between the house's beams. They had escaped her vigorous scrubbing, this time at least.

Lucille still tucked and pulled at her self, half listening to Serena behind the door's netted screen, scratching and pulling at her earlobes in anticipation, like she didn't already know how all Serena's stories ended. "Do you know about the sun and the moon? Do you know their names? How they love each other and us? Let me tell you—"

Víví's shrill excitement cut into Lucille's eavesdropping. "Nye sí, are you there? I was starting to think you had changed your mind about the party."

Lucille's face flashed a mischief. "I was thinking about it, but last minute, I decided to grace you all with my glory."

They fell forward into their laughter, still doubled over as Víví led Lucille out towards the festivities. "Nɔvinyewo! Siblings of mine," Víví began in a booming voice, like the madame of ceremonies at a fête she was, who wanted to be sure even those who stayed home could hear the goings-on. "If you would please turn your attention to the front, un moment s'il vous plaît!"

As they turned to admire and cheer for Lucille, someone—probably Sans-Souci, who by now had lost count of the number of glasses she had polished clean—started a rowdy rendition of one their carnival songs:

> *Volez, volez, volez!*
> *Petit oiseau, volez!*
> *La fête, c'est pour vous! Volez!*

Lucille let the crowd propel her forward, lifting her off her feet and into its midst. They pulled her into hugs scented with lemongrass, lavender, the remains of the garlic frying smell that wouldn't come out no matter how much one washed, talcum powder, and sweat. If they remembered nothing else from their arrivals, they remembered her pushing unfinished bowls of soup or ricewater back across the table—"Ao, you're not done; you need this cherie"—or the click-clicking of her pocketknife steady and light like a clock's hands doing their work. If she wasn't there right after the landing, she would definitely be there as soon as she was able, with new clothes, a firm hug, a moment, and some space to collect one's self.

She was the sort of person who made people strut proudly down the street if they were fortunate enough to know her closely, to sit on a porch somewhere with her sharing glasses of sweet tea or some roasted plantain and peanuts, or swapping stories for laughs over someone's fence—Nyatefee? Vraiment?—or bouncing someone's baby on her knees enough to make them squeal without spitting up their lunch. People's attachments to Lucille looked all kinds of different ways, but there was no denying most islanders had one, and Lucille loved it. She loved to be needed and admired until it began to feel like a swarm of small hands holding onto her arms and legs, their grip turning clawlike and impossible to escape. There was a certain distance she felt was necessary to hold people away to delay the inevitable fatigue, a wish to remove her self from their needing grasp. And she did, so she could bask in the love without their need consuming her whole self and her sanity.

"Ah, elle est là, toute belle!"

"Que les esprits te bénissent, my dear."

Sans-Souci tried with one hand to shift her fascinator of feathers and flowers back to the right amount of playful over her right eye, and with the other hand, she waved wildly: "Let the birthday girl through! Don't keep her all to your self!"

The music floating out from the house had turned away from its languid moan into a more spirited clash and bounce of drums and strings:

> *Walk soft, child, live wild*
> *This is sweetness, this is life*
> *Walk soft, child, live wild*

Lucille felt her self an exquisite procession of one, ever-smiling as she paused to shuffle a few dance steps with someone here or to hold out her hands for others to pour into her palms bracelets made out of sea glass, beads, and shells, and envelopes with fragrant and medicinal herbs pressed between their folds. Friday's Child handed Lucille a small figurine carved out of some sweet-smelling black wood: a woman with solid arms resting on her hips and her head flung back in laughter. Friday's Child was a sensitive soul who kept so much to his self except when he ventured out on fête day once a year. The neighbors would see him sometimes chipping away at hunks of wood in his backyard, but he would only nod and mumble a soft "ça va" as they passed. They said the whites of his eyes used to be so red—not like rust, more like a fresh wound spilling—that back where he had been before, no one would look at him, so he kept his eyes lowered even after they'd cleared.

"Mr. Vendredi, thank you. She looks so real!"

Friday's Child's face opened into a rare and radiant smile: "Anything for you, mamzelle."

Someone handed Lucille four small containers of flour cut through with the gunpowder that most people on Blue Basin kept at home, a reminder of the yet-to-be-unbroken inside of time and the rituals they used to try to open the way between the living side and the spirit side. There was a jar from each of the Amegawó, who had probably settled into their usual retreat to recover the energy they had marched and danced out all day at the fête.

"Saint-Antoine, Toussaint, Saint-Pierre, Saint-Christophe," a pair of dye-darkened hands shook as she handed over the jars one by one.

"Que les esprits te bénissent." Elsie Loiseau's voice was a quiet scratch in all the commotion, and Lucille would have missed her if she had not accompanied her wishes with a squeeze of Lucille's upper arm.

"You gave your voice away to the fête, non?"

Elsie played with the gold hoop earrings weighing on her earlobes. By the wing design pressed into the gold, Lucille could tell Elsie had made them her self. But beyond the fact that she was both sika gbede, gold smith, and eze mela, potter, and she had arrived just a few new moons prior, Lucille didn't know Elsie well. Together, they laughed the kind of airy laugh of people who rarely said more than a "salut" or "lekee" or "how far" to each other as they passed in the street. Lucille caught glimpses of Elsie's teeth between laughs and saw how they sat jagged and not quite fitting in her narrow face, skin like a photograph washed in sepia, and altogether lovely.

Sans-Souci and Antoinette stumbled into the pair, leaning on each other and swaying like clothes waving in a frisky breeze but still sober enough to offer Lucille a cluster of shiny crocheting needles tied together with white ribbon. If there was any sort of crowd gathered, whether in celebration or in chaos, Sans-Souci was likely to be at the center of it, or at least at a prominent place on the sidelines egging on the action. Antoinette was the untroubled water's surface to Sans-Souci's tornados on most days, except for the fête, when they both indulged in celebration of their time living free on Blue Basin. It was understood, if unspoken, that Sans-Souci took the horrors to which they had borne witness much harder than Antoinette, that she still woke up calling for her lost sister, smelling like the singe of hell they had lived, that in the dips between her highs, she was still hoarding the grief of being lost to all who had known her inside of time forever. "Que les esprits.... Vivent les esprits! Vivent L– Joyeux . . . esprit!"

"If I had free hands, I would clap for you! Bravo mesdames, and take it easy on the bottle now!" Lucille winked at Sans-Souci and Antoinette and kept on through the mass of party-goers, slowly now, hindered by the ever-growing collection of gifts she clutched to her chest. Most of the guests competed for small grasps of Lucille's time to give her their well-wishes and tokens of appreciation. There were other people who were too far surrendered to the fog that followed so much enjoyment, holding onto each other by the extra pleats in their skirts, swaying always half a step in front of the music.

Lucille almost missed Miss Yvonne half in the shadow of a tree full and weighed down with lemons, her hands like worn leather folded around pieces of paper as fragile as the creased skin on her fingers. She spread out the papers towards Lucille like an open fan, speaking for themselves in a way Miss Yvonne's quiet evangelism never did: "La Déesse," a broad-shouldered woman standing with one leg in a raging sea, the other in an empty green field, fury lying dormant in her wide-open eyes; "Le Sauveur," a pale man with limp waves tumbling past his face, too mournful looking, Lucille thought, to be any kind of savior. Miss Yvonne took her quivering hands from her grey ringlets rinsed purple, to her pencil, to the thin paper on which she had drawn her holy portraits and copied out verses from her sacred book, and back again, always in that order. The tremor didn't leave them while Lucille pressed them close together between her own, bringing both pairs of hands to her chest, "Madame Yvonne, tout va bien? Thank you so much for these."

After Miss Yvonne walked away into the garden's dark, Lucille turned and gave a sparing nod to Ma-Reine and Glory, even though she and Ma-Reine were far past cold nods and hellos, even though what she really wanted to do was to show Miss Yvonne's drawings to her to marvel at how she was one of the only other people on the island who could make beauty on paper anything close to what Ma-Reine could. Ma-Reine's face was as inviting as her husband's was closed and impervious to feeling. Her eyes were black buttons, and inside of them was soft and liquid, as though whoever she was looking at had the power to move her to tears if they said the right, or wrong, thing. She was not stunning so much as haunting, the kind of person who would leave somebody unsettled for the rest of the day after passing and meeting eyes with her on the road. Glory had pale skin pulled over his knife-edge jaws and tight knots of hair coiled and sprinkled over his scalp the color of the bright Keta Afeme shore that met the Gulf of Guinea. He looked like he would rather drown where any of the seas met than be in Lucille's presence. At first, she hadn't known what to make of his unknowable nature. Sometimes she would come across them working on the shallot patch the couple kept where the Afeme merged into La Paroisse because the soil there was rich, and he would extend nothing more than a mumbled greeting and a smile that left his eyes like two pieces of glass that swallowed the light. Lucille preferred to believe her concern for her friend did not feel more urgent than for anyone else. But in truth, when it came to Ma-Reine, she felt a love and fear that knocked the breath out of her sometimes, especially because of the way Glory's face bent light away from anywhere he stood, and any light-heartedness along with it.

Lucille was drawn to Ma-Reine because she was one of the very few besides her sisters whose vision was so wide she could see farther than any given here and now. The two would spend hours in Lucille's home in the friendly quiet of each other's presence, with only the scratch of Ma-Reine's pencil tip against rough sketch paper or the soft thud and hammer of Lucille's sewing machine. Every few hours, one of them would get up to stretch and refill glasses with tea or with wine or to show their works to the other, the perfection of a stitch, the shading on a portrait of one of her neighbors, or the sun setting over the Katye Hills.

Ma-Reine could see the universe from the outside, like looking into a valley from a mountain summit, and she drew and painted and carved this view all the time. Ma-Reine's grandmother, Mama Hadzila the teller of tales in a small town somewhere inside of time between a sea and a lagoon, could see and know things no one else could, and she taught them to her daughter, Mama Aida, who taught them to her daughter, Ma-Reine. A crack. A fall. Then the people died. They died day in and day out. Unbent backs. Shoulders high and stretched open. Winged or not. They went forth. Ma-Reine's maman had an eye most people could not believe, like she could see the whole world for all of its edges and surfaces, like it was in a small glass globe sitting in her right hand. And when she turned that eye to the work of her hands?

Mama Aida imagined Ma-Reine, swore she saw her daughter before she was born, brought her to life on paper and on the chalk-covered walls and into the world, then taught her how to do the same, taught her how to imagine themselves alive and free. Most importantly, it would have destroyed her to know Ma-Reine had made it all this way outside of time only to endure suffering at the hands of Glory. No, not in this place, not for someone like Ma-Reine, whose maman and grandmother had dreamt a life far beyond suffering for their child.

Finally, Lucille was able to remove her self from the eager and wanting arms around her shoulders and her waist. She set her load of gifts in an empty chair and sat down next to it. Lucille had relished in the merriment at first, but she had begun to feel like the whole world was in Víví's backyard pressing against her. She needed some reprieve. The decorative lights had at first winked naughtily from amidst the bushes and tree branches where Víví had scattered them. Now they felt more like needles threatening to pierce the surface of her skin. She was grateful for a moment to lean against the back of her seat to catch her breath and to let her practiced elegance lapse until she felt ready to interact with people again without letting them see the lull in her spirit. She was nestled far enough underneath the flame trees' cover that neither Víví nor Serena was likely to notice her and would probably assume their sister was still swallowed up by the people desperate to spend some time in her presence.

Now that she was seated, Lucille was aware of the full force of the pain charging through her body from spending the entire day on her feet stitching and cutting and zipping. Even in this little sliver of solitude she had seized for her self away from the evening's fun, she couldn't quiet her mind. Her thoughts raced with the intensity and urgency of the endless requests she had to attend to all day:

"Ma Lucille, please help! My zip is stuck. Can you fix it?"

"I tore a little hole in my sleeve just now, me ɖe kuku."

"Please Lucille, I've lost two buttons!"

"You need some help with that?" Lucille was caught mid-motion, trying to reach a spot on her back where it felt like several mosquitoes were having their own feast and hadn't noticed the person standing in front of her. She looked up past the pointed tips of his black shoes, the silver buckle standing out against the highly polished black leather, the careful pleats in his black trousers as precise as folded sheets of unused paper, the matching shirt tucked in and secured with a simple black belt.

"What do you mean?" Embarrassment washed over Lucille's face with its ticklish warmth, and she was convinced this stranger could tell. Her hands wandered up to her hairline, then to the low bun fixed behind her head, then her collarbone, in a failed effort to not betray the awkwardness she suddenly felt.

"I mean, you look like you could use a little assistance. And I have two capable hands." He turned his hands, palms up, then down, as if to justify his boldness with some proof. "So? Mademoiselle?"

His voice was a smooth hum that was still loud enough to cut through the music and gossip and the tinkling of cutlery colliding with porcelain. She felt his speech in her chest like a booming bassline, each note dropping to the floor of her stomach like heavy fruit to waiting ground. "I can't accept help from someone I can't look in the eyes. And whose name I don't know."

"Samedi Amegbetɔ. I'm sure you've seen my little office in Keta Afeme."

Lucille rose to his height and took off his hat, flipping it over in her hands like she was appraising its quality. She searched this face definitely belonging to a stranger. She was certain she would remember if she had seen this man before. And she didn't know what to make of his name. Amegbetɔ, a person. Names here often spelled out the futures that parents wanted for their children, Klenam—shine for me. They told of triumphs and failures or could even describe the way the sky looked on the day of one's birth, or just the day of the week, like a Kojo or a Kodzo born on a Monday. Names held pieces of wisdom or even prayers: Xɔlali, my savior lives; Sefakor, God comforts me; Seshi, protected by God; or simply the pure satisfaction of bearing witness to new life: Enyo, Eyaedzem, Eyram—it is well, this one pleases me, God has blessed me. Maybe whoever gave him his name wanted him to be his own person, whole and unto his self. She studied his face, his high forehead and a smile free of chips or any other imperfections, and with incisors that were a bit too pronounced, too much of a point to them. She liked something about the look of them.

"I'm Lucille."

"As if I didn't already know." Samedi caught Lucille's wrist in his hands as she reached up to place his hat back on his head.

"Eh heh! Amegbetɔ! Is that you?" Miss Geneviève disrupted the space between Samedi and Lucille, resting her lean frame on the gnarled cane she needed to walk.

"Madame Jeune-vee-ève!" Samedi pulled out each vowel like toffee from a stick.

"You're never one to miss a fête, are you?" Deep wrinkles pulled the skin on Miss Geneviève's face from either side of her nose down towards her chin. She fixed her face into a frown, and her soft, sagging skin seemed to harden into a rugged surface like the bark of an old tree. Miss Geneviève was widely respected and feared for her inflexible character. Despite her years, she carried her self around Blue Basin like her skeleton was constructed of steel bars and fire and not regular human bone. She insisted her name be pronounced the right way, with every syllable given its due attention, and her disdain for Samedi threatened to make storm out of drizzle at his exaggerated mockery of her. "Listen here, you mal-élevé! I sent my granddaughter to you yesterday and she woke up this morning even worse than she was!"

Samedi took Miss Geneviève's free hand in his own, massaging the fingers knotted and twisted by time against their intended direction and stained black and blue with cigarette ash and dye like so many other hands on the island. "Madame, I'm no one's ordinary medicine man. It's not my fault if my remedies didn't sit well with your granddaughter . . ."

The metal in Miss Geneviève's eyes turned molten as she snatched her hand away from Samedi, teetering on her better leg and her cane. "I came to this mess you call a party just to find you, you hear me? My granddaughter threw up all day and couldn't dance in the fête. Just about brought up her entire insides; couldn't even keep down soup or even water!

"Not your ordinary medicine man," she spat. "No kind of medicine man at all! Amegbetɔ indeed. Amebala! Cheat!"

Friday's Child had by this time pushed his body between Miss Geneviève's fury and Samedi's careless laughter. "Madame, it's late. Let me walk you home. Save your energy."

Friday's Child laid a firm guiding arm around Miss Geneviève's stooped shoulders and led her away from the shadowy place beneath the trees where Lucille still sat and Samedi stood, apparently undisturbed by what had just taken place.

Lucille looked a question at Samedi, "So?"

He shone a huge smile in return, revealing dimples that seemed so misplaced for all their sweetness in a stark, angled face such as his. "So?"

Across the yard, Víví was clearing space on the veranda to make way for the jazz trio to take over from the record player. Serena stood cradling her saxophone like it would easily tumble and break if she were to loosen her hold even for a moment. Sans-Souci helped Antoinette carry a double bass out from the house, before settling behind the drums and tickling the high hat, *tsssssss*. Pausing briefly from all her arranging and fussing, Víví turned towards the guests and squinted past them into the darkness at the end of the garden. She could just make out flashes of white from Lucille's dress when she moved, and the tall figure before her, now laughing, now twirling his hat around, now reaching for Lucille's hand. An ugly wail sliced through the night—one of the peacocks that often stood around Víví's garden like they were waiting to be worshipped. Víví pressed her lips tightly together and turned back to the task at hand.

"Allez, are you all ready?"

*break open*

*inside of time, after the break*
*Between a sea and a lagoon in Keta, "Gold Coast," 1777, before Marie-Ange turned Sans-Souci (how did we lose you?), she was Afi-gã with her little sister Afi-ví*
*Can you hear us? Entendez-vous? E mía nkɔ sem a? We are called so many names we gave ourselves for all the many lives we have led:*
*"Are you sleeping?"*
*"No, but I should be. And so should you!"*
*"But . . ."*
*"But nothing! Ðo to!"*
*"Aren't you curious? What happens if the snakes get tired and slither away?"*
*"Afi-ví! Will you stop!"*
*"Think about it! Or what if they sneeze and their grip around the world gets loose?"*
*"Now you're just being silly."*
*"I'm not! Can they die? What if they die?"*
*Afi-gã caught her breath. She seemed to be taking her little sister seriously for the first time since they had been plunged into the alluring turmoil of the creation myth only to be yanked back*

*out too soon afterwards and sent to bed. "Maybe we would all fall through the cracks?"*

*They had heard the story denying them the serenity of sleep from Mama Hadzila, whose real name they could not have mentioned had they been forced. They only knew her as the woman who sang their imaginations alive and whose stories set fire to the otherwise unremarkable hum of their day-to-day. The only time they were around other children was when they would all gather to listen to Mama Hadzila. The night of the story, it was as if the stars, winking and mischievous, and the too-tall grass, restless like uncontrollable giggles, conspired with Mama Hadzila to try and make the sisters believe the world's existence relied on the infinite strength and will of two serpents holding it all together.*

*Both Afis, the older and the younger, knew their mother cherished them more than anything in Mawu's universe. Because of this, they had no need for anyone else beyond each other and the walls of the house their mother's wealth had built. Their disinterest in other people was not malicious. It never occurred to them that their immersion in a world of their own making was experienced by others as haughtiness. Kpɔ wo ɖa. They think their mother is rich and so?*

*Known to everyone in Keta, including her own children, as Mama Yevúbolotɔ, their mother had a laugh that spread to fill any space she occupied. Her voice started as a low rumble deep inside her chest before coming out like an echo, even under open sky with no hard surface to bounce against. Neighbors who were envious of her success spat their contempt into covered hands every time they walked past the house where she kneaded and formed dough into bread every day without fail.* "Kpɔ ɖa! *She spends so much time in those pans she's started to look like the bread itself!*" *People called her "Ɖa foɖo gã" in secret because of the roundness of her belly, but she did not so much as sniff at the name-calling, knowing her form was the attribute she treasured most because she radiated lushness and wealth everywhere she went, even lending her gold and less precious silver to people for special occasions for which they otherwise would not have had the means to adorn themselves. Everyone knew the bitterness of hardship had never crossed her lips and secretly believed any proximity to her could bring them a small piece of fortune too.*

"*Afi-ví? Are you there?*"

"*I'm here.*"

"*Did you hear what I said?*"

*The younger Afi did not reply in words. Instead, she patted the ago blanket until her hand found Afi-gã's. The only thing with the power to shake them more than this latest tall tale was the man called Efo Nkudzē who came back from war with the whites of his eyes on fire, so deep red the sisters couldn't stand to look his way and ran away shrieking any time he came to buy bread from their mother until he stopped coming by. Usually, Mama Hadzila's stories were sweet lies they could relish to put themselves to sleep, little joys they could spin around and around with until they grew dizzy and fell to the ground laughing. Sometimes, if Mama Hadzila's baby was awake, they would each take one of her small chubby hands in theirs and spin and spin so she too would be caught up in the thrall of their ecstasy. Mama Hadzila's worlds were often strange in a way that still felt enough like home not to be terrifying: frogs arguing with flies that would be their prey, fish with scales like jewels, people flying by opening up wings by the sheer will or necessity or belief that they could. Their least favorites were the tales with lessons interrupting the delight of simply listening, like don't sing while bathing at night, here is what to do if your totem animal crosses your path—for their family, this meant staying far away from any dogs—as if they were being tricked into obedience. But this new story about their world breaking into pieces felt like a threat, and they could not sleep for fear the snakes would let go, and they would all fall.*

*By the time they woke up, their fright had retreated far behind their rush to play. They were picking flowers to decorate their hair for hours that would feel like minutes by the time they would have to turn back, when Afi-ví cried out and sucked her index finger into her mouth.*

*"So is it because of this tiny thorn that you want to cry?"*

*The angry creases on Afi-ví's face rearranged into a sneer. "Just wait for me to catch you!" With her uninjured hand, she tried to tug one of the threaded locks of hair that had escaped the stiff lattice on top of Afi-gã's head.*

*"Ungrateful! As I'm trying to help you? Then let me leave it there rather!"*

*Afi-gã started to let Afi-ví's fleshy hand slip through her more sinewy one, and she hunched her bare shoulders to signal her abandonment of the injured finger. The younger sister stood with her palm outstretched hurling desperate pleas and praises after the older and then insults when she wouldn't turn back, Afi-gã's step wavering only so her body could vibrate with laughter.*

*"Useless girl! Just wait!"*

*Afi-ví brought her hand up to her face until it nearly touched the tip of her nose and focused her eyes on the red spot where the thorn had left its mark and then sunk into her flesh. She pressed* the skin around it, one last effort for relief, before shrugging much like Afi-gā had just done and running after her.

"Slow down! Blewu!"

They raced in the direction of home, their feet pounding the ground and little puffs of sand jumping up with each footfall like miniature explosions. Afi-ví was surprised when she began to catch up to her sister with her longer, more solid legs. She almost bumped into her before realizing Afi-gā was standing still, her arms hanging stiffly by her sides and tapering towards clenched fists.

"What . . . ?"

An ominous rumbling drew Afi-ví's attention to the ground ahead of them on the path and a ragged brown dog baring its teeth at them.

"Careful!"

"I know! Can't you see I'm trying?"

They had to find a way to get around the animal without agitating it further. Only trouble would follow if they let it touch them in any way.

break open

*Inside of time, the sly dogs who called themselves white masters turned bloodlust and the promise of gold into forts and castles interrupting coastlines all up and down the Gulf of Guinea and the Bight of Benin, outposts for the easier execution of their most violent fantasies, limestone walls turning green with mold and natural life trying to right ancestral wrongs, and they held church and prayed to their ice-hearted god in chapels just floors above cells where you, our beloveds, yet-to-be-unbroken, adjusted your eyes to a dark so total you swore they had been swallowed by a monster too immense to be perceived in full. And as above: the feet of the sly dogs who called their selves white masters shuffled across the chapel's dusty floors, and so below: our beloved somebodies were refusing as much as they could their current condition, no way to conceive of what lay ahead, but the foreboding rumbling in their down deep told them it would be worse than anything they had ever seen.*

And outside of time, someone woke up and wondered if the black-blue tattooed all around their lower lip and chin looked like it had grown faint, a little greyer than usual. And one lover turned to another, "Regarde, can you tell? Does it look faded to you?"

# 5

*outside of time, after the break, on Blue Basin*
*second full moon, or turning Love's Face can be all-consuming*
*and costly; one pays with the self*

"Mamzelle, you don't have to look at me like that." Samedi lay
on his back, his legs stretched far past the straggly thread at the
end of the blanket Lucille had brought outdoors for them. She
was sitting upright, her legs crossed one on top of the other in
front of her, the sun's heat sinking into every place skin met
skin: the corners where her arms bent and the backs of her
thighs. She cracked peanuts with one hand and sorted out the
shells from their sweet insides, and with the other hand, she
played in tufts of grass, staying stubbornly in the always sodden
bayou ground, no matter how strong her pull.

"Like what? What am I doing?"

"Like you're trying to shake me up and put me back down,
whole self in disarray."

Lucille laughed so long and loud that the sound shook up
the day's quiet, tangling itself in the weeping vines hovering
close enough to the water's surface to kiss and fluttering a
little bit more than they would on such a day without wind.
"Comment ça? A different way? Ribcage where your kneecaps
should be, crown on the wrong way, huh. Everything out of
order. Détruit."

"Dé-truit," and with each morsel of the word she shook

the empty peanut shells in cupped palms like she was looking
through cowries for a loophole into their future lives.

"So you confess, that's what you're doing, non?"

A small bird hopped by and paused close to Lucille's knee.
She tossed some nuts towards it without looking away from
Samedi. "Eyes can be terribly powerful things, Efo. But I don't
think mine are capable of all that."

"I don't know if I believe it. But cherie, I cannot complain.
I'll take as much of your attention as you'll give me. I see how
you are with everyone. But maybe . . . I don't know, I can be
special to you."

Lucille's hand wiping the back of her neck was no match
for the steady trickle of sweat winding its way down to her
back, leaving damp patches on her flimsiest cotton dress free of
sleeves, or zips, or anything that would irritate her more in this
heat. Her laugh was more nervous now, staccato and stuttering,
a tiptoe rather than a hearty stomp onto the ground.

Lucille said nothing.

She was studying him so hard because she also felt
misaligned. She usually didn't go about the business of living
in just any old kind of way, not no basa basa sort of person.
Her inner world was unknown territory, a map of main streets
and shortcuts not just anyone could navigate. Lucille felt her
self deeply, as in she loved to inhabit and believed she was in
complete possession of her self. And most of the time, she
was. Her soul stood up and stretched wide and into every
corner of her being. She was also acutely aware of the way she
made people feel. Wherever she entered, she would feel all the
breath in the room stretch tight and thin like a guitar string
frozen mid-play. Sometimes, it could be tasking, franchement,

to have to pull her hands out of the grasp of other people, to be compelled to smile and pat and pamper while pretending to ignore the desperate tremble in the other person's voice, laden with want, want for more and more than she sometimes wanted to give.

But mostly, she delighted in and relished the self. She listened for the flirtatious tinkle from the rows of earrings she wore hooked into her ears by multiples on the left side. She lingered against her self often when bathing or dressing, in praise of the dimples in her upper arms or the flesh sitting comfy on top of the waistbands of her clothes. She wore a face that invited, that said a little closer, a little more, and a face that warned of the danger of getting too near and staying too long because you could lose your self in her presence or find your self the object of her wrath was she to find that you had hurt one of her beloveds. She moved around the world like she made it, and to some extent, hadn't she? Lucille had called her self into existence, her own offspring and ancestor at the same time, her history a circle uninterrupted.

And yet, here she sat, with this man who thought he had already found his way around. She, complètement à l'aise, had eased into the sweet crawl of the days she had spent with Samedi since her birthday. It was a welcome kind of normal, still crisp like freshly tie-dyed fabric a long way from creasing and wearing thin. They would always sit on Lucille's balcony or on his, with Lucille on his lap, one arm thrown around his neck, eating from the same plate, sometimes fried plantain or slices of after-dinner oranges. Passers-by on their way up towards the hills or down further into Keta Afeme knew to always look out for them and would call up, "Hey! Are we not invited? Save a bite for us!" Or someone would shout, "Lucille, cherie! Some people should be landing soon, I woke up with my knee aching like a storm's coming!" Ah, they would say, they are wearing Love's Face, and wearing it well. Love's Face, this is how they described people in love on Blue Basin. They never, ever "fell" in love. Absolutely not. Falling was too careless and impossible to control and almost always ended in hurt or loss, or in regret at the very least. Blue Basin people showed one another Love's Face. Love chose people's heads for her crown, just like the spirits did, and it was a choice to let love shine out of one's face and onto someone else.

Lucille saw and wore Love's Face everywhere. The ways she showed and felt love and the way she understood her self were as expansive as all the different ways people appeared in the world. She was most enamored with people who, like her, lived in the in-betweens of things. Calling themselves into being out of the gaps of a breaking world made them craftspeople of the most divine order, craftspeople of experience and of self. In those breaks, there was no Noah, no ark, no two-by-two match. They saw their selves and the world through a prism, and if other less complicated people were lucky, some of the refracted rays would fall onto their grayscale lives.

For Lucille and for many other people on Blue Basin, making a life there meant slipping out of the rigid grip of definition; it meant nyɔnu, femme, man, person, amegbetɔ all at once and not at all. And showing Love's Face was easiest for Lucille when the person returning the loving gaze moved through life like this. Lucille loved women for dancing far too close than was holy with their hands in each other's back pockets, loved people whose multiple spirits would only be satisfied with a new name every few new moons, those who left offering to a deity standing at a crossroads wearing a skirt sweeping the ground and a top hat rising high.

She felt most ambivalent about men like Samedi. Usually, she would just watch them slapping down checkers or slapping the sides of their thighs in between laughs, whistling around toothpicks or kola or cigarettes, or hitching their trousers ankle-high to cross puddles or ditches after a heavy rain. She was more interested in the tiny details of their ways, noticing things like their nail beds, the more oval-shaped and distinct against slender brown fingers the more beautiful, especially on the hands of the ones who lived to make art or to make things to take the edge of life—frivolous end tables with legs so ornate they could barely stand, or musical instruments—one could always tell what they used their hands for. She noticed men so pretty it made no sense, so pretty they made her laugh by just being, with long eyelashes casting thin shadows on the tops of their cheeks when they looked down to the page they were reading or the box of matches or some other fidgety thing in their hands.

But Lucille's observations were always from a distant height, a sort of casual curiosity that was not personally invested nor was it even in the spirit of admiration. These men were most interesting when they were far away, and she could imagine those nail beds and those earlobes and those eyelashes washed in early evening light, meditative or rocking with laughter, much safer or full of more possibility than when they were up close and wanting to build altars out of women only to trample them, standing on top of them in an attempt to reach closer to themselves. Men like these recognized Lucille's cool curiosity, and they were both infuriated by and frightened of her because they knew she had no pedestals in her life for them and also because she never hesitated to stand between their danger and the people in their lives they tried to harm.

These men like Samedi, their arms moving slow and wide away from their bodies when they walked, liquid night flowing in the daytime, were also too haughty to admit they bowed down on the inside to Lucille's detached interest in their existence. Like they knew she was watching and waiting for those who couldn't refuse the violence after which they had learned to fashion themselves, like they knew her greetings and winks were only shaky placeholders for the hidden pocketknife flicked open, in case any of them succumbed to the sort of cruelty they knew they were capable of. Lucille was as amused by their fear as she was bored by their bravado. Yet, here she was, with a man like Samedi. Samedi himself.

As for her sisters, they didn't look as kindly on Lucille's new love as everyone else seemed to or with as much dreamy-eyed sentimentality as Lucille herself had.

"A stranger at the door! It's been a while, has it not, cherie?" Víví mumbled her disapproval through teeth clenched tight around the pins she was using to fix Serena's locs in place.

Serena fidgeted in her seat on the step below Víví's and reached impatiently towards the front of her head to see how much more hair there was to smooth and re-twist into shiny ropes and coils. "Me, I didn't come here for all this foolishness. Lucille can do whatever she wants."

Víví went on like she had not sensed Serena's warning her to back down. "Are you the only one who knows how to wear Love's Face around here? You really think this Samedi person is worthy of all your glory? You don't have anything better you could be doing than messing with all kinds of—" Víví swatted Serena's impatient, reaching hands away from the half-done hair, and Serena sighed deep dissatisfaction.

"Nye sí, you just want to be a little careful. I think that's all Víví is trying to say."

"What is it? What could you two possibly know that I don't?"

Serena squeezed out her words, her thin lips drawn into a severe line. "You know the other, real meaning of Lɔlɔmo, Love's Face? Lɔlɔ le mo. It means things are often not as they appear."

"Of course I know the real meaning. Say what you're really trying to say, please, and stop riddling." Lucille's pride was probably the only part of her self that could best her capacity to love, and now it snapped shut like a heavy metal lock on a trunk, closing Lucille off from her sisters' concerns. It was possible Lucille's love was too vast, too profound, and too necessary for so many other people on Blue Basin other than Samedi. But she could handle her self through whichever messy twists and torments that may come. She was grown.

"Lucille. I'm just trying to ask—"

Víví stood up from behind Serena's half-retwisted head of hair and stared Lucille down. "I don't know what Serena is afraid of. She wants to know, what about vengeance? What happens to vengeance when you are so consumed by love?"

"Víví, don't—" Serena was standing now too, the comb and pins in her lap fallen and forgotten on the ground, as she tried to pull Lucille back towards them by the shoulder.

The sister spirits were so infinite; it was rare, if not

impossible, for their spirit selves' responsibilities to be at odds with the fleshly form they had taken on Blue Basin. For Lucille, in particular, the force of her love and the fury of her vengeful side were both powerful enough to threaten worlds if she swung too far off center towards either. She had never had to exact vengeance on Blue Basin, not because the island's people were angelic by any means but because they brought to their new lives outside of time a willingness to handle each other tenderly and to make amends when they were rougher than they should have been with their neighbors and lovers. At most, Lucille would intervene on behalf of the wronged or the hurt with a simple warning that everyone knew concealed blades melded in fire beneath the words, but nothing beyond that, not yet. The space she tried to maintain between her self and other people was not a mere formality but rather a necessity, for her own sake and for theirs. To make sure she didn't spin them and the worlds they inhabited off their axes, she had to take great care not to live in the extremes to which she was inclined, and now with Samedi, she was feeling more deeply than she had in several lifetimes that this responsibility required a denial of her self, of her selves, rather.

"This is not my first time turning to someone with Love's Face, so what's the real problem? What at all has he done to you?"

Víví pointed the comb at Lucille's forehead like a dart to a target. "First of all, cherie, you know that man's 'medicines' have been making people sicker?"

"Víví!"

Víví ignored Serena and kept on: "The other day I saw love-me-now flowers scattering every which way instead of blooming as they should. What do you think is happening inside of time? Shouldn't we be worrying about that?"

No one had ever seen anything like the love-me-nows before they got to Blue Basin, but no one questioned whether they were possible either. The purple flowers started out life floating around in perfectly round balls of fluffy shoots and feathery leaves. They needed just a gentle nudge from the breeze, or for someone to blow on them like a birthday candle, and they would bloom right where the shoots landed, no matter the sort of ground, open wide with full petals like fistfuls of different purples.

Lucille carried on as though she was having a conversation with her self and expected her sisters to pick up the thread. "You heard about what the wind did to Miss Yvonne's house? I need to do something. She didn't come all this way from the inside to the outside to live like this."

Everyone on Blue Basin knew Miss Yvonne lived with death as a permanent lodger, like she had her own coffin sitting lined and ready in her lounge, surrounded by all her other wilting things. The way they saw it, she was the main one to blame when her roof caved in because she was so preoccupied with the afterwards of life that she had not noticed her roof had started to sink in some places and to disintegrate in others with each passing rainy season's fury. Some of her neighbors threw judgment her way:

"Celle-la! So she was really going to let her self rot away in that dump?"

"Me be dɛ! Life is wasted on that one, I swear to you!"

But kinder and more patient souls would disagree. "Now

hold on . . . we don't know how she came to be here and why she is this way . . ."

They couldn't know she found her self weakening from breathing in the stale, damp outside air that had invaded where it should not have been, had no way of knowing who she was missing and how she lost them.

"I know no one else is rushing to see about Miss Yvonne, well, everyone except maybe you and Friday's Child," Lucille went on. "He has been putting the roof back together piece by piece, as best he can, anyway. I don't know who asked him to do that. There's all that empty space next to my house, and I really think I could—"

Víví's impatience had been swirling around the room gathering more heat and more fury, but Serena had decided to pick through the talk at hand like digging through sand without disturbing tiny crabs buried just below. "Yes. Yes. Why not? These days, the wind is like something I haven't seen since . . . well, since we first opened the way to this land. Anyways. About this Samedi?"

Lucille and her sisters were wary of the wind, what it was doing to people's houses and to the flowers, and what happenings inside of time could be causing these tiny tumults on Blue Basin, but it was as though Serena and Víví couldn't help but mask these fears behind doubt over Lucille and Samedi's love, easier to deal with than the island's little daily ruptures.

"Yes? You still haven't answered me. What at all has this man done for you to despise him so?"

Serena stepped between Lucille and Víví and took the comb

away. "Ma sœur, it's nothing. He's done nothing. It's just . . . we know you. And we worry you can drown so deep in this . . . love that you end up outside of your self entirely."

"How do you know I'm going to drown? What if I am buoyant? Can't you see it in my face? Shining. Épanouie."

Víví shot her words out like blades between the gaps in her teeth: "Sister, please don't be foolish. Écoute-moi bien. The only place you're going with that man is nowhere fast, all the way over the edge of your own life."

"And I'm asking you, how do you know?"

"Miss Geneviève told me. She talks about it all the time." Most anyone who sat in Víví's chair felt compelled to spill all their thoughts, whether obscure or troubling or petty, like lemon tea on tile, and Miss Geneviève was no exception. She had been going to see Víví to get her hair rinsed blue since she had decided to let it go grey and quickly run through the usual pleasantries—"Ca va? Lekee? Et la famille?"—before moving on to her favorite subject of discussion, Samedi and his quackery. "Did I tell you, my grandbaby was never the same after that, that—are you listening?"

"Yes Madame Jeune-vee-ève, I am, but please sit back before this stuff gets all over. She was never the same, how?"

"I sent her to him with a running tummy, only after trying peppermint tea first. How hard could it be to cure? Why can she no longer keep real food down? All is well for a few days, and then her stomach turns inside out. Rice water and seltzer for every meal. My baby!"

Serena put on the voice she used for the fussiest babies, trying desperately to bring back still waters to the storm swirling between them all. "Sisters. Careful before you say something you can't take back."

Lucille was a cyclone enfleshed. "Oh please, so is it because of one Miss Jeune-vee-ève"—she dragged out each letter with a meanness she rarely if ever showed—"that you're talking like this? That lady always has something to say. She is never ever satisfied."

"Lucille, it's not just her! You of all people should know how dangerous it is to play with people's healing. That man doesn't know what he's doing, and his hands bring far more harm than help—"

"Me of all people should what! Don't talk to me about what I should and shouldn't do. Where were you when we were spirits, breaking our selves against the seabed to make this place possible? Concerning your self with how perfumed the flowers smell and how in tune the birds are when I was thinking about bone and flesh and life and death. You think you care more about anyone's healing, about keeping this place and everyone here unbroken, than me?"

Víví turned to leave so fast she almost fell over. "Serena, on y va? Or you agree with her?" She was gone before Serena could answer.

### break open

*Can you hear us? Entendez-vous? E mía nkɔ sem a? We are called so many names we gave ourselves for all the many lives we have led:*

*Lucille, the spirit who was, is, and will be love and vengeance, once grew fearsome with razors for teeth and blood for tears. She was so full of fury, the smell of smoke lingered in the air behind her as she paced and paced. Her flame was not quietly luminous but rather loudly blazing. She raged because of the failure of the spirits who were serpents and the suffering they had caused—that they had created a break in the world, and all the souls inside the bodies had fallen through, had broken their fall against each other. Her rage multiplied and boiled over itself when she saw what was being done in the name of love and vengeance, how greed and power swelled and swelled inside the break. No plague, no flood, no fire was enough to vanquish the pink-skinned specters—as ungodly as she was divine—who appeared on blessed shores and took them, her beloveds, to a deadly beyond. No threat, no promise, no thundering voice from above was enough to soften the hearts of those who made objects to be sold out of other people—sometimes their own, sometimes their enemies—who sent them away in exchange for more wealth, swelling and swelling inside the break. With their own survival paramount and the power they had tasted so sweet, they did or could not conceive of how soul-destroying their actions would turn out to be. She stood in the break because she was the spirit with the grandest stride and stance, because she curled her self into the hot ears of the never-satiated, the enraged, the dangerous, the yet-to-be-unbroken, the ungovernable. She was there when some of her children refused to die quietly or refused to die at all or chose to die as human as they could ever be, refusing to buy or sell or barter other people, or be bought and sold and bartered over in a market heaving with livestock and sickness. Those children made fortresses out of slow seaside towns and stole themselves and each other back from cells and stocks and planks and ships, emerging from the belly of the beast even more whole than when they entered, making bonfires out of those cells and stocks and planks and ships and warming their bodies with the heat.*

*She stepped inside of time and hurled her self earthwards, towards anyone facing a raised fist or the end of the gun that meant dying, and there she bore witness to all kinds of upheavals, both intimate and public:*

*inside of time, after the break*
*"Provencal, Louisiana"—agoo we greet, mia tɔwò Natchitoches, mia tɔwò Caddo, mia tɔwò Natchez, mia tɔwò Osage, rightful and careful custodians of the land—1600s*

*The spirit who was, is, and will be love and vengeance was with you, at the only moment you showed hesitation, at the door of the child's room, left cracked open in case of late-night cries or nightmares. There was very little room within you for compassion for this white child, who at the age of eight was already making orders and flinging insults towards the people he knew he would one day inherit, including your self. Any moments of joy and light that crossed the child's face did not last long enough to make it worth sparing him—yes, a child, but one who was being raised to torture and destroy just like his parents had done. The spirit was with you in the threshold. She was there with you because you wore her crown. She saw your left hand flat against the door and the other gripping the neck of the bottle of clear liquid.*

*You had been moving around that curtailed world, bound by dense forest on three sides and a fence succumbing to the insatiable appetite of so many termites, with a blade hidden inside your left cheek and fire simmering in your fists and in the curves of your ears. You had always left little fires, out of curiosity to see what the flame would do to paper, or because you were some sort of devil, if your mother told it. Some people believed your footsteps singed the ground you left in your wake so no one could collect the dust and use it to send you trouble. They all kept some distance from you but still lingered close enough that they were convinced they could feel the heat prickling the air around your body. They knew they would need your fire when they decided they could not and would not live these dying days any longer.*

*You were next to the child in two strides, and you drenched the bed in kerosene. You spilled more on the floor around the bed and in each corner of the room, in the same way you had done with the rest of the family, the man and the woman who claimed dominion over that land and everything growing and grazing on it. You didn't look back at the flames you threw towards the house now soaking in fuel. Instead, you took a comb out of your pocket and ran it through your hair, then gathered all the fallen strands into a feathery ball and set it alight after striking the match against the box three times. You sat there on your own back steps, watching your shed hair flaming first between your pointer finger and thumb and then in the palm of your hand, and the spirit who was, is, and will be love and vengeance was in the small fire of the match and the giant fire that was its mother. You did not flinch when the last sparks kissed your skin.*

\*\*\*

*Remember, the spirit stepped inside of time and hurled her self earthwards towards the break, and there she bore witness to all kinds of upheavals, both intimate and public:*

*inside of time, after the break*

"Boston,"—*agoo, we greet, mia tɔwò Mashpee, mia tɔwò Wampanoag, mia tɔwò Massa-adchu-es-et, rightful and careful custodians of the land*—2016

*The spirit who was, is, and will be love and vengeance sat next to you that night, lifting your heavy head off the pages you had tried to read so they wouldn't bend, and she was with you in the morning standing just on the inside of the day, looking over your shoulder and out at the man who had brought all the world's violence through your bedroom window when he found the door locked. She was the lag in your footsteps, the hesitation, the faint reluctance beginning to gather in the farthest corner of your self where you didn't even know the spirit lived. She was with you on the stairs back up to the small place you called home, three rooms and no door save the one leading to outside. There, she made her self a space on your chest of broken drawers, good only for holding mismatched earrings and chains that turned the sensitive skin on your neck green. She pushed aside a porcelain jewelry box with more chips than remnants of the original design—a bust of some grand woman who had truly lived—and sat, watching.*

*She said: Daughter, bearer of my crown, this is where you can slide in the knife I brought for you, sharpened too, just so, between his ribs.*

*She said: Daughter, custodian of my deep fury long past and yet to come, look, I filed your nails when you weren't looking, just enough to draw blood; here, now scratch his eyes out, it won't take but as long as the time between blinks.*

*She said: Daughter, carrier of my infinite tomorrows, here you are, existing, the fact of your humanity worthy of celebration,* just because you are. *Your self is grander than this moment and at once deserving of the comfort of a thousand chants. You will never be brought this low again.*

She was there with you when you said no to him and when he did not listen nor did he stop. She laid down next to him and tried to force the knife into your hands, but you did not strike. You were absolutely still, frozen in place by the false belief that you had invited your own destruction into your bed, a place where you and sleep would never meet again. Afterwards, you could not bear the smell that clung to your days' old nightclothes, to the curtains, and the towel fallen and pushed to a corner in the bathroom. But she stayed for you, perched on the slippery edge of the bathtub while you tried to dig out his filth from beneath your fingernails. He was gone, and you remained, suspended between the "no" you wished you had uttered and the "not really" that you convinced your self should have been a slap, a razor to his veined throat, a knife in his slippery back.

For months to come, you didn't know you were encountering the spirit until you noticed one day she left the smell of burning behind her where misery and decay had been. You didn't see that you walked past her on the corner by the store you used to get coins to pay for washing your clothes.

She said: *Daughter, your vengeance will eventually turn against you. Let me take this from you.* And the spirit showed you her pipe stuffed with his ashes. He had been found in front of his house, his body burnt to the bone. His neighbors swore the fire started in his right ear and wound its way around his neck and down his body. Apparently, he did not move once, did not attempt to fight it. He could not have resisted even if he wanted to.

*He should've known better than to try and squeeze you, this broad horizon of a person, into his narrow, empty desire. And the spirit was there, front row for his demise, both the char in the air and the scream on his dead lips. And she saw that all was well.*

\*\*\*

Lucille and Samedi went on, letting the sluggish late afternoon hours wash over them like the sunlight changing from hour to hour and listening to the saltwater splashing at the mangroves in the Afeme beyond the nonstop frenzy of the street where Samedi's store sat and the houses push up against each other like a crowd pushing each other for a view of the show. The ground there was perfect for sitting because its yellow sand was light like sawdust but didn't stick to the skin and itch. Many nights, she luxuriated in the feeling of the warmth blooming between them and of the hard tips of her fingers over the velvet of his body and of always hurling towards ecstasy, with many more hours left for them to maybe love again.

"It's almost my favorite time." The brightness in her voice was more short circuit than shine, but she held onto slight hope that she had been able to settle her restlessness enough to distract Samedi from the glaring evidence of her nerves.

"What do you mean, your favorite time? Egɔme ɖe?"

Lucille opened her arms wide as though she was unfolding grand wings only she knew she possessed, wings that could carry her across the slow-flowing water and farther. "Four o'clock on a Saturday! Can't you see?"

Samedi sat up and looked around at the snarled tree trunks coated in green, at a distant ripple in the water far enough away, they needn't worry what kind of life lurked beneath, and then up at the sky, a vast yawning wide nothing. "What is it? What is there to see?"

"I can't force you to see through my eyes mon cher. Just know you're missing out." She shrugged, a faint twitch in her shoulders like she was discarding the anxiety of what it meant for her to be free and easy, truly, in the company of someone who seemed to want nothing more than just that, free and easy. For Lucille, Saturday at four in the afternoon was wrapped in gorgeous possibility, in the anticipation of an evening with friends drinking under the trees in the Paroisse, perhaps, or stripping down and laying on the floor near the window for the late afternoon heat to rise off bare skin, and thousands more tomorrows to breathe, to do, to love.

She adored this moment in time for its special softened sun, not brazen and merciless like it had been just hours before, as much as for its quiet. In almost every house on Blue Basin, lunch dishes would be washed and set out to dry, with the entire street settling into a light sleep, just enough to miss the hottest hours. Even the flies would appear glutted on their meal of leftovers and discarded crumbs, and Lucille took pleasure in listening to them as they knocked into the empty bottles lined up outside like a parade's drum line. Some restless souls still roamed the island at this hour, people who didn't want an afternoon doze to steal the night's rest for them, choosing instead to watch the empty roads running by their front steps in the hopes of delaying the odd neighbor in conversation.

"Salut mon ami, where you headed?"

"Tu as bien mangé?"

"Awwww why the hurry, stop by a while? There's nothing else going on in this sleepy place."

"Je suis là. Just watching the comings going and the goings coming..."

At times, she could hear a child giggle and squeal somewhere close by, indifferent to a parent's earnest pleas for the infant to let sleep come. From farther down the street in the Paroisse, there may be a tune issuing from someone's flute and a tapping foot keeping time on brick.

Samedi put his head in Lucille's lap and tried to get comfortable on the scratchy cotton of her dress. Her hands troubled the rough brush of hair on his face, her fingers moving freely and with no direction from her mind that was still wandering away from where they sat, dancing in the light that scattered itself through the trees. She felt his jaw tighten and still when she reached the slim line of scars cut lightly into his skin where he should have had sideburns. "Why won't you tell me what happened to you here?"

Lucille felt Samedi's face stiffen into a treacherous and inaccessible terrain, more difficult to reach than the northern-most side of the Katye hills, a wall of rock falling steeply into mystery. The previously softened planes of his face shifted and locked together, denying Lucille any entrance into his depths. "Samedi, why do you get this way with me? I thought you were my special somebody?"

On Blue Basin, everyone knew who your people were and where they came from inside of time unless they didn't, and unless you wanted to be cruel or your nosiness knew no bounds, you wouldn't ask but would rather wait until the person was ready to tell you, if they were ever ready. Still, her insistence was precise, sharp, concealed by the gentleness of her fingers still playing across his face.

After a time, she felt the stone in his face crumble and collapse as he tried to conjure humor out of the tension gripping them in the moment.

"Always examining somebody." His laugh was an uncomfortable twitch that ended almost as soon as he had tried to force it.

Lucille was unconvinced and undeterred, pressing on through her steady fingers like the slow but still-flowing current onwards into the trees. "What is it you don't want me to see—"

"Lucie-lu! You home, cherie?"

Samedi sat up sharply like a trap snapped open. "Lucie-lu? Who is calling your name like that?"

Lucille was swiftly on one bent knee, and then on two feet, shaking out the wrinkles formed in her clothes from sitting all day. "It's almost like I'm a shape-shifter. My name sounds different in everybody's mouth depending on what they need, n'est-ce pas?"

"See . . . what did I say? Isn't it too much? If you're giving out so much, what will be left for m— for us?"

"What will be left? Samedi, how can you hide parts of your self and expect to have all of me?"

"Who told you I was hiding?"

Lucille dusted off Samedi's question like the last specks of earth's debris still sticking to her. "Tswww. You think I just love this? Out here mothering grown people like they came from me?"

"Don't you?"

Lucille's back was already turned as she walked back

towards the house, each step a beat in the restless pounding in her ears, her free and easy dissolved in the murk of other people's needs and hurts.

That night, the wind had claws. It scratched its way into the open windows, bringing with it dust and dead insects who had succumbed to its sweeping force. The flame tree outside Lucille's window was long overdue for a trim. Its fronds reached into the window frame, playing a lazy shadow puppet show behind the gauzy curtains on the side where they were still drawn. The room's cool dark offered a pleasant refuge. Lucille and Samedi found respite from the day's heat, from the current chill, and from arguments that touched a little too close to truth. Each searched for the other's body, the papery surface of the bed sheet slipping and stretching beneath them. This was a different kind of seeing and being seen—his smile half-sunken in shadow, a braid straying from its bun and falling onto her shoulder, one of her ear piercings plugged with the very tip of a broomstick. The lack of light meant they had to rely on the memory imprinted into their fingertips to lead the way through motions they had been rehearsing. The set of scars etched into his face on either side, the slick skin tucked into the crooks of her arms, and after a long enough time of their bodies pressed and moving together, the ridged pattern imprinted into his lower belly from the beads she wore around her waist.

*break open*

*Inside of time, the water was tainted and the air was more carbon than fresh, and the rain stung when it came down in the wrong season and for far too long. The taps still ran, but anything that came out of them washed all the rust and sludge and poison from the innards of the city's pipes and threw it up into your sinks. So you, our beloveds, collected it in buckets and basins and small bowls for hand washing and mouth rinsing. It didn't burn as much when you let it sit for all the dirt and poison to settle, so you could fetch just enough to use and not a drop more. And you cried to a vexed and stormy sky for anything better than this, for some water that didn't make the skin itch and ache and peel back on itself, for something not heavy with lead and the promise of sickness, for an answer to the question, where can we really live?*

And outside of time, in the middle of dinner, blue flowers and birds started to disappear off the plates the people were eating from, first in little flecks like shreds of petals and feathers and then in larger pieces until the plates became almost translucent where there had been blue, and they could see past the food to the table beneath.

# 6

*outside of time, after the break, on Blue Basin*
*fifth full moon, or what they call "Decembre" or Dzome inside*
*of time, when the yet-to-be-unbroken are fête-ing all kinds of*
*fêtes under the guise of "Christmas"*

Víví had peonies on her mind all day. Specifically, the way she
loved them so, at least until the petals opened far apart from
one another and began to wilt, drooping and shredding like
crumpled tissue paper, none of the dignified slow browning
and decline that roses and most other flowers endured at the
ends of their short lives. Though she had the knowledge and
the ability to cultivate and breed peonies that would stay
whole even through their dying, she wasn't very interested in
tending to green and growing things and keeping them healthy,
sometimes in a way that seemed like it was against their will
to droop and surrender to the same elements they needed to
flourish—too heavy a rainfall or wild a wind could decimate
flowerbeds planted with painstaking intention and hands
buried and turning wrinkly in wet black earth.

She didn't shrink from difficult or even dirty work, but
she preferred to create beauty in the world in ways where the
meantime of the creation, the actual doing of beautiful things,
was also purely pleasurable. Taking care of hair, her own and
that of others, was one ritual she relished, as was cooking
decadent meals for her own and other people's enjoyment.

Both inside and outside of time, Víví's main reason for being was to witness and maintain any and all things sweet and luscious: a grapefruit pink in the sky, a candle's light split through its glass jar and onto the wall, plants unbending their thirsty stalks after watering, glimpses of smooth and solid thigh from a high slit in a sundress, curly wisps of hair settling themselves around the curve of an ear.

Víví was finding it more difficult to avoid both her sisters than she let show, even though she had not seen them since she and Serena had argued with Lucille over her insistence on turning resolutely towards Samedi with Love's Face. When people came by Víví's house for their hair appointments, to do up their faces just because it was a Wednesday and the sun shone a way so they felt like it, or to borrow her gold necklaces for the weekend, she would answer their questions—"Et Lucille? Et Serena? Haven't seen you three catching fresh air together in some time now. Núkà edzɔ? Everything alright?"— with questions, "Baby, you see how cool the breeze is even with the sun so high? Why don't we take the chair outside and get your hair done under the tree? On y va?"

She would spend the whole time rattling on about how she could not wait for the forget-me-not flowers to bloom all velvet and yellow so this twist of trunk and vines would have some reason for taking up so much space in her front garden; about which oils to use to calm skin too long in the sun unprotected; about how much she had to talk to get her latest lover out of bed that morning: "I had to tell her, listen, these heads won't do themselves. Come back later, amour. Do you know she sat on the veranda for three hours just in case I wasn't serious!"

She had her pride, her resentment of what she saw as

Lucille's selfishness, and this hot, itchy feeling on her arms with so many neighbors trying to pry into their business and hanging heavy over all these was her concern that she might cut through to the bone with the edge of her words if she didn't first take the time to settle the stormy surface of her spirit. So, she would occupy her self with more of what was pleasurable and honeyed and perfumed. Far easier to think about peonies and their too-softness than about the fact that the other day, her reflection had started moving slower than her body, a glitching shadow following her lead, just like it had when Mawu-Lisa called them to bring the land that would become Blue Basin earthward. So, today she was thinking about peonies and about anything else that existed purely for delight.

### break open

*Can you hear us? Entendez-vous? E mía nkɔ sem a? We are called so many names we gave ourselves for all the many lives we have led:*

*Devotees to the spirit that was, is, and will be sweetness and luxury were responsible for taking care of these little pleasures so everyone might enjoy them. Among them were the more obvious: hairdressers, makeup artists, perfume counter girls, shoemakers, a woman who dressed wounds by day and sold sex after the day shift closed, lovestruck teenagers spraying their grandmother's eau de toilette on letters they would never send, clothing store clerks and the window display stylists. There were also grandparents who sat on their sagging verandas and watched neighborhood children growing from round and giggling to long-limbed and stunning; lonely women in attic apartments who noticed every*

*newly painted house and freshly mowed lawn on morning walks
to the boutique for bread; and people who repaired weaving looms
for a living just so they could be present when the kete stoles and
blankets were finished. These lovers of all things gorgeous and
too much were responsible for all kinds of wonders, grandiose
and commonplace alike, and the spirit who was, is, and will be
sweetness and luxury would make her self manifest wherever these
little delights were found:*

*inside of time, after the break
"Jacmel, Sud-Est," Ayiti—agoo, we greet, mia tɔwò Taíno, rightful
and careful custodians of the land—1999*

*The cap of gold covering your left incisor flashed from your
mouth every time you squinted and frowned in concentration. In
your left hand, a tiny mirror with only enough room to show one
eye at a time; in your right, a stub of a black pencil shorter than a
thumb. You were lining your eyes so their slant upwards towards
the side of your face was even more dramatic than what nature
had carved. The spirit was drawn first to the glimpse of gold, then
to the delicate turns of the wrist, the smooth strokes across the eye,
brushing the pencil's flakes away every few moments, and then the
spirit noticed the stone block you sat on was at the entrance to a
cemetery. It was near noon, the sun far too high and hot in the
sky for people to be roaming the streets outside the graveyard or
winding through the scattered headstones in search of the resting
places of loved ones. At your sandaled feet, a plastic bag spilled out
sunflowers and a short broom; you were there to pay your respects,
and the spirit loved the beauty even in rituals for the dying and
the dead, for the way sweetness can be teased out of grief like chaff
through a sieve. The spirit would make sure that grief would*

*never outweigh the sweetness of the memory you shared with a grandmother now crossed to the beyond. When you went to dust off the perfume bottles your grandmother kept on top of her heavy chest of drawers, the spirit of sweetness would be in the dust; when you sprayed some of the scent from the only unrusted bottle, the spirit of sweetness would be in the scent; when you went to rub oil on your own legs like your grandmother used to do, the spirit of sweetness would be there in the shine.*

***

*Remember, the spirit stepped inside of time and danced through the break, making her self manifest wherever little delights were found:*

*inside of time, after the break*
*Keta, "Volta Region, Ghana,"—agoo, we greet, mia tɔwó Eveawo, rightful and careful custodians of the land—1956*
　　*The spirit who was sweetness and luxury was lost in a maze of courtyard gardens that connected one end of the town's biggest houses. The gardens might as well have been in a different realm, not just for their abundant green but because they were between walls with the wide sky for a ceiling and built deep enough inside the house where you couldn't hear the Atlantic crashing against the town all day. Each garden was dedicated to one type of plant: crops for eating and for selling, flowers for adornment and for altars. There was one with scallions planted in rows across the width and breadth of the room's square, the young stalks so bright green their newness hurt to witness. The next had grapes, purple and full and winding all along the wooden beams of the pergola running across the courtyard and scattered along the ground*

*where they had become too rich and too ripe to stay on the vine. Another was for pineapples—you, the woman of the house, were allergic, but all the children you looked after loved them and they sold like nothing else in the market—their spiny leaves like slim cacti bursting from the round of the fruit itself. Yet another was full of hibiscus bushes, the air so thick with the scent, with the pollen spilling from the flowers' middles, with the sound of bees buzzing lust and longing, and the spirit of sweetness and luxury lingered on the neat gravel path snaking around the room in no rational direction until it eventually arrived at the door to the next courtyard. The spirit kept passing through doors from one courtyard to the next until she arrived at one that was only for roses in colors most people didn't know were possible in nature: deep magenta folding into lilac folding into white at the center of the flower; orange streaked with yellow; yellow streaked with orange; sky blue and lavender alternating with each petal. The spirit became a soft breeze ruffling the petals, lifting the leaves so the dry ones fell, parting the feathergrass and sweet grass and silver grass and sending the fragrance across the courtyard and up into the open sky. She was about to whirl from breeze to wind and away into the outside of time when she noticed you, the woman of the house and garden, entering the rose courtyard, your stride decisive and upright so you looked much taller than you really were, your wrapper tied tight around your waist and over a white nightgown, a rare mundane way of looking for the usual grandeur that was your everyday posture towards life. And when you began to prune the bush with the bluest roses, the spirit was in the smell of fresh green, and when the sap dripped down your hands, the spirit was in the sticky sweetness, and when the petals folded themselves close to keep in as much life to sustain them away from the rest of the plant, the spirit was in the fold, and when you placed the cut bunch in a jar full of iced water at your bedside next to the heavy Bible with the pages warped together from age and humidity, the spirit was in the sweat sliding down the glass.*

\*\*\*

Darkness fell slow like heavy eyelids slipping into a doze, and now Víví was thinking neither of her sisters nor peonies or sweetgrass. The only other kind of lush thing she was concerned about for the moment was the air alive and light at her back, her thighs astride the thighs of this week's lover (or maybe this month's, if all went in a way she found she craved more of), peach wine on his breath and on hers, lemon balm and bergamot sticking to her fingers and to his chest, her hands on her breasts and his hands on her breasts and her hands in his hair and his hands on her back, and tears in his eyes and humor on her face and wanting and him in and out and in and left and yes and there and yes and out and her lost for one or two seconds, suspended in air above him and somewhere outside her self, standing at the foot of the bed to get a better view of her self in ecstasy.

Víví continued to hover somewhere between her self on the bed and her self outside her body, trying to savor and luxuriate in the sweetness that she was, in the sweetness of the in-between where pleasure was the means, the ends, and the meantime. Her fingers played over the idea of letting him stay past dawn; she felt most benevolent when she was in bliss. She wasn't fool enough to think this dallying was turning Love's Face to someone else beside her self. In the entire universe and all the worlds within it, the only other beings she showed love to were her sisters, and even then sometimes her own delight obscured her view just a little. In all these lifetimes they had led, all the sisters had turned Love's Face or something like it to other people, at least halfway.

"Cou-cou, it's time to go," Víví said and then got out of bed as light started to leak in like a faulty tap dripping onto dry ground.

"Víví, nye Víví, is that what you really want? You want me to leave?"

She couldn't stand how "my sweetness" sounded coming from someone other than her own reflection in any of the highly shined mirrors in her house. It sounded like a threat, like someone else was laying claim to the way her spirit should sway or still itself. This lover's unwanted grasp towards Víví's self had helped her decide what she knew she was going to do anyway.

"I'm not for you or for anyone here. You know that. Vas-y. I think you're feeling a little too comfortable. Allez."

She gathered her sheer robe about her self without knotting the belt, parts of her skin showing through the fabric as she moved in and out of the dawning light collecting their clothes in bunches off the floor around the bed.

"Vivienne. I didn't mean . . ."

"I know you heard me the first time. Be gone."

She didn't feel much remorse for talking to him that way. He couldn't have known what was really troubling her, and she knew it wouldn't take much for him to forgive her, again, and to come by the next time she called for him, or to call for someone else if he said no. She didn't have time to waste on wallowing anyway; she had to get ready to go and attend to Miss Yvonne's hair, and she was dreading it something bad, but not because of anything to do with the sweetly sad lady. Miss Yvonne's house had fallen so far into ruin, the only comfortable space for Víví to do her work was on the veranda, going back and forth from the stream out back with buckets for washing Miss Yvonne's hair and rinsing out the dye.

Víví realized she wasn't even as angry as she felt her self to be; she just wanted to be in her own presence for a while. Alone, she could sit with her frustrations like they were guests she had begrudgingly invited into her house, only looking them in the face for passing moments, hoping they wouldn't overstay their welcome the way they were threatening to, settling into the cushions and sinking their bare feet deeper into the rug.

What was disturbing Víví more than the prospect of she and her sisters losing sight of their duty to the island and the yet-to-be-unbroken inside of time, more than Samedi, was Lucille devoting her self so much to other people, of hemming her power in between walls made of the needs and wants of other people, transforming that power into something like generosity, when she could be limitless. Víví was disgusted, but beyond this, she was horrified. She had been looking for her self in the mirror of her sister's face and only saw what looked to her like an unfamiliar selflessness, or weakness even.

*break open*

*Inside of time, you gilded your self for Sunday morning in an opal-buttoned skirt suit, with wide hat and mesh veil, satin scarf and gloves to match, all white. You wrapped your cleanest linens from crown to full skirts, not just to visit the altar or the temple or the crossroads where you left the last offering but for everyday living, to go to work on the land, elbow-deep in red earth and somehow still spotless. You veiled and folded and cloaked for masjid on Friday at noon, all white for your own funeral. Your people wear white to mourn when your life has been long and laden with delight, to match the white halo you put on around 75 years old, to remember we wear grief and mourning light on our shoulders even if the thrum of the silence where your laughter used to live will never subside. Lately, we've been waiting longer and longer for you to return from mass and masjid and temple and crossroads; we've been soaking and bleaching and hanging more often and for longer; we've been wearing white so often we decided to stop taking it off at all.*

And outside of time, someone woke up with the white pillowcase wearing most of the blue dye Víví rinsed into their hair and thought, "I washed it with the special soap. She told me it would last longer than this. C'est bizarre, this."

# 7

*outside of time, after the break, on Blue Basin*
*fifth full moon, and dry season sounds quiet like a hollowed out*
*body waiting for a soul in a sister's absence*

The last time Serena had to come and hold the baby so Sans-Souci and Antoinette could sleep, they had just landed and were still staying with Lucille. It was Lucille who had done a lot of the actual holding and soothing and swaddling the child; Serena had been there to sing. As soon as the baby started fussing about something that wasn't hunger or tiredness or heat or fluster, Serena would draw as close to the baby as she could, whether it meant sitting on the floor with her head resting soft against the child's, barely moving because it was hard to believe the lightest touch wouldn't bruise or dent the child's crown still coming into form. Sometimes she would sing: *walk soft child, live wild*, but most of the time she wouldn't even have to open her mouth or do more than hum the melody somewhere high in her head, behind her face, and the notes would leak out slow like rising steam and settle over the baby, who would fall asleep before the next cry could escape the soft bow of his new mouth he was still learning how to use.

The baby could now answer to his different names: Raphael, Saint Ra, Rafa, Rara, Saint-Raphael-child-of-mine, if his mothers were frustrated and lacking sleep like they were on this day. He was in the in-betweens of infanthood where he was still absolutely and totally sure he was not just the center around which the satellites that were his mothers fussed and hugged and spun, he was the entire universe: the stars streaking across the sky that they pointed out to him through the window by his crib; all sides of the moon, the luminescence and the shadow and all that lay across and beyond; planets that his eyes had not yet stretched to be able to perceive but his mothers assured him were suspended in the ether because they had seen them on their way down. There was not a trace of malice in his needing of his mothers at any point of the day and night and his expectation that they would be present without fail—he was only a child whose self-perception for the moment still rested on the fact that he could look into his mother's gazes and see his self—but it meant they were often exhausted and needed another pair of hands to make sure Saint Ra still felt safe and held while they slept.

Saint Ra wasn't the only child who needed Serena's help to fall asleep or to bring them some calm when their own parents could not. For children wriggling with more energy than could possibly be contained in their own bodies, she would try to tire them out with never-ending chants that she would call for them to respond to:

"When you stir the tea it goes . . . ?"

"Clink, clink, clink!"

"When the honeybee flies we hear . . . ?"

"Bzz, bzz, bzz!"

"When the dog's tail wags it goes . . . ?"

"Woosh, woosh, woosh!"

"And when maman struts in her boots we hear . . ."

"Ke, ke, ke!"

Of late, Serena's neighbors had been asking her over more often to talk or sing to their babies, to soothe them after daymares, to quiet gasping sobs, to mind them while they stole sleep in the other room. But the smoothness and stoicism of the still water that was Serena's spirit was troubled because her hums and calls didn't seem to be working as well as they usually did. Even the little ones who were old enough to repeat some version of the words back to her, however babbling and jumbled they might be, were answering her in cries that sounded like fear, that went on long and desperate even after the actual tears had dried out. The parents couldn't know their children were hearing lullabies like they were chairs scraping across unpolished wood floors, and even their beloved Serena's voice hurt like cough medicine where it used to go down like honeysuckle syrup. Some of them, new to turning their dreams and terrors into words, tried to explain:

"Maman, it hurts bad. No more singing. Me ɖe kuku. I'll go to bed now."

"Last night I kept falling and falling and falling and falling, and I never came back down, and everywhere it was blue and blue and blue."

"You see the paint falling, there? Like rain?"

And the adults wouldn't send them to bed alone, tucking them in instead tight between themselves, or sleeping on the floor next to the crib or the little bed until morning, reassuring, "Cou-cou. I'm here. You will not fall. Nothing can get you."

Today, too, Serena's singing wasn't enough, at least the singing like joining words to notes of music and letting them dance out of her mouth wasn't, but there was so much more she could make possible than songs any old body could whistle or coax out of keys or strings. Her spirit was also weighed down with the discomfort of the fight between her and her sisters, so burdensome was the silence that she felt like she was moving about her life slower, like she was trying to walk through high tide waves wearing shoes filled with stones. Serena preferred to focus on being and making the sounds Saint Ra needed rather than Lucille being just one door away. Even with her being so close, she was sure she would not see or speak to her that day, with the same silence that had stretched between them since all three sisters had fallen into discord. Holding Saint Ra in her lap, Serena felt a rhythm first in her stomach before her feet caught up *tap-tap-tap*.

*break open*

*Can you hear us? Entendez-vous? E mía nkɔ sem a? We are called so many names we gave ourselves for all the many lives we have led:*

   *Devotees to the spirit who was, is, and will be saltwater and sound were concerned with committing to memory song, folktale, riddle, snippets of wisdom for everyday use. They included those one might expect: griots in grands boubous with one fist tightened around crumpled bills and the other raised overhead; opera singers; a boom-voiced radio presenter; a daydreaming schoolchild lost in words like espadrille, escargot, zinnia, xylophone; saxophonists whose music sounded like mourning; whistling fishermen; and poets. There were also beginner pianists still confusing their flats and their sharps; the one child on the playground always ready with tales taller than the schoolhouse when it was time to go back indoors; the cashier at some town's oldest poissonerie; a would-be jazz club star who lost all her possible radiant selves in the orange haze of a pill bottle; the one man sitting by the window in the barbershop, keeper of all the street's secrets. They were the kinds of people who were just as likely to obsess for weeks over the closing overtures of a song they had just heard for the first time as they were in the forward, back, and again of the ocean's waves and the spirit who was, is, and will be saltwater and sound made her self manifest anywhere they were enthralled:*

*inside of time, after the break*
*"Port-de-Paix, Nord-Ouest," Ayiti—agoo, we greet, mia tɔwò Taíno, rightful and careful custodians of the land—1989*
*Tap-tap-tap and the spirit was there as you tapped the jar of Epsom salts trying to get as much out of it into the bowl of water as possible, the steam rising into your face and misting over your thin-rimmed glasses. After what it took to get from the capital to your house on the hillside, your desire for relief was more than the good sense telling you that you should've bought a new bottle on your way back. You had been less and less willing to leave the safe and soft of your home to travel all over the island to sell jewelry fashioned out of gold, silver, bronze, amethyst, ruby, and opal and to drape and pin and tuck fabrics across the bodies of ladies who lunched and didn't do much else because people like you, Nadaline, and the armies of helpers and the tailors who would turn your fabrics into gowns, made their lives run seamless and unblemished like the finest silk.*
*That day had started for you at three in the morning with a walk to the only station at the foot of the hill that would take you close enough to the capital to walk to your first appointment*

*at seven, so early because this madame had only a minute of free time to meet with you, between her lover leaving her bed and her husband returning from his night shift at the hospital. Walking down the hill in the dark would've been a march towards death for someone who didn't know the land like you did, but you had trekked that way for all your years living there and knew every groove in the rock, every stepping place where the sand shifted like it was water, every root gnarling and knotting its way away from the tree trunks to interrupt an otherwise clear part of the path. And the spirit was with you in every crunch-crunch-crunch of the sand beneath your heels and in every sniff-sniff-sniff of you trying to clear your nose from the dew-heavy, near-dawn air. At the place where the hill sloped into valley was the station that wasn't a station, just a metal table, folding chair, and a yellow umbrella with peeling white lettering for le patron, whose job it was to mark in an old notebook the times of departure and arrival of the taxis that came to carry working people back and forth from town.*

*The capital was worlds away from your hillside sanctuary: motorbikes, goats, pedestrians, people balancing what looked like twice their weight in wares all fighting for space on the pavements, all losing to each other, to the smog hanging over them, to the cars speeding past so fast they looked like they could lose their way out of the fading white lines traced for them on the tar. The first madame's house might as well have been in another dimension, tucked into the greenest corner of the city in a neighborhood only accessible by two sets of heavy gates on either end, both guarded by men who you would not have been surprised to learn had once been employed as mercenaries for this dictator or that tycoon. You spent the day in and out of salons where any breath of fresh air had been completely displaced by incense smoke, powder, imported perfume, the scent of that afternoon's lunch, the windows clasped tight against any intrusion from the chaos of the city outdoors.*

*By the time the sky began to sag under the city's smog and night's cloak, you were on the back of a moto, all your bags empty and your head leaning against the damp back of the rider, with no energy left to bother that he was a stranger to you. And the spirit was in every engine revving and coughing and sputtering, and she was in your exhausted sighs that would have turned to cries had you been alone. You had missed the last taxi going back to the hill and had to beg a ride in a truck with sun-reddened tourists coming to mind everyone's business and call it a holiday. The guide didn't take much convincing—you knew his mother and had given her more jewelry than she could measure with broken promises of repayment.*

*To roll out your voice flat, unthreatening, smooth, cost your pride, patience, the sense of self that lay between what you had to do to keep your breadbasket somewhat full and fresh fruits in the kitchen. Usually, by the time you returned home, you felt hot and prickly like you had grown thorns on your body, totally outside your self, sometimes sweeping all the rumpled laundry, unwashed and clean alike, onto the rug next to your bed before climbing in without a bath, without a clean cover for your body. Other times, you would spend almost all the money you had earned before you even made it halfway up the hill just to replace the irritation with some kind of rush, even for a moment. You bought things like soaps and oils you knew would make your skin crust and itch, or fried fish fritters you knew would turn your stomach inside out, enough to feed all the children in the houses around yours.*

*So now you, Nadaline, were at home with your self, but without knowledge that the spirit who was there in the tap-tap-tap on the window—fireflies trying to get inside because the glass was so clear they mistook it for air. And you cried because you were compelled to sell the works of your hands to people who with no care or understanding for how long it took for each clasp and hook to take shape or for how to ward off the eventual cloud of tarnish, grandes madames who could afford new sets of earrings and matching necklaces for the birthday of each family member, three for Easter weekend, and who's counting by the time the Christmas season arrives, anyway.*

*Tap-tap-tap, and the spirit who was saltwater and sound was standing by the window when you threw the still steaming and unused water swoooosh splash out of it, along with the mostly empty jar of salts clink-cli-cli-clink. And the spirit who was love and vengeance was in the sting of your furious tears, fresh with resentment and exhaustion, and the spirit who was sweetness and luxury was in the glimmer of the gems scattered across the work table, and you looked at the confused fireflies and wondered if it would ever be possible for you to grow wings.*

\*\*\*

Serena was sitting half on the rug and half on the tile, still carrying Saint Ra on her lap, and they had both dozed off. When she opened her eyes, Sans-Souci was standing over them smiling. "Even you, you can see how tired he makes us. Merci, nye sí."

Serena yawned and adjusted the baby's weight on her, still waking up.

Sans-Souci went on, "You won't ask after Lucille?"

"You won't ask me about your child first?"

"I can see he's fast asleep, non? He's fine. Answer me?"

Serena felt her self bristling, becoming prickly and irritated like she had too many clothes on during a heatwave. It wasn't Sans-Souci's fault her sisters shared a stubbornness that sometimes expanded too wide for them to move around, leaving no room for them to show Love's Face to each other the way they knew they needed to. "Have *you* asked her how she is?"

"Listen, it's not me who will force my way into business that is not mine. But you are loved. You love each other. It's so uncomfortable to see you sliding past each other. This blue bowl is only so big."

Serena's voice had a rasp that was unusual for her, even deeper than the aftermath of her longest storytimes: "Sorry this is causing you discomfort. I can only imagine what it's like being a watcher in this."

Sans-Souci sighed and bent down to lift Saint-Ra, still sleeping and snoring light as a whisper, into her arms, but before Serena let go, she tried to soften the impact of the sharp needlepoint of her temper. "I hear, I do. And I'm sorry I said it like so; you don't deserve that."

Serena's embarrassment wouldn't allow her to speak it aloud to Sans-Souci or to either of her sisters, but she hated how far this quarrel had stretched, and she found so much delight in the way Lucille's voice swayed and swooned when she was turning Love's Face to someone in the way she was currently turning to Samedi. She wasn't anxious about what could happen if Lucille's equilibrium tilted too far towards either love or vengeance, at least not as anxious as Viví seemed to be. Neither Samedi nor anyone else was anywhere near as powerful as Lucille was, not enough to skew her off center. Serena was most preoccupied about how long it had been since she was lulled into an afternoon nap by her sister's voices clinking against each other like champagne flutes, so long since Víví clapped her hands on her thighs when Serena had told an especially tall tale, so long since Lucille had made her tea slightly past the borderline of too sweet, just as she liked it.

She had just turned to the door to leave when she heard Antoinette call out from the bedroom, her words leaning into each other like she was still fast asleep. "What's going on out there? Serena and her sisters finally decided to forgive each other, oui?"

*break open*

*Inside of time, in the same place where Ndɔkutsu paid for his betrayal with his life, all kinds of lives had sprung into being, fed by your desires and your fears. In narrow, shingle-roofed houses the color of reddened dry season sky, you slept and ate and loved and wailed and split and worried about last month's light bill and next month's school fees while the lagoon and the sea drew closer to each other, swallowing a little more of the land you had carved out for living and for dying, whenever the time came for that. The town was a wedge of beach bearing the ocean's world-ending power and pressure on one side and the lagoon's patient but deadly saltiness on the other. Those of you who were old enough to have heard about Ndɔkutsu from your grandparents' stories could see this next catastrophe would look more like floating too far out to sea on a raft where you had dozed off and less like being stolen away by the specters who came before.*

And outside of time, hibiscus flowers bled crimson all over the bushes and onto the dirt. The petals were left feeble and drooping, the stems shriveled and bloodless too. In as much time as it took to blink, to turn one's head left, right, and left again, life rushed back into the plant, lush and ready for plucking to adorn a head or for drying then boiling then chilling to quench one's thirst, only to wilt and turn pale right after. "You saw that? I swear that bush died, came alive, and died again right as I looked at it, just-just now."

# 8

*outside of time, after the break, on Blue Basin*
*fifth full moon, or the road that resentment walks stretches*
*towards the threat of a loveless eternity; it's never too late to*
*turn back*

It was not long before sunset, Lucille's beloved hour, full of sunlight like warm honey spilling over the windowsill into the room, down the wall, and splashing softly onto the floorboards, prime for floating in and out of hours' long sleep. But on this day, Lucille was resisting sleep's seduction. Trapped inside her unease, she looked on, sulky, and her beloved late afternoon sunshine bouncing off the empty bottles lining the shelves of Samedi's room was not a sufficient distraction from her discontent. She rubbed her belly rounded with the rice and beans she had for lunch and not quite yet because of the soon-to-be child coming into being inside her. Each passing day since she found out she was pregnant deepened the discomfort sitting inside her chest and fusing to her ribcage, making her breath uneven and difficult, at least so she felt. She looked over her shoulder at Samedi sleeping next to her. Her new annoyance towards him was walling her off from him, placing one brick of aloofness carefully on top of another and constructing a barrier no contrition on his part could break. Just his gentle rumbling breaths and his heaving back irritated her. He was the reason, Lucille was convinced, that she felt as though she was carting around a bad omen rather than a promising future within her.

During their lunch, Lucille had tried, again, as she had been for weeks, to leave some sort of crack in Samedi's ego, enough to fit in her apprehension. "You think I just love to complain." Lucille stuck her fork like it was a weapon into her food as she spoke, with such force that all she succeeded in doing was scattering rice and beans in every direction across the plate and onto the table. Samedi offered what he must have thought was a reassuring grin, but to Lucille he just seemed smug in the face of her anxiety.

"I don't think you love complaining, ma cherie. But I keep telling you . . ."

"What? What should I do?" Lucille cut in.

"Baby, this child is already magic. Half you and half me. There's nothing for you . . . for us to worry about." Samedi's pride at the prospect of fatherhood hadn't stopped growing, burgeoning to the point of bursting, while she only grew more infuriated, because Samedi seemed more interested in producing a miniature version of his self than he was in being kind or even present to Lucille. This may have been one of the reasons why, instead of flaunting chubby cheeks like was expected of her, Lucille's face hollowed more than anyone had ever seen, and she was fighting off scars left from one pimple after the next on skin that should have been glossy and clear. Every person she met believed they had the remedy to set Lucille's pregnancy on the joyful course that had so far evaded her.

"Have some of this. It's what you need, especially this early on," Sans-Souci insisted, presenting countless spoonfuls of what tasted more like chalk dissolved in lukewarm water than the soup Sans-Souci claimed her concoction to be.

Antoinette bore peaceful and slightly amused witness to Sans-Souci's high-handed instructions, the memory of when she gave birth and Lucille's quiet care still spring-green fresh: "Let her alone, cherie. It's only been two moons, and far too soon for you to be hassling her like this."

Lucille allowed her self to feel the fawn and fuss of Sans-Souci and Antoinette, imagining it was Serena and Víví. She was so ready to surrender to how lovely it was to be pampered for once, she started to think to her self that maybe the soup wasn't so terrible, until Sans-Souci interrupted her before she could be totally entranced: "Lucille, ma poupée. I don't want to get into your business."

"But? You are going to anyway. I'm listening." Lucille tapped the base of the bowl with her spoon until the sound of metal on porcelain filled the whole room, racing away from its measured rhythm like a bell warning of a fast-approaching threat. Sans-Souci paused and looked to Antoinette, questioning whether she should continue, though all three of them knew she would anyway.

"Et Serena? Víví? What about them? Are you really going to keep them shut out? Even when the baby comes?"

"Am I the only one to blame? They know I'm going to have a child, and have you seen them over here?" Without giving Sans-Souci room to respond, Lucille closed the door on the conversation. "Thank you for the soup, for the visit. Truly, I'm grateful, akpe. I'm tired now, let me go and lie down. You two can see your selves out."

Lucille couldn't set foot in Keta Afeme without pieces

of wisdom being pressed into her unwilling hands, especially because everyone seemed to think they knew something about her own self that she didn't or couldn't. But even these pieces of advice were easier to bear than Sans-Souci's reminder that she was growing this life without her sisters. Everyone she met had a word or three for her.

"Some aloe, baby, to clear those dry patches right up."

"You shouldn't be walking up and down like this! Menyo kra kra kra o!"

"It's still so early on baby; I'm sure you'll be alright."

Amidst this tangle of unwelcome advice, Lucille couldn't pick out one solid piece of hope to hold on to, not a single firm word she could use as incantation to summon some relief in the midst of her unease. Even with the devoted hovering of her neighbors, the absence of her sisters made the earth beneath her even more shaky. She hadn't spoken to them in three waxings and wanings of the moon, though she still felt their love from afar every time she found gifts and notes from them at her doorstep. From Vívi: a pair of purple velvet booties for the child, a tin of ointment for Lucille's aching lower back, a bottle of orange blossom essence to sweeten the air in her house. Serena left an opalescent shell with the sound of a cheerful whistle inside it, a book of praise songs for the child that could also be lullabies, and a bottle of soaking salts for Lucille's swelling feet. She found her sisters' mistrust of Samedi drove her to near madness, she was so angry. How could they possibly think they knew better than she did about how she turned Love's Face and who she turned towards? Then there was also their fear of what could become of all the worlds they were holding, as if they could be more afraid than she was of what could happen to all their beloveds both inside and outside of time if one of them became too involved in making a little, singular life as Lucille was preoccupied with doing at that very moment.

Lucille was transforming from being her self to just somebody's maman. She would have a child, a whole person she would have no choice but to see about, all the time. She would have a child, another person in the world who would add to the number of people who already used her name like a cry for help and a chant for relief, an extra on a list of the needy and demanding that wound its way around the island again and again.

Guilt planted itself inside her, a stubborn root, anytime she thought about this new fragile life she was supposed to be willing to die for. The roots grew a little anytime someone smiled their sly knowing and hid their awareness of her pregnancy behind innuendo. It expanded so much, Lucille barely had any room around it to exhale. With or without the presence of her sisters, she had to accept she was on her way to being somebody's mother.

Eventually, she had to surrender to how much she did not want to mother this child she had yet to meet. She let her self be so full of her unwillingness, it pushed its way to all the corners of her being, further than her usual generosity could reach to try to clear it out. Why wasn't the love she and Samedi turned with enough? Why couldn't they let it well alone, to waft in the smoke above bonfires and race with falling stars, like the spirits of unborn children did?

Samedi rose at about half past seven, oblivious to the turmoil brewing an arm-length away from him. Lucille felt

Samedi's movements behind her and tensed her self from the crown of her head to the tips of her littlest toe, a most unnatural imitation of a body in deep sleep. She focused on slowing her breathing enough for Samedi to leave her alone or to at least participate in a charade that simply meant she was still dissatisfied and in no mood to speak with him. "Lucie, my Lucie. Will you stop this? I know you're up."

Lucille maintained her pose, lying stiffly in the same position and trying to ignore the numbness on the right side of her body that had been deprived of space to stretch for too long. "What do you want from me, man?"

"Man?" Samedi sighed like he couldn't belive Lucille hadn't slept away her irritable mood. He walked round to the side of the bed where he could see Lucille's face. "Les gars m'attendent. I'm running late. Join us? I'm sure we can find some lemonade for you instead of whiskey?"

"You go on. I'm not up for any of it. Va yi. I'm fine right here." All Lucille could see of Samedi was the tiny knots of hair sprinkling his thighs and legs, left uncovered by the shorts he had worn to bed. She fought the urge to tilt her head upwards so as not to look into his face because she knew she could only keep the sarcastic remarks she wanted to make about his melodramatic sighs trapped behind her teeth for so long.

So Lucille lay, still and sure that her right leg would be permanently locked in its place if she didn't move around soon. Each of the nerve endings snaking their invisible paths across her skin were on high alert, tuned to Samedi's presence as he walked around the room, tossing piles of folded laundry apart in search of his white linen shirt before adjusting his self in the mirror nailed to the back of his bedroom door. She felt, too, the faint mist of the cologne he sprayed generously around his self, and on a different day, she may have teased, "Why don't you go ahead and baptize your self with that stuff? Take a bath in it even!"

Instead, she remained firm in her determination to extend her indignation as far it could go. She understood that Samedi could only know what she allowed him to know, but she couldn't be sure he would be careful in the way she needed him to be, to listen and soothe rather than to joke until the worry receded behind laughter. She also knew it was unlikely Samedi would own up to staying by her side only when he felt like it and when it felt like that four o'clock on a Saturday type of possible and was so carefree and absent when it didn't. In the strained silence, she thought she felt him pause at the door before yanking it open and heading downwards in the direction of the hacking laughter of his friends outside. Though she couldn't see them, she knew who would be waiting. Redeemer, cracking his large, darkened knuckles between sips of palm wine, his hands still showing the slight tremors from working around iron and in fire all day and tuning the string of his tired old cello all night. Then there would be Nouvelle, his broad face and wide back and shoulders to match, with small sparkling eyes sinking into the tops of his cheeks that looked like they belonged in someone else's head, and Tomorrow Baby, who never grew out of the name his aunt gave him because no one knew on what day of the week his mother, long dead as far as he knew, had given birth to him.

Samedi's friends called Lucille Samedi's afenɔ, his "old lady," because they knew she hated it and would duck away from her doubled over in laughter as she tried to hit back at them with a heavy hand. "I'm no one's anything, you hear me! Don't play with me!" She knew where each of their egos had pressure points she could jab with a teasing finger, Nouvelle's shabby trousers that always seemed to come up short because he insisted on sewing and hemming them himself—"Boy, will you just let me fix these for you? So damn proud—"

Before sleep pulled Lucille behind its heavy curtain, she heard Nouvelle greeting Samedi, mischief all around the edges of his voice she could practically see without seeing, his tongue inside his cheek, "Watcha saying, my good man Saturday! Ça va? Dis-moi, Serena been by? Seen her lately?"

The last thing Lucille heard was Samedi laughing from deep in his chest, "Maaaan there's nothing you have that Serena wants . . ." She moved through a daze somewhere between sleeping and waking. She must have drifted off before she had braided her hair and tucked it away beneath a scarf, so now it stuck out in dry clumps around her face, tickling her cheeks and neck. The darkness of the room felt desolate without Samedi to share it with, and Lucille almost felt sorry she had chosen to remain at Samedi's home rather than go out to enjoy the evening with him. She may have been sitting on his lap, his arms cradled around her rounding belly, stealing sips from a drink she would have forced him to take soft; no way would she suffer the flavor of juice with no liquor unless he did too.

The next time she woke up, it was to the painful sensation of the skin on her lower back being pummeled every which way, so strongly it was like a dozen mean little hands had taken aim at her, refusing to give up until her flesh was beaten soft and helpless. She sat up sharply or, rather, was pulled upright by hands controlling her like she was a ventriloquist's companion.

Her attempt at screaming was muffled, and panic flushed through her body at not being able to raise an alarm for help. The hands relaxed their hold for a brief moment in which Lucille believed the horror to have subsided, only for them to bring her backwards with a violent tug. Expecting her back to meet the mattress, she felt instead a free fall, wind rushing upwards past her face and the little hands scratching away at her skin no matter how furiously she tried to swat them away. She awakened in time to find her self halfway off the edge of the bed and was able to stop her body from meeting the floor. Her housedress was soaked with the sweat that also streamed down the back of her neck. She knew Samedi was still not back, but she reached across the bed for him anyway. She rolled over and rose to her feet, thrusting her face into the bowl of rosewater and heaven knows what else Samedi had mixed, claiming it could dispel any sort of fear and unsettled emotions for the person who inhaled it. She turned the pillow over to its dry, cooler side and returned to bed, shutting her eyes tightly and waiting for relief to descend.

Morning invaded the room in all its brassy newness, and Lucille squinted against the light pouring through the uncovered windows.

"Lucie cherie, you still mad?" Samedi smelled like he had been soaking in a tub of liquor for hours, but as much as she would have loved to maintain her practiced coldness, she was genuinely pleased to see that he was there and that she had survived the frightful night with all its shadowy hands taking her hostage and keeping her trapped and just beyond the reach of sweet rest. "Ah efo, did you drink last night or fall inside the bottle?"

"Why don't you find out? Come here baby, take a sip?" There was a pause, like the room itself was on an inhale, to see if Lucille's disposition was still laced with the same acid she had been pouring onto Samedi or if they could return to the harmless teases to which they were accustomed to showing affection.

Samedi reached for Lucille's hand and tickled the sensitive spot inside of her wrist. Lucille's laugh tinkled in harmony with the small bell one of the ɖekákpùi was ringing up and down the island to rouse those islanders who still went faithfully to worship every Sunday morning. Samedi exhaled a big gust of breath and the tension in the room dissipated along with it. "Ah, there's my girl!"

Samedi sat up and pulled Lucille onto his lap, facing him, groaning theatrically as he did at what he called their extra weight she had brought on board. He rested his chin on her shoulder, and with every breath in and out, his cheek rubbed against the side of her neck. She leaned into this feeling of several days' worth of skipped shaves grazing her skin and craved the same kind of rub on her belly and on the inside of her thigh.

She leaned against him, inhaling deeply past the booze and sweat to the sweet vanilla that clung to his skin, a result of spending hours each day elbow deep in bowls of his medicines and mixtures, and something else, a rich woody sort of scent like he had spent the night sleeping outside with leaves and trees as his cover. Samedi's hands played on Lucille's back, tracing abstract patterns between the stretch marks and faint scars from insect bites and other little injuries that marked her skin before moving downwards to knead her lower back. She winced and pushed him away. "Allez . . . you need to wash up! Laisse-moi!"

Samedi stilled and released Lucille, moving his hands up to her face and looking long and slow, examining her for signs of more worry to come. He held her jaw in his hands and rubbed his thumb over her face. Next, he moved his fingers to her upper lip's right side, where he lingered over the nick right next to her cupid's bow, so slight like a fingernail filed too sharply had pinched a bit of flesh where it was simply meant to scratch an itch.

Lucille considered sharing the terror she had faced overnight and her apprehension about her pregnancy accelerating from quiet concern to total chaos, like foamy sea water coalescing into frightful tidal waves, but she decided against it. It was difficult for her to allow her self to be loved by anyone, to fold into the sanctuary offered by someone else's kindness, even as much as she longed for that kind of safety. To be anything other than the way she was, always dependable, when there were so many hands to hold and split souls to stitch and so many people with far more complicated dilemmas riding their heads. And how could she be certain another person would really care for her in the way she did for them? She was reluctant, even with Samedi, who had walked his jaunty walk into her life, but instead of finally being able to undo some of the knots stiffening in her body from holding her self so close to her spirit, she now feared that Samedi's promise of "viens, on va passer des bon temps" would mean more trouble for her eventually. If the column standing rigidly at the core of Lucille was built out of a deep desire to secure the well-being of other people, to make sure their souls were not bowing down but sturdy and upright, some of its concrete was mixed with Lucille's pride. She relished the rush of vigor and adrenaline coursing inside her fist when it was clenched around the solid handle of her pocketknife and lived for the kind of power that could shift lives back into balance and bring comfort where only destruction once ravaged. Who else could do what she did, either inside or outside of time?

*break open*

Remember, the spirit stepped inside of time and hurled her self earthwards towards the break, and there she bore witness to all kinds of upheavals, both intimate and public:

inside of time, after the break
"Jeremie, Grand'Anse," Ayiti—agoo, we greet, mia tɔwò Taíno, rightful and careful custodians of the land—1992

The spirit who was, is, and will be love and vengeance was with you, child, watching as you continued to burn the wrong kind of incense for so long it was a wonder you could breathe through the smog. The hanging smoke had taken over the air in the room so there was none left to keep your white candle lit. The spirit came mainly because she did not want you, child, to accidentally end yourself in pursuit of connection with the world beyond life and death.

In the corner of your room closest to the window, there was a small table covered in a blue cloth. Next to a candle sat a doll with a scratched-up face and a glass of rum. Some red roses stood broken-necked to the right of the other sad things. Child, you didn't know what you were doing. Still, the spirit came forth anyway, stood by the window, and lit a cigarette on the last lingering sparks of the candle on the altar. And waited.

You would barely cross the threshold of your room before your body flew to the altar, the place you were trying to make for the spirit in your life. It wasn't even that you were too scared or didn't have the heart, but you were not yet in a place to be able to recognize the spirit. You were desperate for an encounter like what you had read in some books and conjured in the wide, rich plains *of your imagination; the spirit with eyes aflame, legs astride the universe, nails and double-edged knife sharpened to lethal points, face marked with scars, the spirit as Ezili Danto.*

*And the spirit who was, is, and will be love and vengeance, the spirit you called Ezili, was all those things, and she was also holding your shattered self together with more tenderness than the human heart could understand. In any case, you weren't quite ready to experience the grandeur of the spirit you craved. You had not traced a path on the floor in flour or chalk or gunpowder. You could not bear her crown; you just weren't ready. The two of you meeting there would have meant two spirits like wide skies cramped inside too small a house.*

# 9

*outside of time, after the break, on Blue Basin*
*fifth full moon, and turning Love's Face isn't always fraught,*
*even if the neck creaks from scarce use*

"Nye sí, since when did you start smoking?"

Serena didn't look up from the step just beyond her feet
where she had laid out some snuff and a pipe, hazelnut-smooth
except for the bowl that looked like it was being cupped by two
hands carved into the wood. Feigning iron-clad concentration
gave her more time to act like her heart had not skipped out
of her chest, down the stairs, and halfway down the beach at
the sound of Vívi's voice. "You heard me? Where from all these
things?"

Head bowed and neck stiff, Serena didn't flinch when Vívi
squeezed into a seat on the step next to her. Serena did not
push her sister away when she moved to put her arm around
her and only sighed when Vívi's hands made her way to Serena's
roots. "You've been retwisting on your own? I can see that."

Serena didn't realize she was crying from laughter until she
tasted the salt on her lower lip. She rested her head on Vívi's
shoulder because it meant they didn't have to look each other
in the eye. Ever since Sans-Souci and Antoinette had said what
they said, Serena had on several occasions started down the slope
from her house in the Katye, towards Vívi or Lucille. One of

those times, she was empty-handed except for some of her most carefully chosen words with a few well-placed huffs and puffs to accent her speech, something like, "Cherie, when have we ever been this petty? What is the fight even about?" Or maybe, "Have you seen Lucille? Tout va bien? Let's go to her together?" Another evening, she went with the lyrics to Víví's favorite song, humming on the inside of her cheek like saving a toffee for later, *sing a little sweet song for me, sweetness.* Yet another day, she went with a jar of honey infused with vanilla and a tulip she saw blooming in the dust just outside her fence. She never made it down to Víví's because the closer she got, the higher her anxiety bubbled up in her chest, up to the top of her throat, threatening to spill over in more wicked words she couldn't afford to say and would most definitely wish she had swallowed when it was too late for sorry. She hated being the level low-tide water all the time where her sisters had space as wide as the horizon unfurled twice over to rage and desire and burn and storm. If either of them wanted to talk, they knew where she was. The road to her house both came and went, after all.

If she was expecting anyone to come bearing the laughter of commiseration and apology, she would've thought it would be Lucille and not Víví, as proud as she was.

"I wasn't expecting you." Serena felt Víví's body grow tense, joints and nerves knitting together and bracing for whatever daggers Serena might throw with her words.

"What are you trying to say?"

"Sister, I didn't mean any harm . . . just—" Serena was never one to fumble with what to say. She swallowed deep and started again, "Forget that. I'm so glad you are here, Víví. Vraiment."

Víví picked up the pipe and turned it over from one hand

to another and back again. She was thinking about how her reflection was still behaving like her shadow, lagging so far behind now that her physical body would be standing in front of an empty mirror while her image lingered in the glass in the doors of her fine china cabinet or in the shiny side of a mixing bowl. The business of making people feel their most beautiful wasn't enough to turn Víví away from her growing fears because the heads she was dressing were far more tender than usual, and not just the babies who were still growing used to the feeling of strange hands braiding their too-soft strands down to their scalps. Even Miss Geneviève, the most exacting and stoic person to sit in Víví's chair, squirmed like Víví was scrubbing her hair with lava and not lukewarm, sudsy water.

"Madam Jeune-vee-ève! I beg you, be still. What is the matter?"

Miss Geneviève flung her self forward and away from the sink, spinning around to face Víví and sending water flying all over the kitchen and down her own back. "What is wrong with you, rather? Are you using boiling water to shampoo?"

Víví had never seen this madame in such a state of panic; the only emotions she knew her to express being disgust or anger and, very rarely, quiet satisfaction. She plunged her hands directly into the water she had been using and said, "See? You see how I am not flinching? This water is no hotter than the air in this kitchen, je te jure."

By the time Víví had convinced Miss Geneviève to test the water for her self, it had run cold.

"Sorry, cherie. You know I would never act out for nothing. You knew my darling?"

"Of course, madame. I remember him. May he rest well."

"He could never rest, that one. Even now that he is no more, I know he is still with me when my scalp tingles like it used to when he would rub in my oils for me. But of late, it hurts, and I can't understand why."

Miss Geneviève wasn't the only one who was sensing the presence of loved ones much more intensely than usual, much more disquieting and less like loving. Víví was noticing more and more that people would recoil from her hands before she had fully laid them on their heads, wincing at the first touch of henna or dye or even at the brush of the towel on their shoulders. For many of those whose loved ones remained in all kinds of intangible ways, hugs from behind, taps on the shoulder, neck kisses, the pulling taut of a fresh braid, Víví found that she couldn't get near them without them trying to back away. Some even complained that uncountable hair washes couldn't get rid of the smell of cigarette smoke or cologne or freshly cut garlic or whichever scent their lost loved ones used to make sure they were never forgotten.

Víví flipped the pipe with the bowl facing downwards, her fingers running over the carved embrace etched into the wood. It made her think of the spirits who were serpents and how they had failed and how things might have been different if her and her sisters' spirit selves had been the ones keeping the universe in one colossal piece. "En tout cas. Everyone is better off here."

As if Serena was following the thread of Víví's thoughts, she said, "I guess so. But at the same time, do we know how bad things can get outside of time, considering how it is inside?"

Víví shrugged so Serena would have to stop resting on her and sit up straight. "Sister, what are you saying?"

"I'm saying . . . the other day I was singing to Saint-Ra, and my voice kept getting stuck in my throat. Like I knew the notes but somehow had forgotten how to make them sound."

"Serena, ma sœur, I'm sorry."

Serena nudged her younger sister's shoulder with her own. "What's there to be sorry for? You've been terrible so many eternities over, but you aren't to blame for this. I'm sorry too. Et Lucille?"

"You know if you haven't talked to her, I definitely haven't." Before Serena could interrupt, Víví raised both her hands. "No, cherie. My anger is long dead. Franchement, I feel shame. You heard what I said to her? And there will be a baby, and we are not there to help or hold."

Serena put her head back on her sister's shoulder and carried on like she hadn't heard Víví. "So. Dis-moi. What beauty have you been feasting on over these many silent moons, without your sisters?"

"Oh, you know. Why are you acting like you weren't there with me?

*break open*

*Can you hear us? Entendez-vous? E mía nkɔ sem a? We are called
so many names we gave ourselves for all the many lives we have
led:*

    *Though their body selves were in temporary disagreement
outside of time, their spirit selves were always in unison, watching
over all the yet-to-be-unbroken inside of time. The spirit who was,
is, and will be sweetness and luxury and the spirit who was, is,
and will be saltwater and sound danced and swam through the
break, to wherever little delights were found and wherever the
water was deepest and the waves loudest:*

*inside of time, "New Orleans, Louisiana"—agoo, we greet, mia
tɔwò Chitimacha, rightful and careful custodians of the land—
2019*
    *On a street corner with a robin's egg blue hatchback parked
outside, in a house with haint blue on the porch ceiling and
splashed across the one metal chair, inside a room with peacock
blue walls and a midnight blue ceiling, there you were, rolling
up to smoke after a long day cycling uptown and downtown with
other people's grocery orders and on other people's errands, all over
a city that felt like several worlds in constant collision, the heat
a result of the lives within worlds constantly rubbing up against
each other, tension enough to start a fire. You took as much care
with this early evening ritual as you did sharing tea with your
aunts and painting seascapes to decorate your house or teaching
your young students how to touch their paintbrushes to the canvas
with the lightest hand, a way to open a door inside your own
mind through which you could pass to a world where the work*

*of your hands was enough, and you didn't have to cycle back and forth with other people's lunch orders to keep your life as blue and blissful as was possible. When you opened the chest of drawers to look for your stash, rolling papers, and grinder, the spirit who was sweetness and luxury ran her fingers across the bubbles of blue where you had painted cornflowers on the wood, impressed at how much time it must have taken to make those flowers bloom blue across the furniture, and the spirit who was saltwater and sound was in the soft creak of the drawer closing and in the trill of next door's bell ringing. When you unraveled the paper onto the tray you had placed on your bed, the spirit who was sweetness and luxury wrapped her self around the gold handles of the tray and felt the ridges engraved in them, and the spirit who was saltwater and sound was in the sweat beading in the valley at the base of your throat and in the tap-tap-tap of your nails against the tray. When you sprinkled the herb into the grinder and twisted it shut, the spirit who was sweetness and luxury was in the scent filling the room, and she was in your satisfied sigh when you licked the paper and began to roll and in the warmth of the paper's seal. The spirit who was saltwater and sound was in the click of the lighter and your cough cough cough as your body adjusted to the burning inhale, and the spirit who was sweetness and luxury was in the perfect plumes of smoke circling your head as you leaned back against the sky blue of your pillows and of the bedspread, arms outstretched, like flying.*

# 10

*outside of time, after the break, on Blue Basin*
*sixth full moon, or how far will a spirit stretch before it is*
*eternally distorted and spent?*

"Lucille, the wedding is tomorrow, and my baby—yes, my last—ripped a hole in my lace. Please. I need your help."

There Lucille would go, scarf still fixed tightly to her braided head, sleep still crusting over her eyelids, through the mist hanging from the trees, through the Paroisse like a funeral parlor with flimsy shrouds for curtains, up on the Gran Promenade and onto the rocky ground of the hills, to be met by a pair of eyes peering through the bars of the closed gate to her house. "Ah, my hero, Lucille! You are, truly!"

There Lucille would go to answer the door, Sans-Souci's face twisted with worry and half hidden by the waning light. "Lucille, she could be out there, my baby sister, Afi-ví. Can't you do something to help her land? It's so cold, and she could be up there lost in the wind."

Sans-Souci's hands, still wrinkled from being constantly submerged in basins full of soapy suds and soggy clothes, lay trembling in her lap as she watched Lucille brewing tea, as she listened to Lucille's measured consolations. "Cherie, you are driving your self sick over this. If she is out there, we will be waiting for her to land. She will not fall. T'inquiète pas, ma sœur. Me ɖe kuku na wó."

### break open

*outside of time, Afi-ví flies and flies and flies and then she does not*
  *Can you hear us? Entendez-vous? E mía nkɔ sem a? We are*
*called so many names we gave ourselves for all the many lives we*
*have led:*
  *Afi-ví would be lying if she said she knew when and where she*
*was. In Keta, they used to measure time passing with the moon.*
*Every new moon meant a month had passed, but she could*
*no longer remember how many new moons made a new year,*
*how many years she had lived, if she was still living at all. And*
*anyway, she couldn't always see the moon from wherever she was.*
*She had been with her big sister Afi-gā, and they were running*
*away from a dog, their totem, trying to run faster than bad luck*
*moves. Then they were at home, eating fresh bread their mother*
*had baked for them, pretending as if it wasn't scorching the roofs of*
*their mouths because it was too fluffy for them to deny themselves,*
*so sweet they almost forgot the story Mama Hadzila had told*
*them about the world ending with a break. They were asleep*
*on their mat. Then they were not. They were the center of their*
*universe. Then they were not. Then they were dragged screaming*
*until they deafened themselves. Then they were walking through*
*a forest they didn't know was on the other side of the lagoon. They*
*did not know what a horizon was until they did. Then they were*
*walking and walking and walking and bleeding and crying and*
*crying until they were too weak and too spent to produce any*
*more tears or sounds or pleas or sighs. They were together. Then*
*they were not. They were alive. Then they were not. Afi-ví didn't*
*think being trampled would feel like being slapped from all sides*
*by heavy, invisible hands, because before it happened, she hadn't*

*thought about being trampled at all. She was hurting. And then she was not. And then there was now. She was whirling so much in open air, she felt like she was the wind itself. It was always night wherever she was, which she supposed was good because she could feel her body and her self without seeing what had become— or not—of her. There was a baby crying and some grown-ups wailing, but they would soon learn to stop when they realized, like Afi-ví had, that no one was coming for them.*

\*\*\*

"Hé Lucille! You there? Girl, open up quick! I need you!" And there Lucille would go to Ma-Reine's door, armed with pieces of gauze roughly cut up with her pocketknife, and tea tree oil for the swelling, and sharply edged words of caution.

*break open*

*outside of time, Ma-Reine in flight towards her wide open future*
      *Can you hear us? Entendez-vous? E mía nkɔ sem a? We are called so many names we gave ourselves for all the many lives we have led:*
      *Ma-Reine was sure she had died again. She and Glory had crashed into each other so hard that she felt if she were to let go, her body would be dust and debris falling out of her left ear and over what used to be her shoulder. The impact was unlike anything she had ever known, not like bumping into a wall at night, because those kinds of walls gave way a little beneath groping hands like they knew you had made them possible, because you yourself had coaxed the clay into bricks, then into something to live in. Before she realized what she had collided with, she just knew it was all*

over; she just knew the unforgiving ground had risen to meet her falling body.

The shock of the crash did not recede, even when she understood she had not died and the wall or ground was actually another person. Instead, it hovered like a glare around her head and took her an infinity of seconds to notice the arms wrapped tight around her. They had collided, and their bones did not turn to powder and fall to their end after being scattered to, fro, and farther in the wind like ashes, or chalk dust, or gunpowder traced on the ground to open and close the gate between who they were and who they would be.

"It's Glory."

She couldn't hear his voice for the wind, but she thought she heard, "It's glorious," thought they must have reached the part of flight where they would come back to life, thought they had reached their destination. They landed on their backs but did not break. It was as though they had simply woken up on another weekend morning and rolled over in bed. Several hands reached down to them, hands with dark-tipped fingers, hands calloused and toughened, polished and perfumed, hands at the ends of scarred forearms and forearms without blemish. And somewhere over their heads and behind them, a brass band, shrieks of delight, and something else fainter and more delicate but no less joyful, like fireflies drunk on atmosphere and bumping into glass, like bells, like new life.

"Bienvenue mia tɔwò. Miawoezɔ. We are so glad to see. The name is?"

Before Ma-Reine could answer, Glory was up on his feet. "It's Glory, and this is my wife."

***

"Nye sí, I'm not mad at you. It's not your fault, ma chère. No way should that man be putting hands on anyone. You can come stay by me for as long as you need. How long has this been going on?"

The nights when Ma-Reine did stay with Lucille were not always the same kind of fear-ridden, window-watching kind—though so far, Glory seemed to be lacking the courage or the audacity to try to follow Ma-Reine to Lucille's house. Especially now that Lucille was making a little one, Ma-Reine often spent the evening at Lucille's trying to convince her to paint a starry sky on the ceiling of the room she was yet to start preparing for the child. "It won't even take me that long, Lu-cherie! We don't have a shortage of blue paint here, and it won't take me long to mix some gold for the moon, the stars, maybe a few shooting ones, bolts of lightning?"

Lucille acted like Ma-Reine's ideas were unnecessary and unwelcome, but really, she was moved that Ma-Reine was so excited on her behalf that she was willing to use her gifted eyes and hands this way, and especially when her sisters should have been there to fawn over and hold her in the same way. "Don't you think it's a bit too much for a baby? They won't even know what they'll be looking at. Stars and lightning bolts." Lucille shook her head but didn't hide her smile.

"You're joking? We all know that children, especially those newly arrived into these worlds, inside and outside of time, have their minds more open than the most ancient of us. If anything, growing up is an exercise in closing the mind until it lets in only the smallest snippets of any kind of magic or light or silly. I'm only able to dream and make like this because my maman and her maman tried their hardest to make sure the gates of my mind and spirit didn't close too tight for my imagination to get in."

Any time Ma-Reine talked about what Mama Hadzila had taught Mama Aida who in turn taught her and about how their wisdom had shaped the open and artful spirit Ma-Reine carried, it felt like sunrise in a shuttered room, like her whole being beaming the first rays after a destructive storm, like a wish on a birthday candle, like a grove of trees that would never die. Lucille admired Ma-Reine's radiance only a little more intensely than she despised Glory for laying his heavy, cruel hands on Ma-Reine's bright and loving self, threatening to extinguish her glow.

As far as Glory was concerned, most everyone now shrugged their shoulders, resigned to the impossibility of trying to redeem Ma-Reine, someone who seemed for the moment unwilling or not yet ready to redeem her self. She was her own somebody with her own mind after all, and while they had not lost hope that she could still be unbroken, they were all out of patience and all out of the air in their lungs that they were willing to use to talk Ma-Reine onto her feet and out the door. And if they were honest, it was Glory who was the truly irredeemable one. They had called meetings with the Amegawó and pleaded with Lucille to join, as they always did with these sorts of matters; they had threatened and warned Glory to keep his hands to his self; they had shamed him in public, hooting and booing when he walked out into the Afeme or underneath the window of the room he shared with Ma-Reine; even gentle

Vendredi had held Glory by his shirt collar, loose enough around his neck so he could still breathe but tight enough to know he was not playing, and Samedi, Nouvelle, and the other men avoided Glory's presence totally since talking and laying on of warning hands were not enough; but any possibility of resolution was extinguished when the couple told them to step out of their household and mind their own affairs. Shunning Glory then meant keeping Ma-Reine at the end of a long arm, but they still opened one watchful eye towards her and trusted that ultimately Lucille would be the kind of protection for her that they could not.

So Lucille went to the door anyway, no matter who knocked, even after Samedi walked onto the stage that was her life, even as the as-yet-unrealized life she was carrying started to feel too heavy, not as much as Ma-Reine and rest of the people she cared for, but close, and dangerously so.

*break open*

*Inside of time, there was a road between Cave Hill and Aburi, built steady and unbending by centuries of you, our beloveds, with your wide brown hands, aching shoulders, laughing eyes, and dreams that never end before the best part is over. The road carved itself into being through wetlands, through rainforest, through bayou and plain, without disturbance to nature sprouting, vining, dying, and blooming all over itself. But then those greedy, pale somebodies decided that care for everything green and life-giving was less important and less necessary than steel and glass structures soaring over treetops, altars, and temples to the bloodthirsty god they invented in their image. And the road between Cave Hill and Aburi began to eat itself, or the sea began to eat it and it collapsed in places, and the sea kept rolling over, insatiable, taking with it front porches with decorative block carved into hearts, low flat-roofed houses and the aluminum roofing them, cribs and dining chairs and kitchen stools, and finally you, the people who had spent hours sitting on them.*

And outside of time, blue paint was flaking off inside and outside walls, not enough to attract notice or alarm, at least not yet.

# 11

*outside of time, after the break, on Blue Basin*
*sixth full moon, and ask if it's really possible to turn towards*
*your self and another with Love's Face at the same time*

One slow Sunday morning followed a humid Saturday night, where Lucille had spent the night at Samedi's and he was actually there, drunk, not on wine but on the smell of the air between their kisses. Lucille was at the rusty sink washing a pot to boil water for some tea, but she was really in the night before looking down into Samedi's wanting, open face, her hands buried in his hair. She almost forgot she was carrying dread where she was supposed to feel the flutter of a new self as a mother, until Samedi turned her around and bent to press his lips against her belly before he spoke a word to her. She went rigid and tried to push him away with still wet hands, but he rose and pulled her in. "Why do you have to be like that, cherie? This is a magic baby, Lucie, my Lucie. How many times should I say it? Ours. Part of you and me. What is there to make you worry so?" She felt like the shadow behind his soothing was his real question: "What else could you possibly need?" Lucille wished to belong to her self, fiercely, and she didn't think she needed any more of Samedi's charm, no matter how well-intentioned, in this moment, despite the fact that this was their child causing her all this worry. "I'm fine. Just a little sore. Probably your lumpy bed that's to blame."

His smile was some kind of wicked, and his hands slid over her shoulders and down her back like he would be able to feel through his palms where the aches and pains began. "The rock pool will still be there tomorrow. Or the next day . . . ?"

"Samedi. We're going."

He looked into Lucille's smiling face for a moment longer and then jumped out of bed, having decided he was satisfied with Lucille's disposition, dismissing any suspicion, at least for now, that she may be keeping some trouble hidden from him.

Keta Afeme was alive with the usual background hum that vibrated over the neighborhood, its air a thick mesh of noise, dirty water sloshing from basins to the stone slabs lining the streets, shouts from porch to yard—"Stop by for a bite! Ok oui, but after mass"—children forming whole orchestras of roadside musicians out of any scraps of things they could collect, upturned buckets and knobby twigs and their hands striking the sides of their own thighs ke-ke-ke-ke, hard heels striking the ground in time to the rhythm the day had set. There was a funeral, unusual for a Sunday, but that was one of the only instructions Dimanche the flautist had left for his burial. Everyone knew Dimanche as Aseye, and true to his name, he rejoiced each of his days on Blue Basin, savoring every moment of enjoyment on the tip of his tongue like sugary shavings of ice melting away. Dimanche's other wish was to come back to life as the feeling of secret joy and satisfaction a person would feel hearing a tune that conjures the memory of past pleasure. Any time Dimanche's loved ones both inside and outside of time experienced this feeling, they would know it was him.

Lucille and Samedi paused in front of Samedi's house to make way for the pallbearers, stepping and swaying in time to the music, their white-gloved hands never once loosening on the metal bars around Dimanche's coffin. Two young girls and an older man stood apart from everyone, watching the fanfare and holding each other's hands like they would grow unsteady and fall if they let each other go. Lucille noticed their wool coats too heavy for the island's humidity and the streaks of dry grey marking their skin like they could do with a nice warm scrub and cream. The man's free hand worried a string of dark beads, a gris-gris he had wound through his fingers and around his wrist. They must have just arrived. It was usually easy to tell. Lucille knew there would soon be open arms calling to them, a room for now, but later a house, lighter clothing, hot soup, and some tea to warm their bodies. Lucille would have done more than smile a rushed "Bienvenue" to the three newcomers had Samedi not cleared his throat and pressed one of his hands into her lower back.

"Mia tɔwò," he said, "You're very welcome. Mia yi, mia va. Lu, on y va?"

Lucille and Samedi walked until they reached the northern edge of Afeme, where the stony side streets kissed up to the Gran Promenade's fierce red. A grove of orange trees stood staunch guard over the road, but its thickness was deceptive, far overshadowed by the jagged cliffs reaching up behind them into the heavens. They walked through the green corridor the trees built around them and out onto the loose sand that shifted around one's feet so you had to shuffle and pause every few steps just to make it across.

"Chou-fleur, you should have built your house up here in the Katye."

"Why is that?"

Lucille tipped the fruit she had picked into the sack Samedi had made out of his shirt. "I mean, look at the view. You can see the Gulf of Guinea even from here. En plus, it's so quiet. Maybe you'd actually get somewhere with your potions and things."

Lucille laughed at her self scrambling away from Samedi on this ground, slippery like desert dune sand, and at him, juggling his feigned outrage and the oranges weighing him down. "We have all day. I'll get you back."

The walk got easier the further they walked into the Katye, even as the ground slanted upwards, changing from drifting sand to smooth layers of stone that massaged the feet with the warmth they had soaked in from the sun. Lucille led the way, stopping to roll up the legs of her overalls as she went, in anticipation of paddling into the pool that was at their destination. "This is it. On est là!"

Samedi found the flat rock where they always placed their food and shoes so they would stay dry. Before he had slipped off his second sandal, Lucille had moved into the water far past her ankles and calves to the point where the light blue fabric of her clothes had now darkened into navy. She tossed more laughter over her shoulder in Samedi's general direction, "So when are you going to learn the way here? How many moons and you still need me to show you?"

Samedi didn't respond, choosing instead to savor the thrill of Lucille teasing and joyful, not brooding with a face closed tight like a steel gate with cement dried into its locks.

Free and easy.

At least, for now. Lucille stretched up and out, the worrisome cramps from the previous night chased away by the cool water lapping at her body gently with none of the latent rage the sea's waves held, even at low tide. She pushed upright and turned back to look at Samedi, who was tiptoeing his way across the smooth pebbles. "Why do you walk that way? Springing off the balls of your feet like so?"

Samedi stood immediately still, his feet rooted solidly like he was trying to dig his self into the ground. "Does it bother you, miss?"

"Non, monsieur, c'est mignon."

He leaned back into laughter, rocking now on his heels. "My family used to tease me about it all the time . . ."

All the time, and his voice faded off to some other place to which Lucille didn't have an invite—what his life had been like inside of time—no matter how long she had spent loving Samedi.

His hands furrowed deeper into his pockets, the deeper he seemed to dig to draw out the story of his family still only half told. "My maman would always say: 'This boy! Will you step down! Step down, child, you're too tall now to be walking like your heels are scared of the ground. Step down, you'll hurt your self if you keep going on this way.'"

He continued, "But most times it was a song."

*Samedi my Samedi*
*Why are you the way that you are?*
*Samedi my Samedi*
*Saturday's Child*
*My beautiful boy*
*Why are you the way that you are? Beautiful boy, eyes*
*lurking low and deep like violet night sky, skin shining so*
*black*

*Footsteps springing off the balls of your feet, lifting off*
*heaven-ward*
*Saturday's Child*
*Why are you the way that you are*
*Beautiful so . . .*

"What else would your maman sing to you?"

*break open*

*Can you hear us? Entendez-vous? E mía nkɔ sem a? We are called*
*so many names we gave ourselves for all the many lives we have*
*led:*
　　*tutu. closed. fermé.*
　*Sometimes, we choose silence.*

Gently, Lucille asked, "What did it feel like to fly?"

*break open*

*Can you hear us? Entendez-vous? E mía nkɔ sem a? We are called*
*so many names we gave ourselves for all the many lives we have led:*
　　*tutu. closed. fermé.*
　*Sometimes, we choose silence.*

Samedi snatched his hands out his pockets and held them
out, palms up, half praying, half pleading, it seemed. "I—Je ne
comprends pas. Why can't you just let this go?"

He studied his palms as if the lines and creases crossing
and curving away from each other in patterns would somehow

make themselves legible and reveal the answer to Lucille's questions. "It's kind of funny. Kind of like one of those old lies people on this big blue bowl love to tell. About how our suffering began because the world cracked open and we kept falling and falling? You know that one, Lucie? Right? I shouldn't have let go. I shouldn't."

"Let who go? Dis-moi, Samedi." Lucille was now standing in front of Samedi, and they both looked down at their toes touching beneath the glassy surface of the water. Lucille felt as though she was flitting around the edge of Samedi's unknowable past life, like the termites dancing about after the rain, quivering and then shedding their four wings. As she had wanted to do many other quiet moments before, Lucille was tempted to insist, looking to help Samedi to piece these shreds of his truth together and hand them to her for safekeeping. But she also had more than a few of her own unknowables. Samedi had never thought to ask her about what had happened to the rest of her family aside from the sisters he knew and about her own flight. It was more important for her to keep her multiple lives—not only secret but eternally in tension—tight to her chest than to draw closer to a somebody with whom she was still on the edge of trust. So instead she said, "What if our baby walks like you?"

"What if they do?" Samedi muttered, his head still bent towards their feet.

"I'd love it." Lucille smiled. "It looks like you're always dancing."

They stayed for hours, paddling and resting until their hunger surpassed the delight of each other's company, gnawing at stomachs they had only filled with fruit. The fright from the night before reclaimed its hold on Lucille by the time she and Samedi had found their way around the outskirts of the Katye and back to the Afeme. A tiny figure sat on the stairs to Samedi's store, her white Sunday frock wearing the dust and tear from a day's worth of play. "Bonsoir! My Grandmama is asking for her bottles."

"Beau-Soleil, is that you? Tell your grand-mère her medicine isn't ready yet." Lucille disappeared into the dark interior of the store with a brush of her hand over the short, just-growing-back kinks pushing up from Beau-Soleil's scalp. She snatched her hand away when she felt a sorrow sinking inside her self. As Samedi sent Beau-Soleil home to explain her empty hands to her grandmother, Lucille stood in the middle of the living room in nothing but the white button-down shirt she had worn under her overalls, a loan from Samedi too comfortable to return.

"Lucie my Lucie! Lucie!" Lucille heard Samedi whistling his way up the stairs. She had spent the entire walk home fantasizing about the warm, salted bath she was going to soak in to try and drown the dread settling in her insides. The climb into the Katye had pushed her alarm beneath the relaxed joy of their Sunday morning, but now that she was home with imminent relief firmly in sight, it was as if the vicious little hands from her nightmares had recovered from their rest and were back to their cruel work. Samedi found her down, lying like she had fallen asleep right where she had dropped.

"Lucie!"

Lucille stared into Samedi's silhouette and watched his playfulness transform into horror when he saw her lying in a crumpled pile of her self, her torso turned in the opposite direction of her legs. She didn't feel like she had it in her to untwist. "Samedi, can you please . . ."

Before Lucille could whisper her request, Samedi was off, leaving behind nothing but the whine of hinges as he slammed doors behind himself.

It may have been hours or days before Lucille became aware of a brisk presence whisking around the room. The midwife, Miss Mathilde, didn't look any less imposing outside of the cream trouser suit she always wore, with bits of broken shells as buttons holding the perfectly tailored jacket together. Her fierce authority stood out like the one unbendable tree in the middle of a storm, with Samedi's agitation as the backdrop to her poise. It took a few blinks and a few more moments of clambering her way back into consciousness for Lucille to remember the foul taste of the drink Miss Mathilde had tipped into her mouth, a taste more like poison than remedy to Lucille's tongue.

"No baby, you need this," Miss Mathilde's crisp voice an uncharacteristic croon when filtered through Lucille's daze. "You'll feel better when you wake up. Je te jure."

"Just let me rest. Please . . ." Lucille thought she said, but her words came out in a gurgle of nothing and a faint cough.

Lucille fell back into her restless half-sleep, lulled by the firm comfort of Miss Mathilde's low tone but still acutely aware of the cramp gripping, releasing, gripping, releasing inside her.

Lucille mumbled again, her pleas still failing to make it from her mind to her lips: "Miss Mathilde, me dᶒ kuku . . ."

"Quiet now, cherie mine. Save your energy. You running your self ragged every which way across this island is what got you here in the first place. Should I send for your sisters?"

"Ao, je veux pas! Please." Lucille thought she said, but instead of an acknowledgment of her attempts at speech, all she received was the pressure of Miss Mathilde's hands pushing her shoulders backwards and pinning her to the mattress.

"Alright baby, I hear you. Okay. This is sweetness, this is life. Walk soft child, live wild."

The next time Lucille fell forward into lucidity, she was surrounded by the heat and panic Samedi gave off, a low-frequency buzz hovering over a mournful gathering, maybe a wake-keeping or the last living moments of an ancient loved one. Miss Mathilde broke the lullaby she was humming off-tune and turned towards Samedi. "Oui?" Her unrelenting hands still pressed against Lucille's damp forehead.

"Lucille, tout va bien?"

"Amegbetɔ. What do you want?" Miss Mathilde still had her back turned, an impassable barrier between Samedi and Lucille, her hands even firmer as she felt Lucille's temperature, damp forehead and neck, thin pulse in her wrist.

"You're ok, oui? I mean you and the baby?"

Lucille struggled against Miss Mathilde's metal grip and pushed her self up off the bed, her weight on her elbows.

"Lucille ma chère, the guys are waiting, and since Miss Mathilde is here ..."

She looked at Samedi, her head tilted to one side and lips twisted to the other. Seconds passed, suspended on the edge of the answer Samedi would not get. Lucille eased back down to the mattress and turned on her side, bringing her knees up towards her chest, her own cocoon of solace.

"Tswwww." Even the sound of Miss Mathilde sucking her teeth was no-nonsense, more like a zip yanked shut abruptly than a long drag. Miss Mathilde bristled, irritation crackling the stray hairs from her tight top-knot, "Baby, if leaving right now is what you feel you need to do, you go on and do that."

*break open*

*Inside of time, the earth coughed up empty husks where seedlings should have curled up and out, shy at first then luscious and reaching far across the topsoil. The land cracked under the pressure of hot air and windstorms and crashed itself valleywards in landslides, no longer able to remain stable and together with so much hunger and so much nothing sitting where you should be bathing in and fetching from hot springs and eating the fruits of your hands so new and so fresh there's still grit on the skin. The youngest of you, our beloveds, ploughed sun-starved earth for days and hours and lifetimes to produce the cacao and the cane that makes it possible for the youngest of the cruel, pale somebodies to gorge on sweetness until they feel the bite and burn in the farthest of their back teeth.*

And outside of time, someone woke up on a Sunday morning cloudier than they'd ever seen on the island, and the dress they had hanging on the wardrobe was dripping blue flowers and blue dye all down its front, puddling blue on the bedroom floor.

# 12

*outside of time, after the break, on Blue Basin*
*sixth full moon, or when the split blood of a beloved ran slow*
*and far*

Lucille felt it like the edge of a blade on a cut still open and weeping blood. She had been sitting on her balcony, her feet elevated and resting in the gaps in the metal trellis. She was back in her house, alone, in defiance of Miss Mathilde's best judgment and most stern looks over the thin rims of her glasses. "Girl, if you're going to be so stubborn, at least let me just walk you back. I swear, I've not seen someone like you before." Lucille weighed her pocketknife in the palm of her hand, running her fingers' calloused tips over its glossy handle, following each scratch and bump in the enamel. She flicked back and forth between the two blades and teased the sensitive skin at the base of her palm with the sharp point. The night screamed a cacophony of sounds, crickets' song underscoring the softer sounds of bowls of used water emptied into gardens, laughter bouncing off dinner tables, bicycle bells announcing loved ones' arrival. Slices of all kinds of interior lives spilled out onto the street between half-open curtains and cracked windowpanes to be mended one of these days, which meant probably never.

Old Saul, who taught every musician on the island to play, had finally shuffled indoors after a day of tuning and playing his clarinet on the veranda, and half of his small self was visible, bent over the kitchen sink as he splashed cold water onto his face. Toussaint stretched her broad shoulders back and let out a sigh so deep it was as if it rumbled all the way down the street before reaching up and untying the white cloth she had tied around her head. She paused mid-motion and closed the heavy curtains like she could feel Lucille's curious gaze reaching into her private space and seeing her in a way that was forbidden of most people other than her fellow elders. On the corner, Lucille saw Friday's Child with his shoulders rounded over what was probably his latest wooden masterpiece, surrounded by the warm glow of a lantern flickering weakly like it too was preparing for sleep. No one on the island, not even Lucille, knew that Friday's Child's constant woodworking was a continuation of the only thing that had kept him something like alive inside of time, when he returned from war to find his town empty and in scattered remnants of the households it had been. At least, until his despair led him to swim to the deepest part of the water, so far from the shore he was certain he could maybe touch the elusive no-place called the horizon. That day, he found out sinking and flying had a similar weightlessness, and when he washed ashore on Blue Basin, he wasn't at first sure if he had conjured a mirage of his old town to lighten the unbearable load that was his grief.

*break open*

*inside of time, after the break*
*Keta, "Volta Region, Ghana,"—agoo, we greet, mia tɔwò Eveawo,*
*rightful and careful custodians of the land—1777*

*Can you hear us? Entendez-vous? E mía nkɔ sem a? We are called so many names we gave ourselves for all the many lives we have led:*

*Before he was known as Friday's Child, he had been a young man whose eyes had not yet begun to redden. It happened after the first war, the purpose of which had long dissolved into the pool where memories went to drown, never again to be retrieved. He returned with at least his physical self intact, a surprise to his family who had been long resigned to never seeing him again. His private self, the one that laughed at mundane joys like a baby's chubby fingers reaching for bread she couldn't eat, or at a dog chasing its own tail like it could catch it, or at the tickle of a morning breeze on his back, was buried next to the rotting bodies of warriors who would never make it home. Before going to battle, he had been bright-eyed and loud-voiced, Mawusi, and he had walked like he knew for sure that his life was cradled in God's hands and could not be ripped to shreds and sent flying to corners of the world unseen. He had left with a smooth shine to his head, bald except for the patch of rough curls at the back, just above his neck. Now here he was, Mawusi in name only, with the dying shouts for help, for pain relief, for revenge, sounding in his ears whether he was awake or asleep. His daughter noticed the change first and felt it most acutely, even though she was too young to speak her fear in words. For months after his first return, Bébé would scream pure fear whenever he tried to hold her, twisting her head away from him every which way to avoid looking him eye to eye.*

*"Ao. It's alright, she's probably just fighting to remember you. Give it time." Sena would say, cooing and cradling to vanish their child's distress. "Wò ŋkúo biã lo. They're so red. Your eyes. Have you been washing your face with that thing I gave you?"*

*He ducked his head to leave the house, seeking a break from the heat trapped between its clay walls, unseasonal and unusual for a home built to remain cool no matter what. He muffled a frustrated sigh with the back of his hand as if he was stifling a yawn.* "I have, srɔ nye. *I'm sure they'll heal, whatever it is, soon enough.*"

*The red didn't fade, intensifying instead, to the point that anyone who tried to hold his gaze would have to look away because their own eyes began to water; it looked so painful.*

*"Efo, you can't carry on this way. Do you see how you're becoming?"*

*Mawusi heard the rising panic in Sena's voice, and it agitated him to the point where it felt like someone grinding a slab of stone against his nerves. "What am I becoming? Am I not a human being?"*

*"Are you? It's harder to tell with each day that goes by since you came back."*

*Screaming now, she added, "Aren't you in pain? What kind of person just sits there and lets their pain kill them slowly?"*

*And this is how Mawusi would leave again, a lot less like his self than he had been the first time around. By now he was no longer Mawusi, but Efo Nkudzē or Mr. Red Eyes, and Sena had no more room within her self to absorb his self-pity and no more patience to defend this grim decline to genuinely concerned neighbors and nosy gossips alike. She left with her baby, better off tuning out her parents' nags and her siblings' taunts than listening to this grown man crying his self to sleep only to deny it in the morning.*

*"Good luck to you. I hope you find whatever you need to get better. Mawu bless your troubled heart."*

*With his family gone, he ventured beyond the small square that was his yard less and less, ceasing eventually even his errands like buying bread from Mama Yevúbolotɔ because her two daughters' screams and laughter caused shame to rise up his neck like he was drowning and reminded him of the daughter he would not get to raise. So he left, this time to fight again.*

*Efo Nkudzē, no longer laughing, sensitive Mawusi, with his fearsome eyes flaring red, knew their enemies' power had nothing to do with their skin. The specters were armed in a way none of them could imagine, and their sharpest tools and most stable shields stood no chance. The booms of distant cannon blasts were death calling each soldier's name, warning them they would be blown away to the other side, one broken body after another. The warriors all looked to Efo Nkudzē, who stood tall no matter the threat, like some divine pull was drawing him always upwards and not round-shouldered and hopeless like the rest of them. But as they stood soaking in their own terror and the lagoon's stagnant water, they knew it was only a matter of time before those warning shots would be upon them, threatening to break open their eardrums and then the rest of their bodies. Who would fall and remain festering in the water and who would survive to tell what he had seen would be left only to chance.*

*Efo Nkudzē returned again with a heavier load of horror on his back, like he had carried the weight of the dead all the way from the battle's front. He pushed his door open and met surprising resistance. The flimsy wood wouldn't budge and rather threatened to snap into splinters under the force he was exerting on it. He eventually had to smash the door open, and the chickens idling around squawked away in surprise, the only living things around to witness the wood succumbing to his frustration. He had lost track of the time he spent away after the third month, but however long it was had been enough time for Mama Yevúbolotɔ's kiln next door to be nothing but bricks of red-earth crumbling back to dust. Tall weeds soared over what was left of the low wall around the neighbor's house on the other side, not a trace left of the swirling chalk designs that she had spent her days etching and perfecting.*

*"Useless," he muttered through his kissing teeth. It was obvious the money he had given to one of the town's young people to clean the house once a week had been for nothing. Whatever-his-name-was had gone the way of his payment and of the rubble where his neighbors' homes used to sit.*

*The inside of the house matched the desolation outside. The bed was broken in half down the middle. A piece of cloth, blue and grey kete woven together with silver thread, a gift from their wedding Sena forgot to take with her, was strewn in bits across the floor, between little mounds of dust and shriveled skeletons of mice and other small creatures no longer recognizable by their remains. He stood with his hands on his hips. He didn't know where to start to put back some type of order into his life. He did nothing. Besides, his eyes ached from lack of sleep and from the dust grating away at their insides like sandpaper rubbing away at sensitive skin.*

*He walked back into town, following the direction of the sea, a sharp blue arrow into Keta proper, and he was sure Sena wouldn't let him see their baby, walking and talking by now. He wandered for a few hours, the flaming red of his eyes cast down to the ground to prevent the alarm he knew would come, children scattering like skittish ants evading his gaze. Efo Nkudzē is back! Look! É gbɔ! Kpɔe ɖa! He found Sena's family house, set back from the stony main road, behind a flame tree that had freshly shed all its flowers. He saw Bébé rolling around on her chubby legs, clapping and shrieking delight in her own language, the sweetest sound he had ever heard. He couldn't look at her, would never slash through her joy with his evil-looking glare. Sena was sitting under a mango tree just inside the yard, clapping a rhythm for Bébé's dizzying dance, ke-ke-ke ke-ke ke-ke-ke ke-ke.*

*Efo Nkudzē left them in their pocket of heaven, under that tree, in that sandy yard, but he kept hearing the sound of Bébé's gurgling attempts at real words in his mind all day, a welcome change from the last howls of dying men surrendering life for a cause they had not chosen to fight for themselves. He might as well have walked out of Keta and onto the next battleground, because the horn blaring the call for soldiers to return to post came no more than a week after he let his self catch sight of the life he could have been living. He rubbed his eyes, still sore and even redder than they had been on his return, and shut the door even more warped in its frame than he had found it. Efo Nkudzē longed for a time when he could shut his tender eyes to a world set to implode. He knew someday both Mawusi and Efo Nkudzē— and just Efo, who would not be able to see at all—would cease to exist, would be forgotten, but his mourning cries would echo here and here and here, in places he could never imagine, always more blood flowing and more life spent.*

\*\*\*

Pain beat against Lucille's abdomen, snapping her out of her pleasant reverie. An uncomfortable wetness slid from between her thighs onto the foam cushion she sat on. She hummed the lullaby like a chant through gritted teeth, "Walk soft child, live wild," slipping the knife into her pocket and trying to still the panic that was roaring inside her. She pushed as much energy as she could awaken into her arms and legs and stood up, turning to the screen door and back inside the house. Her teeth crashed together as she concentrated on crossing the room, her bed and the clothes littering the floor now more like an obstacle course that was proving impossible to navigate.

Here she was, terror groaning deep from the center of her spirit, a future to be concluded before it could grow to be more than just an abstract idea, more than an occasional flickering in her belly, like a newly lit candle licking a palm.

In the living room, Lucille steadied her self on the navy blue back of the brocade-covered armchair Víví had gifted her, as stiff and unwelcoming as it was shiny but finally serving some sort of purpose: something for Lucille to latch onto, a moment of pause in the midst of a solitary procession through her empty home towards another loss. There was no Samedi, and there was no Miss Mathilde, either. Miss Mathilde with her firm, massaging hands unyielding to Lucille's pull away from their grip. She didn't think she would be able to manage the walk out the door, down the stairs, and down the Gran Promenade towards Keta Afeme to fall into the midwife's sure and steady healing hands.

But she could at least make it to the bathroom. The cramp now felt as though it was stretching its reach beyond her belly, pulsing in her abdomen in the hot, familiar way it did when she saw her moon's blood. Her teeth now clamped so tightly together she feared they would break against each other, she stepped into the bathroom and onto the frigid tile and started to strip. She cringed, trying not to feel what had now dripped its slow way down her thighs and legs, soiling the pale blue floor rust brown and red. She bent forward and braced her weight against the edge of the tub and bled. She bled three moons of re-stitching scraps of futures, of wishing a joyful dawn into existence, of another beginning.

She resolved to mourn for eight days and no more, as many days as it would have taken for her child to be given a name with which to move around this world—Kekeli, the dawn is here.

On the first day, Lucille filled the tub with vinegar and cold water as close to icy as Blue Basin's humidity would allow and soaked the stained scraps of cloth she had used to wipe the trail of her self and her love she had left through the house the day before. Later, she would scrub. She sat on the floor, one hand gripping one of the tub's clawed feet, the other clicking her knife open and shut, waiting for the blood to flow out of the fabric's fibers and away. It took a few hours for her spirit to grow restless, to start stretching its wings and preening, itching for some space to expand. She got up and wrote a note to anyone who may stop by, another fête season approaching as quickly as it was: "Mes chèrs, I'm very busy trying to make you all beautiful. No fittings for a week. Leave clothes for alteration on the steps. Bises."

The piece of paper felt as fragile as the excuses she was trying to hide behind. She tacked it to the wooden board that read "Tailleur" in peeling blue cursive. Lucille was as sure as she was of her own name that no one would knock in search of the answers obscured by her spiraling handwriting—not even her sisters—except Ma-Reine, whose calls to her through the cracks of the door grew from concern to pure desperation as the days went on.

"Nye sí! This is Ma-Reine cherie, open the door."

It was easier to imagine them in peace, without the burden Lucille was terrified of becoming: Ma-Reine sitting with her latest work, her hands and face so smudged with the colors from the canvas, it was a wonder there was still enough left for the painting; Serena tapping a steady beat on her thigh, keeping her own time as she practiced with her various instruments; Viví with her hands pressed into one head of hair after another, moving in and out of tubs of oils and creams, or pressed into the back of her latest love, something to soften the edge in the air just a little bit, "Important in this wild world, n'est-ce pas?" she might say, winking.

On days two and three, she barely moved except to strain thin cups of tea from their leaves. She reclined in bed, closing her eyes with each burning gulp close to ripping off the insides of her mouth. She dreamt about Samedi's hands sticky from the oranges he would peel for her, Samedi's hands kneading away the pressure knotted into her spine, Samedi's hands blending with the night's dark and only giving away their next move with quick flashes of the light inside of his palms, Samedi's hands holding instead of letting go.

Now, there was no Samedi, and Lucille was sure there never would be again. Samedi with a mouth full of sugar and hands full of burning, a special kind of fire that didn't rise and destroy but licked her skin and engulfed her in its heat. The last time she saw him was two weeks prior, when Miss Mathilde had just brought her home after she had passed out. Samedi said he had come to see about her, but he stood two arms' lengths away in the doorway leading from the house to her balcony, right foot bent and resting left leg, as if he was so impatient he could not bear to stand solidly, his feet seeking a swift escape.

"So you said you're going where?"

"Fishing with the guys. Bring us back something for the table?"

Lucille glared at him through the tangle of eyelashes on her squinted eyes, shaking her head so slightly that Samedi could have chosen to ignore her annoyance had she not continued to speak.

"Right now? Mon cher, I don't need anything for the table. And if I did, I would go fish myself. We both know you can't fish worth a damn."

Samedi held his hands out in his usual gesture, half pleading, half praying. "Listen, baby—"

Lucille inhaled a mighty breath, hoping to exhale composure. "I'm not angry. I just . . . do I have to beg you to care? Weren't you always saying *our* magic baby?"

"Lucie my Lucie. I just don't know if I can do this right now. Just give me a couple hours. I'll be back."

On the fourth day, she left pale pink spots of blood on the filmy blue shawl that lay over her sofa. Her insides swirled, and she thought she would throw up. She knew Miss Mathilde would have glared admonition over the wide brim of her wire glasses: "Baby you've lost blood. You need iron. You need to replenish. Don't go losing your whole self, now."

The next day, Lucille sat at her sewing machine with her back turned away from the door to the bedroom and away from the mismatched furniture positioned around her front room, as if in denial of her need to rest and restore her ebbing energy. Her knees pressed into the cold metal of the table's spindly legs, imprinting its curly patterns into her skin. The machine itself was formidable, more like a weapon of war than an appliance capable of spinning elegance out of plain pieces of fabric. She rubbed her hands across its shiny black surface, feeling her way across its gold engraving; a three-headed woman close to the wheel, with flame, knives, and a snake spewing from each mouth towards the face plate. She placed a white skirt between the bed plate and the needle, hoping to reduce the pile by folding away one more item belonging to one of many neighbors who had left their clothes outside for Lucille to mend. She spun the wheel and immediately felt regret. The hammering sound that usually marked the rhythm of her working days now felt more like she was caught in an endless crossfire, an insistent pounding she could feel all the way back in her wisdom teeth.

She tried to remember when her dread for motherhood had become longing. It pained her so to look directly at her own truth, that she had only begun to long for her child, to dream of starched white bows and socks on Sunday morning, to dream of a child when she realized she might lose them. Or even worse, perhaps she had started longing a little before she should have, whispering her child's too-hopeful name when she was alone, *Kekeli*, far before she should have done, before the child had safely entered the living world.

On day six, she coated chopped-up chunks of pork, fat intact, with salt and cayenne, and a random selection of other fiery flavors she could get out of the bottles gathering dust in her kitchen cupboards. She listened to the sizzle of frying like the buzz of insects rousing themselves after rain. When it was done, she tossed the meat down one piece after the next into her mouth, barely chewing or tasting, relishing the bite of the still scorching pieces as they went down her throat. Not more than half an hour later, she threw up into the sink, her fingers leaving streaks of grease on its metal side.

Day seven arrived, and Lucille opened the shutters overlooking the back of her house, over to the serenity of the bayou, interrupted only by a frantic cicada that must have lost its way; this was not the right season for their swarm. She looked at the trees hunched over the water like protective mothers over their vulnerable offspring, guessing which one would have been best to hang a tire swing, to push a child into the air, to hear the child's thrilled peals of laughter dropping into the water's calm. *Kekeli*. Perhaps all of her fantasies had bound her reality in a jinx. She only had her audacity to blame, for daring to dream up a future for a child with a name like this one, when she had no guarantee this child would not choose rather to return to the other spirits to show off this name sounding like a new beginning, *Kekeli*.

It was dawn on the eighth day, and she wrapped her shoulders in her brightest shawl, even though the world was still too dark to catch the light of its thread. She took the stairs down from her house, one careful step at a time, before passing below the pergola leaning against the left side of her house, the vines tickling her forehead where they had grown too low. Though soaked from dew and yet to dry rain—why had it rained, at this time of year—the ground was still solid enough and reassuring to the soles of Lucille's bare feet. She walked up to the Promenade, and trying to avoid the wind's livid slaps, she turned her face south towards the usually boiling waters of the two Gulfs, still only a simmer at this time. She climbed into the Katye towards her once-loved rock pool, as close as she could get to the ancestors' cliffs with their mounds of red sand marking lives both cherished and destroyed. On her way, she tripped over her own feet as she tried to stop her self from treading where she shouldn't, on the white pattern someone had traced into the ground, lines and hearts crisscrossing, a secret message shared spirit to spirit across worlds.

And then she stood by the water, at the boundary between night and day, around the same spot where she had spent more careless afternoons giggling into Samedi's neck about all kinds of lovely nothings.

"Kekeli."

She had brought with her three small vials of clear liquid, almost identical except for their distinct scents and tastes. She spilled the first one, filled with schnapps, on the rocks in front of her: "Kekeli, this only in moderation. Be careful."

Next was a cold drink, translucent and bubbling: "This is sweetness. Refresh your self once in a while, Kekeli."

Finally, she spilled water: "This is life. Drink this always; you need it to live. Spotless fluid for a spotless soul."

Lucille's mind was carried so far away from her present that it was still on the night side of dawn as she headed homewards while the day had opened up to the sun.

"Cou-cou! Lucille! E le afi ma? You there?"

She clutched the now empty bottles in the crook of one arm, swinging the other in a brisk march towards the calling voice, occasionally readjusting the scarf around her shoulders.

"I need a fitting badly, cherie! My grandbaby's outdooring is coming just now! I know you said one week but . . ."

Lucille pushed her face muscles into a smile, surprised she was still capable. "You're right on time, baby. Get you some tea? You ate breakfast already?"

*break open*

*outside of time, Lucille's spirit grieves and we grieve with her*

    *Can you hear us? Entendez-vous? E mía nkɔ sem a? We are called so many names we gave ourselves for all the many lives we have led:*

    *My eyes are always aching, so red from grieving you, and you, and you. Kekeli. Many times over and eternities apart. Your name fits snugly in my mouth and it sounds so sweet to me. I should not be here, kicking my feet in stinking water, in the same funeral clothes I have not been able to fold away, or even take off to wash, for centuries, or days. Kekeli, you should be cutting the soles of your feet on the sea glass I told you to watch out for. I should be holding your small, hurting feet in my hands and kissing away your tears. Don't go out there again, at least not just yet; stay here by me, let me boil some water for your bath. You should be here, playing shy for the neighbors like they don't hear you thrilled and shrieking at games you invented for your self, spending hours in worlds only you know how to enter.*

    *Playing shy, clinging to my right leg and trying to hide your face in my cloth, trying to disappear into the side of my body, only when the neighbor extends agbeli kaklo fried fresh and still sizzling do you turn one sly smile out and up. You should be here, with me, on the daytime side of dawn, Kekeli, the right side, the living side, your brown skin deepening still the longer you stay outside and hot from the sun's shine and your own energy ever bubbling inside you. You should be here, growing into your own person, belonging to your self, your laugh now less a ring and more a bellow, the sound of ground shifting and coalescing to make way for new life, a whole world inside a person, my whole world inside a person, my only person inside the whole world. We should be together, me listening to your ringing-bell laugh pulling me from sleep: What is it now baby? What do you need?*

*Instead, I am here, and here, and here, pitied first and hated later; we've all moved on they say, children die and they are born, they say; we've all lost someone after all, they say; we tried our best and our people still stayed gone, they say, what more could we have done?*

*They say, regarde celle-là. Just look at her, going mad. Tsúkúnɔ.*

*I am here, and here, and here, my hair sticking together in dry tufts I see no use in combing, my nails cracking at the edges and falling to the ground, my back cracking when I try to get up too suddenly, whole self cracking because I can only sit here and cry.*

*My entire self aches. I can barely uncover my bowed head for fear that light will pierce me straight through. We should be together, Kekeli, child, and I should not be in forever mourning, here, and here, and here.*

### break open

*Inside of time, babies shrieking into life on terrazzo, the tiles covered with the slime of antiseptic and all the outside people have brought into the ward on the underside of their shoes. You, the mothers, try to make out of your arms incubators for your minutes-old children against the cold of the floor, against any infections that might work their way into these soft, new bodies. Tears don't fall easy or fast or at all when your head is thrown back and hard on a solid floor when you know this isn't the way to open up for your child to enter the world. Your mothers and their mothers and their mothers may have been living the ancient ways that are now outlawed, but at least in those days they would be at home surrounded by warm towels, warmer hands, herbal baths to regain strength, fragrant oils to knit the skin back together. Instead, you are wondering whether you and your baby will make it out of this den of illness and death pretending to be a place that can heal the sick, a place where the upper floors are reserved for people with enough in the bank or the right last name to birth their children in peace with no fear they will die mid-scream or at night when the infection settles too far into the blood to be redeemed.*

And outside of time, the blue bottle trees turned clear and shattered in some places, and the people thought the wind sweeping across the land the night before had done it. But even the wind did not wield enough power to make bottles lose their blue.

# 13

*outside of time, after the break, on Blue Basin*
*seventh full moon, on the occasion of the sublimation of all Ser-*
*ena's desires into her voice and her stories, much more a way of*
*life than a singular occurrence*

"Next time, a little lighter on the salt, d'accord? My mouth feels like the water out there." Víví waved towards the water frothing and breaking outside Serena's kitchen window like she was shooing some insect or cobweb or some such nuisance away, but Serena didn't mind, because the noise her sister's bangles made sounded like church bells and cutlery striking a plate after a meal shared with a loved one and wind chimes in a sunlit room. Her mind didn't file away sounds in neat rows like a librarian of memory and meaning. She experienced them deep in the part of her self that couldn't always find words to describe sensation. She felt them the same way one feels the right hand holding the left, especially when her mood was lifted, like it was that day, so ecstatic she didn't care one bit if Víví disliked her food. There was no single cause for her joy; it was more so that her ears had been filled with all kinds of small pleasures all day: bees whirring in the bush outside her bedroom and their tap-tap-tap against the window pane, drunk on nectar, the zzzzziiippppp as she got dressed, water against metal when she made her morning tea, the clink of the teaspoon on the inside of the cup for Víví's coffee, their laughs dancing around each other, bouncing against the table, the tiles, the walls, and out the door.

Serena said a sorry she didn't mean because they both knew Víví had enjoyed the food even if she would rather eat gravel than admit it: "Pardon, nye sí, I didn't hear the right sizzle so I added the seasoning you gave me at the wrong time."

"This is why no one is coming to this house to eat," Víví said between cackles, "because who listens to stew?"

Víví's laugh sounded like a promise kept and the morning's first bird call, and Serena was feeling through what else her sister sounded like when a tap-tap-tap at the door interrupted.

"I hear you in there, Serena! C'est moi, Nouvelle."

Serena had been running into Nouvelle in parts of the island where she typically encountered no one, and while she was sure this uninvited knocking was about to tap-tap-tap on her last calm nerve, there was also a part of her that was always pleased, or at least amused, by his presence. One day, she took her pirogue, painted blue with white and pink seashells, out into the shallows to fish for her dinner. As she took her boat nose-first back to shore to anchor, Nouvelle was standing there trying and failing to look as though he just happened to be walking on the part of the beach that just happened to be behind her house. Another time, she was taking her slow, sweet time on the Gran Promenade on the way back from rocking one baby to sleep and telling her tallest tales to a few other young ones, and Nouvelle was ahead of her, just before the road branched off towards her house, trying to look like the hibiscus and rose bushes were the most interesting thing he had ever seen on the land.

"Man, what do you want here?"

The sisters could hear him jostling the doorknob from the other side between words. "Someone told me it would be a good day for fishing; they're practically jumping out the water. Let's go?"

Because she was talking through laughs, her words had a lot more blush and bumble in them than she would ever own up to when Víví would tease her later: "Someone who? Don't say a little bird, I beg you."

"You're not the only one who can hear what other people can't. Won't you let me come in so I can tell you?" Nouvelle would have realized by then that the door wasn't locked, and Serena was surprised his pushy self still had enough decency to wait for her to say, "Come in."

He stepped into the room with his head bowed so he wouldn't bump into the door frame, and Serena considered for a flash-quick moment whether his presence was really as much of a nuisance as she first thought. He was such a beauty; it didn't matter that his childish trousers hovered somewhere around his shins instead of grazing the floor. He wore his hair shaved low to his head, which made his forehead seem even higher, and the planes of his face were totally smooth except for the entire left side, which was covered with neat lines scarred into the skin in a pattern of concentric arches that grew as they moved away from his wide nose and closer to the side of his head. The marks stood out from his skin, shiny and darker than dark, calling out to be traced and touched by loving, wanting hands.

"Ah, I didn't know my sister was here. Bonjour, mesdames."

Víví's smile was part pity for a man she knew had absolutely no chance of getting her sister to turn towards him with love and part impressed by his persistence. "Efo, you didn't come here to see me. Sister, I'll be at the beach. If he decides to be foolish, just shout. I have a knife."

Nouvelle took the seat Víví left empty, crossed one ankle over the other, and looked up at Serena, still standing by the door. "Won't you sit, mon bijou? I hope I didn't interrupt your meal?"

"So you've sat down, crossed leg, and now you're offering me a seat in my own kitchen. And you didn't even lotion your legs before coming?" Serena's laughter came out in gasps and threatened to steal all of her breath when Nouvelle tried to cover up the ash grey covering his feet. "It's too late now; it's all out there. That's why you need longer trousers."

As tempting as it might have been to take Nouvelle seriously as someone she could turn Love's Face to, all Serena heard when he spoke was the squawks of a brace of ducks fighting each other. It had nothing to do with the actual rolling deep of his voice, and she was sure no one else heard this discord when he spoke, but Serena heard what she heard, and she couldn't imagine keeping a straight face with him trying to speak sweet and slow to her.

"So. Fishing?"

Serena walked over to Nouvelle and braced her left arm on the table, still covered with the morning's dishes, and bent down in front of him, touching his scars with her right hand.

"Oh yes, the fish called you personally to come get them, isn't that so?"

Nouvelle held Serena's hand where it was and laughed into it. "No, it was a bird, remember? A little one, specifically."

"Not today, maybe not ever, or at least not anytime soon, dear. And I promise it's not because of anything you did or are." Serena was very familiar with how the voice bent itself when the inkling of infatuation turned into something more, and she could hear not one tinge of that no matter how hard she listened. She cared more about what she heard, or rather didn't hear, in his voice than she did about him being Samedi's friend, because her grudge against Samedi was not really about his character, virtuous or otherwise. It was not personal; she just found that there was nothing holding his or any other person's body, or turning Love's Face to another person, could offer that singing and telling her stories couldn't. As infinite as she was, as boundless her spirit and her memory, she found she only had or was only willing to make room for desire and love when she was singing and telling about it because the singing and telling itself felt like loving to her.

*break open*

*Remember, the spirit stepped inside of time and swam through the*
*break, making her self manifest wherever the water was deepest*
*and the waves the loudest*
*inside of time, after the break*
*Keta, "Volta Region, Ghana,"—agoo, we greet, mia tɔwó Eveawo,*
*rightful and careful custodians of the land—2002*
*. . . tap-tap-tap and the spirit who was, is, and will be*
*saltwater and sound was there after one of those rains so heavy it*
*folded the horizon flat and made the sky, the sea, the land, and*
*the falling water one unending stretch of cloudy grey. And with*

the rain came the light-hungry afrekete with their translucent wings too big for their slim bodies, throwing themselves against the tube of fluorescent light in the veranda until they died, burnt by the heat of their curiosity and their fixation on the bright and burn of the bulbs. Tap-tap-tap and you were a boy called Koku, sitting at a side of the table where the lights couldn't reach, and so all Yayra could see was the flash of silver as you tapped the borrowed signet ring—your father's—against the glass top of the table.

"He got it from Senegal. He said the metalsmiths there are better than he has seen anywhere, because they learnt from their fathers' fathers' fathers."

"The what? What are you talking about?"

"The ring, Yayra. You've been watching my hands since we sat down. By now you've even forgotten what my face looks like."

Yayra drew her seat closer to the table but kept her hands on both arms of the chair, feeling the scratches and ridges in the white plastic. The light fell across half her face, enough for you to see that the dying afreketes had dropped their thin wings into the puff of hair Yayra was wearing high on top of her head. You loved the way her hair sat like it was its own entity with its own mass, like something needing strength and a straight back to carry without falling, and you loved it especially now with the wings all over it like a bouquet of flowers. You reached across to pluck one of them, but she flinched like even the suggestion of you touching her was unwelcome, like it would hurt.

"Wow. You have some of these wings stuck, and I was just trying to help."

"Don't. I don't need—" Tap-tap-tap, and Yayra pushed back so fast she nearly sent her self, the chair, and the table falling *backwards. She turned to listen for the source of the sound, not the flies, not your nervous, unresting hands, but someone making sure the bottom of a bucket of rubbish was totally empty by tapping it against the side of the house.*

*"Yayra, listen. It's not that I didn't want to talk. It's that I couldn't."*

*You reached out again and Yayra raised her self up like a warning for you not to come any closer; she would close her self behind both doors to her grandmother's house and resume her pretense that you didn't exist, which you might as well not have since you had not spoken to or seen each other since her birthday two months ago.*

*"If my grandma sees you with your hands anywhere near me, you might not leave here in one piece. E sem a?"*

*"What's the meaning of that? It's not like I did you harm—"*

*"Didn't you? Last I heard you were on your way with my cake. And then nothing. Honestly, I don't know what you could possibly say to me that I would listen to."*

*Tap-tap-tap and you didn't know, but the spirit was in your unstill hands and in the quiet buzz of the bulbs a few flickers away from short-circuiting.*

*"Yayra, I don't know if you will even believe me if I tell you."*

*"Listen, talk or don't talk. Stop stalling. Trying to come up with your longest lie yet, or?"*

*You breathed heavy, and the spirit was in the breath, and the spirit was in the salty sweat drying on your shirt collar.*

*"I deserve this. And you deserve to be angry. First let me say. . . . So, I was driving from my father's house in Woe. And I was so scared to meet your whole family. I don't know what it means to have people the way you do. I mean . . . coming from abroad*

*and all, just for your birthday? And then to meet me? It felt like so much pressure."*

*"So you're a coward? Good to know. Wish I didn't have to find out on that day of all days. Happy birthday to me."*

*You moved your chair closer to her, and the spirit was in the scratch of plastic against concrete, and the spirit was in the tears building in the corners of your eyes.*

*"Yayra tɔnye, that's not fair. And too easy. It was more complicated than that."*

*"Tɔwo? I'm no longer yours when you can't even open your mouth and talk to me. So what? What at all?"*

*"So I was driving. And I was nervous to meet everyone, but also . . . I was scared and ashamed, and I felt so bitter I could taste it. Bitter because you had this whole crowd of people gathering for you last minute to celebrate you, when I have only my father, who is only ever passing through. Bitter because it felt like I have no one."*

*She slammed her hand against the tabletop, and the spirit was in the slap, and the spirit was in the tears sticking in her lashes like dew.*

*"And who am I? I am no one?"*

*"Please I beg you, let me finish. When I got to the lagoon, now remember the road is dark-dark. Those streetlights haven't worked since-since. And then I saw someone who looked like they were drowning, so I quickly parked and got out. Or rather I heard them first, 'Me le blanui, me le blanui, I have so much sorrow, I have so much regret I'm so sorry.' I kept following the voice but couldn't see anyone."*

*"Wait. Was the person drowning or trying to—"*

"*Have you heard some story about a man named Ndɔkutsu and his ghost?*"

"*Ghost?*" *Yayra's speech was clipped, abrupt, like she was snatching her self back before she fell for the story you were spinning.*

"*Yes, will you just hear me out? Long long time ago when the white man came here, Ndɔkutsu betrayed the town and drowned his self because he couldn't take what he done. And now he's stuck over there crying and crying, begging for someone to forgive him so he can rest. Yayra, I was stuck there too, for hours. Like someone had buried my feet in wet sand. Ndɔkutsu was my great-great-grandfather.*"

"*Mawu. How come you never told me this story before?*"

"*Shame. I didn't think I could feel more ashamed about my ancestor until that night. I couldn't come here after that. I went home and tried to call. I kept trying. I just couldn't.*"

*Your voice lowered enough to where the only other sound besides tap-tap-tap and the rush of the sea somewhere, which isn't really a sound if no one can tell the difference between the swissshhh and the swissshhh in the back of one's own ear, and the spirit who was saltwater and sound was the only witness to this faltering love trying to find its feet, to history crying out tomorrow and yesterday, to the spirits of the yet-to-be-unbroken wandering and wailing for something freer than this life, even if they didn't know it.*

\*\*\*

*Remember, the spirit stepped inside of time and swam through the break, making her self manifest wherever the water was deepest and the waves the loudest.*

## inside of time, after the break

*A place called Sorrows, sometime in the 1990s, somewhere on an island, somewhere inland from the Caribbean Sea, somewhere on the road from Cave Hill to Aburi*

*And you were there, tuning pianos for a living. The job was bearable, and you might have actually tolerated it more or even loved it if you could hear anything other than notes played in a minor key. As far as you were concerned, Happy Birthday, any number of national anthems complete with trumpet-backed choirs, dawn birdcalls, and love songs where no one dies or hurts or leaves might as well have been funeral dirges, sweet somethings whispered in your left ear where you heard better, Good Friday hymns or threats slurred through whiskey on the row of bars where you did most of your work.*

*That your hearing was off-key from the rest of the people in the town (or theirs was off-key from yours) was not the source of your frustration. Rather, it was the fact that they were audacious and entitled enough not only to complain about how you made their Saturday nights feel like keeping wake next to a dead body but to demand to the owners, bartenders, security, or anyone who would listen that you should be let go. They said they had gone dancing to forget, to feel and be felt, to move until their feet no longer touched earth, or at least until it felt like it, but your music sent them home longing for people they had never met yet missed and places they had never seen yet longed to return to at the same time.*

*To you, if everything was a minor key, then distinctions between major and minor, between cheerful and somber, meant absolutely nothing. And after all, the music and dance teachers didn't seem to mind. For whatever reason, their students took to your eccentric tuning fiercely and with total seriousness; every note they played or step they took around the room measured and carried out with the same delicate and precise touch with which you handled the hammer and key you used for your work. The teachers would have preferred to leave class without shedding tears during scales practice or leaps across the room; still, they wouldn't complain because the young dancers and musicians who had trained their ears to these heavy notes dropping through their chests all the way to their feet went on to have long and ranging artistic lives, though people who knew them could never tell the difference between their laughing and crying.*

*On a Saturday afternoon around four o'clock, you were sitting on a wrought iron bench watching the statue of Our Lady of Sorrows and the fountain playing, the water pouring from the stone face and down the body, finally ending in liquid topaz rippling around the statue's feet. No newspaper nor book, no toothpick to worry your gums with, no handkerchief to attempt to stop the sweat rising at your brow, just your two rough hands, and next to you, a satchel fraying around the edges with your work tools inside. And to your left, a woman all in white laughing in a key you had never heard in your life.*

*All of a sudden, her voice became your favorite sound. Before hearing this voice, you had no understanding of the difference in timbre and feeling you heard and tuned into Sorrows' pianos and what everyone else heard. You did not know you were experiencing a major key for the first time ever, and the spirit who was saltwater and sound was there in the laughter, and she was there when your breath fell out of step with your heartbeat tap-tap,*

*tap-tap, tap-tap. You wanted to lay your head in the woman's lap and never stand upright again; you wanted to be rocked to sleep on the cradle of her voice; you wanted to grow out your hair so she would have something to hold onto and play in while you lay; you wanted to hear her voice in verse; you wanted to hear your name from her mouth; you wanted to sit next to her in a field of nothing but lemongrass as far as you could see and no other sound except for that trilling laugh.*

"*Excusez-moi, madame. You said something?*"

*You leaned over so far and kept folded forward even though you knew you were probably more jester than gentleman in the moment. You didn't care.*

"*Hello? Do I know you? Is everything alright?*"

*Tap-tap, tap-tap, tap-tap, and the spirit laughed along to the beat inside your chest.*

"*I mean—*"

"*Man, what is the problem? Qu'est-ce qu'il y a?*"

"*I mean . . . I need you to say anything to me, and I'll listen.*"

*The woman in white laughed and you saw you and her in the field of lemongrass and the scope of your imagination widened and then focused, a sharp lens on the life you could live on the edge of that field where the only sound that mattered was her laughing.*

"*I should be scared of strange men . . . bowing? Are you bowing to me right now?*"

"*I don't know. Is that what you want me to do? Are you laughing with me or at me?*"

*Tap-tap, tap-tap, tap-tap, she tapped the heel of her sandal on the ground and the spirit rode the air around you and this strange woman to whom your new favorite sound belonged.*

***

After Nouvelle left, that heart of his that he had extended to Serena palm up and open now in his pocket, Serena left through the screen door and found Víví sitting on a big piece of a driftwood stuck in the sand. "What happened? Don't tell me you sent the man away in pieces. Why do you always do this?"

"Me de kuku! He will be back here in a few days with something else silly to say. On y va? Walk a little?"

Víví tilted her head, smiling sly and slow at Serena. "What is it? You don't like the sound of him? Don't feel like you have the need for him to turn to you with Love's Face?"

Serena stayed silent, but they both knew that having accessed the deepest, most unreachable depths of their power as the spirits they were, they had no need to seek satisfaction in someone else's flesh. Still, Víví wondered if there wasn't some desire and fulfillment that could only be found in the arms of someone else, a real somebody outside of the spirit and imagination, on the night side of dawn, just one more time before daybreak.

Serena pulled Víví up from sitting, and they hadn't walked far when they saw Ma-Reine sitting on a blue blanket woven with gold thread, probably Lucille's handiwork, surrounded by pencils, pieces of charcoal, and loose sheets of paper. The sight of her stung some because it reminded them of their missing Lucille, but they were also pleased to see her. Víví loved Ma-Reine and the works of her hands because every line she drew, whether curved, straight, or wobbling, and every brushstroke, all smudge and smooth, was carried out with precision and with an obsession with beauty that Víví's sweetness-loving-self admired. Serena, on the other hand, was less interested in what Ma-Reine made than she was impressed by how she made it, the way she lost her self in the doing the way Serena did in story and song.

Víví stopped short of the edge of Ma-Reine's blanket. "When are you going to make my portrait? I've been asking you since-since."

Ma-Reine laughed a greeting, "Bonjour, les soeurs. I was even coming to look for you when I got done with my work. Any time you want, as long as you help me do something with this mess I call hair."

"It's not a mess, sister. You're looking cute these days." Serena added, "Anyway, me, I don't need a portrait. A drawing lesson will do."

"Et Lucille?" Ma-Reine's question split the sweetness of their talk, and discomfort and defensiveness spilled out instead.

"What about her?" The sugar that had previously laced Víví's voice had crystallized and turned immovable as rock.

"Have you seen her lately? She talked to you? How's she doing?" This prolonged period of separation from their sister had the hum of care and concern nonstop just beneath the surface, and shame too, for letting it get this far, but where Serena was breathless and grasping for any glimpses into Lucille's world, Víví was closing her self off behind a metal wall of stubbornness.

"I don't know, please, that's why I'm asking. Lucille hasn't said much about you beyond that you are busy with your own matters. I know better, but I also know enough not to put my nose too far into your sister's business. I was with her one or two moons back, and I would see her around with Samedi, normale. But it's been long, so this morning, I decided to stop by and see. Door, windows, everything locked. And a sign on the door saying she would be 'back soon' or something like that."

Shame and worry prickled at both Serena and Vívi's necks like a hot compress from a rough towel because they had let their pride drag this argument on for so long without knowing what Lucille might be enduring without them, the ways she might need them to hold her. Their thoughts spiraled quickly towards the worst possibilities because it wasn't like Lucille to lock her door or be missing from Blue Basin's day-to-day, at least not for as long as it sounded. And what about the baby? Leaving her silent gifts was one thing, but it was only now occurring to them that they didn't know what it would look like when Lucille brought forth this new little life.

## break open

*Inside of time, sand dunes roll and wave like the sea, but here, the death will be hot and dry and long, not instant and freezing like the drowning that awaits those of you, our beloveds, who make it through the Sahara. This death is long and punishingly slow, losing water and hope and eventually one's life from the inside out. How you have survived on a journey with no clear path and no certain reward at the end is beyond us, and we watch with our hearts in our hands as your bodies fold inwards, how the wind whisks away what's left of your clothes, how the land eventually claims your bones. Those of you who survive do so in name only, because you are never the same after traveling for months through a place with nothing green and life persisting out of spite and not purely for life's sake. We wail and wonder what we could have done to make the former side of your departure feel full and loving and possible, because you wouldn't have marched headfirst into your own graveyard if you had known something other than endless wanting and needing but never finding safety and satisfaction. But because we are spirit and not god, we can only make breeze out of our voices and still, clean water out of our arms and hope your sojourn in that sandy grave is not eternal, or that the sand rests lightly on you if it is.*

And outside of time, one vat of water and indigo dye stands still and waiting to be stirred and stirred until white cloth turns blue, but "that dye look grey to you?" "Not grey. Maybe a little reddish. Like it's tainted. Bloody."

# 14

*outside of time, after the break, on Blue Basin*
*eighth full moon, or imagine someone believing they could fold*
*love and vengeance into hiding in their pocket*

"Sister, how long did you think you could hide?"

Lucille ignored the gentle probing in Serena's question and instead frowned over the patch of slippery white fabric in her hands, so soft it could have been made of cobwebs strung together. She stitched on one silver bead after another as fine as grains of sand. She fixed her eyes solidly on the needle and thread sliding back and forth in her hands, her gaze pointing only towards her work so she could avoid her sisters trying to poke and pry into her hurt.

Lucille had brought a stool from the kitchen to the balcony to sit on so Serena and Víví could have the two iron chairs. Those chairs could be awful for sitting after too long but were perfect for looking at the Caribbean Sea in the distance, so bright and clear in some spots it almost shone emerald. Serena sat with the mouthpiece of her sax and a rag idle in her lap, and Víví picked impatiently at her nails, breaking some of their sharply manicured tips with her rough touch.

"What did you think you were doing, sister? What did you think we would say when no little one came to meet us after nine new moons? Or you don't know how the body you live in works?" Víví's voice had a lot less calm in it than Serena's, and Serena slid a warning eye her way, the memory of their last falling out still heavy on her spirit.

"Baby, I know you didn't think we would just let this go. You know this would have been our baby too?"

Lucille could tell Serena was struggling against her frustration at the same time as she was holding Víví at bay, trying to restrain the rage they would have liked to fling towards Samedi for causing their sister's doubling grief. Lucille had spent all her time since Kekeli was no more alternating between discarded sewing patterns and laying down in a cave of grief of her own creation, her focus on her work and the coolness of the clay tiles against her body and the curtains shut to daylight as her only comfort. She had gathered her self together enough to remain elbow-deep in feathers, sequins, and bowls of blue dye for hours each day. The spirit she sent outwards was vibrant as anyone would expect, no dullness detectable around its edges, as she held babies in her lap while their parents tried on their costumes, tossing around Hey baby-s and teasing—"Need some tea to drink with all that sugar?"—so breezily that anyone who even took notice of her neglected curls standing away from her head in a misshapen halo and the dry darker patches where her skin wanted moisture would assume she was expending too much effort stitching beauty for everyone else to make time for her own vanity. Her masquerade was so airtight, she had fooled her self into thinking her sisters would fall for it just like everyone else did.

Lucille sighed her frustration as the patch of fabric she was working on slipped out of her hands yet again. "I'm not completely senseless. I knew everyone would start talking the minute I showed up flat-flat-flat where my belly should have been. But I just needed some time with my self. And what right do you have to ask me these kinds of questions? I didn't think you would care, franchement."

Serena tried once more to spin reason out of agitation. "Lucille, ma sœur, you can't mean that. What are we for if you can't tell us this?"

Víví's patience was as thin as the scraps of chiffon Lucille had left unswept around her sewing machine. She itched at her scalp so hard it looked as if she would come away with blood and skin under her fingernails. Her cropped curls had grown up to a thick bob hovering just above her shoulders, and her head was suffocating from being covered by more hair than she usually cared to have. "Lucille cherie, it's you we care about. Samedi can drown in the deepest, most godforsaken corner of the Gulfs for all I care. It's you that worries us. We want you to stand up in your self again. At peace. Free and easy."

"How did you know what happened to me and my—"

Lucille cut her words short behind her teeth, but her sisters still knew what she wouldn't say. Her current spiral away from them and into her self was their primary trouble for the moment, so even Víví didn't mind that Lucille kept crossing over questions with even more questions, drifting far away from the talk they were trying to have. "We saw Ma-Reine by Serena's the other day. She said she hadn't seen you in too long and wanted to know if we had. I don't know if I've felt shame like that before, not having any sensible answer for her."

Serena put the saxophone parts on the table next to her and took the piece of fabric and needles from Lucille, placing them down as well.

Lucille covered her eyes with her hands and pressed, her breathing stuck somewhere between gasps and gulps. "Don't . . . you'll get them dirty. And you just spent all this time polishing your sax, now look—"

Serena took both of Lucille's hands between her own and brought them to her chest. "Nye sí. Please tell us what you need. Let us stand in the break with you. We truly are sorry that this is how it ended."

"Are you? Aren't you a little glad you were right after all? This is what you saw coming, non?"

Even Vívi was stunned silent for a moment by the razors wedged between Lucille's words. "Sister, how could we be glad to see you suffering so?"

Lucille left them holding air and started getting ready to go back inside, gathering her box of sequins, her needle and thread, and the cloth she was working on. She wasn't sure she was ready to take her sisters to the depths where her loss was buried. Meanwhile, her sisters wanted nothing more than for Lucille to trust them fully and in all ways, not just with other people's dilemmas or with the infinite problem of worlds breaking and making and breaking again. They were ready to hold her and each other's spirit and fleshly selves without letting anything fall through the breaks, as impossible as Lucille thought it was for them or anyone else to really understand the source of her grief and her tired and the bends and branches where that grief and tired spilled into unsettled seas. She was inclined to keep trying to understand other people's suffering, to find where it was worst in order to get rid of it, no matter what her own state of mind was, because it was easier and less painful than tending to her self.

Serena had started to cry, though neither sister noticed it at first because her sobs were inward, swallowing sorrow rather than letting it wail aloud, but Víví kept going. "How could we be glad? Why would you even say that? Sister, I know we said . . . I said so many wicked things to you and I'm so sorry. I'm holding so much sadness, so much regret. This is not how we love each other, I'm sorry."

Lucille's tears started where her sister's had subsided, and Serena spoke through sniffs. "We should've been there with you. I'm sorry. For all of it. Truly. And Samedi? At least he was there with you, oui?"

Lucille felt a thud inside like a gate closing, like all the tender things she was about to say being locked back into a safe beyond anyone's reach, even her own. "Please, not this again, not now. Me ḍe kuku. Can you two help me with something?"

"Anything. Whatever you need," Serena jumped to answer before Víví said something that could break the peace trying to restore itself between them all.

"Miss Yvonne." Lucille adjusted her things into the crook of her left arm and walked around her sisters and up the stairs. "Come and let's go. I've lost count of how many moonrises and moonsets have passed since I said we needed to do something to help. Let's go see her now. I can't imagine how much lower the roof could sag without falling in on her."

And so Lucille went, as always, except this time not alone but with her sisters beside her, burying her own heartache in the ground of someone else's suffering, as if it was possible that she could taste the fruit of healing by vicarious means, as if turning towards other people with Love's Face required turning away from her own life.

*break open*

*inside of time, after the break*
*"Jérémie, Grand'Anse," Ayiti—agoo, we greet, mia tɔwò Taíno,*
*rightful and careful custodians of the land—1789*
   *Can you hear us? Entendez-vous? E mía nkɔ sem a? We are*
*called so many names we gave ourselves for all the many lives we*
*have led:*
   *She was only ever called "celle-la" or "ça," but as soon as she*
*was old enough to understand, around the age of three, her older*
*sister, Yvonne, gripped both her arms and shook her. "That is not*
*your name. You are not a 'that.' Your name is Enam. You hear*
*me? Enam. It means 'God's gift.'"*
   *It would be years before Enam would find out they were not*
*sisters by birth and that she had quite literally fallen into Yvonne's*
*lap when she was a baby. "Why didn't you ever tell me?"*
   *"Ðo to and keep digging."*
   *Enam put down her shovel without looking, and it slid down*
*the pile of dirt she had built up next to the hole she had just*
*finished making. Though she was younger and smaller, she always*
*finished any sort of work they had to do. Yvonne had hurt her*
*shoulder in a way she never wanted to talk about, and Enam had*
*been too young at the time to remember, but Yvonne still refused*
*any help.*
   *"No. Please tell me why."*
   *Yvonne kept hacking at the ground, unforgiving as ever in this*
*cursed place, her back and shoulders heaving like they were living*
*things separate from Yvonne herself. Enam was scared she would*
*snap in half.*

"*What is it?*" *Yvonne snapped.* "*Eh? So now we are not sisters? What now. Where did you even get this?*"

*It wasn't that Enam was shocked by Yvonne's raised voice. It often happened when they were writing together and Enam's lines kept leaning to the side. Yvonne's words made worlds anyone would want to live inside if they set eyes on them, and she had been trying to teach Enam to do the same, though she lacked the patience to train someone who wasn't crowned with her sort of natural talent.*

"*So? You can't speak? Who told you we are not sisters?*"

"*The woman shouted at me today. I was hanging up clean curtains, and she was angry that there was a hole. She said: 'You are nothing. You have no one. You see Yvonne carrying you around like some golden egg? She is not your blood sister.'*"

*Yvonne stopped digging, rested her hands on her knees, and took a few deep, heaving breaths.* "*Enam. I can tell you whatever you want to know. But we need to finish this work first. And stop standing around like that. Before they see you.*"

*Later, Enam parted Yvonne's thick hair, shrunken from the biting cold water she had just washed it in, into four flawless parts after greasing her scalp with the last bit of castor oil left in the jar. Enam's hands struggled with letters, but she could braid in patterns like no one had seen. It was the one Saturday night a month they had some space to breathe. Once a month, the woman traveled to attend her special church up in the hills, with the overseers and their dogs left back to make sure there was no trouble. It took the woman almost a full day to get there, so she left on Saturday to be on time. She had only started going when her husband's travels back to France became more frequent. Everyone knew she was no churchgoer and that it took too much time to get to France for him to be going there so often, but who cared? They did not feel a pinch of sympathy for the woman and her crocodile tears for a husband who probably never loved her because she believed those who were forced to till that land belonged to her just like the horses and the land and the house it stood on. In her eyes, they were not feeling, thinking people, so why would they spare any feelings or thoughts for her?*

*They spent their Saturday nights trying to forget why their arms and backs ached, why the soles of their feet peeled to the point of bleeding. One would think Saturday night would be the best time to run away, but if you were caught, which was often, you probably didn't live to tell about it. Yvonne and Enam were trying to forget that earlier the same day they had been digging not to plant but to bury the people they had lost to the man's temper, the people they had lost because they dared to yearn for the taste of something like an actual life. Yvonne and Enam were trying to forget so they could remember that their spirits belonged to their selves only.*

*Yvonne tilted her head sideways and up to look at Enam. "So what do you want me to tell you?"*

*"You know."*

*"Bon. They had started calling her Odessa in this place, but your mother's name was Sena. The day she flew away was the day you were born. Before she went, she told me she was going back to where you had both been stolen from, somewhere between a lagoon and the sea. She said she had to go because she woke up with a certain taste in her mouth and an ache in her lower back, and she just knew. She also said I should make sure you knew you could save your self after she was gone, because you were in her*

*belly when she was stolen and somehow survived the sea journey that had carried you both from life to death."*

*"And my father? You knew him?"*

*"Non. I only know he went to war and his spirit was destroyed. Your mother told me that when he came back, his eyes had turned red and stayed that way. She said she had another bébé who died on the march to the ship, and she never got to tell your father about you. I don't know what happened to him. Funny, he was called Mawusi, 'in God's hands.' But when he came back they started calling him Efo Nkudzē because of his eyes."*

*Enam kept the comb against the part, but her hands were dead still. "Another bébé . . . so you are saying my mother left me on purpose?"*

*"You have to understand, she just had a way of knowing. And she couldn't be sure it was safe for you to go where she was going. So she gave birth, and then she flew off."*

*"So she died?"*

*"You could think about it like that."*

*"So if she flew, then she is somewhere out there? Farther than the last fence? Beyond beyond?"*

*"Oui. Something like that."*

*"So can we go too? Fly, I mean. If she could do it, maybe I can too."*

*Yvonne stood up, and her hair and the wooden comb sprung out of Enam's hands. "No . . . you can't—"*

*"How do you know? How will I know when you're just now telling me?"*

*"Enam. Me ɖe kuku. Stop shouting."*

*Enam's voice sounded low, a nascent threat turning from simmer to boil. "How can I know anything? What is true? You told me the man took us away from our mother, my mother, when I was too small to remember. That we were in some other place before—"*

*"Enam. Please." By now Yvonne had backed into the doorway, stuck, framed by it like she was suspended in the force of Enam's confusion, galvanized and made dangerous because it was combined with anger.*

*"You can't stop me. What will you do? You're just a liar."*

*In one step, Yvonne was nose-touching close to Enam and bent forward slightly at the waist; she could look the younger girl in the eye. "Fire should not tempt you. Don't do it sister. Don't call me that."*

*Enam flinched and squeezed her eyes tight shut to find some stillness in the shaking she felt coming. Instead, what she felt was wet and opened her eyes to see Yvonne in tears. "Enam. Sister. Listen. Your mother did not birth me. But she was the closest I had to it. The little she was able to remember in our language she gave me to keep, and I gave it to you. We are sisters, even if it's just in the spirit way."*

*Enam was not convinced. Now that she had heard about flying, it was like she hadn't heard anything else. "If my maman could do it, then maybe I can too."*

*"Enam. Dzigbɔdi. Have patience—"*

*"No. Let's go now. Tonight. The woman is not around. Now."*

*Because she saw her furious demands were getting nowhere, Enam swallowed her desperation and honeyed her voice. "Sister. Let's try. Please. I'm sure we can go together."*

*"But how do you know? Let's wait until the next Saturday night. You've just heard everything. Let it settle in your spirit first."*

*On the next free Saturday without the woman, Enam had not*

even cleared sleep's gravel from her throat and the corners of her eyes before Yvonne started her appeal, "It's still too soon. Me ɖe kuku. I'm not ready yet. What if you can't do it?"

So another Saturday passed without the woman. And there was nothing in between for Enam; there was nothing but heat slapping her face to wake; there was nothing but her desperation like a ball of wool stuck and ever-expanding inside her head, blocking her from any other coherent thoughts except for her obsession with flight.

She lingered in hallways, inevitable even as the wrath of the man or the woman seeing her idle was, and under trees after the too-short rests for too-little water, and in doorways trying to gather any shreds of story about people who had flown. So you know someone who could? How? They had wings? What color? How wide? How did they hide them? How was the sky when they went? Stormy? Cloudy? Clear? You said you knew someone? Do you know where they went? They didn't tell you? You knew someone? But why didn't you go with them? Do you want to go? Now?

One Saturday turned into another and into six months during which the wool inside of Enam's head expanded to the point where she swore she felt a split starting to form in her forehead, and Yvonne rubbed and wrung her hands so much it hurt to touch anything. Still trying to dissuade Enam, Yvonne asked over and over, "But how do you know you can? If you had what your maman had, why haven't you taken off yet? Eh? On one of these windy days?"

And so the Saturdays became harder for Enam to distinguish from any other day because they all felt like dying, as more flightless time elapsed.

*"Where is she? Celle-la!"*

Enam's breaking sleep cracked open and she fell out of it and onto the floor. It was meant to be a Saturday, but she knew she wasn't dreaming the woman's voice. Past the rows of earth buckling into itself, the plants bent at the neck and drooping, the flowers lining the path up to the woman's front steps pale and weak. Everything looked to Enam to be bowing close to the ground, surrendering to the cruelty that thought it could force life and abundance out of death.

*"Wash these. And I don't want your lazy work either. We are expecting someone very important."*

She went round back to start the work she despised the most, disappearing the woman's filth from her clothes, now much worse for wear than when Enam first started washing them with childish hands. And she despised it even more knowing that she could be off, away, in flight, soaring, gliding through air, slicing through air like a cleaned and sharpened knife ready for cutting. She understood that her fate and the destinies of Yvonne and the rest of the people waking up to the death on that land were in flux, at the mercy of the man and the woman and their make-no-sense whims and temperaments. This understanding led Enam to the conclusion that the "something important" the woman spoke of would probably mean their doom.

At night, she turned on her side to face Yvonne. *"I just know something is going to happen here. Something terrible."*

Yvonne didn't open her eyes and barely parted her lips to say, *"What could be worse than what we have now?"*

*"Nothing good and alive can come out of this place. We will die just like all those things planted outside if we don't leave. Please. I promise I can take the two of us."*

Yvonne sat upright as if she had an arrow for a spine. "Someone told me the man is finally leaving the woman. Leaving altogether. They heard her crying and begging him to remain. That was no marriage. Just a lie they were telling each other."

Enam's impatience choked the air in the room. "What has that got to do with us? I'm trying to tell you we need to go, and you're talking to me about those useless somebodies."

Enam felt she might as well have been reasoning with the blank walls blending into the room's darkness.

Yvonne went on, emotionless, like she was reciting memorized incantations. "They said he's going back to where they came from and leaving her to her fate. What does she know about the land? What about us?"

"If you go with me, you won't have to wonder about these things."

"Bon. Let's go. The next Saturday."

Enam got out of bed and struck a match. She held it to the candle standing in a cracked saucer with flecks of blue and gold paint clinging to it as the only remnants of its design. "Not the next Saturday. Now."

She tried to push the sudden rush of fear behind her determination. She didn't know what to do next, but she knew any sign of doubt would give Yvonne another excuse to stay. So she gathered a few things; what would they need? How to prepare for something like this? The comb they shared, most of its teeth broken, and the bits of chalk and charcoal they needed to write and draw wrapped in a handkerchief, some stolen fruit.

Enam didn't look to see if Yvonne was behind her as she walked away from the only thing like home they had, the wooden structure inside which they died a little more each day. They marched to the edge of the land, the farthest bit of fencing termite-eaten and tangled with thorny bushes, green and brown and dying and already dead, as far out on the land as either of them could remember going because they had never left and they barely remembered arriving.

Though she had the longer legs, Yvonne had struggled to keep in time with Enam's relentless pace. "How will we know what to do?"

Enam stuffed her left hand into her pocket and tightened it around the comb and the chalk; she held her right hand open, fingers spread wide. "You are in my hands. Let's go."

Yvonne's doubt froze her arms behind her back so Enam could not grab them. Enam's star of a hand remained open and inviting, willing Yvonne to trust. The air between and around them turned cold then turned wind, but it did not touch or trouble anything near them, not the overgrown grass, not the stubborn weeds, not the flimsy fence that they could not imagine had been keeping them confined to this land of the dead and dying. The wind lifted them from beneath their feet first, and they were so upright they did not feel at first that they had left solid ground behind.

"Kpɔ da!" Yvonne's shriek broke a brief opening in the wind's roaring rush. They had left the stingy ground and those Saturdays between dying, but Enam did not know what they were heading towards and whether the flying mother she had never known would be at their destination waiting, and if she was, how they would find and know each other. And because of all this, she did not want to see what Yvonne had seen to make her shout like that. She couldn't turn her head, and she couldn't have seen through this swallowing type of dark even if she tried. There was only the *cold wind—their carriage—and there was only up to go and then more questions, like how would they know the right place to land? Would it be in the same way the wind knew to carry them?*

*"Yvonne! Núkà edzo? What's that up there?"*

*Enam felt Yvonne trying to draw her hand away from her own, slipping gently at first before pulling so hard Enam just knew her sister would tear her arm away from her shoulder and tear the two of them out of the air altogether. So there was the dark and the wind. And just above the flying sisters and a little to their right, there was a host of figures with wings twice as wide as the broad shoulders that carried them. Beneath the wings: smooth black backs, uncut, unbruised, unsullied, unbent. Above the wings: necks upright and steady, and above, heads adorned with perfect tufts of hair coiled around themselves and falling to one side.*

*"Sister—"*

*"Sister—" Yvonne's echo, sister, was swallowed by the wind. The last of her that Enam saw was an open mouth shaped like the end of the word sisterrrrr—*

*Enam lost track of how long she spent roaming the void looking for Yvonne. She was not even sure if she was still intact or if she had started to disintegrate one numb toe after another, followed by the rest of her foot, the ankle bone, and eventually, the remainder of her self falling after her sister. Wandering in what she knew deep down was fruitless pursuit gave her mind something to do that wasn't panic or fear; it was a purpose now more urgent than finding her much-dreamed-of destination, whether it existed at all or not, whether her mother had found her way there all those years ago and would be there waiting or not. Most of all, searching for Yvonne meant she wouldn't yet have to accept that Yvonne wanted to be lost, that she had jumped. With time, Enam's aching body went past numbness and back to pain, and the knowledge settled reluctant and heavy, more overwhelming than the never-ending night through which she flew, and she gave her body over to the wind to decide whether she would fall or land. The wind sent her over and placed her onto a piece of land so blue and so green it looked like it was part of the water. Her mind and spirit had been in disunity since the moment she realized she wouldn't find her sister. This had to be the reason why, when asked who she was, she kept repeating her sister's name, "Yvonne, Yvonne, Yvonne . . ."*

***

Lucille, Serena, and Víví took the Gran Promenade down from the Katye and through the Paroisse to the Afeme where Miss Yvonne's house was. When they reached it, Miss Yvonne was standing with her back turned to her yard, on the farthest left-hand corner of the veranda that wasn't drooping like a fruit left to ripen and rot on a vine, just like the roof and the rest of the house on that side since a storm had come and torn its way through. She was setting up a glass pot of tea and two glasses with lemon slices on a table with three termite-ridden legs, the fourth too short and propped up on a brick. They now saw why Friday's Child was not on his own veranda in the Paroisse huddled over some new sculpture or piece of ordinary something he would turn into some little wonder. He was in the midst of the wrecked side of the house, holding a small, smooth wooden plank in one hand with the other in his pocket, staring up at the place where the roof had opened up to the sky and all the elements.

"Miss Yvonne, ça va? Monsieur Vendredi!" Lucille called out. "You've done well, taking care of this lovely madame like this. Can this be saved?"

Friday's Child looked at Miss Yvonne first, his eyes as red as ever, taking his usual pause as though he needed to be sure of his thoughts before he shared them with anyone else. He turned to face Lucille and her sister, opened his mouth to speak, then seemed to change his mind, saying nothing. He jumped down from the veranda and walked close enough to them to be out of Miss Yvonne's hearing, though she didn't seem to be paying them any mind, still tinkering with the tea things and arranging the broken-down chairs just so around the table.

"I've been meaning to replace that porch set. I don't think it's safe to sit on, but she insists we have tea any time I come here to work, insists we sit just there." These were the most words that any of the sisters had heard Friday's Child utter at once, and none of them interrupted, in case it discouraged him from going on. "As for the house, unless I use magic, I don't know what else I could do. Imagine a body with bones turned into paste. That's this house. Been open so long, the termites have chewed up what the rain didn't soak up. I've tried to tell her I can build her something, somewhere else. Actually, you see the space beside your house, Mamzelle Lucille—"

"On est ensemble!" Lucille slapped Friday's Child on the shoulder and laughed open-mouthed and full of relief. "Exactly what I was thinking. N'est-ce pas, les sœurs?"

*break open*

*Inside of time, you are beautiful, somebody's child, all wide, gapped grin and sturdy legs and dimpled arms and face, all beaded ends and freshly edged up, all bathed and lotioned and new-socked like it's Sunday morning. But those no longer exist for you. Your days are an interminable stretch of the worst kind of Monday morning when the courtroom is full of the pleas of those who loved you enough to miss morning shift to bear witness to what they hoped would be your salvation. A judge who looks like a deacon you used to know orders the bailiff to take you somewhere they believe you will no longer be a danger to your self or anyone else; meanwhile, they are walking you directly into the beast's mouth and no one knows if you will come back the same or come back whole or come back at all.*

And outside of time, the people who had once spent most of their days inside of time with their hands soaking in water and indigo woke up to the blue dripped clean out of their fingertips and their tattooed lower lips and chins, staining instead their bedding and nightclothes.

# 15

*outside of time, after the break, on Blue Basin*
*first full moon in a new year, when Samedi thought he could*
*get away with killing Lucille's spirit and dancing amongst the*
*ashes*

Another year, another fête day had come around, and an especially boisterous hoot from a trumpet jolted Lucille out of sleep. She sat up and rested back on her elbows, squinting into the glare from the open window. If the fête had already reached la Paroisse, it meant she had slept past 10 o'clock, far too late for someone who usually sprinted straight into her day as soon as daylight cracked the sky. Her hands roamed about the bed as if to try and find something secure to hold onto amidst the storm of chants and mirth brewing just outside her home. Lucille could tell she had been exhausted the night before because she had been able to sleep deeply with the sheets twisted and rumpled so much they had exposed the mattress in some places, and usually the slightest crease would prevent her from letting sleep carry her away until she could smooth the mess back to its rightful neatness. She threw her hands behind her head and breathed in, stretching her body until she felt the ache that always throbbed in her back, intensifying if she reached too sharply to pick something off the ground, or when she sat for too long at her sewing machine, but this time dull and almost comforting because she lived with it every day. This morning, she was home alone, and there was no second pair of hands to massage relief into her muscles. Her grieving had evened out into a dull thump, the kind of pain that ebbed or grew depending on her present circumstances, like a weak knee in the rainy season.

The voices outside were quickly turning into croaks from singing at their highest volume all morning. Their cheers clashed with the heavy boom of drums, the cymbals' airy hissing, and the whistles' shrieking marking every beat.

> *No day for the devil!*
> whistle
> *Fire on his head!*
> *No day for the devil!*
> whistle
> *The devil is dead!*

Lucille crawled across her bed and hopped off the end. The air in the room was heavy with the nights' worth of worry and sweat and the stink of the dying flowers sitting in the center of the night table next to the bed, so far into their rot she could no longer identify what kind they had once been. Lucille couldn't find a scrap of enthusiasm anywhere in her dejected self to match the spectacle unfolding itself on the streets out there. If she sniffed long and hard enough past the staleness of her room, she was sure she could smell the vapors lifting off the sticky sweet icing Víví had whisked for the special cake all the way on the north side of the Paroisse.

Lucille breathed in deeply like she had been holding her head underwater for hours and was desperate to push life back

into her lungs. She looked to her left, up the road and towards
the hills, and fixed her attention for a moment.

> *Volez, volez, volez!*
> *Petit oiseau, volez!*
> *La fête, c'est pour vous! Volez!*

Now Lucille was sure she could distinguish Serena's
saxophone from all the others, her tone more harsh and
somehow somber even in the midst of all the sounds competing
to be heard. She knew, too, the feathered crown bobbing back
and forth and on the brink of toppling off the head it adorned
must belong to Víví, who always danced so hard, it was as if the
drum's pulse was coming from inside her own body.

"Oh, oh careful! Atansyon!"

"Watch out, now!"

"A le le le . . . kpɔ nam da!"

"Poor thing! Someone get him!"

Shouts of warning and alarm broke through the exuberant
trance of song and dance, and Lucille stretched over her
balcony as far as she could without risking a fall to see what
was the cause of the disruption. A child had fainted, and the
inquisitive neighbors watching from their windows and stoops
soon identified him as Jean-Jack. Jean-Jack had been lagging
behind the children's group all day, but they had all brushed
his complaints off like dust on the sleeves of their pristine
white marching band jackets. He said his outfit was too tight,
the jacket was pinching him in his armpits, the trousers were
riding up into the space between his butt cheeks, and the
other children rolled their eyes and kept swinging their arms
and twirling their batons. He said the sun was burning down

on him as if he was the only target and the pebbles were boring holes into his feet, and the other children shook their heads and shook the tassels hanging from their sleeves in his scrunched-up face and kept on ahead. And then Jean-Jack let out a small yelp and fell onto the pebbles he had just been lamenting about. The other children didn't break formation, their heads soaring with the pride of being out in front as if they were the finest and most important participants in the festivities, the guests of honor. The island's elders arranged the fête lines this way because children never walked behind their parents. They were too cherished, and someone doesn't have one thing only to let it fall in the sand. The other children skipped and footworked on, weaving in and out of their lines in tandem like they had practiced. Some of them felt sorry for doubting Jean-Jack, but most were too high on the cheers of their audience and the anticipation of the big feast at the end of the day to care.

> *Volez, volez, volez!*
> *Petit oiseau, volez!*
> *La fête, c'est pour vous! Volez!*

Lucille watched as Mama Jean-Jack pushed through the throng screaming like she was being chased by spirits from the parts of hell even the devil wouldn't venture. The screams were like a muffled alarm in the back of Lucille's mind, like there was some anxiety she should have felt, the cruelly pleasant moment of vague memory between forgetful and aware. Then she remembered her own little one who never was. *Kekeli.* If only she had been more patient and not hasty to name the child before they decided they would stay. If only.

"Let me pass! Let me through, I need to get my baby!"

From a spot below her balcony, half hidden from Lucille's view, Sans-Souci let out her loud cackle like wooden shutters crashing against each other on a windy day.

"Woy woy woy! Will somebody look at this for me!"

Mama Jean-Jack threw her disdain in Sans-Souci's general direction but didn't stop parting the crowd to try and reach Jean-Jack. She was Mama Jean-Jack not in the way mothers lost themselves and became recognizable only in relation to their children, but because she thought her self a formidable person and therefore worthy of a junior. She didn't play about her self, nor about her child, Jean-Jack the junior. "Sans-Souci, why can't you worry about your own life for once?"

"Baby, it's my business to look at anything passing in front of my house."

"I could give you some real business to see about. Don't play with me!"

The parade became an avalanche. Whistles spilled over cymbals tumbling over drums and trombone blasts over voices, fringed umbrellas twirled in dizzy spirals, skirts swished, and beads and feathers ground into dust. In the chaos, Lucille's eyes still managed to settle on a solitary figure, his white linen shirt and trousers radiant against his skin, liquid night flowing in the daytime and dressed in lightning. While others were attempting to rearrange themselves after Mama Jean-Jack had cut through the crowd in her panic, this man towered over the scrambling bodies around him, his lean elegance standing out like a statue at the center of a busy square. He neither danced nor walked but rather glided along on the balls of his feet, with an ease that seemed to spread from his shoulders to the tips of the slender hands he was waving at no one. Lucille bore grudging witness to this one-man show, and she hated it and hated the fact that he had snatched her attention, even after how he had done her. She was startled by the way her heart jumped up and down inside her, like the muscle had been replaced with a fist knocking against her chest in a bid to escape and do its desired damage. In the time that passed since Samedi had vanished, she had made acquaintance with the gaping emptiness of abandonment, but this, this was pure rage thumping in the veins at the side of her neck, surging through her ears with the force of river rapids coursing around and over boulders.

A dry little man with wrinkles lining his skin so plentifully Lucille could see them even from that height danced along with a whistle clamped between his lips, blowing it to punctuate each one of Samedi's movements with such force that the veins on his forehead threatened to pop open at the next blow. Samedi two-stepped forward and paused every few beats to do a shimmy starting in his shoulders and moving all the way down to his thighs. "Hey, hey, go, go," the whistle-blower egged on Samedi's every step, and Lucille rolled her eyes so far upwards she felt they would dislodge from their sockets. She could almost see Samedi's ego from where she stood, growing like a giant bubble with everyone else trapped inside.

> *No day for the devil!*
> *Fire on his head!*
> *No day for the devil!*
> *The devil is dead!*

A flock of birds cut through the sky and swooped towards the cliffs, not breaking their formation until they flew back upwards, scattering away from each other in every direction. Lucille turned her back to the pandemonium and stepped back inside. Behind the screen door and the filmy curtain like cobwebs knitted into a sheet, she stood barefoot and as still as the room's stale air. She wondered if some of that fleeting August rain would soon make one of its unpredictable appearances, cool enough to lift some of the unrest brewing everywhere.

*break open*

*Inside of time, your hair has now outgrown the lines and waves cut into it, and only one cracked bead remains tangled into the end of an old braid, and you are still beautiful, somebody's child, sitting on the floor in a cell as wide as you are tall on Rikers Island, just across the peninsula from Guantánamo Bay, a short walk away from a town called Nsawam. We weep, and you are multiple places and nowhere at the same time: in this room with the walls pressing too close against you, and buried into the furry couch grandma has kept longer than you have lived, and in a bed belonging to the bed bugs and not to you, and trying to remember your name is not a number and your voice lives in your throat and not in the static of a phone call you cannot afford. We call the name we gave you, and you are trying not to feel the grime from the ground sliding onto your legs and you do not answer. We rage, and you decide you can hold your breath long enough to swim off the island and past the peninsula so you can walk through that town and through the back door of the house where we will be waiting to remind you that you belong to your self and your favorite food is on the table, fresh and ready for you to eat for the rest of your free life.*

And outside of time, the morning was quiet, not the usual silence weighed down with waiting and birdsong soon starting but hollow like the week after a funeral when every dish from the repass has been washed and returned and the last relative packs their bags and leaves. Not a wheezing wind, not a chicken scratching dirt, not a howling dog—empty, as if a colossus of hands had covered the entire island and closed it into fists.

# 16

*outside of time, after the break, on Blue Basin*
*first full moon in a new year, or scorn is so sweet when it is*
*justified*

Lucille fixed a narrow stare on Samedi across the empty breadth of his desk. His charm and nonchalance, feigned or not, was even more annoying than it had been from her balcony at the fête that had just passed. He adjusted in his oversized chair, shifting constantly like the leather was singeing his skin through his clothes. Her disgust stretched between them and hung in the air of the one-room shop Samedi liked to call his office, and he cleared his throat several times as if to get rid of the troublesome fog. "So, how have you been? Long time!"

Lucille remained silent, knowing she would have little control over her next words or actions, as deeply immersed as she was in her righteous anger. She looked at the few items decorating the room: a clear glass ashtray, a silver frame around an empty space where a photo should have been on display, and a dimpled tumbler with the sticky brown remains of the whiskey he had thrown back for breakfast stuck to the base. She looked at the peeling cream wall behind Samedi's head and at the two hats hanging side by side on two hooks, one black with a silver ribbon, the other had been part of his costume for the fête, its feather now bald. She took a quick inventory of the bottles he claimed could get rid of almost every disease known to have settled into a human being's muscles. The bottle labels read more like worldly vices and threats of harm than remedies: "Liquid Resentment," "Envy," "All-Over Body Pain." Lucille had always thought Samedi kept these just for show because she couldn't remember a time when she had seen anyone consume the contents. The dusty film and rust rimming each vial supported what Lucille presumed to be true about Samedi's dubious healing abilities. His role on the island was to provide temporary solutions to minor health gripes. Mostly, he was a symbol of the scare tactics that parents employed for stubborn children.

"Of course your stomach is paining you, when all you know how to do is eat toffees! Allez! Start walking to Samedi before I carry you myself!" And along would come the child steeped in regret of a little lie gone too far, her hands balled into fists with a tremble matched only by her lower lip. Inching slowly up the stairs to Samedi's place, the spot on her arm where the injection would soon be administered already twinging in anticipation of the bitter pinch of the needle.

Lucille considered how she could show Samedi what her vengeance felt like. She could break the glass and force him to chew it until his tongue bled down his chin, or shatter the photo frame over his head, or sweep her arm across the tabletop and bring all his things crashing to the floor, or she could reach for her pocketknife and carve her name into his fresh haircut until he screamed for mercy. Lucille didn't often wish violent retribution against people who had wronged her, mostly because no one ever dared to. Her rage wasn't cheap and flashy like the violent fantasies she was entertaining. It wasn't melodramatic, not any kind of tightly packed spring ready to explode without warning. Her anger was rigid and contained. It was the tension of her lips pressed as tight together as they would go to prevent curses from flying out, and the embarrassing tears she knew would come after her fury subsided, like torrential rain chasing away a scorching sun.

She ran her fingers through her braids from the roots, which had already lost all their tautness and shine so soon after they'd been done, to the ends resting just above her waist.

"Long time. It has been a while hasn't it?" She sighed. "Where on this damn blue bowl have you been?"

Three new moons since Samedi chose some lie of a fishing trip over caring for her. Three new moons of complete silence without explanation or apology. Three new moons without a single trace of Samedi Amegbetɔ. Three new moons—but what did the time matter with betrayal like this—since she found the door to Samedi's store padlocked and bolted, the steps leading up to it covered in more dust and fallen leaves than usual. Three new moons since the night when grief had invaded Lucille's life, every new instance of remembering bringing with it a little more pain than the last.

Blue Basin Island was small enough that one would think it would be impossible for anyone to dissolve into obscurity in the way that Samedi had managed to do. Blue Basin people spent their days leaning over their balconies or wooden porch frames and into their neighbors' business. Everyone knew who preferred someone else's bed to their own and who was too strict to feed their children sweets after dinner every night. They knew Lucille had lost who was to be her and Samedi's child, somehow not able to dissuade them from going back to the world of the unborn, but no one had seen them together to share their condolences or to feed their curiosity. In fact, they hadn't seen Samedi's shop open since-since.

It was also common knowledge that Samedi Amegbetɔ was as charming as he was untrustworthy. Lucille hadn't needed her sisters' advice or the rustling of her neighbors' hushed gossip to convince her Samedi would never be capable of extending his care for another person beyond the point where he was satisfied after wringing them dry, having no more need for their presence in and service to his life. But the warnings had only circled her ear's curves before fluttering away into the contentment of her oblivion, and no matter what cruelty of his other people had tried to expose, she still hadn't believed he would eventually abandon her.

"How are we?" He smiled a slight, smug smile, showing only a quick glimpse of teeth.

"Which we?" Lucille rose in her seat, her anger swelling in her chest like hot air threatening to break free, and leaned over as close to Samedi as the desk between them would allow. "Samedi, which we? The 'we' you went out fishing for many moons ago? You've been fishing all this time, oui?"

Samedi never lifted his eyes from an unlit cigarette he was twiddling between his forefinger and thumb, like this fidgeting was a task demanding a laser eye.

Lucille was unrelenting. "Samedi look at me. Does it look like I'm carrying *us* with me?"

Shock flashed in Samedi's eyes, a sudden flare of light in a dark room. "What?" His cool act was wrecked. He looked like he was former fragments of a whole self sliding out of the frame that had been his body, once straight lines and edges giving way to confusion. Lucille watched him scramble for some way to hold his self together. They sat inside the aching silence until Samedi seemed to recover from the jolt of this news, tracing non-existent creases in his linen shirt before leaning to the right and dislodging a box of matches from his left trouser pocket.

"I'm sorry, ma chère. I'm not sure what I can do now. I feel so guilty, but I just . . ." He struck a match, and his words were punctuated by smoke curling over his bottom lip, as casual and uncaring as his attitude appeared.

"What will your guilt do? Will it make the sun come up tomorrow? Can it replace what I . . . *we* have lost?" She shook her head, knowing the only consequence of unfurling all her hurt onto the desk between her and Samedi would be her further humiliation. Lucille gathered the extra fabric in her full skirt and rose to leave.

"Efo, I don't have the energy for this. You've gotten away with being wicked, as always. Well done."

She stepped into the afternoon mess of Keta A*f*eme. The air was stagnant and thick with layers of smell and sound. Children faced each other in two lines slapping hands right to left, left to right, and chanting,

> *No day for the devil*
> *Ke-ke-ke-ke*
> *Fire on his head*
> *Ke-ke-ke-ke*
> *No day for the devil*
> *Ke-ke-ke-ke*
> *The devil is dead*

A man strolled past Lucille on the paved path from Samedi's store through the heart of the town, his shoulders sagging under the burden of the heat and the wooden box he carried on his head, alerting anyone who passed by that he could shine or mend their shoes. Tap! "Shoeshine!" Tap! Even his voice seemed to droop in the heat and the lethargic hours of the day.

Oil on high heat sizzled and spat from the front of nearly every house. "Beignets, viens! Viens!"

"Lucille! Daavi Lucille! I know you like my fried yam! Hot pepper just for you!"

"Not today, tatie, but maybe tomorrow! I'll have that fabric for you, too!" Lucille forced a grin resembling teeth gritted in distress, only if you paid close enough attention. She was sure everyone could see the feigned glee sticking to her teeth like a layer of sugar after dessert.

It had been a week since the fête, and the houses' wooden siding, doors, and shutters showed signs of losing their luster. The acrid smell of fresh paint sat on top of the food aromas drifting down the street. Where people had danced too hard, porches would need repairs. But the sanding, patching, painting, would go on indefinitely, long after the frenzy fizzling in the air calmed to a slow normalcy, like sugar taking its sweet time turning into caramel. They were trying their best to guard against the tiny—and growing every day—breaks opening on their island outside of time caused by the cosmic break from which they had fled, back where the yet-to-be-unbroken suffered and dreamt still. These days, it seemed their fixes were lasting for less time, their care requiring more patience and more detail, more paint and more hours spent on hands and knees sanding wood, as if the rising tide of crisis inside of time was now so intense they had to work harder to keep it at bay.

A few houses away from Samedi's, Mama la Patissière's husband was bringing out a colander with agbeli kaklo still sizzling for the teenagers who were scrubbing the stairs of their house. Mama la Patissière followed with a pitcher of lemonade, its sweat dripping onto her skirt.

An infant teetered along on the road ahead of Lucille, a ball of butter on wobbly legs, trying to chase after a hummingbird whirring just above his head and out of reach. His flustered mother hurried after him. "Me be ɖe! This child is going to kill me!"

Lucille felt a faint brush at her back, as if someone was blowing gently over her skin through pursed lips.

"Madame, ma déesse . . . que le rasoir coupe toujours. May your blade be the sharpest." A whisper turned into a slow hiss, and fingernails gripped the softness of Lucille's left arm and pressed inwards. "Ma déesse, take a bottle. Take a bottle for what haunts you."

Lucille snatched her arm away sharply and immediately regretted her outward display of annoyance. Her disgust for Samedi and for her self for still craving his support had settled over her skin like a film she knew she wouldn't be able to wash off anytime soon. She immediately felt guilty for her reaction when she realized it was just Nanewɔ, trying to entice people towards her trinkets, shells with slips of paper tucked inside for the names of loved ones and sea pebbles polished so they gleamed as if they were precious.

The sun caught the gold thread in the scarf Lucille readjusted over her shoulders, sometimes blue, sometimes green depending on how daylight struck it. She paraded her false confidence away from Nanewɔ and down the road after mumbling her disinterest, her breath held in tight until her lower belly muscles begged release. She believed she was striding with purpose, unwavering and unapproachable, her sandals clicking almost the same rhythm as the children's chants, *ke-ke-ke-ke*. In her mind, her glide was airy, her head lifting as far as her neck and shoulders would allow. She could make it through town, where the chaos broke open to the stillness of the street where she lived, up the rusty staircase, and into the safe solitude of her home. She could make it, if only she didn't let her act lapse to reveal the molten mess of anger and despair she was hiding.

Lucille came upon a game of checkers at its most impassioned moment. A group of old women, settled on their haunches and cheering on their chosen players, turned their heads occasionally to spit tobacco into the sand. Their head wraps were streaks of bright in their cigar smoke, so dense and dusty that Lucille wondered how they could see the board or the faces open with delight and anticipation before them.

One flashed a sly smile embellished with gold at Lucille. "Hé ma belle! Where are you rushing to? Join us for a game!"

Another twisted the bulky rings she wore, moving from one finger to the next until each one had been adjusted to her satisfaction, and mumbled through a smirk, "This one . . . can you not see where she's coming from?"

Lucille swayed on down the road like she hadn't heard, not bothering to ask what she meant. She was done talking to or about Samedi for the rest of her days if she could help it. Her casual demeanor denied the chafing of her thighs and the sweat gathering between her folds sitting snugly on top of the waistband of her skirt, and she left the women in their own world, smothered in smoke and aging glamor. "Enjoy, mes dames, while you can! I only play if I can win."

At the edge of Keta Afeme, where the dusty path skirted the edge of the thick trees standing guard over that part of the island's coast, Glory and Ma-Reine approached Lucille. The closer they got, the more apparent it became that there was something awkward about their walk, as though they were tied together by the ankle, the only competitors in a three-legged race. They came nearer still, enough for Lucille to notice Glory's left arm was hooked through Ma-Reine's so that she stumbled every few steps, her one free arm trying to make up for the other with its swing.

Ma-Reine's shock did not fade for days after the first time Glory hit her. It was some afternoon hotter and quieter than most, but she preferred to be entranced with the works of her own hands than force a restless siesta inside the stuffy house. Her paints were spread around her in a circle, the only witness to what she would create. She was trying to paint the feeling of first realization that the dry season had arrived, the air that could scratch if you inhaled too deeply and smelled like anticipation, that midday light dimmed to a soft orange, like a bonfire's after-glow, like white light through an orange screen. At that point, all she had to show for hours bent as close to the canvas as her body would allow were smudges of the orange she was attempting to conjure and the white she was using to conceal her mistakes, the canvas of never-ending possibility for her to test and pass the limits of the pictures she could dream.

So when he struck her, her heart dropped into her pelvis because she did not see the raised hand, the lines knitted into his forehead, the jaws' clench pulsing in his cheek. She did not see it coming because she was too busy thinking about what her maman would say about how to draw a scent or a feeling.

"You didn't hear me calling you? Too busy to mind me?"

She was stunned into a state like a nightmare, but unlike the aftermath of their first crash, she felt no hope when she looked into his face, only a profound doom more than she had ever felt before, not even when she lived at Tɔgbí de la Cimitière's place. This would be the only time his hurting her was followed by a sort of remorse, with a hug taken rather than given and hot tears spilling into her hair and down the side of her still-sore face.

Lucille now stood in their way, and their stiff conjoined walk faltered to a stop. "Salut ma sœur! Where to in such a hurry?"

Ma-Reine's face creased into something short of a smile, almost genuine, almost, if you didn't know her the way Lucille did, all vestiges of a frown vanished except for three feathery fine lines above her broad nose. Her hair was wrapped in a high tignon, a vibrant red reaching far up like she was carrying fire on her head.

Glory cleared his throat as if in preparation for a response, his mouth working around his pipe, but Lucille tilted her head slowly towards him before looking back at Ma-Reine, reminding him that he was not the one she was addressing.

Ma-Reine's laugh was halting, almost embarrassed at its own forced gaiety: "No hurry! Just taking in the daytime. A little stroll, a little afternoon delight."

Glory cleared his throat again.

"Well mamzelle. Let's not hold you up eh?" Lucille stepped aside and as they passed, Glory called back to her, tossing his words one by one like boomerangs whose return he did not really care about. "How's Samedi doing? Haven't seen him around in a while."

Before she could think up some salty reply, they were already too far away, back where Lucille had come from, too far for her to say anything to him that would have as much edge. Lucille clenched and released her right fist around the handle of her knife in her pocket. Its imprint would be left in her palm all day.

She reached the point in the road where Keta Afeme touched the Paroisse, and the houses grew stories higher and retreated from the street behind metal fences. She considered heading north on the Gran Promenade towards Víví's highly perfumed sanctuary, her little yellow house standing cheekily amidst the uniformity of its blue neighbors. Or maybe, she could climb higher still, up into the hills where Serena lived, and sit on the packed clay floor listening to her sister playing a whistling tune. She chose neither.

*break open*

*Inside of time, those of our beloveds who let fire and power tempt them towards treachery kept a polished loafer on the necks of the rest of our beloveds, leeching out the breath and life from their chests like a cruel valve, a little more tax and then more and more. The treacherous called themselves righteous, chosen, Big Man, do-you-know-who-i-am, elected, convinced themselves and their neighbors turned constituents turned sacrificial lambs at the altar of their greed that someone had to die for another to prosper. The cold glass edifices they called offices, headquarters, and seats of power were tombstones for the last vestiges of the humanity they had forgone to justify their grabbing more and more food out of the mouths of most of you to feed the ever-expanding beast living where their souls did not. The only thing heavier than the cloud of smoke hovering over the places where the powerful burnt evidence of their sins was the mass of discontent and rage forming and settling down in the deep of you, the beloved and yet-to-be-unbroken, who just wanted life free from the threat of being the next on the menu at those Big Men's tables.*

And outside of time, the blue periwinkle and blue forget-me-nots and blue orchids and blue morning glories dripped down their stems and stained the ground, and the petals shriveled and folded onto themselves.

# 17

*outside of time, after the break, on Blue Basin*
*first full moon in a new year, and whether there is grief or*
*bloodthirst, eyes flash red the same*

When Lucille reached her house, she was greeted by an empty chair where Miss Yvonne had taken to sitting since Friday's Child had started working on her new house, under the twisted forget-me-not tree between hers and Lucille's. It had taken him only about one new moon to finish the entire first floor with its veranda wrapped around, working through any weather and deep into the night by lantern, the most committed to the work of his hands that anyone had ever seen him because he wanted to make sure Miss Yvonne finally had somewhere warm and whole to call home. Miss Yvonne usually stayed in the shade from the most sweltering hours of the afternoon until the first wafts of evening chill, her eyes protected by the wide brim of her straw hat and a white umbrella planted into the ground behind her. Lucille played with the idea of going to sit with Miss Yvonne for a while, but almost immediately after the thought flickered in her mind she shooed it away. Miss Yvonne's spirit was sweet and sorrowful, and always fading, her homemade cookies days past their crispness and arranged on plates in flower formations, her faint pencil scratches, her futile insistence on trying to rescue souls that had already found their way in the world somehow. Today, though, Lucille decided she could do bad all by herself and didn't need this sort of company to wallow in the stale air clinging to the curtains and the tablecloths and to Miss Yvonne herself, like stubborn morning dew refusing to melt away. Before she turned away towards her own door, she realized Miss Yvonne wouldn't have even needed her company anyway. Through the window, she could see Friday's Child refilling Miss Yvonne's teacup and then his own, the steam from the pot swirling high and wide around them, a gauzy curtain cutting them off from any intrusion. Since Friday's Child had started keeping her company, Miss Yvonne seemed like she was missing the dead she always seemed to mourn a little less.

Víví was sitting on the staircase, waiting to mind Lucille's business, because her heel had hardly touched the first stair when Víví called out, "Cherie mine! Just came over to touch up Miss Yvonne's rinse, but she's not ready yet. Today is burning up, eh?'

"It is. I'm just going up for a glass of water and some sleep. I'm exhausted." Lucille trailed off with the useless hope that Víví would understand she was not willing to wade into the swampy uncertainty that was her relationship with Samedi here, en plein air.

"So I missed you on fête day. Have some of your birthday cake I made?" Víví's empty facial expression was betrayed by the subtle raise in her eyebrows and the grit underlining each word she spoke. She dragged out "your birthday" long enough to let the guilt she hoped Lucille should feel settle in the moment. She wanted Lucille to imagine her piping elaborate designs onto the cake, the too-hot weather thwarting the sugary swirls that were meant to look like seashells but came out more like the rough edges of waves breaking onto the beach.

"Ma sœur, I beg, not today." Lucille's tone was turning into a whine, so desperate was she to be spared this interrogation.

"I can keep the cake for later, pas de problème. You want some kalamí? Just fried some."

Víví was not in the business of letting go, especially when she felt she knew better, which was always. She brushed invisible wrinkles from the front of her dress, a slow, deliberate movement to try and maintain the homely charade she was attempting to keep up. She continued, a determined matter-of-factness in her voice. "You missed bottle washing too, n'est-ce pas?"

Lucille wrapped the tip of a braid around her index finger and ran her hands across her shoulders as if a sudden chill had landed. Then she bent almost completely forward at the waist to get a closer look at the deep purple leaves of the plant she had been growing to keep away snakes, as if they were suddenly the most intriguing thing she had laid eyes on, as if she had not walked past these plants so many times she never noticed them anymore.

"The plants are looking so full, Víví. Don't you think?" Lucille was now pressing one of the dark leaves so tightly between her fingers that it split in half. She stood up straight, holding the wounded leaf in her palm like there was some way she could knit it back together and place it back on its stem.

"Eh heh! Just wait! This way you're behaving, it's about Mr. Missing-Any-Day-Of-The-Week! Ma chère, baby, what has he done now?"

"Víví, please. This isn't the time for this. Honestly, I don't know when the time for this will be."

"Taflatse, I'm your sister and not your mother. I mean, we are our own mothers, but—" Víví brushed her hands on her apron again, now more of a desperate compulsion than a need to dry her hands. She reached for Lucille as if her arms could steady their talk before it careened into a crash of insults Víví hoped to avoid this time. "Sister, please talk to me. I promise not to go wild like the other time. At least I can try."

"He left me. I was losing the baby and he made his self missing." Lucille said her words with all the viciousness that had been fermenting in her spirit moon after moon, while she had been waiting on Samedi to prove her wrong.

"You said? So you were suffering and he was what? Where did he go? Where is he now? Let me talk to him. How dare—"

"Don't worry your head. That man doesn't and will never know shame. Just leave it. Hear? Just leave it. Please." Lucille was already at the top of the staircase before she could see Víví's shock transform into anger. She shut the door gently, taking care not to disturb the pane of glass embedded within it, cracks lining its face like it was one fierce slam away from shattering. She felt brittle, near breaking too, and although she knew Víví's rage was directed towards Samedi and not at her, she wasn't sure she could survive even the secondhand effect of its force.

Lucille was going to treat her self like she was delicate, carrying her self like an egg. She had met Samedi's apparent indifference nose to nose one time too many. She had stood so close to his carelessness that she could taste the sweat dropping off its nose and onto her upper lip. Now, Lucille wanted nothing more than to dissolve into her loneliness, pooling on the floor in the hopes that any benevolent somebody would eventually come and discover and pull her out of the pitiful person she felt she was becoming. She didn't turn around when Víví closed the door behind her. Víví had decided it was much more urgent and necessary to care for and be a witness to her sister, though it would have also been satisfying for her to unleash her grief-fueled wrath on Samedi the undeserving.

Lucille walked into her kitchen, relishing the feel of the clay tiles and imagining their coolness was soaking into the soles of her bare feet and up through her legs, thighs, and stomach, into the core of her body. She put a small pan below the tap and the water hit the blackened spot in its center where years of burnt oil and food had welded to its silver surface. It wasn't long ago that she had detested the high fragrance of the oils Víví made for her. She found them too sickly and almost suffocating when she combined the wrong ones, a common mistake for someone like Lucille, who had little patience to cultivate this sort of decadent habit. But if there was a time to lavish her self with care and sweetness, it was now, when she was "well," the source of her nausea long gone. Her grief was striking in her in the same spot, so she could not possibly forget that an almost future had eluded her loving grasp.

She would soak her dry feet in the water infused with lavender and mint when it was at the perfect level of warmth, and maybe she could leave some of her worry at the bottom of the bowl with the dirt and flaked skin from her heels.

Víví nudged Lucille and stood next to her in front of the stove. "Can I . . . ? Let me help?"

Lucille's mind conjured the nervous smiles Samedi kept trying to give as a show of goodwill, his teeth seeming oddly too small for his mouth, smaller than they'd looked before, with just a little too much space between each one. "I'm sorry ma chère. I'm not sure what I can do."

Look at those teeth, abe amelã dula, like someone who eats human beings. She felt she was being ground to ashes between the jaws of her own anger, and it terrified her. Why allow her self to disintegrate when she could grind his teeth to ashes instead and sprinkle them to the three seas. After all, he was only skin and bone, and her rage was more than enough to crush him, to make him pay.

The water on the stove bubbled and turned over itself, but it was as if it was inside Lucille's chest, the steam rising and threatening to suffocate her from the inside out. Her rage would be reckless and uncontrollable if she gave it room to spread out, and ultimately of no use if she ended up the only victim of its destruction.

She leaned over the stove to take the pot off and saw the bushy ends of her braids hanging over the water. She was some kind of miserable, letting this fraying at the seams go on unchecked—let Víví tell it—from the ends of her braids to the once tightly woven self she was now scattering around her cluttered house and all over the island. Something else cowered behind Lucille's insistence that Víví leave it all alone, something feeble like a sore only halfway to growing new skin to cover up raw flesh. She had loved this devilish someone enough to place her whole being in his hands, knowing also that she was conferring upon him the power to rip her to shreds and leave her in a dejected pile of her former self. Maybe she had let it happen. And maybe she was now letting her self remain so, torn up and useless, with no real interest in continuing on in this life. And again, she could imagine Samedi to be this invincible monster with claws digging into open wounds repeatedly, but maybe she had become monstrous too, for mourning the abandonment of a mere man more than a child that was of her own making.

She clicked open one of the blades of her pocketknife as she crossed into her living room, choosing to sit on her favorite armchair with its fluffy lining outgrowing the silk covering. She drew one of the braids from behind her head over her shoulder and began picking away at it with the knife's point. She undid the braid past the tapered point that would have been too small for her fingers to tear apart until she reached a place of more reasonable thickness. It would take her longer this way, but she was always so cautious because of what happened to the one neighbor who had once tried to take out her hair the easy way and now wore a misshapen ponytail like a squirrel's tail no matter how long her hair grew as a permanent reminder of her impatience. Lucille's fingers spun quickly up and up, with a motion like hands zooming back and forth over a loom. She watched the first piece drop to the wooden panels of the floor, now just a strand that would later turn into a large cottony mound like a black sheep's shorn wool. Víví took her place standing behind Lucille's chair. "Baby, your hair feels like dying grass in a drought. What have you been doing?"

"Please don't pick me apart. Not today, I can't take anymore. Be gentle, please."

Lucille was sitting with her head bent towards her chest to better reach the middle portion of her head while Víví worked on the back and had finally begun to feel like they were making progress because the ends of Lucille's own hair were tickling her upper back and her scalp felt lighter and able to breathe. When it was all undone, Víví led her sister to her bathroom with its white tiles scrubbed so clean, the shine was painful to the eye. Lucille sat on the thinning towel Víví had placed on the floor next to the tub and stretched her head back over its edge, enjoying the security of its solidness on the back of her neck. With her eyes closed, she felt Víví parting her hair into several sections before rubbing her slender fingers over her scalp, dislodging weeks of dry skin and sweat away.

Víví clucked and whistled a quiet song as she tried to push moisture back into her sister's dry scalp. "Tutu gbɔvi. Walk soft child, live wild . . ."

Lucille ran her fingers over the length of her own hair that had been set free from the braids. She was trying to readjust, to give her self permission to experience the very kindness that she seemed to have abundant stores of for everyone who needed it, often, or maybe always, at her own expense.

Serena announced her presence at Lucille's door the way she did anywhere she went, without the exuberant flurry of kisses and "Ça va" over and over, but quiet-quiet, her usual hum in a tune only she recognized. She pushed the door open and stood in the doorway for a brief moment before crossing the room and sitting softly next to Lucille on the sofa.

"Nye sí, ça va? How goes it?" Lucille's attempt to force levity into the grim atmosphere was unnecessary because Víví and Serena were already sharing in her pain. Serena took Lucille's right hand between her two larger ones, sliding the knife away and closing it in one fluid motion.

"Red eyes. Her eyes were always so red," Serena began in a low tone, somewhere between song and speech, in the careful way she rolled each word over in her mouth, sampling her sounds one by one before sending them out into the world.

"Not the kind of pale pink crossed with fine veins nor the slight tint when you rub your eyes too hard to try and banish a speck of dust from its depths. It looked like she had blood pooling at the brink of her eyelids instead of the tears you would expect from someone in an eternal state of mourning. She was known all over the world, on different coasts, beside different shores, by people who couldn't quite recognize her or trace where she had come from. She was known as angry and vengeful, but this her was a shift away from that fire, unending grief personified.

"*Who called that woman here?*' They asked, sucking their teeth and rolling their eyes they asked.

"*Who called her here? Who knows her?*' They asked, tightening their black headscarves and crossing their arms.

"*Who called that woman here?*' They asked, readjusting the cloth they had wrapped their bodies in and turning the one bare shoulder against her.

"And yet, she remained, eternally poised to grieve and mourn each released soul as deeply and fully as she had loved them in life. She sat on a stone outside what had once been a home but was now more a life-size matchbox emptied of its contents, discarded and trampled under giant feet. A red cloth, empty of any kind of pattern or design, was tied in overlapping folds over her black blouse. Her chin sat heavily in her hands, pushing her lips into a resigned pout. A few minutes would pass and she would shudder, a ripple running from the top of her covered head to her slippered feet crusted over with dust and dead skin. A few more minutes, and she would let out a sustained wail, laden with so much pain it seemed to be coming from the farthest flung reaches of her being.

"You would not be able to take your eyes off her; you know this woman. You were repulsed, but you knew her. She was the woman sitting on the stone outside that house, the day after the whole world slipped sideways and all her children fell off the edge. She was also trailing at the back of the procession winding its solemn way from the dust bowl cleared for canopies and tables littered with used rubber bags plastered to their surfaces with smears of oil, to the graveyard with whole chunks missing from its perimeter wall. Missing as if someone was halfway to barricading the dead in, or giving them space to fly out into the wind, but gave up before they could finish the task.

"Her bloody gaze was unbearable, and so you looked away, but you knew her. So disgusted were you and all the others in this mournful parade that you turned and spat at her feet over her shoulder, the darkened patches of wet in the sand turning into a path for her to follow.

"They all knew this woman. Everyone said they had seen her somewhere before. Some say she was the same one sitting on the stone outside that house, and others swear they saw her on the beach in 'Jérémie' (or was it Ouidah?), chasing the waves as they pulled back and running away each time the tide returned, closer and closer than the last.

"'*That one? Elle est complètement folle!*'

"The townspeople shrugged their shoulders and went back to plodding through their lives, from farm to market to home to church to shrine and back again.

"Her eyes, still brimming over with blood and sorrow, roved the horizon incessantly as if she was waiting for some kind of rescue or for a lost somebody to return. Many somebodies did come back, exactly in the way our red-eyed woman feared. They came back in fragments, almost unrecognizable, a brown sandal missing its buckle, a stomach bloated with seawater, a wad of letters and important documents choked with water and sticking together, now totally useless. Many of her people never even made it into the yevúwo de, the pink-skinned specter's land, on the water's other side, before death sunk them into the ocean's deep, although you could say yevúwo had tried to claim all the water as theirs too. They had given themselves the power to draw boundaries around people's liberty and chain others to foreign land. She wept and wept, her entire face aching from fatigue, but still the people shrugged. They were used to the horror. One day, she would come to her senses, too; they were sure.

"You know this woman; she was the woman standing under the neem tree's wide canopy, as close as she could get to the grave without flashing her blazing eyes at you. She was also the one who hurled her self into the rubble that was the clay home she had built for her children, only recognizable by the remnants of black and white swirls she had painted to beautify what would have been as bland as any other house in the town. She rolled around in the mud and clay until her skin was coated in deep red, and rolled and rolled, and cried and cried until you couldn't tell the blood in her eyes from the clay on her skin. She roamed her hands endlessly over the fragments of rock and dried reeds that had once stood firmly planted into the soil, as if hoping for a sign she had once had a home full of mischief and tinkling laughs, a boy who always scattered her combs, and a girl who found a way to pour half her dinner into her hair and onto her chest no matter how closely she surveilled mealtimes. Her neighbors, burdened by their own grief, were disgusted with hers.

"*They're gone ooo . . . they're gone.*'

"*Are you the only one who lost someone! Kpɔ da!*'

"She flashed her red eyes on different coasts, beside different shores, and even on land the ocean never touched at all. She was the woman sitting on the stone outside the flat matchbox house, and she was the woman under the tree at the graveside, and the one covered in filth and rolling a tantrum all over the town. She was also the one rubbing eyes bloodshot from lack of sleep and the kind of panic that could kill; she was the one opening desperate arms wide to the sky, pleading for respite, for rescue to dry land. All around her was the same desperate sinking in her chest, people hanging on to beams and pillars with one hand, and assorted belongings that surely would be of no use where they were probably going, photo albums and boom boxes and suitcases, all drowning, drowning. . . . *The water is rising, please.* Her tears run red because all their pleas would be unanswered, drowned out by the noise of news helicopters and sirens for those deemed more deserving of mourning.

"The blood brimmed over but did not spill when she took a bat in the ribs for resting in a spot not designated for her kind. The once-whites of her eyes blazed but did not explode when the earth opened and shook and sank under water, burying her children without allowing her the proper rites. Today she is somewhere outside of time, crying for the children she knows who don't know her, who are disgusted by her wretchedness, who mourn as well but have no one to smooth their misery out into acceptance. She has cried so much her own blood runs in the same gutters and streams as the blood of her children and her children's children, spilled because they dare to keep living past the death sentences the world tries to use to wipe out their glory. She has cried her eyes to a red that can never be cleared, hoping you won't have to do the same. Sometimes, they call her Ezili Je Wouj. Sometimes, they call her the spirit who was, is, and will be love and vengeance. Sometimes, it is you they're calling, Lucille. Sister, you can't remain grieving forever."

Serena had barely spoken the last sentence of her story when Lucille let out a groan from deep in the middle of her chest. She pulled her hands out from Serena's grip and used them to cover her face.

"Oh, oh, oh," she cried, with Serena and Víví beside her, anchoring her to the wooden floor so her sorrow would not wash her away in its current.

*break open*

*Inside of time, the black lines and numbers on the large, white-faced clock above the door at your job untethered themselves from the ticking hands and pulled tight and long like the center line on a road leading deeper into the despair where you already lived. At two thirty, you thought about how little you or the work at hand mattered and how no one would notice if you disappeared from your station. At four fifteen, you daydreamed about your own blood pooling around your body, one last ritual, a body of water to cross at the other side of which would be the peace you never found while alive and striving. You had gone to church to call on us and heard nothing; you had gone to the river spewing filth on its banks to call on us and heard nothing; you had gone to a forest of sickly trees to call on us and heard nothing, so you decided first that we spirits did not exist, and then—even worse—that we existed and did not care enough about you to show our selves to you, to help bring you back from the void somewhere behind your ribs where you were hiding and waiting to gather enough will to end your self. We tried to show our selves in the voices of all the people turning to you with Love's Face, trying to hold on to you by the shoulders, by your damp hands, by the low dip of your back, but your soul had already bowed so low and so far away from anyone convincing you to give life another chance.*

And outside of time, leaves still green with promise fell to the ground only to return to their stalks shriveled and brown the next morning and then shiny and green again the next.

# 18

*outside of time, after the break, on Blue Basin*
*second full moon in a new year, and what to do when misfor-*
*tune arrives in your home wrapped in charm and indulgence,*
*refusing to be banished no matter how viciously one scrubs and*
*sweeps and polishes?*

This was the part Lucille disliked most, the impatient picking
at knots in rope cemented in place for too long, impossible to
undo without nearly breaking one's own fingers in the process.
At least, she thought, she wouldn't have to worry about anyone
stealing her canoe. Apart from the tie that had to be coaxed out
of its complicated tangle, stealing wasn't something they did
on Blue Basin when everything they needed was in abundance.
Lucille wanted to be immediately out on the open water,
listening to the creaking calls and light whistles of the bayou's
birds, cutting through the carpets of moss and white flowers
with petals opened up as if in praise to the heavens. But it was
more than impatience that pulsed through her fiddling hands
on the rope. Back here on her own, in the farthest end of the
Paroisse's shadow, she felt oddly exposed, even if no human eyes
blinked open to watch her. One miscalculated step could put
her at the mercy of any hungry cottonmouth slithering close
enough to her to strike, and her nerves shook together at the
risk. She hadn't seen one in years as far as she could remember,
but her fear swallowed her better judgment. The thought of

venom sliding through her veins was one of the few things that made her truly afraid, even if she knew it could never actually kill her. She exhaled and laughed at how tightly wound she had been while she tried to free up the canoe. Lucille placed both hands on either edge of the boat and climbed in, one knee at a time, before relaxing back onto the seat. She picked up the paddle, its wooden handle showing its age with the flecks of itself it was leaving in her palms and pushed it down and back and farther away from the shore and lurking snakes that she may actually have to face another day.

The sun wasn't quite four o'clock on a Saturday, not quite as optimistic and as sumptuous as that honeyed time because of the few clouds in the way, but it would do just fine. Paddle in hand, she could let her mind wander wherever it desired. She could be a musical siren, cane covered in glitter and engraved with her name, strutting through the Afeme, keeping to her walk with its tap-tap-tap and ke-ke-ke on the stone streets. She could be one of the green reeds waving at nothing, content just to be, growing and growing in the cool cover of the bayou, vines and leaves hanging from the trees like tattered clothes or sagging spirits bearing mournful witness to the life continuing beneath them. She could just be, without the grasp and clutch of needy hands pleading for more pieces of her time than she had to spare.

Weeks had passed since her birthday celebration that wasn't, since she fought with Víví about the same Samedi who had trampled over her peace of mind, and they had set aside their disagreement close enough to still see its edges but far enough so they couldn't retrieve it easily and fall back into its grip. Lucille had almost succeeded in convincing her self she was totally through rehearsing her loss over and over, dancing the same steps around the death of her little one who refused to stay living, of a love that may not have been as steadfast as Samedi's touch on her body had her believing.

Lucille's thoughts shifted steadily away from their leisurely wander as they always did eventually, beyond Saturday's Child, to people like Glory and so many others like him who seemed to enjoy breaking their loved ones apart, just for the sake of seeing where the pieces fell, just because they could. And if they were men, the world would often applaud and prostrate before them, for the hurt they happened to leave behind upon their transformation into someone supposedly less brutal and less irresponsible with their power. But even more urgently, there was Ma-Reine. More than most other people she had looked after on Blue Basin, Lucille was painfully familiar with the dimensions of Ma-Reine's distress. She knew where the broken teeth were; Ma-Reine insisted on keeping them in a chipped china jewelry box with a regal woman's bust engraved on the cover. She had rubbed endless handfuls of aloe onto her friend's aching arms, wrapped her in leaves over oils to smooth away the scars, some so steadfast they would never quite fade away, remaining as shadows of past traumas dotted over Ma-Reine's otherwise smooth skin for any who looked closely enough.

She maneuvered the nose of the boat through her favorite part of the bayou, a small corridor where the tree trunks had twisted and bent into meeting over the water, allowing Lucille to move from day to evening and back again with a few short swishes of the paddle. She was almost at the back of her house, with the rest of the afternoon still stretching leisurely before her. Just as she veered the canoe to one side, she caught sight of two bulging eyes inside a scaly black head—Gentilly, the gator she had named and liked to call her neighbor, unusually meek and seemingly never on the hunt for flesh, with a white patch right in the center of his head. She nodded politely, as she would if she was passing a distinguished-looking stranger on the street, before turning away and pushing the boat to a stop on the bank. She took her time unbuckling her sandals, now soaked from a little puddle that had been resting in the bed of the canoe below her seat, and so didn't notice she was no longer alone.

"Ma chère. Hello."

Lucille sat still, like she had changed her mind about getting out of the canoe, about the cold drink she would have with her lunch, about the short walk to Serena's house to hear some sweet singing, about rolling a mat out on her balcony to sleep en plein air on what promised to be a cool night. One too many responses leapt in the back of Lucille's mouth, so instead she said nothing. She stared at her lap and the old white linen trousers she used to knock about, for gardening, for lounging and dozing, stared so long she could probably count the number of threads missing from the worn patches around the knees and hemlines.

"I know there's nothing I can say. That pitiful apology, I know." Samedi's words struggled over each other, none really making any sense, and his voice faded in and out like a candle wick trying and failing to catch alight. "I don't know who I thought I was . . . the attitude . . ."

Lucille stepped carefully out of the canoe, her straight back showing no sign of what felt to her like her bones turning into slush. "Samedi, you sat there blowing smoke in my face after I told you what you ... I ... we lost. ... And where did you go? Where do you vanish to all the time?"

She stared at him straight in his face, refusing to fold him into the warm comfort of her sympathy. She rejected the chatter of his teeth, more suited for a freezing January day up on the cliffs than the bayou's afternoon broil. She refused to see the jagged line where his hair had grown and coiled over its usually impeccable lineup. She resisted the sorry sight of what looked to be his oldest shirt, loose against his body where it should have sat snug, and his unkempt nails, some cracked and others grown too long, dirt buried in their corners. How could she be sure this man crawling in like it was Ash Wednesday was not just another act of the Samedi show, her sitting front row with her gullible self, always ready to forgive? And why was he the way that he was?

"Lucie, nye Lucie. What can I say except I'm as no good as everyone thinks. Maybe even worse. Grown and nothing to show but mess after mess."

She closed her eyes, compelling them not to spill over in betrayal of her resolve to stay aloof and untouched by Samedi's begging to be granted space in her life once more. She pretended she was healed, free of the dull throb of loneliness somewhere in the background of her consciousness like a bad tooth resigned to rot away without the care it needed. "You still didn't answer. Where did you go?"

His voice wrenched from his mouth, an ugly mix of suffering and accusation. "But you're not right neither. You just dropped the news on me like that. Like you didn't trust I would come back to you?"

Just then, a heron screeched like it was also in pain.

"Please. Don't you dare. You're a slippery one. Always stepping out, just for a bit, me yi ma va. With the guys, non? Sliding through any small space you can get, between the frame and the door if you could."

Samedi had now moved close enough to Lucille so she could smell the staleness of neglect on his breath. His eyes were switching wildly between states, one moment glazed over and staring past Lucille and over the water, next wild and dilated, straying all over Lucille's face.

"Lucie, please understand, there are some things I can't even say aloud. Not to anyone. Not even to you. I did go fishing, but not with les gars. On my own. Nothing bit, but I ran into Friday's Child on the way home, and he gave me some fresh shrimp, said he had too much. I was going to cook us up something nice, a little private celebration. Knew we were both scared as all hell and . . ."

"And? And it takes several new moons to walk from Vendredi's on the corner to my house? Samedi, you must think I'm some special kind of senseless."

"Hear me out, tɔnye. Meɖe kuku. I was terrified. But I was also excited out of my mind. I'm thinking wow, our magic brought to life. And then I got all caught up, let my terror eat up my joy. I said what if I just throw my no-good all over Lucille again and this baby who didn't ask for any of it. But I was coming back. Really was. I swear to you."

Lucille couldn't bear to stand still and help Samedi work his way out of his muddle of hurting himself and hurting her. She stepped apart and moved to leave him behind, with the early evening shade already sweeping through the trees and hovering over them. "Baby, I can't take one more second of this.

I'm going inside to rest up. You can go wherever you want, as always."

Samedi caught Lucille by the waist and paused only to sniff away at least some of the tears that drenched his face. Lucille didn't make another attempt to distance herself from him, so he kept talking, "I swear I was, baby. Nyate*f*ee. I wouldn't lie to you. Not about this. I walked up to the door, then I turned back. Said I would spend the night by one of my guys, just until the fog cleared. And then it was a couple of weeks, and I figured you had your sisters . . ."

Lucille turned back to face Samedi and cried out her next words at a volume she didn't think was possible, and the bayou ceased its murmur abruptly, jolted by this disturbance. "You figured? You figured I would be ok without you? What am I going to do with a somebody like you, leaving our tomorrow hanging off the edge of chance?"

Lucille's arms hung stark straight at her sides, her fists closed so tightly her nails could have drawn her own blood from her palms if she kept them so for only a little while longer. She had tried to savor her solitude, feeling out all of its unfamiliar edges and dimensions, like she was trying out a new food, rolling it around in her mouth long enough to make herself believe she liked the taste. She released her hands from their tension and held them open now, weighing her resentment for Samedi himself, for her sisters' judgment, for her own loneliness that sometimes covered her all velveteen smooth, only to smother her to the point of near choking on some nights that stretched too long and empty. She walked away from Samedi and the lazy water, their only witness. She thought Samedi was standing still, stuck, until she heard a few tentative steps shuffling through the grass behind her, away from her and her house, like his feet were scared to touch the ground.

Lucille felt Samedi's return less like the euphoria of cymbals colliding with trumpets and keys, the highest point of her favorite song, and more like the day after a house fire. To her, it was as though they were standing in the ashes of the former selves they had been with each other, with only scraps of memory and affection sticking out of the uncertain haze that had settled between them.

break open

*inside of time, after the break*
*"Cité Citadelle, Nord," Ayiti—agoo, we greet, mia tɔwò Taíno, rightful and careful custodians of the land—1974*

   *Can you hear us? Entendez-vous? E mía nkɔ sem a? We are called so many names we gave ourselves for all the many lives we have led:*

   *Cité Citadelle had little of the contrived grandeur its name held. There was no stone piled upon stone, no towers cleaving the sky in places and crumbling upwards in others, as if pieces of the building had been snatched from up above, no tourists scattered across wide and winding stairways like pieces of scrap paper, their matching short and shirt sets in contrast with the hats they would often lose to the wind and the force of gravity pulling them over and down the side of the hill. Neither was it like the other Cités of working people carving lives out of corrugated iron and shared plates of fried meat and cold drinks passed over fences, places housing the cooks, the drivers, the market women, people*

*who dreamed about finding ways to make enough money to move
out to the suburbs—distant in spirit but near in miles—where
each house was surrounded by its own private green and where
one window's view did not give way to a neighbor's bathroom.
Cité Citadelle was a township of clay and brick houses built
into the side of the hill holding the ruins of fortresses from the
revolution days when free living seemed like it would be forever.
The foundations of these homes were built as far into the ground
as the granite below the earth would allow, and it would take a
particularly powerful flash flood or sliding land to uproot them
from their perch.*

*In one of the houses closest to the valley, Samedi's parents
were living out a marriage that threatened to shake the stone
keeping their house from freefalling mostly with their rage and
only occasionally their desire to be as close together as they could
get without wearing each other's skin. His mother, Brigitte,
wasn't the Cité's only healer, but she was the one whose doorstep
had been most worn smooth by the footfalls of neighbors looking
for relief for their ailments, be it pain spreading between the
muscles and taking root like a crop-stifling weed or mental strife
turning even the shady spots under trees on the mildest days into
malevolent shadows coming to claim an expiring and weary soul
for the lands beyond life. She could brew teas to cleanse the body of
what she called that chaff pretending to be food that was becoming
more and more common, even in their town far away from the
fluorescent-flooded aisles of the stores selling imported food in the
capital.*

*Some of the other local healers scorned what they felt was
Brigitte's favor because "Celle-la, she's buying those concoctions
from the normal pharmacy and adding one-two one-two splashes*

*of sweet oils and calling it sacred. C'est du n'importe quoi. And I hear not much healing is going on over there with those women who keep going to see her. Healing is not supposed to involve touching and rubbing, at least not in that way." There might have been traces of truth between the bitterness; Brigitte did love some of the women who came to her seeking sweetness or respite from their dreary, work-filled days, but any doubts cast on the power of her care were pure envy taken shape in jagged shards like glass baked into the cement of the walls surrounding the homes of those who had something they deemed precious enough to protect from people climbing over and into their yards to steal. If a child played in ivy they did not recognize as poison, Brigitte made a poultice out of orange weed for the itch. She knew how to brew the best sassafras bark tea or asafetida for menstrual cramps, and her hands were sure and steady when she rubbed castor oil on a feverish person's chest.*

*Samedi was a junior, but everyone called his father by their family name, Le Baron. Some joked that the popular rum with the same name was named after him because of how often he got lost at the bottom of his glass, and the little children would clear any path he crossed because, to them, he resembled the spirit of the dead who was also his namesake, the one who haunted their storytimes with threats of dragging the living to a land after life whether or not they were ready to go. Samedi le grand worked in the mortuary of the regional hospital 25 miles away from the Cité as a cleaner and general dogsbody, but if you let Samedi le petit tell it, his father might as well have been a doctor who held people's hearts between his hands, firm enough so they wouldn't fall but soft enough to make sure they stayed beating. Because the hospital was so far from their hillside, Samedi le grand only came home on the weekends, his pockets full of sweets from the bowls in the doctors' waiting rooms and his mouth full of stories more fancy than fact. "Le petit! Come sit, let me tell you how I saw a man breathe his last breath and still walk out the building the next day."*

*"How, papa? Was he a ghost?"*

*Most weekends, Brigitte would pull the junior Samedi away from his father's legs, sometimes roughly by the arm, "Laisse-le. It's time for bed. You have all weekend for these lies."*

*But, if the air was sweet between them, she would tug him gently with one hand, the other winding around her husband's neck, "Le petit, time for bed oui? Let the old folks be for the night."*

*When Samedi le petit grew tall enough to reach his mother's countertop without stretching up on the tips of his toes, she tested his readiness to be her helper by first asking him to wash the bottles hanging on the tree outside their kitchen window.*

*"Maman, tell me again what the bottles are for?"*

*"Aren't you tired of hearing? Or you forgot already?"*

*"Oui! Please, Maman. All I know is something about blue."*

*Brigitte took Samedi's unblemished babyface between her large hands turned leather from years of soaking in boiling water and grinding pestle against mortar. "Yes, baby. Something about the color blue, indeed. It's magic, like this—she held her hands out and showed her indigo- and ink-stained palms—how these can make sickness and sorrow go away with the right stir, the right combination of plants, the right words at the right time of day or night."*

*Samedi pulled his mother's hands back towards his face. "The color blue is magic."*

*"Yes, in a bottle to catch any evil trying to come close to us; in*

*paint that does the same, in the sky and sea that are also paths to some other place where our mothers' mothers' mothers flew to when their here and now became full of dying and too much to bear."*

*"Flying where? Can we go? Is there dying now?"*

*"There is, and there always will be. But we are safe; no need to run or fly, unless for fun."*

*"But—"*

*"It's enough, Samedi le petit. Back to work for now."*

*After every single bottle—long-necked, squat, dimpled, round-walled—was polished spotless and hanging back on their various strings by the new moon's waxing, she began to trust him with washing the jars and bottles she used to store her medicines. Watching over him, she would laugh a laugh like a teaspoon hitting the inside of a glass at him walking back and forth from the sink. "Cherie of mine, it's like you went to bed last night and woke up tall but don't know what to do with all that leg. You know you don't need to tiptoe anymore, oui?"*

*"Maman, laisse-moi!" Samedi would throw his mother's laugh back to her, a lower register of the same tune, less light, surprisingly somber for such a young somebody.*

*"Samedi! Careful before you—"*

*Brigitte's warning fell to the ground along with the freshly washed bottles Samedi had been balancing in his arms, but she only laughed harder and sang to him the words she had been singing to him for as long as he could understand the words, a sort of reminder of who he was and who he belonged to:*

*Samedi my Samedi*
*Why are you the way that you are?*
*Samedi my Samedi*

BLUE FUTURES, BREAK OPEN / 249

*Saturday's Child*
*My beautiful boy*
*Why are you the way that you are?*
*Beautiful boy, eyes lurking low and deep like violet night sky,*
    *skin shining so black*
*Footsteps springing off the balls of your feet, lifting off heaven-*
    *ward*
*Saturday's Child*
*Why are you the way that you are?*
*Beautiful so . . .*

And Samedi grew up with the perfect blend of the best and worst of both his parents. A thornier version of his mother's rasp came out of a mouth as full as his father's, and when he was delighted, which happened less and less the older and more restless he got—just like his father—his laugh echoed his mother's, uninhibited, clear, and clean like water hitting an empty metal basin. From his father, limbs long and tangling as he tried to walk up and down the hillside of his hometown until his teenage self learned Samedi Senior's easy elegance. Like his mother, never ever satiated, an ever-widening void of hunger and desire, and growing wider still the more he ate or loved. From both his parents, charisma that could easily turn into scorn that could easily turn into wrath should he feel threatened or insecure.

As his teens reached closer to adulthood, his wicked beauty was not lost on the neighbors his age and even some of the elders looking for someone to pair up with their offspring so more generations would come to build more life clinging to the sloping land. Young people in search of uninterrupted sleep, or miracles for state exams for which they had not studied enough, or an end to the possibility of children unplanned for would all forget their *various complaints and afflictions when Samedi no longer so petit was in the room where his mother received visitors. And even if he wasn't, they would linger in the hopes of seeing his shadow pass across the doorway before he bent into the small space, even better if he sent a lazy mumble of a greeting their way.*

*The neighbors were almost too busy being enchanted with Samedi to notice Brigitte's medicines were losing potency. At the very least, they would not guess he had anything to do with the belly aches, the unusually sour breath from their babies, the prayers unanswered. To them, it was more likely that Brigitte was getting careless, her teaspoon slipping through shaky fingers and spilling a little more of this and not enough of that, because Samedi Senior was coming back for weekends more and more rarely with every passing year.*

*"If this is what she has for us, then we might as well mix our own. This is rubbish. C'est du n'importe quoi!"*

*There was a universe in which Brigitte's longing for her always already-distant husband would have made her hands and mind less nimble, more inclined to cause discomfort or even damage than was usual. But in the reality where the Cité found itself, the truth was that Samedi did not inherit his mother's touch and deep knowing for which fruits of the earth could harm and which could soothe. Because the work of her hands and the man she had chosen to love both required as much patience as there was water in the sea, Brigitte kept correcting Samedi every time she caught him going wrong, sharing her notes and diagrams that no one besides her had set eyes on to try and initiate him into the knowledge she carried and continued to cultivate.*

*One Friday evening, Brigitte was feeling optimistic, or maybe she was in denial, about the progress her son wasn't making. They were tending to the garden with their backs turned to the house when they heard a brisk tap on the metal gate ke-ke-ke-ke, "Le petit et ma cherie! I'm back! Get up from there, what kind of welcome is this?"*

*Intent on staying in the allure of the promise of the weekend ahead, she was more soft than cutting, sending her son into the house like she did when he was still small enough to hide behind her legs. "Vas-y, le petit. Let me stay with your father a while."*

*The two Samedis snapped each other's finger mid-handshake like they were acquaintances crossing paths in a dingy bar or at a crossroads into town, and they might as well have been, seeing as the father had not returned home for his usual visit in so many weeks they had ceased to count.*

*"Evening, but remember I'm not so petit these days."*

*The son moved into the now-dark house, far enough away from the garden's edge so all he could hear was the lulling and cresting of his parents' voices, every other word extending past the shore of the evening:*

*"... missing from me ..."*

*"... more and more bodies ..."*

*"... you ..."*

*"... trouble ..."*

*"... let's not, Sam ... this ... extreme"*

*"... you know the way ..."*

*"... no ... never ... we ... survived worse ..."*

*"... will you listen ... you don't know ..."*

*Samedi leaned against the counter where his mother did her work, now mostly clear except for a few straggling pieces of lemongrass, some tops missing their jars, dried flecks of hibiscus tea that Samedi missed when he swished a damp rag across the countertop earlier that day. He knew his mother expected him to keep the counter spotless at all times when they were not working, but at the moment, he did not have the will to do anything more than just stand. He was getting older, but his mother's gifts were yet to make themselves manifest at the tips of his fingers. His anticipation had dried up and turned to vapor, and his restlessness moved far past boredom and apathy, landing at cynicism at the truth he did not want to swallow: that he might be a lot more like the father whose name he had borrowed—inept, a little selfish, and absent from his own life—than his fearsome mother with her blessed hands.*

*Because he was winding his anxiety about his inadequacies and his resentment tighter around the inner self who was still his parents' "le petit," it took Samedi a few long seconds to realize his mother had pulled him out of the kitchen into the fading evening light.*

*"Samedi oh oh oh oh . . ."*

*"Maman, what at all—"*

*"Not you, not you, not you. Your father. He jumped . . . fell . . . tried to fly . . ."*

*"What do you mean maman—"*

*"Please! No time for talking; we have to go after him."*

*While Samedi le petit had been indoors catching only wisps of his parents' conversation, Samedi Senior had been telling Brigitte that trouble was boiling over in the capital and threatening to spill their way, possibly all the way to their hillside. The only evidence he had were whispers from behind closed doors in the hospital, so faint they could have been doctors shuffling papers across their desks or patients using their last breaths to make desperate pleas for relief. And there were also the bodies. The only other time he could remember rolling in so many bodies and the wails of relatives in pain crashing against the sound of the steel gurneys was in the wake of the kinds of storms that only came once a century, the one that found and swept away people from their beds and their rooftops from underneath staircases and tables they knew would ultimately be too weak to shield them. Samedi Senior had in the past waved away Brigitte's stories about blue bottles and blue walls and blue waters for warding off evil as fantasies for children who didn't yet know that pleasure and play continued to seep out of life the older one got. But, his restless spirit didn't allow for as much skepticism as his dismissals of Brigitte's stories suggested; in fact, he needed as much room for his soul to roam if his body was going to be confined to this small life on the hillside. He couldn't convince Brigitte to show them the way to the place totally out of reach from the pending horror he was sure would come, the place where some magic blue would cover them for the rest of their lives and the lives to come beyond those. He pointed his body away from his wife, and the wind was at his back and the open sky before him, and he jumped.*

*"But maman, if you knew the way, why didn't you stop him? No one leaves just like that, you could have—" Samedi the son, now with a father absent for good and not just because he was too drunk to make his way home from work that week, would rather turn to blame than to the sudden void that had appeared in their lives in his father's wake. His mother pulled him to the edge of the garden where you would expect the land to slope downwards green and gentle, but it dropped off to the rockface and then nothing.*

*"We don't have time. Spite me if you want. Hold your arms out."*

*That was how Samedi the not-so-petit realized for the first time that as he had been stretching out and growing broader, the force that was his mother had been folding and bowing closer to the ground. She wrapped her arms around his back like she did when he was still le petit and pulled him over the land's edge.*

*Flying didn't feel like Samedi expected—no rising and rising in his stomach like driving over the hills in an old truck, no sinking in his chest like coming down from surfing a high wave. Not even the wind was how he thought it would be, not slow and warm like an overslept Sunday morning after falling asleep with the window open, not like late afternoon right after a heatwave breaks. It was so cold that after a while, he couldn't tell the difference between his arms and his mother's arms, between his forehead and hers, couldn't be sure if any of the parts of him still had life running through them and whether they would get through to whatever blue promise was on the other side of this cold and this dark. Each second passing might as well have been a week, a year, a month, though Samedi was no longer sure whether such measures of time meant anything out there beyond nowhere.*

*The muscles in his arms crossed the threshold of pain towards numbness and back towards pain, then forward past tingling and numbness to agony, and still he kept trying to hold his mother up. Nothing could overtake the wailing wind, so Samedi didn't even try to ask her to shift her weight, to adjust her self, to hold her self up as much as she could, nor did he try to listen to anything she might have been trying to say. When he was finally on land again, he would repeat in his mind that she had slipped and he could not feel it until it was too late, that her weight finally exceeded his ability to keep carrying her while remaining sky-side, that he had not meant to, that he was not that selfish, not like his senior, not ever. Her fall itself happened as slow as grief and as quick as one last flare of pure fear. The last touch of hers Samedi felt was of her nails sliding down his face on either side, deep cuts that wouldn't heal clean but rather scarred deep.*

   *Samedi, Samedi*
   *Why are you the way that you are?*
   *Careful . . .*

***

The day after he appeared behind her house, she was sitting in her kitchen when Samedi again made his presence known at her door, as if it was a suggestion, as if he wasn't sure he should show his face at all. "Lucille, bonsoir."

"Samedi. Salut." His name tasted bitter in Lucille's mouth, like a curse, and not the kind she used to whisper to him when they were all hands inside thighs, finger on pulse, sigh, tremble, laugh, and groan. She had not been able to peel away the sourness coating the inside of her cheeks and her mouth. She felt a lingering disgust towards him for being content to remain somewhere only slightly higher than the lowest level of disappointment and at her self for finding room in her love for him anyway.

She didn't know what else to say, so she said his name again like an abrupt end to a sentence. "Samedi. You're here. " She scratched her nails across the table's grooves and bruises. "Too bad you are catching me on my way out. Dommage."

She placed her hands on the tabletop and pushed outwards and up, preparing to rise. Samedi stood looking as sorry as Lucille thought he was, like he was mulling over all kinds of unsaid words, trying to select the wisest or sweetest, maybe to make her think about staying a while. Knotting her scarf at the nape of her neck in a large bow, she continued past Samedi, out the door, and down the steps, her head still bent forward to secure her headpiece. She didn't look back as she said, "Shut my door as you leave, s'il vous plaît."

Lucille didn't look back to check if Samedi was following her, but she was sure he knew well enough to disappear before she came back. Without turning, she added, "How many times do you need me to walk away before you just stay gone?"

*break open*

*Inside of time, it rained poison in December and snowed icicles like daggers in August. The harvest froze in the ground for so long, people decided it was better to go hungry than to break their fingernails and crack their knuckles against unyielding ground for food that would only cut and cold-burn the roof of the mouth. River waters that once waved and thundered and frothed onto the banks now trickled and dripped and eventually dried, leaving the riverbed cracked and coughing up the last of the naïve fish and plants still holding on for a flood season that was never coming. What had been an abundance of forest green turned brown and grey, gasping for fresh water, what was left of the leaves crackled and rustled against each other until they were kindling, until there was fire, a funeral pyre. Herds of cattle buckled at their knees and fell forward into the dust, lowing and writhing until their flesh was no longer, until they were only bone, until their horned skulls were all there was.*

And outside of time, red grapes spoiled on the vine and bled heavy and sickly onto the ground, and orange blossom over-bloomed and rotted on the branch. The oranges doubled in size and sweetness almost as quickly as mold flowered on their supple skin and took over until they were spongy and too heavy to stay hanging. "Regarde, the entire grove of oranges is rotten. Have you seen something like this before?"

# 19

*outside of time, after the break, on Blue Basin*
*second full moon in a new year, and do you know you are*
*somebody's child?*

Lucille's face pointed firmly far beyond Samedi and towards all the care she had to give to her self and to all the other people who sought her. She knew she should probably see about Ma-Reine. She had not stopped thinking of her since the last time she saw her with that Glory on the Gran Promenade, their arms locked in a way that looked nothing like love, nothing like free and easy. It was pure stubbornness that was keeping Lucille upright, at least until she was out of Samedi's sight. She felt heavy, and she wasn't sure whether she would be able to lift Ma-Reine's hurts and worries off her lap. Lucille's own grief was sitting light but firm around her head like she had walked into cobwebs but couldn't see to take them off. She couldn't do it. Not today.

It was late afternoon, and Lucille was standing in the middle of the Gran Promenade like a signpost, like she didn't know if she was coming or going. She was shifting from foot to foot, clicking her pocketknife by her side, trying to decide where to go, and fast, before Samedi had a fool mind to try to beg his way back into her life.

"I like that scarf, lady. How can I get something like it? The same fabric, but as a shirt with buttons down the front?"

Lucille looked up and into a familiar face, which wasn't saying much in a place where everyone knew each person in passing and intimately at the same time—faces, names, and maybe when and even why they had flown away and landed there.

"It's Elsie. I know you have too many faces to match to names. Ma belle of the birthday ball. I'm not offended." The unevenly perfect teeth, one gold hoop, the other piercing filled with a small piece of twine, the hair straight and slicked down into a low wet ponytail.

"Of course. Elsie. Ça va?" Lucille was taken aback not by her own unusual forgetfulness but by this brazen somebody talking through smiles. This isn't the person she remembered from her birthday all those new moons ago, although there had been a lot to remember and to forget since that night. Lucille gathered her self as bold as she normally was. She rubbed the end of the scarf between her fingers like she was feeling its texture for the first time. "Merci, cherie. I can't let you have it. Maybe you can borrow."

Elsie smiled her sideways way and said, "Borrow. You're a smooth one, lady. Borrow so you'll have to see me again?"

Lucille moved to walk past Elsie, still smiling. "Lady. I have somewhere to be. I live just back there. This isn't even your style, but if you want it so bad, stop by some time and you can have it, d'accord?"

Lucille could have stood there, she and Elsie in a two-person oasis of their own construction—banter, laugh, innuendo, and again. But the awareness of Samedi's desperate self somewhere farther up the road was breathing heavy down her neck. She had to go on. She walked on south towards

Ma-Reine's house, knowing Elsie was watching. She knew her loose pants were hugging her much closer since her appetite had found her again, and she didn't mind if Elsie noticed as well.

Ma-Reine was sitting on the lowest step leading up to her veranda, her body twisted away from the metal gate separating the dusty street from the even dustier land Ma-Reine and Glory called a garden. Her hands were streaked white and blue, and some of the paint had buried itself beneath her nails. Small tins of paint and a red-handled brush with its coarse bristles fraying lay next to her feet.

"Queen of mine. What's this? Who are you trying to out-work when you know everyone else is dozing the afternoon away?" Lucille stepped gently around Ma-Reine's things and sat one step higher.

"Salut, Lucille. Careful now. I've been painting since morning, but there could be some wet spots still." Ma-Reine lifted her arms above her head like she was lifting planks of wood, her muscles locked in the same position for so long that they stiffened and began to ache. She yawned loudly and added, "Glory's round back."

Lucille's lips became a tight line. She saw the greeting for what it was. The anger she felt was concentrated in the fist clenched around her knife in its usual place in her pocket, something she could put to use. "Nye sí. I didn't ask about him. I came to see about you."

"They told me so many lives before this one, my mother's hands were blessed like no one else's. She wasn't the only one in the town painting the walls of her compound in white and ochre, but their designs were childish scribbles next to hers."

Lucille could hear Glory whistling some minor key between the noise of an axe striking a tree trunk.

"Ma-Reine. Mama Aida on your mind? She woke you up early this morning to work?"

As long as she had known her, Lucille was always beyond eager to hear Ma-Reine talk about her mother and all her wisdom. Lucille tried to hide that she was holding her breath. She had to be careful with Ma-Reine. She didn't want to discourage her by being too pushy. She just let her talk. "Other people painted swirling nothings and circles inside circles and slanting lines. My maman brought life to those walls. Each week a new landscape, and all the children would watch and marvel."

She paused and tried to dig flecks of paint from deep in the lines crisscrossing her palms. Glory's whistles grew louder and closer and the cutting-down noises less rhythmic, less like a regular ke-ke-ke beat and more like he was pausing to consider the parts of the rotting tree bark he wanted to strike before hacking into it. Lucille reached for Ma-Reine's shaky right hand and held it between her own. "What would she paint?"

"She painted things you wouldn't even believe. She painted the sun and the moon sitting on top of the earth and the spirits who were serpents wrapping their infinite coils to hold us all together, the spirits of unborn children like little specks of light waiting to take their place among the living. She painted a whole universe on those walls. And she taught me how to do this, too."

Lucille squeezed Ma-Reine's hand tighter, but the gesture seemed to bring her little relief. She still shook as though all of her fear and grief were concentrated into one burning point in her hand. "What happened to her, your maman?"

Ma-Reine went on like she hadn't heard Lucille's question. She was entranced, smothered in a thick haze from her own memory. "She taught me how to do this too, started when I was still too small to understand, to use my hands to bless any surface, wood, canvas, animal hide, clay wall, concrete, the way she had done, and her mother and her mother and all the mothers before had done as well. And now look at me."

Glory cleared his throat like he had dust trapped in one of his windpipes, and Lucille tightened her hold on her friend's hand.

"The day the world turned upside down, she was by her paints and her wall where she felt the most joy. I was standing by her, but I don't remember what she said to me before the wailing and the kicking up clumps of earth and the dragging and the dying. We thought our little spit of land a solid fortress, walled by a raging and protective sea. Until the sea brought us the end of the world."

Lucille held so still she almost forgot to exhale. She was holding onto Ma-Reine's story and onto Ma-Reine herself, for fear that her friend would fall over the edge of her sorrow and back into the gaping unknown of her life before the island. Ma-Reine took her hand back and folded both of them like a prayer.

### break open

inside of time, "Louisiana"—agoo, we greet, Natchitoches, Natchez, Osage, Caddo—1800s
 Can you hear us? Entendez-vous? E mía nkɔ sem a? We are

*called so many names we gave ourselves for all the many lives we have led:*

*In the place where they were, the man in charge was called Tɔgbí de la Cimitière. Tɔgbí, like they called elders and chiefs back when they were still whole and living, back then before they were taken from the selves and began to die, because he ruled over a land full of dying people and things. If he had another name, Ma-Reine only heard dead air when it was called. Tɔgbí de la Cimitière was how she and Mama Aida called him when they were alone and loudly in their minds when they were in his presence. It was their private joke, more tragedy than humor, stolen like hard candy and the chalk for drawing in the night, the only light so liquid it splashed onto their hands like the oil from the lantern. Mama Aida renamed people and things often, pushing aside words in Tɔgbí's language—an ugly something, like a cough gurgling far back in the throat or whistling through your nose—with what she could remember of theirs. She named her Ma-Reine, her queen in those "French" words, a fact both mother and daughter hated but learned to live with because she couldn't remember the meaning in Evegbe, most likely because she was sure they didn't have queens over there where they used to belong, on that land between sea and lagoon. There could be no name for something they did not do.*

*Tɔgbí de la Cimitière. Behind their secret mockery of the way Tɔgbí and his family looked and of the stiff shifting from side to side they called "dancing," they were terrified. Would it be today? And how would it happen? All the hand-shaking and head-nodding and throat-clearing would've taken place inside the room with wood panels like a coffin, and they would not know about their next dying day until one of those other guardians of la Cimitière came to interrupt whatever task was set for the day, to look into their faces—they would rage—to check their teeth—they would bite—to look up and down their bodies with a slimy gaze they could never get off their skin no matter how much they bathed afterwards.*

*Sometimes they would almost forget the terror, like in those months they called "Avril" or "printemps" when it was not too humid and the air lay gentle on their bodies like a lover embracing from behind. And then Tɔgbí de la Cimitière would owe some debt, and one of them would die again, changing hands, to settle it. Total forgetting was not possible, but Mama Aida was always quick to remind Ma-Reine that dying was less painful when you held tight to the parts of you no one could know or buy, the things that brought pleasure and water to the mouth, like the air flirting with the hairs on arms and legs, and the split-second when the sky could not decide between sunshine and moonrise. They may have died, but in their spirits, they were still theirs unto themselves. Ma-Reine was not convinced, but Mama Aida was, and that got her through.*

*Tɔgbí de la Cimitière was a disgrace, she said. Akpe ne Mawu, he was not Ma-Reine's father. Mother and daughter were human while he was an abomination in piglet-pale skin. She would never talk about who Ma-Reine's father actually was, just that he had been an upright person, honorable, one who had not laid down and died quietly. The worst thing about the abomination that was Tɔgbí was his vanity, but it was also the best because he let Mama Aida touch those chalks and paints because she painted his portrait every year on his birthday. Mama Aida was not allowed to sign her name on what she had made, her imagining of his bulbous nose and ears to match, no scribble in a corner of the canvas to say, "I once lived, and still, I do because of this work." So she signed her presence into the pictures in other ways—flowers from back home in the vase next to the disgrace, a white snake coiled around its own body on the hearth in the far left corner of the picture, subtle and in shadow, halfway slithering out of the frame save for its head. The rest of the time, he pretended he did not know she drew during any free moments she could steal and that she had taught Ma-Reine as well. What he could not have known was that they were drawing themselves a way out of that place.*

*"There is a better place. Another sort of life is waiting. We will not break. We will not fall. We will not die." Her words always said less than her pictures could, so she drew the world like she said it looked if you had the view from outside—which she did— blue and green, life begetting life and around the globe of life two snakes wrapped round, holding it all in place. She told Ma-Reine they were impossible and yet there they were still; she told her that they existed because and in spite of the break. She drew the break, the snakes' heads hissing and widening in threat at each other. She drew the specks of the bodies housing the souls that they were, are, and will be falling and falling and then fading into the lower border of the page.*

*Ma-Reine's maman was not born on that wretched land. Like her own mother, Ma-Reine's grand-mère was from the faraway place they could not name. She had only been a baby when they had been taken by the yevú who raided their town, once a sanctuary between waters.*

*"I know she told stories, your grand-mère. Her name was Mama Hadzila, singer of silvery songs, teller of tall tales. She told*

*me the story about the snakes. I cannot tell and sing like she could, but our hands are blessed. They will take us out of here. We will draw it and make it so."*

*Mama Aida swore she could draw their way out of death, well, Ma-Reine's way, because maman didn't live long enough to follow the way she had imagined. But then she remained asleep and never again woke; her breath stopped short in the hollows of her chest, and Ma-Reine knew she could not stay. So she covered her maman's body up to her head with the rough blanket that could scrub your skin raw if you didn't lie stone-still and walked right out. She walked like she knew that the pathways and portals her maman had scratched into the ground led to a place she knew would be there. And she stood on the spot with nothing but her faith in a place where they did not die, and the clothes she wore and her soul unfolded and allowed the wind to carry her away.*

***

By now Lucille had forgotten what she came here to see Ma-Reine about. She had forgotten Glory was standing back there, his shallow breath like a warning, clearly listening and daring them to turn their talk towards him and his ways.

"I knew I had her hands, but I didn't know I could draw and dream my self free until I did. Only for me to end up like this. She would be ashamed."

"Ma-Reine, arrête! She would not be ashamed. You are not responsible for your pain."

"Pain. Sister, you don't know about my pain. See me, here. Like this. With—"

Glory strolled round the corner swinging his axe by his side, and stood over the two women, his shadow rippling over the steps they sat on. He had knocked over one of the tins of paint but didn't even flinch as the white pooled around his feet, destroying all the neat work Ma-Reine had put in since morning.

"Ah, les filles. Welcome to our home, Lucille. I wasn't expecting you. Tu as soif? Can I get you something to drink?"

Lucille placed her hands on her knees and took her time standing up. She looked Glory in the eye, one hand on her hip and the other clicking her knife in her pocket. Her eyes slid from his high forehead, down his torso, to his feet, and back again. "Monsieur, we are not girls and you know that. I'll be going now. Careful with that axe."

Ma-Reine was also standing by now, and Lucille gave her a short hug and kisses on both cheeks and said, "Keep those blessed hands safe and working, baby."

She turned away from the two and made her way home, the whole while her heart turned over and around like a porch chime caught in a monsoon wind, flipping and twisting over itself. She hated to have left Ma-Reine like that on those steps, and she hated even more how she had allowed herself to enter into Glory's foolish display of "I am the man here," like Ma-Reine was a thing to argue over and not a soul twisted into a trap by someone who claimed to harm out of love.

*break open*

*Inside of time, the rubber boat is taking on water, and the bucket next to the window in a small house in Keta is taking on water, and the back room where the children sleep in a shotgun on Dauphine Street is taking on water, and the bloated lungs of the person floating on a mattress across the street from the corner store are taking on water, and all the wide blue and black waters and bays and bayous from Guinée to the Gulf of Mexico are swallowing more and more of the land and you, our beloveds, along with it. The waters are hotter and hotter and swollen with greed and grief and the bodies of those of you we could not save. They are reclaiming whatever they deem theirs, and no ritual or sacrifice or tearful prayer at the shore will stop them from rising until you on the land have to look up at the waves, until you yourselves are submerged, until the land where Keta and Jacmel and New Orleans sit are once again fused together on the seabed like they were before the break.*

And the paint chipped in larger flakes and faster and faster so people woke up with blue in the nests of their hair and dusted blue off their shoulders and picked it out of their mouths. And on the siding and verandas and shutter frames, paint flaking and falling turned into the slowest, not-yet-perceptible drip. One neighbor picked a chip of paint from another's shoulder and looked at it closely: "Didn't we just repaint? Qu'est-ce qu'il y a?"

# 20

*outside of time, after the break, on Blue Basin*
*second full moon in a new year, or you will taste the edge of the*
*blade if you harm the beloved of love and vengeance*

Lucille kissed her teeth and sucked her thumb to try and soothe
the pain of what felt like her hundredth pinprick. Her fingertips
were raw and ruined, dotted with tiny cuts and holes that
looked like the eyelet design she was supposed to be completing
on the fabric spilling over the edge of the table and into her lap.
She was a tiny bird's breath away from ruining the pale pink
fabric with sprinkles of her own blood and decided to set her
work down before she caused even more unnecessary trouble.

She usually wasn't so careless. Most days, she worked with
a rhythm in sync with her own breath—prick, pull, loop, and
again. But she was off because each time she went to loop, she
found her mind sliding around and away from the task at hand,
settling instead on Ma-Reine over there in the shadow of the
Katye's turned back, Ma-Reine with her hands covered with
patches of dried paint and shaking so serious it was a wonder
she had been able to draw anything at all.

Ma-Reine hadn't opened her mouth to ask for help, at least
not in so many words. But for as long as Lucille had cared and
shown Love's Face to people, she knew hopelessness could be
far more powerful than the pull of the earth itself, so you could
be too deep and too far gone from the surface of your life for

anyone to hear you. Lucille also knew people could be prideful, and Ma-Reine was no exception. The dignity Ma-Reine had brought with her from the other side of death was still intact, and Lucille knew better than to step too far into a proud somebody's chaos without being invited in.

Then there was also the ever-present Samedi, like a knot in her back from a rough night's sleep refusing to smooth out. She could spend hours uninterrupted by the memory of him until it was time to deliver a baptism gown for this one's child or take that one's measurements for a Sunday dress.

"Baby, that person is tragic. I haven't seen him so scattered in a long time. Me be ɖe. You been seeing him lately?"

"Daavi, me ɖe kuku, be still so I can get this right."

"Now Lucille baby. You know I usually try to keep my nose squeaky clean, in my own business. But the whole person is derelict; I mean the front of his store looks like someone dumped buckets of sand right on his doorstep."

"Derelict? Lift your arms, s'il te plaît."

"I'm telling you. The last heavy storm must have ripped right through and swept some of the sand inside."

"Your arms."

"And those bottles of his? Knocked right down along with those shelves. Only les esprits know what kind of evil will come from those powers and concoctions mixing up with the dirt and blowing out the door and all over the Afeme. So you said you haven't seen him?"

Lucille had her lips pressed together in half concentration, half irritation. "Come to think of it . . ."

"Oui? You saw him?"

"The weather has been so extreme for this time of year,

non? All this wind doesn't seem to be paying any mind to rhyme, reason, or anything that makes sense."

Everyone seemed to have something to say. Whether they'd seen the gbetɔ or not, they all knew he was in a terrible way, and didn't she just want to see how he was doing? But Lucille would have rather fed her left foot to a shark than to see how Samedi was doing. Her grief and anger had long gone stale and turned into disappointment, mostly towards her self for being too caught up in Samedi to see his trouble coming.

She knew she would go mad if she had to hear one more piece of gossip wearing a mask of concern for her and Samedi. People just wouldn't stop asking what happened. Núkà edzɔ? Even if they could already guess, seeing as there was always something about Samedi. He wasn't so smooth that you could ignore the not-quite-right altogether. You couldn't necessarily trust his medicine to work, but it probably wouldn't kill you. There was just something.

She had other things to think about anyway. Like the uneven edges of Elsie's teeth and how her voice rasped rich and deep like a few glasses of rum after dinner. She was still thinking about Elsie and her strange smile when she heard her name from right behind her in a voice weighed down with contempt.

"Ca va Lucille," more of a statement, an irritating formality to be cleared out of the way quickly, than a question.

She decided to channel all her attention towards the clumps of grass and dirt Glory had dragged into her living room, and how the heels of his clunky work shoes were digging into a corner of her light blue rug, and how he had gotten past two locks and a dropped bolt. Eventually, she forced her eyes from Glory's shoes only long enough to retrieve her knife from the pocket hidden in the pleats of her skirt. "Núkà dím nele le agbe me?"

"Pardon?"

Lucille finally met Glory's empty eyes. "I said, what are you looking for at all in life?"

"I thought you were a dressmaker, not some priest. What are you going to do? Ask me to wear white for a year? Make an offering to the three seas?"

Click, click went Lucille's knife.

"I figure you must be looking for something quite serious for you to come up in here like this, uninvited, so early in the morning."

Glory spat, "Isn't this how you showed up in my place? Just like that?"

"Last I checked, my sister Ma-Reine, that's also her place."

Before Glory could finish grabbing his own earlobe like she was a stubborn child refusing to listen, Lucille clicked her knife again. This time, though, she left the blade out, stepped close to Glory, and brought the cutting side to the tip of his chin. "Do not even try it. You listen to me. Ma-Reine is a whole person with her own mind. So whatever you thought you came in here to do, I'm not about to argue over like she can't fight for herself. E sem a?"

In trying to get free of Lucille, Glory grabbed the blade of the knife. He snatched his hand away and stared his dead stare at the fine line of blood seeping out of the fleshiest part of his palm.

"You think you're so big and bad. I see you running up and down this blue bowl, thinking you can save somebody. Me and my wife don't need saving. Stay away. E sem a?

Click, click went Lucille's knife.

"You wouldn't have come all the way up here if you didn't know you were wrong, if you didn't have something to fear."

Click. Click.

"You're afraid, aren't you? What do you have to be afraid of?"

Glory was gone a long while before Lucille realized she was still standing stone-still with the knife pointing where Glory had been. Then, she crossed into the kitchen and dropped the knife in the sink.

## break open

*inside of time, after the break*
*Somewhere on the road between Central City and Osu, which year, do you know?*

*Can you hear us? Entendez-vous? E mía nkɔ sem a? We are called so many names we gave ourselves for all the many lives we have led:*

*Glory was a young boy in a garden with a dying bird clenched between two still-growing hands that should not have known to hurt this way, but he didn't feel cruel because he would ultimately let the bird go, at least some of the time anyway. He would feel the bird's panicked heart beneath his fingers, and this small thrill turned into a supernova of satisfaction when he felt the heart slow and beat its last. Or, he was looking up into his parents' faces and beginning to understand that his first witnesses, the same people who crowned him with a name like you-are-everything-we-have-and-hold-dear would also be the ones who tried to destroy him with lashes from the ripest and most pliable vines from the same garden; that is, he was his own first witness and his own eventual killer, so he cowered and covered his head and promised to be better so no one would have to try and beat better into him.*

*Or, he was a boy in a concrete schoolyard with metal slides that fried the skin of children's thighs if they dared to climb on at noon, and he was alone in the shade of the neem tree picking up dead, dry pods and digging at the dryer ground around the tree's roots with them, trying to hide from boys who had learnt to turn their fear into shoves and knocks on the head for those who seemed the weakest among them. Or, he was only trying to look like he was hiding because there were now enough dead bird bodies on the street side of the garden wall to confirm his bullies had never tried someone as stubborn and as mean as he had become.*

*Or, he was a young man who closed his face tight and clenched his jaw until the veins stuck where they were, trying as much as he could to distort the image that was the unquestionable resemblance he held to people he could not wait to run away from. Or, he was a young man still, but even angrier and hungrier for ways to fill his emptiness with the shards of other people he had broken. And he was sitting in the glass cube he and all the other bank tellers worked from, feeling the sweet ache of the cracked skin along his knuckles and the scratch on his face just beginning to scab. And he smiled because love was supposed to hurt, and he loved his wife more than he had ever loved anyone, more than the birds or his parents and their heavy hands.*

*Or, he was as slippery as this story and slipping and sliding off the side of the balcony of the house with the garden where he tortured slow, low-flying birds, and he was slippery and slipping and sliding until his body followed the same elegantly tragic loop over the edge and into the waiting garden, and we don't know if this was how he came to find himself hurtling through the air somewhere between the inside and the outside of time. We don't know if crashing into other people the way he crashed into Ma-Reine was a way of breaking his self, whether he thought he would find peace on the other side of the break, whether it was just the exhilaration of seeing how much power a punch could pack, of probing the limits of his own destructive capacity. In fact, we don't know him at all, nor do we know why he became the way that he is, does anyone? Do you?*

*** 

The clock told her it was still early, so she had plenty of time left to restore her space to what it was before Glory disturbed her. She took the rug and shook it out as much as she could over the side of her balcony before hanging it on the railing. She made her way around the room, erasing any signs of him having been there. She lit the white candles standing like guards on the table next to her front door on the left side. Then she splashed a full bucket of blessed water and vinegar across the floorboards and pushed a mop into every corner she could reach, even those that were nowhere near where Glory had stood. She started on her sewing table and had managed to arrange every spool of thread according to their colors before she could no longer ignore the pain pulsing behind her left eye to a point where she felt it might fall out and roll across the floor if she wasn't careful. She sat down at her kitchen table to rest a while.

Lucille woke up with the imprint of the rough kitchen table pressed into the right side of her cheek. The light in the room gave nothing away about the time of day because the sky was an impenetrable grey, heavy, cloudless, a slab of granite covering the sun like a lid. Glory's visit had unsettled Lucille's spirit, but only slightly. She was low tide; she was the sure stillness of a field of new grass on a day without wind. Her spirit, muscles, and bones were all unified in silent but unshakeable conviction. She felt more deeply what she had already known: Glory was dangerous, even though Ma-Reine still hadn't said anything directly to her. Lucille also knew she would be ready whenever Ma-Reine was.

Lucille didn't admit to her self she was heading in the direction of the place where Elsie and the other metalworkers were usually to be found, even though she had been sure to wrap her head in the scarf she was wearing the last time she saw Elsie. It was just a short walk, and maybe she would catch a glimpse of Gentilly. She was only walking on the bayou side path to that place, the path people walked if they needed herbs for dinner, or some flowers for a dye, or just to enjoy the shade of the trees. She was just looking for a quiet stroll to listen to nothing else but her own mind.

The sika gbede had built their workshops where the mangroves behind the Afeme turned into the slow-moving, moss-covered bayou so they could work in peace and without being a nuisance or causing harm to anyone else. Lucille could remember how children would burn themselves catching the sparks flying from the forges, most of them wearing scars as proof of their boundless and sometimes dangerous play. It wasn't until one child was burnt so badly the skin all the way down one side of their left arm had scaled over and toughened that the metalworkers decided to move elsewhere before anyone could tell them to.

Lucille felt the heat from the gbede's scattered fires and

heard the scraping of metal against metal before she saw the six wooden shops leaning against each other.

"Bonsoir les gars. Is Elsie around?

One of the gbede set down the nugget of gold he was polishing with a stained rag. "Ah mamzelle Lucille. Bienvenue. She usually doesn't come around 'til it gets dark. Should be soon. You want to wait? Si vous voulez."

She looked around and wondered where she could even sit. Except for the dark room at the end of the row, the workshops had sparks sputtering and shooting out of their front doors onto scattered metal scraps, sculptures missing parts of their bodies, and iron sheets rusting and returning to the same color as the earth.

"You came looking for me, lady?" Elsie walked from behind Lucille and stopped slightly ahead of her. She looked back at Lucille and grinned. "On y va? This way."

Elsie was in all white, her clothes hanging boxy and away from her body. As they bent to enter her workshop, Lucille asked, "All white for work?"

Lucille watched as Elsie tried to force the warped wooden shutters open. "I don't know why I bother with these. The seawater soaks in and makes them useless." She turned to Lucille. "I left home not meaning to end up here, but I think my spirit knew better."

With the window finally open but still squeaking in complaint, Elsie moved around trying to clear a surface for Lucille. The room was a nest filled with roughly cut pieces of gold and glass in all sorts of shapes. Most of the space was taken up by a table in the middle, covered with glass blown into small bowls, whisky tumblers, ashtrays, and coiled shapes that didn't seem to serve any other purpose beyond decorating or cluttering up space. Lucille saw that regardless of shape, each piece was shot through with bright colors: amber, purple, the sort of blue you could only see where the three waters meet. She tilted her head from side to side, transfixed because the colors seemed fluid, then not, depending on the angle from which she looked. "These are something. How did you do it? You're doing spells back here, n'est-ce pas?"

"This is where I keep the essence of all my victims when I'm finished with them. Souvenirs. Tu vois?"

Their laughter struck Elsie's creations like metal on metal. Lucille took the scarf off her head, wrapped it around her shoulders, and settled in to watch Elsie work.

"So this is really liquid sand? Ma kpo da. Show me."

"Let me get you something to drink first? I was raised right."

"Just some water, lady."

Elsie reached for a shelf an inch or three too high for her slight self and brought down two squat glasses with what looked like silver swirling in their bases. "All I have is rum."

She poured from a bottle rounded like a full belly and stopped just as Lucille said, "Ça suffit. I don't need all that fire in my throat."

Lucille dragged two of the room's mismatched chairs up to the same side of the table and pushed them together so that when they finally sat, their knees touched. "You can't tell me you aren't working magic back here. I'm still waiting for you to explain."

"Not before you explain what you want here. Aren't you still with . . ."

Lucille looked at their hands lined up next to their glasses, her left to Elsie's right, their fingertips lingering near a full touch. She picked up her near-empty glass and drained it, then did the same with Elsie's, smiling behind the rim. "Would I be here if I was? Does it matter anyway?"

Elsie held Lucille's hand and the glass and brought them both down to the table. "How would I know? So what is it? I'm not in any trouble. I don't need saving."

Lucille felt the childish flutter between her ribs turn into a thick, burning feeling. It travelled up through her chest, her neck, her face, and to her scalp, burning the roots of her hair. "What do you mean? Is that what you think I do?"

Elsie went on like she hadn't heard the budding annoyance in Lucille's voice. "I'm not trying to disrespect you, lady. I'm just surprised to see you down here. Let's start again. You just wanted to spend some time?"

"Would I be here if I didn't?"

*break open*

*Inside of time, you are somebody's child, sore to your own touch and existing in variously sized fragments of your self because of the man who used his ego like a sledgehammer to the marble of your spirit; and the next one who used an ice pick and took his time, callous and careful; and the next one who approached you with a velvet cloth in hand and lied that he would be gentle. Your only witnesses tried to convince you that your shattering was just a set of light scratches or maybe some surface-level cracks at worst and that you were being way too precious and expecting too much from people who promised to love you, and had you considered the amount of stress the one who wielded the hammer was under? Did you know the one with the ice pick never knew his father? And anyway, the one with the velvet cloth could not possibly be manipulative because this would mean it was intentional, and he was never the devious type. You think about whether it will ever be possible to recover all of the pieces you have become and reassemble your self into something like wholeness, and another witness tries to suggest—taflatse—that maybe you might need to spend less time thinking about the past and more about why you keep getting into this kind of trouble.*

And outside of time, someone who woke up to see sunrise in the Katye hills saw the oceans break away from each other enough to see sand and stone between the different blue waters. They decided to go back to bed and start the day over at a more reasonable hour when they would be less likely to see visions that made no sense.

# 21

*outside of time, after the break, on Blue Basin*
*fourth full moon in a new year, or when the ancestor spirits*
*climb on and off altars to eat their offerings*

One of the things Lucille loved the most about Elsie was also the strangest—the way her hands made no sound when she clapped. She clapped often, when she found something funny, the claps a metronome to her laughter's music, or when she was impatient or frustrated, like when Lucille tried to rearrange her workspace into some semblance of order that made no sense to Elsie's meandering ways of thinking and doing things. She clapped when Lucille surprised her with a visit: "I didn't think I'd see you 'til nighttime. Ça va, cherie?" She clapped when Lucille shared her latest beading experiment or the new blue she had dreamed of and turned into a fabric dye, and it sounded more like a dull thump than a brisk snap. Elsie said it was because she spent her whole life passing her hands through fire, and so the skin on her palms no longer behaved like it should. Her quiet hands touched differently than anything Lucille had ever felt, which was the second thing Lucille loved about Elsie. Her hands were always warm, no matter if she had just taken a bath in freezing water, or even if she had not gone near her forge in days. They were also calloused all over, a little like pumice, or like the old rocks on the beach on the Guinea

Coast, perfect for sitting and resting because their surface wasn't too smooth and would keep a grip on one's clothes.

Lucille loved Elsie's infatuation with the tiniest of details in everyday things most people would not even blink at twice, like the point where curled designs connected the handle of a spoon to its bowl. She looked so hard and long at objects like these, trying to determine how she could make them herself. She loved that Elsie was able to remind her to just be. She had grown used to being tugged in every possible direction, so much so that she never felt quite whole, never fully her self, parts of her flung all over the island in the homes and hearts of the people who felt they were so desperately in need of her attention. Lucille also loved the special sort of silence living between the two of them. It reminded her of watching old couples in moments when speech had paused, but with their bodies remaining inclined towards each other, heads leaning close enough to hear all the soft unsaids that didn't require explanation, eyes staring into space in different directions but probably focused on the shared experience of years of contentment and being fully one's self in partnership with someone else. Most of all, in Elsie's presence, Lucille felt her self especially embodied. Through Elsie's gaze and attention, she noticed small details about her self that anyone else might have dismissed as trivial, the lone hair sprouting from a mole on her own left arm or the way water droplets took on the color of her skin for a brief moment before she dried off after a bath.

Lucille and Elsie turned Love's Face quickly and firmly to one another, their bodies, their breath, their senses adjusting to one another's in a way that said "woezɔ" and "come sit" and "your spirit sits well by mine." On nights after her work was done or abandoned in various stages of becoming, Elsie would take the bayou way to Lucille's to curl her body around Lucille asleep, folded nearly in half, knees brought up almost right up to her heart. With Elsie, Lucille did not feel she had to be sparing or even stingy with her self, didn't have to hold back and close to her chest or in a tightened fist behind her back to keep safe from greedy, grasping types of love.

With Elsie, Lucille settled into her self and into love, even more so because her sisters also turned to Elsie with an open-hearted acceptance they never showed for Samedi. Víví was growing a fixation on bells and anything bell-shaped and the sounds they made. She had mentioned it only once when Elsie went to her workshop and forged her a gold candle-snuffer, its head shaped like a bell and the handle with a snake wound along its length; gold bell charms that actually rang when hung on an ankle chain; tiny bells for her ears and on a headband for her hair. Elsie got to work on one of Serena's flutes she had neglected and now sounded like it had a breath caught in its neck when she tried to blow into it. When Elsie was done, it sounded even cleaner and sharper than it had when it was brand new. Víví and Serena had not spoken their thoughts out loud, but they were breathing in deep relief—that Lucille had found someone else who seemed to be handling her complicatedness with the same tenderness they did—and also a little regret that they had been so harsh and hostile to Lucille with Samedi, when what she really needed was for them to hold onto her so she wouldn't break.

As for Elsie, she would tease Lucille any time her sisters left. "Careful, Lu, they might end up choosing me over you!"

Lucille felt settled like a house at night, feeling every stretch and yawn past muscle and into her ribcage, half-sleeping in contentment but still deliciously aware of Elsie moving around in a room where the only light leaked around the sides of the door to the kitchen where Elsie was fixing a late-night drink for the two of them, noticing too the blanket or skirt or pair of trousers folded over unevenly and clinging to the arm of a chair, temporarily cast aside to be washed and put way in the morning.

One of their still mornings started late, around eleven, with Lucille and Elsie sitting as always on the same side of a table, this time on Elsie's back porch. The table was glass smeared with paint and circular stains left from the bottoms of glasses. Through the transparent surface, Lucille could see her right thigh snug against Elsie's left, both bare because they had woken up naked and had only dressed enough to cover their upper bodies. It didn't matter much anyway; their only witnesses were the mangroves and the fast-flying birds speeding between land and water like darts of red and blue.

Lucille's morning voice was a secret blues sung from deep. "No work is getting done around here this morning, n'est-ce pas? It's already so late."

"What work?" Elsie rubbed the tough skin on her left thumb against the sensitive space on the inside of Lucille's right wrist. She felt the silver ring Elsie had made, each ridge catching and waking her veins, bringing them closer to the top layer of skin with yearning and expectation.

"Let's even forget about the jobs people are waiting for you to finish: jars for jam, a set of champagne flutes for a birthday, a sculpture of dancing feet for a birth celebration." Lucille reached over and picked a few flakes of light blue paint that had fallen from the veranda ceiling and onto Elsie's cheek and showed them to her on the tip of her pointer finger. "And look at this, your sky is falling. You want evil to come straight to your doorstep?"

"I don't think I have to worry about evil. Wicked already lives here." Elsie lifted Lucille's hand to her lips and brushed her lips across the back of it. Lucille felt her smile against her skin. She wanted to ask Elsie if she had ever seen two old people who had loved each other a long time sitting in their own private silence in the presence of other people or to point out one of the shy and secretive red birds showing unusual boldness by landing on the peeling white metal rail fencing off the house and the garden from the rest of the land. But there was the stillness and the warm and wet of Elsie's lips moving against her hand. She wanted to speak, but Elsie was now using one of her soundless hands to wander over and between Lucille's thighs. Elsie pressed one finger, then another, inwards and deep, over and again, and Lucille felt her like hot water ebbing and pooling in the space around her hips on the inside. She felt full. And there was the stillness and the hot and hunger of Elsie's mouth where Lucille's jaw turned into her neck. Through the glass, Lucille could see Elsie's hand now lying still on her thigh.

Then, back through the screen door they went, stepping carefully around Elsie's half-done glass and clay works that were standing around patiently waiting their turn for their creator's attention. By then it was noon, but after a few hours, they might as well have been beyond minutes and hours and days of the week, lying outside of time with the quiet and crave of their need for each other. They were side by side in silence, each one's skin sticking for a moment to the other's when they shifted on the bed close enough to touch. Lucille turned on her side and watched the afternoon lights dancing through the window and onto Elsie's collarbone, down her chest, and along each rib, retracing the same path Lucille had just followed with her hands and her mouth. She kept on watching as the sunlight played in her lover's ears and along her cheekbones, pausing for a moment on the peaks of her upper lip. The point of her chin did not derail the beam of light as it wound its way down her face and collected in the hollow of her shoulder.

"Something missing? The way you're searching my face . . . I stole something from you?"

Lucille touched her forefinger to the vein in Elsie's forehead, then the tip of her nose, then her lower lip. The urge to fuss, to test the limits of the stillness, felt urgent and pushed against the backs of Lucille's teeth. "I'm just trying to understand how you, so exquisite, are able to live in such mess."

Elsie grabbed the wrist of the hand Lucille had been dancing across her face. "Mamzelle. What did I tell you? I'm not someone you can fix."

Lucille wrestled away from Elsie's tightening grip and cradled her arms to her chest like she was nursing a wound still stinging to the touch. Even though she knew her intention had been to provoke and that Elsie was only responding in kind, the taste in Lucille's mouth soured. Her soul, previously stretching out inside her body like she was just waking from heavy dreamless sleep on a full stomach, now shrank into a corner, somewhere in the back of her head, mean and bitter because Elsie kept poking at the soreness of all the weight

Lucille had been carrying for everyone else. Who did Elsie even think she was? She had no idea about Lucille, or at least not enough of an idea to be hurling judgment at her feet like flowers wilted dry.

Before Lucille could get all the way up and out of the rumpled bed, Elsie put her arm around her waist.

"Elsie. You're not about to lecture me this afternoon. Me ɖe kuku na wo. I don't care what you think you know. I don't want to hear it. Not now."

Elsie's arm slid away in less time than it took to blink or to kiss teeth before Lucille felt Elsie shift to sitting, her legs enclosing Lucille's from behind, the same arm wrapped tighter and farther around so that her palm was open and warm against Lucille's belly button.

"I'm not judging you, ma chère. I just wonder when it gets too heavy?"

*break open*

*Can you hear us? Entendez-vous? E mia nkɔ sem a? We are called so many names we gave ourselves for all the many lives we have led:*

*The spirit who was, is, and will be love and vengeance, who we also know as Lucille, Lu-chérie, would like at times to step down from the altars built in her honor, out of the shrines that can sometimes feel like traps, and into the place of delight and desire where she is worshipped with only pleasure—and no one's salvation—as the motive.*

\*\*\*

Lucille didn't try too hard to hide that her defenses had vanished, leaving only the contentment she wanted to feel if Elsie would just stop talking and let them lay back down.

"Lu-Lu. Chérie? Don't be mad."

"Do you want to go somewhere tonight?"

"Ce soir? You want to go outside? To do what?"

Lucille laughed and leaned back into her love. "Why? Scared of the dark?"

"There's very little that scares me, if you must know. I just don't enjoy this time of year. Akpe."

*break open*

*tutu. fermé. closed.*
*Sometimes we choose silence.*

There was no slippery irony in Elsie's voice, no teasing slant to her lips, no sight of those teeth, but Lucille felt a prickling that she could not resist, her pride shaken, even if Elsie had been right about the weight she was carrying. She was reminded of Samedi's face snapping shut anytime she tried to pry into the life he had lived outside of time and decided to retreat before Elsie did the same.

"Just wondering, mon Elle." Then, as pride dissolved into shame, "Elle, that was unnecessary. I didn't mean it. I'm sorry."

She watched Elsie's face flicker like trying to light a match outside on a day in November, like she was trying to decide between anger and understanding.

"Lu. All I want to do is to show you Love's Face, carefully. Can you do the same for me? Me ɖe kuku."

It was either All Saints' Day or Fête des Ancêtres, depending on who you asked, a time at once sacred and wicked, again depending on who you asked. For some, the only special thing about this time was that it was when the cold haze settled in place of the usual hot, damp blanket usually covering Blue Basin. Some believed in different spirits or didn't believe at all. After all, if something celestial was really keeping watch, would they have died and died and died before ending up here on the strength of their own wings and dreams? It was a time to be still and listen, keeping watch for signs the several-times-dead had left to be remembered by. Underneath a favorite tree, sitting at the foot of the bed, at the roadside, feet in sand just washed over by high tide, waiting for that sound, that smell, that feeling that would say, "I didn't die. We didn't break. I am with you."

So they got dressed in each other's clothes and laughed all the while but did not speak until they forgot or put their disagreements away enough to share in each other's pleasure. Lucille adjusted an old and now ill-fitting skirt on Elsie's hips so it could sit in as flattering a way as possible, and Elsie wrapped a purple tie around Lucille's neck and made sure her hat sat on Lucille's head at the correct angle over the left eye. "On y va?"

"I'm trying to play the part." Lucille held out a white-gloved hand and hooked Elsie's arm through her own. She stiffened and tried to keep her hips centered rather swaying slow half-circles. She raised her shoulders up high by her ears and tried to turn her chest concave as far as it would go. "How am I doing?"

"That's what you think I look like?" Elsie laughed so wide, so long, and with her whole body, and she had to rearrange Lucille's scarf around her shoulders pushed back and proud.

Now trying to mimic Lucille, she swung her arms much too far back and forth like she was trying to stretch a tight muscle and rolled her body as if through a hoop.

"Cherie, I'm sorry. You don't have enough of what you need for all you're trying to do."

All Elsie was able to catch was the tail of her dress shirt Lucille had left hanging behind her.

"Well, Lu, what's our first stop?"

Spending all day indoors meant they had missed all the real work of honor and remembering. They couldn't see from where they were in the Paroisse, but the tombstones up in the Katye were most probably gleaming a grey so stark they appeared white, all clods of dirt kicked up by footfalls of visitors—still grieving and at peace—the weeds forcing their way into any empty space their roots could find to settle in the breaking marble now cleared away and added to the pile of fallen leaves for burning.

Lucille and Elsie joined the ritual wandering from house to house, the passing greetings back, forth, and again, sipping a little aliha brewed special for the day, declining an offer for a little something off the grill, usually guinea fowl, promising they would be back for the crawfish boil next weekend, taking some boiled sweets for the road—yes, even if you were grown—hugging and kissing right side then left, clapping a little at and with those entranced, overcome by spirits who had chosen them.

Their stroll brought them finally to a quieter part of the Paroisse, where every set of front and back doors had been flung open so you could see straight through to the backyard, leaving a clear path for any spirits to pass through unhindered, their way lit with tea lights, kerosene lamps, blessed white candles, any light that could be shone. At the first house, Lucille and Elsie exchanged kisses, once, twice, and again, and looked for empty seats in the circle of people sitting in the front yard, their feet stretched towards a low, slow-burning fire in the center. Then, the sound of metal striking stone, the tip of a walking cane against the pebbles and seashells buried in the path leading up to the house.

"Ah, who's there? Baron Cimitière, is that you roaming around?"

Laughter tumbled like dominoes around the circle. There were few spirits who would inspire fear on Blue Basin, if any at all, and in any case, the guardian spirits had more important matters to occupy themselves than to appear embodied at such a gathering, on this night of all nights. The closer the figure came, the more details Lucille thought she recognized, the hat tilted on one side, the suit jacket very much the worse for wear, the white shirt with buttons mismatched, the stiff angles of the shoulders.

"Bonsoir à tous et à toutes. Evening, Elsie."

The firewood crackled and shot sparks into the air, and someone got up to calm it.

"Lu, this is . . . she's also a sika gbede. Like me."

With her building worry dying down, Lucille stretched out her hand. "Enchanté." Lucille shook hands with the person she initially believed to be Samedi, as she felt the sika gbede's mottled skin. "What's this? Still healing?"

This newcomer snatched her scarred hand away from

Lucille, adjusting her hat with it and gripping her cane with the other and spat, "This warms my heart, Elsie. Vraiment."

"That knot metal knocking about in your chest, is it a heart?" Elsie's response was sour with accusation.

Trying to place a soothing arm around Elsie was useless; all Lucille caught were the tassels at the end of the scarf Elsie had borrowed. Elsie was standing close to the stranger, half-gone in the shadow beneath the rim of the woman's hat.

"I'm not the heartless one here. Have you told your new mamzelle Lucille about what you flew away from? Mamzelle, this woman is not who you think she is."

The circle of people had melded with the night. They had walked away in twos and threes, some laughing, some holding on to slippery glasses, all trying not to turn what they thought was a lovers' fight into more of a spectacle than it had to be, not on this night of reverence and opening ways for the spirits to pass through.

Lucille pulled Elsie by the edge of the scarf: "Baby. Let's go. We still have so many people to visit. It's enough. On y va. Please, Elle."

*break open*

*Inside of time, you poured your self some water that smelled like gasoline. You decided to go to bed without drinking it, and when your thirst woke you up before your alarm or the rooster in next door's yard could, you saw solid oil settling at the bottom of the glass. You went to bathe but changed your mind as soon as you saw the same oil coating the inside of the tub. You went about your day rubbing your hands across the skin on your forearms and the back of your neck, trying to remember when you first started sweating petrol. Everything was laced with it; the coffee you bought on the way to work; the holy water in a bowl at the door of your grandmother's church; the communion wine you, the unbaptized, were not allowed to drink; the cheap beer you downed on Friday nights that found you anywhere but home because it was easier to breathe at the outdoor neighborhood bar than in your room; the milk for the baby; even the medicine that was supposed to restore the balance between water and oil inside your body. Everything.*

And outside of time, someone was startled out of their sleep because they dreamt they were buried in sand. The next time they woke up, it was because they felt like the bed had become a raft sinking fast in the middle of the sea. In the morning, they rubbed grit and dried salt between their fingertips, maybe from the window left open next to the bed, maybe.

## 22

*outside of time, after the break, on Blue Basin*
*fifth full moon in a new year, maybe try seeing your self clearly*
*before you try to look outward*

They didn't rise from bed until the third time the sound of shattering glass reached them from somewhere at the back of the house.

Lucille got to the veranda before Elsie did, eager to leave the discomfort of their blooming argument behind and not caring what new fiasco was waiting with the noise.

"What made you think you could do something like that?"

Before Lucille could answer her, Ma-Reine brought the brick she held above her head with shaking arms down on Elsie's glass table. This fourth time, the table gave way.

"Sister—"

Ma-Reine would not hear it. "Today, I am not your sister. Entendez? Answer me, who do you think you are to do something like that? Do you know, the skin at the place where you sliced my Glory's hand open has turned all kinds of colors it shouldn't be?"

"Ma-Reine. What are you talking about?"

"I'm talking about you and all the nerve you had to touch my Glory with that rusty knife you carry around. He didn't tell me anything about it, le pauvre, until weeks passed, and I noticed it was festering, and even then I had to ask before he told me you were to blame."

"Your Glory? Le pauvre? Ecoute-moi bien. Did you think about why he didn't tell you at first? You think it's because he cares about you or our friendship? You don't think it's because he was ashamed, because he has been walking round playing god, like he can't hurt the way he has hurt—" Lucille stopped before she could let out the sort of spite that would be impossible to swallow. She had already gone farther than far.

Through a deep breath that sounded like it came from a shrinking spirit, Lucille began again. "Ma-Reine. This isn't even my place. You can't come down here tearing up Elsie's things when she did nothing to you and your Glory. It's not right."

Lucille looked back towards Elsie who was leaning against the frame on the inside of the screen door, as calm and complacent as a vine content to grow and twist around the same tree trunk for the rest of its days. It could have been the door's netting warping the expression on Elsie's face, casting shadows and drawing a smirk where there wasn't one, but Lucille was sure she could feel the smugness, and it made her temper boil past its rim and over the sides.

"Today you don't understand the meaning of not right. I see you, sister, and I know you see me. But you will not destroy me and my life and then tell me it's for my own good. E sem a?" Ma-Reine's turned back did not grow smaller the farther it moved away from Lucille and Elsie's shattered table. She was a stone wall to the cracked glass of Lucille's self-righteous care.

Lucille sat down on the step closest to the ground from the veranda and planted her heels in the broken glass until they bled.

Elsie came and cleaned the fine cuts with soap and water and Lucille never spoke, even trying to hide her flinching away from the sting of the warm salted water that followed. Elsie swept away the shards before laying down the broom and the piece of failed glass sculpture about as wide and as deep as two cupped hands she used as her dustpan. Then she laid her head in Lucille's lap. Or tried to, but Lucille twitched and flinched and would not let her, then she stood up. Elsie got up too, and Lucille rested her head in the curve between Elsie's neck and shoulder.

The night brought with it an unbearable weight. Lucille felt small and suspended in it like the prelude to a scream trapped in the throat of someone frightened. Because she believed down to the roots of her self that she was only to soothe, to heal, and to protect those who needed it, she understood she could not force healing onto Ma-Reine. And what was healing to her if she did not feel she was in danger? Lucille's mind and her spirit were rotating obsessively around this rejection, and she did not, or chose not to, hear Elsie pleading with her to at least make sure her shoes were on properly before trying to walk home on cut-up feet.

She took the bayou way home and stepped over and around the snakes slithering backwards, side to side, all kinds of ways except forward. She kept walking as if she didn't hear the usually nocturnal birds, wailing and desperate in the daytime. She carried her self homeward on feet she could no longer feel by the time her back veranda was in sight and did not blink at Gentilly swimming backwards, against the slow-moving but never-dead current, his scales glowing crystal even with no moon shining on them.

How Elsie beat her home she could not tell, but sure as the

three seas met, Elsie was pacing by the back door like someone
determined to collect on a debt long past due.

"Did you run here?"

Elsie didn't answer.

"These stairs are rusted beyond salvation. If you're coming
up, wait for me to climb first, e se a?"

Elsie's anxiety barely made a nick in Lucille's solid self-
protection. So stubborn, she tried to hide each wince from
sensation and pain returning to her feet.

"Lucille. Ma chère—"

"Ecoute-moi. I don't need any more I-told-you-so about
Ma-Reine and Glory right now. Is that not what you came for?"

"Ma chère, your feet. I just don't want whatever is growing
outside in the mud and bush to find its way into your body. Let
me."

*Can you hear us? Entendez-vous? E mía nkɔ sem a?*

*Lucille—the spirit who was, is, and will be love and vengeance is
breaking into pieces at the possibility of going too far to stand in
the break for those she loves.*

"Let me."

Lucille let Elsie lead her to the sofa, let her hold on to one
of her hands while she cleared space on the cushion, piling
fabric scraps, a half-done shirt with no collar or buttons, and
samples of different silks in the opposite corner of the seat, let
Elsie bend her gentle-gentle-gentle into a sitting position.

*Can you hear us? Entendez-vous? E mía nkɔ sem a?*

*Lucille—the spirit who was, is, and will be love and vengeance is
breaking into pieces at the possibility of going too far to stand in
the break for those she loves.*

"Let me."

Lucille watched Elsie moving about the space with a sort of purposeful care like she belonged, stepping over Lucille's work materials and around the side table, the stiff armchair, and the sewing table like she had always lived there; watched her putting water on to boil and pouring a little into a mug with some mint leaves and the rest in a big enamel bowl, chipped and rusting all around its rim, on the table behind her; watched her switching between checking the tea and checking the water for the soak.

*Can you hear us? Entendez-vous? E mía nkɔ sem a? We are called so many names we gave ourselves for all the many lives we have led:*

"Let me."

Lucille let her head drop back as far as she could, let her self feel the pulling between her shoulder blades, let her self lose sight of Elsie's hands below the surface of the water, let her self smell the castor oil and follow in her mind the path of Elsie's un-sounding hands on her calf muscles, on the backs of her knees, on the tops and the insides of her thighs.

*Can you hear us? Entendez-vous? E mía nkɔ sem a?*

*Lucille—the spirit who was, is, and will be love and vengeance is breaking into pieces at the possibility of going too far to stand in the break for those she loves.*

"Let me."

Lucille let her feelings coalesce into thoughts, into the desire to speak words, into the need to be understood. "Why didn't I know you before?"

"People wander over here from the sea or the sky all the time. You really think you can know everyone?"

"Pas du tout. But everyone needs something from me at some point. You never needed anything from me."

*Can you hear us? Entendez-vous? E mía nkɔ sem a?*
*Lucille—the spirit who was, is, and will be love and vengeance is*
*breaking into pieces at the possibility of going too far to stand in*
*the break for those she loves.*

"What do you want me to say? You need to let your self be loved and stop worrying about being needed."

Lucille knew there was not a spiteful razor nor knifepoint in Elsie's words, but she didn't want to hear what would come next. She made to lift her self up and away from Elsie. "It's not like I'm sick. Let me stand."

"Let me."

Thinking twice and a third time about letting Elsie carry on, Lucille lifted one slick foot out of the water and oil mixture, then the other, careful to step on the bare floorboards and not the rug, then walked to the rug's other side slow and careful, so she wouldn't slip.

"What did you fly away from? What are you hiding?"

Elsie wiped her hands down her trouser legs.

"Đo ŋtsi nam. Answer me, Elle."

"Lu-cherie. What did I just say? What do you get from digging so deep into other people's business?"

"You're not other people. I look on you with Love's Face, Elle. That means your business is mine also. What was that woman talking about the night of Fête des Ancêtres?"

"At least sit down so I can tell you. I can't talk with you looking down on me like that."

## *break open*

"Lucille. First, understand that I am not ashamed. No one can tell me about me, about what I had to do when I died, about what I left behind to get here, about why I didn't look back.

"Both my parents were sika gbede in our town. The works of their hands were stunning and so people started to whisper that they were dancing with devils to create it. I didn't blame our neighbors for thinking this way, anyone would after seeing their hands passing through the fire as if it was water, molding metal like it was clay. How on earth could there be a way to explain this?

"When I was old enough, they held my hands inside the flames and all I did was smile at the warmth. Because the heat did not turn into pain, they knew I was ready. It didn't matter that I was a girl; in our town, we did not separate ourselves that way in order to live. Around that time, we started to hear from nearby towns that the devil had clothed his self and his demons in something like human bodies, almost like raw flesh without skin to cover them. People stopping for a rest before continuing to flee inland tried to warn us. Some of our neighbors followed them into the hinterlands, believing even the devil couldn't cut through forest so thick.

"I did not worry, because my parents told me where we were—deep lagoon on one side and sea on the other with rocky cliffs and caverns—meant we could not be taken easily. Earth herself was on our side. Me be ɖe. So even when the devils found us, I did not believe the devil would turn our town into ash, or that I would die while my parents refused to die the way the devil and his men had planned. I refused to believe even after I saw what the devil did to their bodies, even after the same lagoon and sea carried me and so many other soon-to-die people to a place we couldn't begin to make sense of. It didn't matter what I believed anyway. Part of my soul had laid itself flat and rolled itself limp like rope. I left it in all the ash. I wonder what happened to her, that soul, that self.

"I want you to know I do not feel shame. I tried my best to remember that my self was mine alone, what was left of it anyway, even soulless like I felt. I am not ashamed. I was not ashamed when I spent those dying years using my hands for works I had no room to refuse. I was not ashamed when I had to lay down on my back like that, and not when I searched at night for the right roots to brew and drink, and not when I twisted a piece of wire at the right angle to empty out all that was unwanted in the hollow I have inside, whatever I needed to do so that I would not give life to a child I could not love. I was not ashamed when they forced me to let the offspring pass into the world. I was not ashamed when I let it cry out of hunger and fatigue, and a more wrenching cry, the total absence of love and nurture. When someone told me they knew how to fly out of hell and into a pure blue freedom, I did not wait to think or feel, I left the child I could not claim right there on the mat like I left my flattened soul back where I used to belong.

"The person you saw at Fête des Ancêtres was that child. She found her way to Blue Basin on her own, and she hates me for leaving as much as I hated her for surviving. Lucille, I was not ashamed when I left. And I am not ashamed now. You must understand."

"You left the child behind? Your own?"

Lucille thought about Kekeli the unborn, always and never

her own. In her spirit, she was always smoothing the child's hair back and not, feeding the child their favorite soup and not, always and never together.

"That child was not and could never be my own. And I refuse to feel shame."

Lucille's feet had dried in the time it took Elsie to declare her self unashamed. The oil slip had become sticky, and it took some treading like marking time before she could move from where she stood to open the door. "Va yi. I don't know what to say to you right now. Vas y."

Later she would wonder when Elsie actually left. Lucille only closed the door when she noticed the crickets' screeches pouring in along with the dead cold of night air. She ran a bath hot enough to make her feel faint just from the steam, and it did its job before she could even step in. She woke up on the bathroom floor, her still-sticky feet nearly welded to the tiles.

Pride and defiance were like a new dress for Lucille, one she would never admit was often ill-fitting to the point of discomfort because she was convinced it looked perfect as long as she sat or stood up straight and haughty. She *break* the *break* spirit who was *break* love and vengeance, *break* didn't need to let anyone do anything to her. The spirit who was, is, and will be love and vengeance—Lucille—didn't let Samedi happen to her; she didn't let her self avoid the deceit hiding in the few spaces between his too-even smile. She didn't let the idea that would have become Kekeli nestle into her home of a body. She didn't just let things happen to her. The world didn't act on Lucille *break* the spirit who was *break* love and vengeance in ways she did not desire or approve of. She chose to wield her power and offer her care where necessary, no matter the toll on her self. If she was indeed so self-possessed and purposeful, then it didn't make sense that Elsie's confession of abandoning her own offspring inside of time had made Lucille's stomach twist around itself.

### *break open*

*Inside of time, you coughed five beads of blue plastic into your open palm and picked out two more from the corner of your eye. You picked out one more from between your two front teeth and tried to convince your self it was just the vestiges of your lunch stuck in the gap only your loved ones could see when you smiled. Your child ran soft-boned and turn-footed towards you, and you expected another unusual gift, some morsel of chewed-over food or a doll's shoe. But, in the plump, outstretched hand were three more beads, a different blue than yours but with the same shine and shape. You took them from the child and threw them into the container you kept to separate cans from bottles as though it still made a difference and decided to make some tea, chamomile, to chase away some of the despair. After a few minutes of boiling and brewing, you raised the cup to drink, but your eyes were open and you saw two more beads dancing in the golden brown water.*

And outside of time, one lover kept sending the other to the living room to check on what had fallen off a shelf and broken. "There's nothing, ma chère; maybe it's from the next house, from outside somewhere."

# 23

*outside of time, after the break, on Blue Basin*
*fifth full moon in a new year, when Ma-Reine turned land into*
*canvas into portal*

Ma-Reine had covered the entire length of the Gran
Promenade up through the Afeme and the Paroisse, all
the way to the orange grove in the Katye. Lucille hadn't yet
realized because, from her house, she could only see as far as
the Paroisse trees standing close and thick, but she knew it
was Ma-Reine because she could just make her out on hands
and knees, shoulders rounded like a shield above the ground
she was working on. Lucille followed from a short distance,
keeping watch over her friend and making sure she would not
be disturbed.

Very few people were awake early enough to bear witness
to Ma-Reine littering the ground with stars, and if they
were worried, they did not show it beyond a nod in Lucille's
direction before fixing their heads towards the water, intent
on getting to fishing in time for the first clearing of dawn haze.
Lucille and Ma-Reine moved on up the Gran Promenade, like a
noonday sun shadow and the body responsible for it, until they
reached the part of the road bringing itself to a sudden end at
the steepest drop of the Katye's hills. By this time, Ma-Reine's
hands were ashen with chalk dust and sand. "It got harder to do
the higher up I walked."

Lucille crouched next to Ma-Reine, who was finally still, finally exhausted, maybe. "Nye sí. Qu'est-ce-qu'il y a?"

"I ran out of paper at home. Ran out of canvas too. Then I covered the table we don't use for meals, the chairs we don't sit on, the floor, and the walls in every room. The ceilings were too high, so I moved to the veranda and down the stairs. All covered. Then I just kept on. Opening my mind wide. I needed a canvas wide enough to match."

There wasn't much that could surprise Lucille when it came to undoing other people's distress, or so she thought, until she herself had been undone by Elsie's story and now by Ma-Reine. Even with all she had held for Ma-Reine, for the first time, she felt fear spreading like illness slow but determined through her body, from her tingling scalp to the itching soles of her feet. But what she did know was to let Ma-Reine speak freely. "I had to open my mind wide. Draw out something I saw in the sky, an opening, draw out the portals, maybe I could draw Mama Aida through the open break. Maybe I could push him through."

"Nye sí. I am not understanding."

"I didn't live beyond Tɔgbí de la Cimitière, beyond my maman herself, only to endure this. Not here. My lot will not be to endure until time unravels itself when it is tired of running. Especially because we are already eternal." Ma-Reine's voice was an echo, as if she was standing apart from her self and shouting the words through cupped hands.

"It's Glory, isn't it? You will not endure. Your eternity can be as beautiful as what your mind tells your hands to do."

"Several new moons had passed without him hurting me, and it had been so long I thought he had gotten tired and decided to show me Love's Face without it hurting. That's why

I could open my mouth to shout at you to defend 'ma Gloire' that day. Me be ɖe. My hands are filthy so I can't show you well, but..."

Ma-Reine turned her head to the side and opened her mouth, and Lucille looked over her own shoulder and away from this physical evidence of what Glory had done. "You don't have to show me. I already know what he can do."

Trying to swat a slow-moving blue-bottle fly from her face, Ma-Reine left a grey smudge on her cheek. "You wouldn't be able to tell if I hadn't told you, n'est-ce pas? And you know, he said he was sorry, and the aliha was too strong for him to have had on an empty stomach. But he hadn't touched anything all night, not even water. I don't know why this one got to me. You know this isn't the first tooth I've lost. And it's not as if I don't know he hasn't meant his sorry for a long time."

"What do you need from me, Ma-Reine? Núkà dím ne le?"

Ma-Reine opened her mouth and again and shifted her jaw left and right. She looked like she had a thought she ultimately decided to swallow.

Ma-Reine walked to the path's abrupt end and looked down the steep sheet of rock falling into the ravine. "I don't remember the last time I walked up here. I almost forgot this open space was hiding up here."

"On y va? Let's get you cleaned up cherie. Serena and Víví are not far. They won't mind having you at all. E se a? As long as you need."

***

The next morning, by the time Glory had set down his net, taken off his hat, and shifted the pipe from one corner of his mouth to the other, Lucille had gotten up from her perch on a beached canoe. "Morning Gloire. Comment tu vas?"

She didn't look at his face, her gaze turned down instead to pick out any splinters from the canoe's long-dead wood from her clothes. "Are you not behind? It's late to be coming out here looking for fish, isn't it?

Finally looking up, Lucille watched Glory turning his pipe over and over in his hands. "That's beautiful. Ma-Reine carved it for you?"

Glory's unyielding eyes did not unsettle Lucille. She was standing in Ma-Reine's stead, standing in the break that Ma-Reine was trying to mend in her self, standing in the break for all the people who had needed to borrow some of the fire of love and vengeance when theirs dimmed into embers. Extending her hand, she did not look away when she asked, "Ma kpɔ da. May I?"

Ma-Reine had carved an entire landscape in miniature into the pipe, something so vast for so narrow an object. A snake coiled around the neck of the pipe, each scale etched into the wood in perfectly symmetrical diamonds, and its mouth opened up around the pipe's bowl.

"Nye sí has blessed hands indeed."

"Mamzelle. I know you didn't come here to talk about Ma-Reine and her blessed hands."

Lucille kept on turning and turning the pipe in her left hand and rubbing it with the thumb of her right hand. "I mean, the snake is moving through grass, through vines. She even added the leaves."

She slipped the pipe next to the knife in her pocket.

"What is your problem? Núkà? You don't have enough of

your own mess? What happened to your baby? And Samedi? Or who is your latest person?"

Lucille adjusted her trousers, her thumbs between her skin and the waistband. She felt once more for the things in her pocket. These were the tired knockabout trousers that sat down to sew, climbed into canoes, and lay in the grass, and she needed to be sure nothing would fall through any holes there might be. She brushed her hands over her wrapped head towards the knot of the scarf at the back of her head, even though it wasn't possible for any strands of hair to escape the wrap. She saw to her self like she would with her reflection in the mirror in the morning, as if Glory and his insults didn't exist.

"Donne-moi. Give it back and stop playing with me."

She went on as if not even the air had stirred, as if he hadn't spoken, as if she was not facing the force behind Ma-Reine's breaks.

"Girl, I'm not playing with you."

Lucille turned away as Glory's threats became a steady whine.

"Just give me my pipe. Why can't you just leave me and Ma-Reine alone?"

Beach pebbles and shells crunched beneath Lucille's sandals, and on a less urgent day, she would have made each footfall gentler in case she found anything precious enough to collect and keep. Her steps were so loud, they blocked out Glory's complaints: "This is—arrète—I don't have time—I'm here fishing—how will your so-called sister—stop this—me ɗe kuku."

Still, she went on, her arms swinging only when they hit

her body, a strolling pace. "An odd time to fish, non? You never answered me."

Lucille led them farther away from the part of the beach where they had started, far from the point where you could look one way and see the flat-roofed houses huddled together against spray and wind, and the other way, the Caribbean Sea waves shifting and winking in the light, at once witness and accomplice. She stopped short at the point Glory did not know Ma-Reine had shown her, raising a hand without turning because she knew Glory would stop too.

"You know you will not lay a hand on me. I know you won't. It's not that I'm stronger than my sister. But you cannot smash my spirit the way you have tried to do hers."

The air was not plentiful where they were, and Lucille could hear Glory gasping for what little he could get.

"What at all do you want, Lucille? For me to say I'm sorry?"

"Are you?" Lucille looked down at the top of Glory's head, the part of his hair that was the most sunburnt red-gold. He was bent over and heaving, his shirt sticking to his perspiring body all down the back of it. She walked around him.

"I said, are you? How will I know? What will you do to show my sister your sorry? Your sorry will not close her breaks."

*Can you hear us? Entendez-vous? E mía nkɔ sem a?*

*Lucille—the spirit who was, is, and will be love and vengeance is breaking into pieces at the possibility of going too far to stand in the break for those she loves. The spirit that is love or vengeance does not give or take life. She is only supposed to ignite unquenchable fire in the hands of the yet-to-be-unbroken so they can save themselves.*

"So, are you?"

*Can you hear us? Entendez-vous? E mía nkɔ sem a?*

*Lucille—the spirit who was, is, and will be love and vengeance is breaking into pieces at the possibility of going too far to stand in the break for those she loves. The spirit that is love and vengeance does not give or take life. She is only supposed to ignite unquenchable fire in the hands of the yet-to-be-unbroken so they can save themselves.*

"Are you sorry?"

Glory set his self upright and looked at Lucille. She saw the way his eyes blocked out the light and knew he was not. The part of Lucille that was more love and another chance and less vengeance and break-what-broke-you wanted him to try to at least speak his own way to redemption.

*Can you hear us? Entendez-vous? E mía nkɔ sem a?*

*Lucille—the spirit who was, is, and will be love and vengeance is breaking into pieces at the possibility of going too far to stand in the break for those she loves. The spirit that is love or vengeance does not give or take life. She is only supposed to ignite unquenchable fire in the hands of the yet-to-be-unbroken so they can save themselves. She cares first and solely about the relief and redemption of the yet-to-be-unbroken.*

"What kind of somebody are you?"

Now Lucille and Glory had changed places, with his back to the open air, absolutely nothing behind and below the shelf of rock they stood on.

"Who are you to question me like this? Give me back my pipe and let me be on my way."

"What kind of somebody is not sorry for giving cruelty

where Love's Face should have been? What kind of person takes pleasure in spitting in Love's Face?"

"Donne-moi and stop this foolishness. Foolish . . ."

Before Glory could reach for Lucille, she had reached for him and pushed him off the edge of the rock. Lucille had not intended to kill him, just to send him into a limbo from where he could do no harm to Ma-Reine for a while. When she pushed him, he didn't fall but rather retreated into the air, the sky's wide blue mouth swallowing his screams. She found a crack as thin as a hair between the seabed-turned-land and the sky and shoved Glory and his cruelty through, where he would be neither inside nor outside of time. He was suspended and flying, a waning morning star with no destination imminent, indefinitely somewhere between dying and living anew for a few eternities and whatever lies beyond, between the inside and outside of time, for as long as it would take for Ma-Reine's life to cease to feel like endurance, for her to actually start living, for him to actually be sorry.

Lucille did not look back. She already knew where she had left Glory and knew he would not be able to find his way out without her help. She returned on the same route they had walked and kept on past his abandoned fishing things. She tossed the pipe into the tangled net and continued homeward.

The children were the only ones on Blue Basin to see the figure suspended up above in open blue space. It was not a Friday or a Sunday or any other holy day set aside for worship and for turning inward to meditate on the quiet divine speaking from within one's self. This meant the children had the entire day to fill with play and to explore the infinite dimensions of their wonder at the world. They took out their kites to amuse themselves with the birds' confusion at these playthings that looked so much like family, at least until they flew close enough to see the empty, glassy eyes and the beaks glued on a little off-center. They were in the Katye hills, better to launch their kites skyward and for the wind to keep their creations buoyed and soaring, and all the warnings of "Don't go climbing too high! Fire should not tempt you" already out both ears and lost to the ether.

"Kpɔ da! What's that?"

"Tswwww stop wasting time."

"I'm not. Look there! À gauche!"

"Is it not someone trying to land?"

"Maybe? But that's not how they look."

"Who told you there's a way they look? I remember it and I'm telling you—"

"We need a grown person. You don't know anything."

They were too busy to recognize that it was Glory, and not glory, glory hallelujah or glooo-ryyy like elders would cackle while telling each other stories not meant for childish ears. Even if they had seen that it was Glory, they would not have known what to do. There were few grown people they feared and tried to avoid more than Glory, not even Miss Yvonne, who made you feel sleepy or hopeless if you lingered too long by her veranda and she looked you in the eye, not even Friday's Child with his always downcast flaming eyes because he carved them all kinds of marvels out of wood for them to play with, not even Samedi who made "medicine" that tasted worse than sickness and made them sicker still. And so it was days before anyone started to look for who or what might have been flying over the hills. Not because the children were not believed but because they eventually abandoned their kites and the weak wind refusing to hold them up. They did not run home to tell the grown people what they had seen, chasing instead some more fun and laughs, forgetting they had ever seen a body that was not a bird nor a newly arriving, free-flying soul like they had become used to.

Then, a few evenings afterwards, the youngest in the group slipped the discovery into bathtime conversation between giggles.

"Baby, you said? You saw what?"

"There was someone up there with the kites. Someone flying!"

"Flying... chou-chou! You heard the baby? There's another person out there!" The parents did not waste time on lecturing the child about their blue island, about freedom dreams, about their responsibility to each other. Instead, they joined the people in the Katye and started searching amongst the hills and down the ribbon-narrow paths between their houses, hoping whoever it was had landed close by. They told the people in the Paroisse who told the people in the Afeme that everyone needed to take extra care until this person was found with body and soul intact. They searched all day for days on end, after even the sun and the moon had grown weary of helping them search for someone all the heavenly bodies and elements knew was not there. They would know; they were always the first to know.

When someone asked, "Lucille, you heard someone took off and never landed?" she did not respond right away, kissing her teeth and frowning deeper.

"Blue Basin people are always up here telling stories." But

there was no air in her laugh when she nudged the conversation away and pointed out the sort of fabric best suited for the desired dress.

Most people on the island cared far more deeply for Ma-Reine than they did about her husband, even though they kept her at the very end of a long stretched arm because of him, and because of this, they did not realize Glory was missing and would not have noticed anything had gone even more wrong in their household if Ma-Reine hadn't kept showering the island with little white stars.

She covered the turned backs of the houses and all rocks with broad enough faces to draw on. She covered the outer trees of the orange grove and then as far into the thick of it as she could go. They did not think she had lost her self, because they knew life came out of her fingertips when she touched them to some chalk or some paint. They did not even mind when she drew on their gates, their front and back steps, the low walls dividing one garden from the next, on the seats and the backs of the chairs that had been left outside for neighbors dropping in. They left her glasses of water, lemonade, and bissap—all iced—plates of tidbits, plantain chips, and roasted peanuts, and refilled them until she moved on.

By the time Lucille found Ma-Reine again, she was drawing on her self, up her legs and thighs and onto her stomach, and had just started on the right arm. "How will you do the left?"

"I told you I ran out of room."

"Cherie, I thought we were finished with this."

"Where's Glory?"

"Egɔme de? Why are you asking me this, sister? Why now?"

"It's been a few days and I haven't seen my Glory. This place is too small for him to dare slip into another somebody's bed."

"You said you did not want living your life to mean endurance."

"And you thought you would help me to live?"

"Ma-Reine, I look on you with Love's Face, and—"

"So to you, Love's Face means deciding for your sister? You asked me what I wanted, did you let me tell you? Your protection can turn dangerous. I fear you."

"Will you listen? I took care of things for now. But it is not for good. I did not kill him. No one dies here at the hands of another, Ma-Reine; you know that."

If she knew or even heard what Lucille had said, Ma-Reine acted like she had not and collected her chalks, leaving Lucille standing amidst her stars—white, then yellow and blue when the first color ran out.

# 24

*outside of time, after the break, on Blue Basin*

*when does the moon rise and how do we count when time is
bending onto itself? Or, when the spirit who was Lucille began
to fracture and Blue Basin tested the limits of its own
possibility*

I *break* Lucille *break* the spirit *break* of *break* love and vengeance *break*
*I am standing in the break*
*I've been standing in the break so long*
*I've been standing in the break so long I have become the break
spirit, mind, and body disunified*
    Lucille knocked at her own door, ke-ke-ke, right on the
crack in the glass, and she looked through the break to see her
own self standing there. She had been standing in the break on
behalf of other people for so long and had now gone further
than she ever had to protect Ma-Reine; she found her self with
spirit, mind, and body in disunity. Her spirit split and found
its way out of the body—Love out of her left ear, Vengeance
out of her right. Love was a bloody-eyed woman with a head
tie and wrapper sewn out of black fabric with red stars stamped
on. Vengeance had a righteous air, pristine, the only signal of
the danger she posed being her fingernails sharpened to lethal
points, attached to smooth hands resting in her lap.

Lucille was at her door, on both the outside and inside of the threshold, looking out at the trees behind her own head and looking in at the furniture behind her own head. She was at the door, and she was sitting at her sewing machine spinning the wheel, watching it with boredom lying flat in her eyes until the wheel slowed. She spun it again. She was at the door inside and outside and at the sewing machine, three Lucilles, until Love and Vengeance got fed up with waiting for her-them, for one of her selves to recover from their scattered state and speak out loud.

"This chair is not for sitting, is it?" Vengeance gathered her black silk dress in two fistfuls and stood up to open the door for the outside Lucille before guiding her and the inside Lucille to the sofa. Lucille at the sewing machine also rose from her seat and came and sat at the feet of her self and her self. She put her arm around her self, and she put her hand on her own head, and she put her hand on her own knee.

Love sighed and went to stand by Vengeance. "Will one of you look at me? You've been turning my face to people left and right. Look here."

Vengeance added, "You mean you are here and here and here and outside of time and inside this house and you couldn't think this far? What did you really think was going to happen? Look here!"

"I pushed Glory over the edge of a cliff. I thought this is what Ma-Reine would want. I thought it would make her safe, finally."

Three Lucille faces turned to the Love and Vengeance who were part of their essence, and countless spirits of the yet-to-be-unbroken pressed from inside of her head, jostling for space to see out of her eyes.

The Lucille who had pushed Glory spoke again, "I really thought I was doing what was right, what I've always done inside and outside of time, protecting the yet-to-be-unbroken from all kinds of dangers. But I think I have gone too far this time. I thought Ma-Reine could use some more Vengeance, but now I don't know."

\*\*\*

Lucille was on the brink of time, neither inside nor outside of it. She was red-eyed and mourning a flattened home, she was brandishing fire and kerosene, she was taking back her self, she was in endless pursuit of connection. She was not obliterated in Samedi's arms, she was always and forever grieving her would've-been dawn-child, she was holding her self too tightly to make room for Elsie and her trouble, she was here, and here, and here. What Lucille had done to Glory was not the first time that standing in the break, that showing Love's Face, that avenging another's hurts had meant vanishing someone else. But it was the first time she had done this from here, from the safety of Blue Basin, only for Ma-Reine to turn out more broken than before. Isn't this what she wanted? This was completely new, even for this spirit with a body wide enough to be astride the universe. Threatening or attempting to take another person's life was unheard of on Blue Basin. The people living there chose free, chose life, chose death for themselves, on their own terms, and in trying to get Ma-Reine away from Glory's heavy hands, she might have done the unthinkable. The world had been broken apart for thousands of moons, a century and some days more. The pieces lay in the hot hands of a no-longer-grieving woman with red eyes, a woman who was everywhere and nowhere at once, a body standing on her feet outside of time so she could position her self within the break, the spirit who was, is, and will be love and vengeance, the spirit who was Lucille. The universe was always breaking open.

***

While Lucille struggled with her fraying spirit, *break* the spirit *break* saltwater and sound *break* Serena was at home tending to her instruments, as yet unaware that Blue Basin itself was in crisis. Serena was focused on the rag she was using to clean her flute, a task requiring her undivided attention to make sure her touch was firm enough to polish but not to the point of damaging her instrument, so she didn't realize her pursed lips produced dead air instead of a whistle and no sound was coming from her mouth at all, until she went to call out to the children playing too rough on a lethal-looking mound of rocks. Ðevíwo! Attention! Watch yourselves out there! When the children continued to push and climb and jump, Serena *break* saltwater *break* sound *break* shouted again, this time with less indulgence honeying her voice. The children stopped, but only for a breath, and wondered why Tatie Serena was yawning so big in their direction before they turned back to their game. When she went to test the flute after she was done cleaning, she realized she had fallen mute. She blew and blew with nothing to show for it, but it was only when she looked out the window and saw the ocean's waves receding far past their natural line and returning too close for safety to her house that she knew all was not well.

Víví *break* the spirit *break* sweetness and luxury *break* had grown bored of her hairstyle again. If she was honest with her self, the real problem was not boredom, nor was it her ever-wavering tastes in hair dye, dress necklines, people; it was that the bleach had fried her short cut to within an inch of what used to be her healthy scalp. Through narrowed eyes, she concentrated on cutting one forlorn curl after another, working through the ruin carefully but with determined speed. She stood before her mirror self, running her hands over the new and as-yet-undamaged growth, and it wasn't until she bent to sweep up the snipped strands that she noticed her reflection did not bend with her. Víví on the mirror side blinked seconds after the fleshly self; the fleshly Víví raised her hand to her head and then out towards the glass several moments before her reflection did the same. Knowing what had happened the last time her mirror self shadowed rather than copied her, she turned away from her lagging image for a moment, for as long as it took for the mirror Víví to do the same. She opened the door to Serena's first knock and said, "My selves are out of step again, sister. And you? Ça va? Et Lucille?"

But Serena could not talk back or explain that the moon had risen and set three times on her way over. She stepped into the house and went to hold Víví's hand, but the mirror beside the door showed only Serena's reflection grasping at empty air.

On Blue Basin, there was a frightful clamor, worse than a storm gathering and breaking the sky above and the earth beneath it into an unrecognizable scramble. It was sound, color, smell, sensation, and taste colliding with each other continuously until they fell apart like burnt husks. Blue Basin's people experienced their world at its ultimate and all at once. The presence of those who had chosen to pass in body alone was so strong it hurt to be awake and conscious: shouts of "hey,

hey, hey" cheering someone on the dancefloor, honeysuckle scent, cool water running through the parts of carefully braided hair, unending knocking on a door ke-ke-ke-ke-ke, a fresh stick of incense, how it sounds when warm slippers shuffle on dusty clay tiles. Sans-Souci swore she heard someone calling her *Afi-gā, Afi-gā, Afi-gā*, desperation lining every word like a song's beat. There was only one person who knew her by that name from two lifetimes ago. Afi-ví?

Serena and Víví tried with all the power their spirit selves possessed to get to Lucille's house, to check on their neighbors on their way, but every time they stepped outside, it was like the force of the island's crisis would not allow them to set one foot in front of the other. They tried for days that felt like hours, and hours that felt like days. Sometimes, they made it as far as the Gran Promenade only to take one more step and realize they were back in front of Víví's mirrors or even farther, on Serena's back steps. Once, they had only closed Víví's front door when they found themselves floating on a raft in one of the Gulfs, the wood disintegrating as fast as the wind could eat it. Another time, they left Víví's house in daylight and arrived at Lucille's door in deadly night, only to find there was only a blank blue wall where the door and its glass pane and knob should have been. Yet again, they tried to reach their sister, but when they reached her door, it sounded like she was screaming and crying and laughing at the same time, and she wouldn't come to the door no matter how loud Víví called for her. "Sister, please, we don't have time for this. I can hear you in there. Serena, let me—your knocks make no sound anyway." They needed Lucille because all three of them had made Blue

Basin possible, and all three of them, together, had to make sure it could remain intact.

And the air was black and blue and black and blue, black where the wings of people trying to pass from inside of time to the outside swooped back and forth, and blue when the sky showed itself a few seconds at a time.

All over the island, the people asked, "Has anybody seen Lucille and her sisters?"

"I saw the sisters, but Vívi looked like she was fading, ghostlike, and Serena refused to speak."

"What are we going to do with so many of our people landing? Where are they?"

"What will happen to us? Did we come all the way here only to die another time?"

It was a day when stepping outdoors was like trying to stand up inside of a kaleidoscope and walk in a straight line. The lights and colors were edible, and the sound tasted like unsweetened lemonade without ice. There was no smell, no sea-salt, no fish, no ripening fruit bursting in the heat, no wilting leaves. One neighbor told the next: we couldn't sleep in this house because it was hard to even draw one clear breath, like someone planted honeysuckle inside the walls and decided to set the flowers on fire.

Time bent back on itself in a way that wasn't frightening at first because they were already used to living outside of time as they used to know it. Yesterday and tomorrow became impossible to distinguish from each other. They woke up to twilight and laid their heads down with the noon sun shining high. Dawn lasted for days at a time, so they were always balancing on the edge of night and day no matter how many times they closed their unrested eyes. Below the water's surface, away from the eyes of anyone on Blue Basin, all the fish feeding on seaweed and on each other were temporarily startled when the three seas began splitting from each other, inching steady-steady away from the point where love and vengeance had drawn them together.

*break open*

*Can you hear us? Entendez-vous? E mía nkɔ sem a? Inside of time, our beloveds are witnesses and targets for all kinds of cruelties, and our fear that the horror will bleed onto this land outside of time, this Blue Basin, might come to pass. Inside of time, somebody's loved one dozed off and awakened to the smell of vinegar, in a house somewhere in Takoradi, or in Salvador de Bahia, or maybe it was Baton Rouge. Wherever this loved one was, it was their first sleep in weeks, and still guilt gnawed at their stomach because the missing somebody wasn't coming back. It didn't matter how hard they had scrubbed the clay tiles in the kitchen or that the homemade cleaning solution was so potent it could burn the print of fingertips. The missing somebody was gone, never again to track mud or beach sand onto the newly spotless floor. A mother in Chorkor, or maybe a boyfriend in Port of Spain, had sliced the after-dinner oranges into a flawless set of six wedges, knowing full well their beloved would not rise from the mortuary to come and eat. Can you hear us? Listen closely: we are trying to tell you that so many of our beloveds simply did not make it home one night, or they made it to the front door only to be sent into eternity with two shots in the back, or they never got out of bed the next morning because that wicked world inside of time requires our beloveds to die over and over in order for it to continue turning, to feed their greed. Can you hear us? We are saying we do not evoke the names of our dead beloveds carelessly, nor do we remind those of us who survived of the gruesome ways they died. We say instead that even one of our beloveds would have been too precious to lose, and there will never be enough time, enough wreaths, enough foil-covered plates at the reception or the repass to reignite the light we are losing each time the world the sly dogs made takes one of our own from us.*

\*\*\*

"Et les sœurs?"

"Are they hiding under their beds?"

"Where could they be at a time like this?"

"Did you knock?"

"No, I tried to summon them out of thin air."

"What kind of question is that? What is doing you?"

Blue showered the tops of their heads and their shoulders; blue came off on their hands and their clothing if they brushed against the walls in passing. No problem, there was always paint, there were always brushes, and as long as they had their health, new blues would lick over the flaws. No problem. Only when the flakes of blue turned into clumps and then turned into liquid did they begin to panic. The blue flowed down the walls like waterfalls and then like rapids, like the blue was trying to find its way back to the sea.

The bottles they relied on to trap evil in its tracks broke right on the branches they hung on, and the people found the shards scattered around the roots of the trees. The strings of jewelry around their wrists, waists, and ankles tore in place and the beads got caught under their fingernails and burrowed into their skin as they tried to sleep. Their clothes frayed like a string from the hem had caught on a jagged nail, pulling and pulling. The stars and spirals and arrows Ma-Reine had drawn on the walls, on the roofs, on the ground itself were all washed away when the moon's light turned liquid and fell like cold rain.

*break open*

*Can you hear us? Entendez-vous? E mía nkɔ sem a? Inside of time, our beloveds are witnesses and targets for all kinds of cruelties, and our fear that the horror will bleed onto this land outside of time might come to pass. Inside of time, in a sea called "Mediterranean," it stormed so long and so hard and heavy that you, the beloveds, could no longer tell the difference between the slick sides of your canoe and the floor of it filling slow and steady. You, the passengers, the beloveds, having left behind lives and family in Dansoman and in Mermoz Deuxième Porte, still believed you would not sink because you had no other option but to float, even if your vessel and your own bodies eventually betrayed you. You, beloveds, rowed on because backwards was no longer a reality available to you, all that remained were sights you wished to forget of all the Sahara sand under your tongues, inside your noses, in your eyes, sand as far as you could perceive and all the dangers it hid, and the memory of a home holding nothing but endless yearning and failure and hunger and the disappointment and the pain of relatives going hungry another night because there were no coins or hope to be had. You, beloveds, could not entertain*

*the thought of what-if-we-don't-reach, but down in your deep-*
*deep, you wondered who would tell your mothers and brothers*
*and fathers where they found your bodies.*

***

Et les sœurs? No one has seen them? Still? This is no time for
them to vanish. But it's not like we haven't seen these things
before. No, we haven't. Not like this. Pas du tout.

Friday's Child sat on the stoop of Miss Yvonne's house
with his wood sculptures scattered in pieces on his lap. Having
finished the roof, complete with wooden white herons sitting
at every peak and gable, he had started carving figures for Miss
Yvonne to display indoors whenever she was settled. Núkà
edzɔ? Qu'est-ce qu'il y a, Vendredi? What's happening? What
have you done? He didn't lift his head or so much as sniff to
acknowledge his anxious audience. He cast his eyes—especially
reddened on this day—on the haughty face he had carved out
of rosewood, the narrowed gaze and pursed lips now detached
from the body and the legs and miniature drums and pots
for carrying all asunder. He did not blink when these pieces
continued to disintegrate until they became sawdust. He
scooped the dust in fistfuls and stared like he could still see the
whole entities they had been. The neighbors backed away, just
like Friday's Child's neighbors had done when he still lived as
Efo Nkudzẽ on that land called Keta, inside of time.

They thought the Gran Promenade had turned to liquid
until those whose houses lined the road went outside to look
closer. What had looked like liquid silver was actually hundreds
of snakes slithering backwards. They moved in perfect concert,
one unified serpentine mass stretching from the Katye to the

Gulf of Mexico coast as if conducted by some unseen force willing them to act against their own volition. Gentilly the ivory alligator waddled tail-first out of the bayou, moving in reverse until he reached the Gran Promenade now turned lake of silver.

"Et Lucille? She needs to help us face whatever this is."

"Someone should send for Samedi; he should know."

"Me ɖe kuku. Don't you mean Elsie? You can't see past your nose on this island eh?"

"No because I keep it out of other people's business and inside my own house, cherie."

***

*break open*

*Can you hear us? Entendez-vous? E mia nkɔ sem a?*

*The spirit who was, is, and will be love and vengeance would like at times to step down from the altars built in her honor, to remove her self from the curves of the ears and the heat of the fists of the yet-to-be-unbroken and the ungovernable, to stop being the first to arrive on the scene of other people's disasters. An altar is a pedestal that can easily be toppled; a shrine is a sacred prison is a trap. The human-divinity who is Lucille desires admiration without negating her self. She wants to be cared for with no hidden caveats, to be made Love to, to make Love with, to be shown Love's Face without the condition that she secure her Loved one's salvation first. She has stood in the break so long, she has become the break. She can no longer sustain this way nor does she wish to.*

# 25

*in the break between the inside and the outside of time, when
Lucille must learn the limits of her own power*

*when does the moon rise, and how do we count when time is
fraying until its unrecognizable?*

Lucille, Love and Vengeance, and all her other selves pressing
in to look out at the world through her eyes, still scattered,
continued to struggle against the righteous and necessary
power they wielded for the protection of the yet-to-be-
unbroken, the souls trying to step from within time to without,
beyond the break and into an eternal free.

"Too known. Too much. Too full of your own power."

"Too dangerous. Too enamored of your own power, you
might get lost inside of it, you might crave it just for its own
sake, you might supply the poison and watch it fester, just so
you can then present your self as the remedy."

"How will you gather your self?"

"How will you turn my face to your self and to other people
without destroying your self and those people, and so you will
not fall through the break?"

Love continued, "Do you know you don't have to stand in
the break on your own?"

"But who else? I am capable."

Love and Vengeance continued in unison, "Just because

you are capable does not mean you should continue. You, a divine-humanity, are not anybody's martyr. You have done well to stop the break in the world from widening, but you couldn't possibly believe you were the only one. You have fortified your beloveds inside and outside of time; you have borne witness to their freeing of self and spirit; you have been helper, comforter, oracle, but you need them just as much as you are needed. Even Mawu-Lisa needed help, remember?"

The Lucilles who were there inside the house on the big blue bowl had heard the sharp knocks on her door, heard the glass groaning and near shattering, much like Lucille herself. She heard the chorus of life and those who had already lived; she heard Víví's wailing rage high in pitch like a bell out of tune; she heard Serena, barely, as if she was trying to form her words around a ball of wool stuck in her mouth. She did not hear Elsie though she hoped she would. She heard a rustling of leaves but did not see Gentilly coming backwards out of the bayou and past her house; she heard surging water but did not see that it was the blue running off the walls of her house and all the rest of the houses; she heard waking birds singing at night as time on the island splintered and re-ordered in whatever way it chose to do. She was well aware she was needed, but for the moment, she had to be at peace with being a disappointment, a mighty task, as used to embodying rescue and salvation for the people as she had become. This time, she would not have eight days to grieve and repair her self like the time she spent reckoning with her child dying before they could ever be born. She did not have the luxury of undisturbed days with which to reconcile her self with Love, Vengeance, and all the other shards of spirit-self still recovering from the aftershocks of power gone awry, power she had wielded in a way that may have caused damage far beyond any noble intention she believed she had. She needed to remember what it meant to stand in the break without becoming of it and breaking her self apart.

The impulse to feel the ground and the water at the three places she had shifted seas to join together was as forceful as the power in her hands the day she and her sisters had brought Blue Basin to be, out of a break. Needing to test the point where the work of her hands met the love and the undying will of the yet-to-be-unbroken, she waited for the cover of a night that looked like it would not lift before leaving home. She didn't notice until she was at the bottom of the stairs from her front door that Serena and Víví were there waiting, moving in and out of gloom as the trees waved back and forth and again across the moon, blocking then spilling its light.

Serena reached out both hands to Lucille to fold her into her self, her voice lapsing between a crackle, then a whisper, then nothing, then whispering again. "Sister, you didn't pull this land above water alone; you don't have to break under the weight alone. Me ḍe kuku."

Víví continued, as thought they were in duet. "Lucille, do you disappear because you think you need to shrink and bend your self—your selves—to stand in the break? We tried and tried to reach you. Where did you go?"

Lucille wrapped her arms around her flesh self.

"I didn't choose to vanish. I was stuck inside the break, stuck between the inside and the outside of time, neither here nor there, neither void nor whole. Inside of time, the suffering is so much that it is spilling over here on the outside. We brought this land together in the beginning. We know how to keep it so."

They walked first to the Katye, relying on memory and each other's steps rather than lantern light to guide their path so they would not be seen. With her sisters on either side of her, Lucille was holding out at arms' length the confusion and disappointment everyone was surely feeling towards what they thought was her abandonment of them in their worst time. They walked to the point where the Gulfs of Guinea and Mexico and the Caribbean flowed into each other, and Lucille dove in, right at the seam of the waters, pulling them taut together where they had separated. She did not see Glory up in the air.

Love and Vengeance said: *An altar is a pedestal that can easily be toppled.*

Serena who was saltwater and sound and Víví who was sweetness and luxury said: *Let us stand in the break with you.*

Then they took the bayou way to the Afeme so the vine-heavy trees would shield her in case the darkness lifted. It took all the conviction she had to refuse the guilt scratching at her heels, the strangeness of not making her self immediately and totally available to whoever needed her, and right now, the entire island needed her something desperate. Her final stop was the point where the Gulf of Mexico flowed into the Gulf of Guinea. And there was Glory, up in the sky, where Lucille had left him, distant like a star that died before it got to live but present still, stuck floating for the moment. Weeping by now, she thought about Kekeli and the child they could have been. The child was the only being whose existence absolutely relied on hers, and yet Lucille had been treating everyone she encountered, even the grown ones, Ma-Reine included, like they were helpless children only she could rescue, like they would perish without her strength, like they had not been holding themselves up and together with their own will all along.

Love and Vengeance said: *An altar is a pedestal that can be easily toppled.*

It was dawn in the Afeme while the rest of the island remained in nighttime. Serena and Víví left Lucille near the sika gbede workshop and told her they would be at home waiting for her.

*Remember, you are not standing in the break alone. You are not broken.*

She came up to the doorway of the sika gbede workshop and stood there a few breaths watching Elsie's turned back. "If someone wanted to come and steal, by now you would have nothing left."

"I don't have time for this. You see the state of this place?"

Lucille entered the room fully and drew up a seat at the worktable. "Should I keep talking to your back?"

Elsie turned and threw the scraps of metal in her hands to the floor. "What? What can I do for you madame? You're here to finish your judgment, isn't it?"

"Elle . . . madame? I'm madame now?"

"I don't have your time today. Don't you have more important things to do around here? You saw what it looks like outside?" She stopped and swallowed air. "Why are your clothes wet?"

Before Lucille could answer, Elsie held out her hands openpalmed. "I felt heat for the first time in this life and the one before. I felt the heat and burnt my self."

"Ma kpɔ da. Let me?"

Lucille took hold of Elsie's wrists and brought the reddened palms close to her face. "Mon Elle à moi. I can't even imagine this pain. I'm sorry. I'm so sorry, baby. Let me?"

At first, she felt Elsie's body stiffen when Lucille pulled her close and rested her face against Elsie's navel. Her voice was a gentle muffle. "I want to be able to show you Love's Face without negating my self, without tying your problems around my neck to the point where I am both carrier and judge."

Elsie separated Lucille's arms from her waist. "What do you mean? I never ever asked you to do that. I told you I don't need rescue or guidance. Are you sure you can respect this?"

"I want to try. But I need to tell you about the break I have been standing in."

"Eh? Egɔme ɖe? What's the break?"

"Do you look on me with Love's Face?"

"Why ask this now? Qu'est-ce qu'il y a?"

"The break through which this land came to be. The break, the reason this place is necessary at all. Do you know the story about the spirits who were serpents and how they broke the world?"

"Oui, I know it. But this is not the time for riddles and tall tales. Say what you need to say, baby."

"So we all flew here to this land, n'est-ce pas? Except I didn't. I am why and how the land exists. Moi et mes sœurs, we pulled this land out from under the sea; we pulled the three seas together."

"And then?"

"And then? Are you listening? I am saying I had to put my

body inside the break. I am the spirit with the grandest stance. I had to stand in the break so you all would not fall through."

Elsie sat down hard on the tabletop, and Lucille looked up into her face for what felt like three and a half forevers. "That we are here is such a miracle; nothing you say could shock me. I understand. And I'm telling you that you don't have to be someone's salvation all the time. Definitely not mine anyway."

"I know. And I'm saying I stood in the break so long, I nearly broke my self, and it was terrifying. E se egɔme a?"

"I'm not worried about that. But are you sure you're not killing the divine in you?"

"Mon Elle à moi. You are my divine, my sublime. I want to turn Love's Face to you the way I know how and the way you need. I know I am not standing and do not have to stand in the break alone."

# 26

*outside of time, as Blue Basin repairs itself even as it continues
to break
when does the moon rise and how do we count when time is un-
making and making itself before our eyes?*

Serena could make the harp growl and the guitar sing, and she
felt it might be possible once more, on this day after many days
of no distinction between dawn and evening, all this time of
Blue Basin reeling as though it had been turned onto its brim
and rocked more and more off balance with no sight nor sound
of the sister spirit that was Lucille. Serena, the spirit who was,
is, and will be saltwater and sound, opened her mouth and let
laughter flood over the edge of her lower lip, down her chest,
onto her lap, and then to the ground. There was no one in
the house to hear, and she might not have been sure she was
hearing her self had she not also felt her laugh echoing from the
back of her throat to the floor of her stomach.

   Víví, sweetness herself, was the kind of woman whose
perfume turned corners before she did, subtle but tempting
enough that unsuspecting bystanders would be overcome by
the urge to set eyes on the wearer of this scent and would want
nothing more than to smell the fragrance up close, and not just
in the air, but rather from behind her ear or from the inside of
her wrist. She indulged full in the sight of her self but had been
terrified to look her mirror self in the eye since the world, or at

least this land, had threatened to break open once more, while the sister spirit who was Lucille was nowhere to be found. She had covered her many mirrors in white, turning those too small to be hidden with cloth towards the wall, a sort of prelude to mourning. But when she reached a point where self-reflection felt less risky, she decided to look. She lifted the sheet on the largest mirror, the one that sat on the floor because it was too heavy and too wide to hang, but only halfway, so she could only see from her bare feet to her waist. She stepped side to side, swaying left, right, and left again, and filled with delight and relief to see her image do the same.

All over Blue Basin, the presence of those who had chosen to pass in body alone but remained in sound, color, smell, sensation, and taste had long since turned from excruciating back to comfort. It had been a haunting, until a pause, like the air itself, and all the heavens had heaved an enormous breath in and exhaled serenity. The presence of les morts, les ancêtres, said, *Hear that? I am the cheers pushing you to the center of the dancefloor. I am slippered feet shuffling on clay tiles towards a beloved waiting in bed.* They said, *Feel that? I am cold water soaking away the dirt on your scalp.* They said, *Smell that? I am orange blossom, lemongrass, fresh bread, rain-soaked soil, sweat-salted skin.*

The noon sun shone at the time they most needed and expected to see it, exactly at noon, and dawn came and went like the blink of red light that it often felt like, and they were no longer always on the edge of day. Light became light again, intangible, and not like water raining from the sky. The red flowed back into the hibiscus flowers like a wound healing at miraculous speed, as did the blue tattooing the fingertips and faces of the people on the island. The walls of the houses shone blue like they had been painted for the very first time, though some chips and flaws remained if you put your face close enough to see. Their fraying clothes joined back together at their seams, as if Lucille herself had taken her needle and thread to them. Gentilly turned away from the Gran Promenade and slid long-nose-first back into the bayou. The shards of broken bottles meant to trap the same evil that had threatened them reassembled and became whole once more.

Outside Miss Yvonne's, the sawdust and broken bits of Friday's Child's sculptures returned to their deft shapes. He did not know, and neither did Miss Yvonne, that she was the spirit of the child who had been Enam, who had been the second baby Friday's Child never knew he had, the daughter of Odessa who had once been his Sena. He could not know that his incessant instinct to mend her home with his woodwork was an offering to the child his soul was too destroyed to care for back there inside of time. What he knew was that the thought of showing his work to Miss Yvonne made his heart grow so big it felt like it was pressing against the inside of his chest for more room and relief, that he wanted nothing more than to sit and sip tea with her on her new veranda, built with his own two hands, while she looked at what he had done for her.

Sans-Souci sat cross-legged on a ledge of rock shaped like an obstinate lip jutting out over the water. This was the only place she felt she could go to put her self back into her own body, away from the horror of this haven outside of time threatening to fall in on itself. And if it did fall, she was ready to fall with it, having felt for the first time since her flight the kind of unmooring that had been life inside of time. At least the baby was safe with Antoinette, perhaps better off without a mother who was trying to reach back one hand into a world where she could not fully return in pursuit of a sister she was sure was no more.

"Mama?" Sans-Souci did not turn towards the sound coming from below, knowing she was alone and was most likely hearing the echoes of other lost spirits caught somewhere between the inside and the outside. "Mama Yevúbolotɔ?"

Now, bracing herself against the rock, she leaned over and down. She was looking into the face of her small me, her Afi-ví, who was shifting from one leg to the other like she did when they had gotten in trouble as children. Sans-Souci's, who was once Afi-gã's, tears flowed without pause or breath, coursing down her face and blurring her sight to imprecision so she was still half sure this child before her was the delusion of eternal longing and not her actual little sister.

"No, I'm not her. Afi-ví, it's me, your big me. How did you find me?"

*break open*

*Can you hear us? Entendez-vous? E mía nkɔ sem a? We are saying that our beloveds inside of time are drinking and bathing poison in their water; coughing ash onto the blue and white flowers on their pristine Sunday evening plates; picking scrap metal from between their teeth from the waste dumped in their backyards; folding themselves down as small as possible without disappearing altogether, too young to die but almost too tired to keep living. The air between the inside and outside of time is thick with flapping wings and smooth brown legs and free dreams and*

*desperation. And still, the way is open, not just for horror, but also for ecstasy. And so, Blue Basin will repair and remain,*
    *because somewhere inside of time,*
*along the tracks halfway between home and work, two friends pick out each other's faces from a crowd moving like one tired and begrudging body, at times gasping, at times heaving. The friends smile so wide, their smiles beat them to their destinations*
    *because somewhere inside of time,*
*a girl runs into the night's open mouth but she is not eaten. Rather, on the other side of her flight is a place she can fashion a new sort of self. She is the sort of soul who makes the universe bow down in reverence when she dances. Two plump feet belie something like a cosmic event. She is too wide, a sky forced inside too small a house, so even when the other women scream and smash and knock the prison walls down, she runs completely away from the rubble and from the direction the rest of them are going*
    *because somewhere inside of time,*
*there is no love in the world he has ever felt like the baby's new hands, not yet practiced and still learning how to grasp, trying to cling to the collar of his shirt. Those hands, nails so soft he fears they will bend and fall out of their beds. This little life, breath still like syrup and not as yet embittered by life*
    *because somewhere inside of time,*
*a person from "New Orleans" and a person from "Queens, New York" and a person from "Blanchisseuse, Trinidad" amuse themselves listening to the way they talk, reveling in the ways words like incandescent and lieutenant sound coming out of their various mouths. Each convinced the other two to sound more like they're singing rather than speaking, they laugh to temper the yearning they feel from not having known each other sooner*

*because somewhere inside of time,*
*there has never been a little girl in the world so loving and as*
*loved as the one being held on a Monday in May of 1993 in a*
*photo studio somewhere in "Texas," with her mother's lips painted*
*an ochre the child will try to find and emulate when she is grown.*
*The child is held, and it is still 1993, but a Saturday in August,*
*on the veranda of her great-grandmother's house in Dzelukɔfe.*
*The child is held, and the vines and leaves hanging behind the*
*great-grandmother's head reached down to hold them both*
*because somewhere inside of time,*
*someone is sitting on the still-damp grass—it had rained early*
*in the morning while they loved each other through and past*
*dawn—content with life and not bothered with the green surely*
*spreading across the back of her white dress. She lays down on her*
*back and presents an open mouth, one accustomed to laughter and*
*much-too-much of life and everything it contained, to the heavens.*
*If she narrows her eyes, she can still catch sight of her love reaching*
*down into one of the little pools of water to take the bottles of*
*punch they had left to cool. Some twigs tuck themselves into the*
*springs of hair as if for bed, and she does not take them out*
*because somewhere inside of time,*
*there is a house with a low roof, roofing sheets one storm away*
*from sliding right off. A house full of women who have been*
*giving birth to each other's children for generations—niece's*
*hands at the end of daughter's arms; auntie's eyes inside great-*
*grandmother's face; granite in mother's voice coming out of sister's*
*mouth; sister-cousins arguing over whose baby face is fading*
*from that one photograph on the wall. In this house next to an*
*ever-sinking beach, they tend to each other's wounds and sing*
*loud to the impossible beyond of each other's triumphs. Needing*

*no father—they had waited once but he never came—they mother themselves and each other, topping up the last few coins for medicine or new church shoes, or violin lessons, watching an infant so the elders could attend a wake, turning Love's Face to one another constantly and with the utmost care*

*because somewhere inside of time,*
*a lost child craving connection with dead mothers finds the right formation to draw on the ground to open up the way, and the spirit of fire that burnt down plantations and prisons spread deadly and liquid like kerosene through the hearts of the same people who will burn courthouses and precincts and every chalk-colored, wide-pillared obscenity called a "seat of power," and the spirit who was, is, and will be love and vengeance has summoned a generation of people with retribution sewn onto the underside of their tongues*

*because somewhere inside of time,*
*a mother with silver and black spooling from her scalp like yarn looks to a child with the same wonder-widened eyes and says, "What's the matter, Beanie?" His own hair springs off his head in coils like it is living—we will see if he will go silver early like his mother—and he grabs it in handfuls at the end of a wide stretch and yawn. "Tired, Beanie?" The land will not break because this woman has her whole life outside her body walking around in the pocket of this big soul of a child in a delicate-boned but strong-growing body*

*because somewhere inside of time,*
*a gold-toothed, thin-browed woman smiled at a mirror and was enamored of what she saw, and a slight woman with the tallest spirit cultivated garden upon garden at the heart of her house, and a person in a blue room in a blue house near a blue bayou*

*inhaled sweet and exhaled sweeter, and the spirit who was, is, and*
*will be love and vengeance was with them*

   *because somewhere inside of time,*
*there is a riot living inside the body of a woman, and she isn't*
*satisfied until the fires she starts first lick, then devour the entire*
*length and breadth and even down into the soul of the place she*
*and her sisters have been sent to die. She is not concerned that the*
*destruction she brings forth will be irreversible. Scorched earth*
*will always rebirth itself into green even if no human being is*
*there to see it happen. She sits on the last step leading up to the*
*dying house, the state penitentiary, the last slab of concrete to be*
*found anywhere on that land, the rest ash, and combs the tangles*
*from her hair. She cannot take off looking like what she has just*
*lived. She picks the falling hair out of the comb's teeth and sets it*
*aflame with the lingering embers in a bush to her left. Then she*
*takes flight, a little shaky, a little uneven, because the riot knows*
*ultimately she can never be still*

   *because somewhere inside of time,*
   *a woman living on a hillside dreams of fireflies and wings of*
*her own, and a man hears a woman's voice in the key of desire,*
*and two young lovers try to turn to each with Love's Face through*
*the veil of history's ever-presence*

   *because somewhere inside of time,*
*brother loves sister as deep as he would have had they remained*
*à lòt bò dlo, except here where it is cold most months of the year*
*and every house is a brick replica of the one next door, the love is*
*quieter and restrained, distorted to the point where it looks more*
*like control, compressed beneath generations of look-what-we-*
*gave-up-for-you and nothing-we-do-is-ever-enough. "Hey kid,*
*you good?" Sister's tears, also restrained, slowed to occasional sniffs*

*as the only answer for the moment. Brother and sister know they will be whole, whether or not mother and father heal with them*
   *because somewhere inside of time,*
there is so much love and saltwater and sound and sweetness and luxury and also so much vengeance and so much retribution to be had. As our beloveds are turning to one another with Love's Face, exchanging tired smiles, combing each other's hair, tasting each other's sweat on their tongues, they are also out for the sly dogs' blood. They started small but with precision, collecting the dust from the footsteps of anybody white, picking too some grains of sand from cemetery grounds, collected canisters of all kinds of other powders, for the gun, for the ritual, to adorn the face for celebration when it was all over. They brewed poison and pretended it was dye for clothes, made like it was dirty laundry water, like it was chicken stock. Biding their time, they put little drops everywhere they could, in the sly dogs' food and bathwater and in the pale ears of their sleeping children. Subtlety does not mean meek and mild; we and our beloveds believe in scorched earth, remember? They bent iron bars and bent time, broke open the swine-pink foreheads of overseers, landlords, probation officers, hostile neighbors, police officers, prison wardens, army generals, presidents, and all kinds of assorted so-called overlords. They did not spare the native-born despots who chose to model themselves after the sly dogs in their cheating, their theft, their bloodthirst, their enjoyment on the backs of the masses of our beloveds. On the "Gold Coast," en Ayiti, et en "Louisiane," wherever there are white lies hiding behind black faces, they let the kerosene flow long and smooth and the flames they lit curled all over the stolen land, a dragon unfurling its fiery tongue and lapping up the fuel. They knew how to heal the charred soil, that would come later.

*Can you hear us? We are telling you that Blue Basin and its beloved people inside and outside of time and somewhere mid-flight between the two places is able to persist not only with the force of love and tenderness but also with the fury of a vengeance that has stirred and seethed for centuries.*

# 27

*outside of time, on Blue Basin*
*now, Ma-Reine gathered her peace and her pride around her*
*self and they fit better than they ever had*

*break open*

*Glory was hovering in open air, neither inside nor outside of time, close enough to Blue Basin to see the island from above, sitting between the three seas. The tears he cried were the bitter, vengeful kind that felt hot at the corners of his eyes. If there was remorse stirring within him, it was buried below his body's struggle against the cold air, deep and deeper still, past his memories of the dead birds and his parents' and bullies' heavy hands. This cold was bone-deep, like nothing he had ever felt before, definitely not on Blue Basin and not even inside of time when he had to cut and haul logs to burn for warmth in the frightful time called "winter," or before that when the harmattan winds would sweep through his hometown somewhere between Central City and Osu. As he continued to float without aim or direction, his only companion was the anger living with him at all times, like a parallel heartbeat ticking in the background but equally as life-giving as the real muscle in his chest.*

*Normally, the anger was a soft pat-pat-pat, a fingernail keeping time on a tabletop. Other times, its intensity increased to a steady pound, like when Ma-Reine refused to listen to him, playing around with her paints and chalks all day instead of doing things how he believed they ought to be done, or when people tried to put their mouths in his and Ma-Reine's house business. Now, in this nowhere that was his trap, his rage had the force of a pestle breaking through the base of its mortar. There was no telling what he would do to Lucille whenever she let him go free from here. He had tolerated her sideways looks and comments, her nose always too far into his and Ma-Reine's lives in the name of "sisterhood," but this current circumstance was far beyond belief. All he remembered was feeling as though he was falling in a dream and woke up before his body hit the ground. He was holding his self taut like a fist set to release a punch, and the tense buzz in his body reminded him of the first time he and Ma-Reine met, when they collided mid-air and landed on Blue Basin.*

*This time though, there was no rush earthwards and no welcoming hands to break the fall. He could see a group of children trying to make a flimsy kite take flight and people standing in the water up to their waists splashing each other and laughing skywards. It was clear the wind slapping him across the face and body was also swallowing his pleas turned screams turned curses, and the people on the ground could neither see nor hear him. He vowed to his self that whenever his feet touched the ground, Lucille would know no peace, walking around this place with her scarf trailing behind her like someone anointed her queen or lord and savior. Always with the intrusive questions, not even allowing someone to come up with an answer to one before she fired off the next. How dare she think she knew more about how to show Ma-Reine Love's Face than he did? What could she know about what Ma-Reine and he had and how patient he had tried to be with a wife whose mind and spirit were always floating elsewhere? How could she know showing Love's Face sometimes involves causing pain, and that pain and power sometimes felt so sweet?*

\*\*\*

*Can you hear us? We still can't tell you what warped Glory's sense of pain and love this bad. Some things are not for us to say. Maybe you know?*

\*\*\*

With Glory gone, Ma-Reine didn't know what to do with her self at first, and her attempt to accept this newness spat out like anger at Lucille. She was still walking around corners flinch-ready, fists balled inside her pockets in her own home, still slid-ing her eyes away from mirrors or misted-over windows or the water's surface, choosing instead the insides of metal bowls or the rounded backs of spoons, the illusion of self granted by blurs and shadows.

She was trying to discover what her own redemption looked like, now that the dead air between arguments over household nothings was no longer bellowing inside her ears, still trying to draw her way back to the person Mama Aida had tried to raise her to be, like plotting the points on a journey; north-west is a lifted chin, south, a smiling mouth—missing pieces be damned—east, a life beyond victimhood, a self more than surviving.

Before she was fully awake most mornings, her body was already carrying her to the corner of the veranda where she had spread out her paints, scraps of cloth, and paper smeared with various blues, shells, and stones she felt curious about. Free to open her mind as far as it would unlatch and see what it would tell to her fingers to tell to the canvas.

This was not until-the-next-time-it-happens, not after-the-last-ache-eases. This was living, not enduring. Maybe when her spirit had finally settled back into the various far-flung corners of her body, maybe she would pay Lucille a visit, her fearsome sister in all but blood (which did not matter), who almost broke her self standing inside everyone else's breaks but ultimately did not fall, did not break, instead running towards and into abundance, Love's Face turned to a bright blue future. For now, she tried to tune out the loud silence of Glory's absence with her own humming. She was not ready to think about where he was just yet and whether he would be gone for good, although she sometimes winced when she swore she could feel some kind of anguish from him out of thin blue air.

On this particular morning, Ma-Reine stepped out onto her veranda with the pictures she wanted to make that day on her mind even before her body was fully awake. Lucille was sitting on the second-highest step like it was any other day for a whispered chat while Glory was in the back garden. Elsie was there too and went to stand in front of the empty canvas, like she was waiting for the swirls of color to materialize on their own, growing out of the blank surface like new shoots sprouting from soil.

"Ma-Reine, nye sí. Ça va? What are you working on this early morning?" Lucille asked. Ma-Reine turned around next to but a little higher up than Lucille on the top step and tightened her cloth around her chest, tucking the loose ends between her thighs.

"It's not early, sister. I'm surprised to see you in daylight. Where have you been hiding? You didn't hear the whole world and her wife calling for you?"

Lucille picked out a pebble that had stuck itself between her foot and her sandal. "I didn't come here to fight with you. If you let me explain, I can tell you where Glory is. I can even bring him back if that's what you want."

"Ma sœur, I know whatever you have done to him can never equal the ways he has hurt me. Laisse-le, let him be there for now. I was angry. I'm still angry, franchement, because I felt like you didn't let me choose what I wanted, like you knew better what I needed."

"I understand," Lucille started, pausing to swat a rogue daytime tiger mosquito away from Ma-Reine's shoulder. "I do. I said you belong to your self, and Glory couldn't step on your future the way he was doing. But I didn't act like I believed it. I'm sorry, nye sí. I really am."

Ma-Reine killed another mosquito against her leg, a drop of her own blood smearing downwards with the crushed body of the creature. "Why are these mosquitoes so thirsty this morning?"

"Do you want to know what I did?"

"I honestly don't know. I know the voice in my head sounds like me and not Glory, not even my maman, not like anyone else. But let me ask you something."

"Please ask me. I'm listening."

Ma-Reine cleaned the bite on her leg with the hem of her cloth. "Remain my sister, but also remember that showing me Love's Face doesn't mean you need to save me all the time. Can you do this for me? Can you try?"

"Absolutely. Absolutely. Je te jure. I will turn to you with love the way you need, sister."

*break*

*We are outside of time, dreaming of you there, inside of it, and we are holding the way open for you for as long as it will take for you to get here. When the sky yawns wide and blue, think of us; when it cracks open with thunder and lightning, know that those breaks are openings too. Whenever you are ready. And we hope you are ready soon. We don't know how long we have—*

*Can you hear us? Entendez-vous? E mia nkɔ sem a?*

*open open open*

# ACKNOWLEDGMENTS

. . . . . . .

I'm incredibly grateful to Sarah Munroe for giving me the chance to bring this book to life and for her gracious and thorough editing eye. Many thanks to Natalie Homer, Than Saffel, Kristen Bettcher, and Marguerite Avery at WVU Press for their dedication to getting this work over the finish line.

I'd also like to thank Mama Essie, my amazing mother and first and most important reader, and my family, especially Grandma, Aunty Lynda, Aunty Ama, Uncle Tunde, Uncle Ayo, Uncle Wonyo, and Uncle Dele, for not allowing me to give up.

Merci mille fois to the Romains for being my home away from home, for hosting me on countless holiday visits, and for sharing your memories about Haiti and anything else I wanted to know.

To my friends, especially Melissa, Sakeenah, Eliza, Abigail, Aminata, my two Jays, Arakua, Lily, Ashikai, Lloyd, and Breauna, I'm so grateful to love and be loved by you.

Thank you to Nicole Terez Dutton, the Serious Judge, and Angélica María Sánchez Barona for the endless light and laughs through those challenging times.

Without Katerina Gonzalez Seligmann's Cuban Literature and Decolonization course and years of encouragement and feedback, this novel probably would not have taken the shape that did it. Thank you so much.

A huge thank you to Kim McLarin for mentoring and guiding me through so many drafts of this novel and for holding on to me and to Steve Yarbrough for cheering me on from my first workshop and publications to my thesis committee and more.

I'm also very grateful for the advice and encouragement of Erika Williams, Maria Koundoura, Jerald Walker, Jabari Asim, Suzanne Hinton, and Ashley Tarbet DeStefano and for the Emerson College Writing, Literature, and Publishing Department for giving me the time and space to practice and to start dreaming up this book. Without Bridgit Brown, I probably wouldn't have started on this path towards Blue Basin Island. Many, many thanks for teaching me about haint blue and about the Geechee-West Africa connection.

To my primary and secondary school teachers, especially Mrs. Baah (may she rest in peace), Mrs. Odamtten, Mr. Kwofie, Mrs. Vanderpuye, Mr. Amponsah-Mensah, Mrs. Ofori, Mr. Morgan, Mrs. Senyo, Ms. Sagoe, Monsieur Hossoh, and Monsieur Abloso, thank you so much for fostering my love for reading and writing.

Thank you to Miléna Santoro and Amadou Koné in the Department of French and Francophone Studies at Georgetown University for the pep talks and for encouraging me to try creative writing in French.

A big thank you to Dr. Mawuli Adzei for the continued support over the years and for helping me with my Ewe terms and translation.

I'm also grateful for the 2017 Callaloo Creative Writing Workshop, where I wrote the first pages that would turn into this book, and for the Virginia Center for the Creative Arts for the space that pushed me towards the completion of my first draft in 2019.

Many thanks to Dr. Sandra Greene, whose scholarship on gender, geography, slavery, and kinship in colonial Ghana helped to shape the universe to which this story belongs.

Thank you to the editors who have published and championed my work over the last few years, especially the editors at *Blackbird* and *AFREADA* and to the agents and book editors whose constructive feedback helped me reach a better final draft.

Thank you to everyone who has believed in me and helped to bring my soul upright and whole out of that bowing-down place.

All honor to the ancestors. I hope you are pleased with me.

Zoë Gadegbeku is a Ghanaian writer. She received an MFA in creative writing from Emerson College and was a fellow at the Callaloo Creative Writing Workshop. Her writing has appeared in *Saraba*, *AFREADA*, *Blackbird*, *The Washington Post*, and the anthology *Pan African Spaces: Essays on Black Transnationalism*. This is her first book.